ONE WAY PLEASE

PART I – THE RUNAWAY

A NOVEL

MEHMET TAMAY

One Way Please
Copyright © 2018
All Rights Reserved

Library of Congress Registration Number: TXu 2-288-396

ISBN (paperback): 979-8-9866278-0-9

Editor: Cari Shane
Content edits, Line edits, Story advice: Cari Shane
High-level assessment and advice: Olivia Parven
Copy Editor: Anne McPeak
Page design, Typesetting: Jessica Kleinman
Cover Design: Mehmet Tamay, Burconur, Jessica Kleinman
Formatting and publishing: Jessica Kleinman

CONTENTS

ACKNOWLEDGEMENTS

I WOULD LIKE TO THANK THE TURKISH GOVERNMENT, THE citizens, and my parents for raising average children like us to go abroad, make a living, and earn valuable foreign currency.

The United States government more than deserves my thanks for giving me an opportunity to come here and for allowing me to stay. The citizens also deserve the same thanks for welcoming me and treating me with nothing but kindness, patience, and love.

One of those citizens is Commy, the owner of the legendary Saloon in Georgetown then, on U Street now, Washington DC. Commy gave me a chance forty-two years ago and hired me, then sponsored me for school. I'm grateful to Commy forever.

Another one of those citizens is Cari Shane. Cari is an established writer and content editor. She had significant contributions in structural, scene, and line edits. She went on to recruit both the ever-brilliant Olivia Parven and most capable copy editor Anne McPeak to help.

Olivia swiftly and shrewdly provided overall assessment and advice. Anne humbled me with hundreds of fixes, just when I was thinking highly of myself—of my command of the English language. I'm grateful to both.

I'd like to thank Jessica Kleinman, a superb cover and page designer and typesetter, a publishing expert extraordinaire. Thank you, Jessica.

Also big thanks to my good friends Donna Lalley and Kaye Nitta, who encouraged me to write and provided advice. Likewise, I'm grateful to my friend Hiyam Akkasha, who read the novel in only three days, and provided valuable feedback. My dear sisters Inci and Nesrin on the other hand, took several months to read and comment on, but they did so, despite their busy schedules. Thank you, Inci and Nesrin.

My colleague and friend Nathalia has also become an early reader, and advised that I include the following: I'd like to thank Bella and Max the cats, who patiently and affectionately kept me company day and night as I wrote and re-wrote One Way Please fourteen times.

Also, many thanks to those friends and family members who contributed and prefer not to be mentioned.

Last but not least, for her patience, ideas, and a full round of copy edits, I'm forever grateful to my wife Amelia.

I thank all the readers. If One Way Please has entertained you, I'm happy. If it went beyond that by inviting you to think about immigrants and the challenges they might face, I'm happier. If it stirred up something in your spirit, that's more valuable than the whole world.

PREFACE

I GREW UP IN ISTANBUL, TURKEY, IN A MIDDLE-CLASS FAMILY. I came of age in 1970s. At that time, Turkey was still very much a developing country. To many of my friends and me, America was a beautiful but impossible dream. Few Turks had the means to immigrate to America; they mostly went to Europe to study or work, as it was closer and more economical.

I was about twenty-one years old when a serialized novel in a Turkish newspaper caught my attention. The main character was a young man, much like myself, who had dreams of going to America. The story ended tragically. The protagonist never made it to America.

The story clawed at me for decades. Even after I had made it to America, I wondered, what would have happened to that boy if he had actually made it to America? How would such a story play out?

It's been forty years since I arrived in the US. And, I decided it was time to write a young Turkish immigrant's tale with a different ending to the novel I read in the newspaper. In *One Way Please*, I tell the story of Adem Bayer, a fictional character, exposing to you, the reader, his plight, as he forges a new path for himself in America.

In part 1, "The Runaway," Adem's story takes us back half a century to glimpse into his experiences in Istanbul in the 1970s—his hopes and disappointments. He is insecure, has little money, and struggles with poor judgment. In part 2, "The Promised Land," his math skills, honesty, and courage will carry him into unlikely situations in 1980s' America.

This is Adem's story.

M. Tamay
2022.

1

THE CLUB

I step through the iron gates of the istanbul horse club. The gatekeeper slides the lock back into place and I feel safe. The air is warm and humid, my shirt is sticking to my skin. Summer is arriving in the Bosporus Strait.

I usually feel uneasy here, inside the gates where only the wealthy and influential belong. But not today.

Today I'm savoring every step along the path between the gates and the Bosporus. I'm enjoying the things I never noticed before—the new lounge chairs, the new sliding glass doors to the game room, and the blooming roses, magnolias, and lilies of the valley that line the long marble walkway—as if I won't get to enjoy them much longer.

The clubhouse is on one side, the changing rooms on the other. I can hear chatter from several small groups of people sitting on the large patio ahead. Others are sunbathing and silent. As I walk along, the sweet scent of flowers gives way to the stronger smell of sea kelp in suntan lotion.

The headwaiter greets me, then asks, "Could you continue with him on Tuesdays?"

"Sure, as long as I'm in town. How did he do?"

"Honor roll, thank God. He's already started on seventh grade math. Do you think he has what it takes to be an engineer?"

"I think so. You know—he doesn't really need tutoring."

The kid is good; smart. *I wish I had what it takes.*

The staff are easier to talk to than the members. Warmer. I continue toward the edge of the patio. I keep my head down to avoid talking with ma'ams and sirs as Diana Ross's "Theme from Mahogany" plays softly in the background. *Do you know where you're going to?*

Ahead, the clean, dark blue waters of the Bosporus Strait, separating Europe and Asia, shimmer under the sun. Yachts and smaller boats bob on the surface. A giant cargo ship marked CCCP slowly makes its way south, from the Black Sea toward the Dardanelles and the Aegean. Beyond the ship, just a few hundred meters to the east is Asia. I want to swim today—and steal a day from fate.

I walk to the changing rooms. "That was Adem, the smart one," I overhear one of the women on the patio say as I pull on my swim trunks. "He's at Technical University, and oh-so-polite. He'll be an engineer in less than two years. I don't know if he's even eighteen yet. Mind you, the Technical University!"

"Ooh! Does he have a girlfriend? He would be perfect for Suzan . . ."

I know Suzan, I really don't think I'd be perfect for her. "And I am eighteen," I whisper out loud to no one. I've been eighteen for a month. Even if I didn't have a birthday party, even if I don't celebrate my birthdays, I'm still eighteen.

I exit the changing room, a towel around my neck, and walk toward the end of the patio. The fragrance of suntan lotion begins to fade as the smell of salty ocean air drifts in. I finally have an unobstructed view of the Bosporus. I look down into the deep, flowing water then slowly look up eastward until I see the shore of Asia, once again. I drop the towel on a chair and jump into the cold but welcoming waters of the strait.

In the water, I'm removed from my troubles—the troubles outside the iron gates and fifteen kilometers to the south. I propel myself forward and close my eyes as Savas Kartal's threatening voice rings in my head: "I will kill you!"

It takes a half-kilometer of fast, deep strokes against the current to wash

Savas's words out of my head. After fifteen minutes, I turn around and swim even faster, feeling like an Olympian, the current carrying me in and speeding up my stroke, back to the club.

A yacht blocks the ladder. *Rich people!*

I swim around the yacht and climb up onto the patio, brushing the wet hair from my forehead then reach around to squeeze out the excess water from the back of my head. *I need a haircut.* A breeze hits me; goosebumps rise on my skin. Standing there, I look up, begging the sun to warm me.

After a shower, I head over to the outdoor dining area. The Hammer waves me over. The captain of the Galatasaray soccer club as well as the Turkish National Soccer Team, he's a big deal. Hammer is sitting at a table in the shade while his wife chases their little son who is, in turn, chasing a ball like a future soccer star. She stops long enough to say, "Hi Adem," and immediately takes off again after the boy.

Hammer's shot is among the strongest in Europe. His fans say, "Before he shoots a penalty kick, the goalie's legs start shaking." They say the goalie is more afraid of being hit by the ball than he is of allowing a goal.

Hammer is ten years older than I am. I'm always surprised by how modest and kind he is. I met him when my team faced the basketball division of his team in the youth league final. He and his wife were there to support my opponents, but we won instead. He treated both teams to pizza after the game.

Hammer rises from his seat to shake my hand, then pats me on the back. "Sit, sit," he says, gesturing to the empty chair across from him. "You want a Coca-Cola?" he asks, motioning to a waiter before I can answer. "Coca-Cola, please. And another mineral water for me, please. And a beer, Efes. Please. And more of this, too," he says, circling his hands over the snacks on the large glass table. "You know what, Adem? Technical University was my childhood dream. I would trade places with you in a heartbeat!"

I laugh, incredulous. "You would give up all your fame and fortune for Technical University?"

He raises one eyebrow and nods while I shake my head. "Outside the gates," I say, "there are thirty-nine million people who want to smother you with affection. And that's just here in Turkey. How about your fans in Europe?"

"I would trade places with you this instant!" Hammer repeats and reaches for the backgammon box on the glass coffee table between us. He opens it and begins to set up his game pieces; I join him in setting up my own.

A waiter brings my Coca-Cola and some sparkling mineral water with freshly squeezed lemon juice on the side, two empty, frosted glasses; and a small bucket of ice along with Hammer's beer. The waiter pours my Coca-Cola, then uses tongs from his tray to drop in a lemon slice. I watch my cola fizz up in response. Another waiter serves toasted bread slices topped with melted *Kashkaval* cheese and small bowls of hazelnuts, walnuts, and almonds.

"Are you going pro?" Hammer asks, as he watches the waiter open his bottle of beer and pour it into his icy glass.

"No," I say, "I don't know. They've brought in a seven-footer. And a new American. Too much competition. And school is busy too."

"Come on, you're the star, you've destroyed our boys," Hammer says, shaking his head. "How fast are you? Man!" He rubs his chin as he contemplates his next move on the board, and asks, "Are you staying for dinner?"

"Yeah, dinner with my parents."

As the game continues with the quiet sound of rolling dice and moving pieces on the walnut game board, only part of me is concentrating on the play. My mind is occupied. I'm having problems at school—my academic standing is sinking. And, the political conflict is intensifying; my classmates are trying to convince me to join the fight. I don't want to join and I hope that I won't have to. I'm consumed with the details of a fallback plan in case I flunk out or in case I have to leave Istanbul to save my life. I open my mouth to confide my worries to Hammer, but then decide to remain silent. The whole thing will sound too ridiculous, farfetched, embarrassing. *Savas Kartal wants to kill me!* No one would believe me. But I heard him. "I will kill you!" he screamed. He was pointing right at me when he said it.

By the time my parents arrive at the club for dinner, my backgammon game with Hammer has turned into a little tournament. As members arrive for the evening, they stop by to watch our game. Most members are retired parliamentarians, judges, ambassadors, professors, businesspeople, actors, and sports stars—old money mingling with the new. My parents belong to neither category.

My dad, Teoman Bayer, or Colonel Teo, is a retired army colonel, a brilliant man in many respects. His friends call him a walking military library. But, he knows more than just military strategies. He knows laws and regulations, accounting, art, history, geography, math. People say he looks like Jack Nicholson. He is fiercely loyal and dependable. The thing is, despite being confident and charming, when it comes to self-promotion, Dad seems clueless. He has "what it takes" but finds the idea of marketing himself, or even making money, almost immoral. He says it's an issue of integrity. But I don't really understand what he means by that—what does integrity have to do with getting paid what you are worth? He believes that people who make large sums of money aren't honest. I throw my hands up when he spouts his theories about money. He believes money is either inherited, which he says is okay, or is gained through corrupt and evil ways. There's no gray area for him. His views on money confound me, especially because he and Mom hang out with rich people.

When he retired from the military eight years ago, Dad was invited to join the club in honor of his extraordinary service. He loves the club. He comes to play bridge here several nights a week. He also teaches bridge. He says he's a better teacher than a player. My mom, Meral, loves the club too. She plays gin. Mom was the most beautiful girl in her hometown and had a good speaking and singing voice. She wanted to be an actress, but her conservative upbringing got in the way. That's what her cousins say. They're like sisters to her. Neither one is married. They tailor clothes for the rich, but also for Mom whom they never charge, even though they use expensive, imported fabrics to make impeccable pieces. I think Mom is grateful that she has these elegant clothes my family would never be able to afford. Sometimes I watch her rearrange her dress or her blouse and smile when someone compliments her on her outfit. I think the clothes help her feel like she fits in with the wealthy women at the club. Mom left school at ninth grade, married Dad at age eighteen, and had her first child when she was nineteen.

Nobody would accuse my parents of being wealthy. Dad has continued to work after retirement. For the past few years he's been employed by a wealthy man who builds luxury condos. The man was a lieutenant under Dad's command in the late 1950s, and now Dad works for *him*, managing his construction sites, employees, and money. My parents paid the club's initial membership fees from Mom's inheritance, and Dad's additional income from the construction work goes a long way toward meeting their daily expenses at the club.

Dad and I don't get along and haven't for years. It could be that we're from different generations. It could be that our political views conflict. Or it could be that he just doesn't like me. My lackluster performance at school bothers him—even though I got into one of the top universities at age sixteen and I'm significantly younger than my classmates. His inflexibility about things, especially money, bothers me. A lot. And I don't hesitate to let him know. My sisters, who are eight and ten years older than I am, tell me, "If Dad ever has a heart attack, it will be because of you." They're not wrong, but it's a pretty horrible thing to say. "Just say okay," they say. "Don't argue."

I don't want my dad to be wrong out there among other people. If somebody else's dad is wrong, that's *their* problem. But to correct my dad, in private, point out his mistakes, and tell him the truth is *my* duty. I want my children to correct me the same way.

Two years ago, just after I started university, things got so bad between me and Dad that he kicked me out and disowned me. That was the word he used: "Disowned." As I was leaving the house he said, "And don't come back, Adem. You no longer have a family. Consider yourself disowned." Oddly enough, I was fine with being kicked out. I could manage my life fine. Yet his words still float around in my brain, especially at my lowest moments. *Does Dad hate me so much that he could utter such hateful words?* Or, maybe I was simply disrespectful; I'd talk back and argue with him, maybe I did deserve it.

Then again, he'd never really wanted me.

Mom told me that. She told me that I, unlike my sisters, was unplanned. "You were an accident," she explained to me on a rainy day when I was about ten years old. She told me the story only once. My sisters were in college then. I have no idea what prompted Mom to give me a backgrounder on my existence, but she did. "There was no way we could afford a third child," she said. I remember that's how she began her tale. I think I was sitting at the table eating a piece of marble cake. It was my favorite and no one was going to stop me from enjoying it, I had decided. "So, every day," Mom continued, "I'd climb up and jump down from a one-meter-high wall. I was trying to get rid of you. But it didn't work." I remember listening and being confused. What did a wall have to do with having a baby? "Then, your father began to pressure me to have an abortion. If I was going to get rid of you, I told him, it would be an accident, like you were. So, I found a taller wall, a two-meter wall. But, you kept growing inside me. When I was three months pregnant with you, your father began to pressure me every day to go to the hospital to have the procedure. I got angry with him. I told him I had changed my mind. 'No,' I said to him, 'I'm having this baby.' . . . But, your brother wasn't as fortunate." I sat mute at the table, trying to understand. What brother? That evening I asked my sister, and she said when I was two years old, my parents got rid of my baby brother. I still wonder what if he'd survived too, what that would have been like.

I'm not sure how much Mom truly wanted me versus how much she hated the idea of going to a hospital or having a procedure. In fact, she had never been to a doctor in her life at that point, and not many times since then either.

When my dad kicked me out, I moved in with some classmates and lived off my tutoring income. It felt freeing to no longer feel like a burden to my parents, not even for food or shelter. I was already sixteen and realized that I'd overstayed my welcome back home. After I had lived on my own for three months, Mom begged Dad to let me move back home and he gave in. I was surprised to hear that. My sister told me. It made me see my mom as strong and my dad as weak and wavering. They'd flipped. Literally and figuratively. I felt glad to be home and enjoy Mom's cooking again, but I never moved back in completely. I'd gotten used to staying with my classmates, happy to be able to support myself and not to saddle my parents with any additional expense. Over the past two years, I've lived with my classmates more than I've lived at my parents'.

I lost respect for my dad when he let me move back in. He had been such a respected and disciplined soldier. I had tried to follow in his military footsteps and had failed miserably. After seeing him cave, emulating him was no longer important to me. Knowing that I had no future in the military no longer bothered me. *Why would I want to be like him?*

When I was younger, I felt grateful for Mom's stubbornness and changing her mind about having me aborted. Now, I'm not so sure. I don't regret that I was born, but something close to it.

One of the most peaceful aspects of moving out was that I no longer had to hear Mom and Dad pointing out my failures. They called it "falling." "We love you, but you always fall," they would say, ignoring the fact that I always got up again. They would only focus on the negative with me. Now I share little with them. It helps cut down on the criticism.

It seemed to me that my parents treated me differently from the way they treated my sisters—my trouble-free, obedient, thoughtful, dutiful, and successful sisters. When I came along, my parents were simply "over it." While they hounded me, they also seemed to expect little from me, their unexpected child. It was more like—grow up, we'll do the minimum to keep you alive, but hurry up and become self-sufficient; get out of the house, have your own life and be independent, the earlier the better. So, by doing little to supervise me, by being what I decided later on was lazy parents, they raised me to be independent, both physically and financially, for which I'm forever grateful to them.

By the time I was six, having skipped two grades, I had a second-grade student ID. That meant I could use public transportation by myself. On Saturday mornings I'd take the city bus across town to visit my dad at the military base. After a forty-minute ride, I'd get off one stop early so I could walk through the zoo. I'd linger there and watch the animals. It was my favorite part of the week. I would get lost in the spectacle of their behavior, sometimes spending hours around the tiger compound or watching the camels eat, counting how many times they would chew before dipping their heads back into the feedbag for more.

But my delays apparently caused no concern—at least that I was aware of. No one ever came looking for me. And, when I arrived at my dad's office well after I was due, he never asked me what had taken so long. As far as I knew, Mom never phoned Dad to ask if I'd arrived yet either. Apparently there was no worry at all. From either of them. I was free. And ever since, I've enjoyed that freedom.

I would simply walk into Dad's office and sit down at a table near his desk and begin punching numbers into his FACIT adding machine. I loved numbers. In the afternoon, Dad and I would return home together on his military service bus.

I still love numbers. I find them soothing. I'm not sure why, but I do. I wonder if *I'm* a number because if I were a number, I could make up a formula for my life. I think having a formula would make life a lot easier. Less room for failure. Numbers don't lie. With a formula I could understand my path forward. Yes, a formula could make things a lot easier.

Even as I got older and spent more time away from home, my parents never seemed to worry about my whereabouts. They never asked me where I was going, what I was doing, who I was with, when I was coming home. They didn't ask. I didn't tell. Come to think of it, when I said "bye" and opened the door to leave their apartment, I hardly ever remember hearing a response. Usually the only sound I heard was the click of the door shutting behind me and my echoey footsteps down the hallway to the elevator. My dad hounded me about my grades—but seems to have given up—and that was pretty much it.

Even in the navy high school, neither my entry nor my departure in failure, failure in judgment, was much of a concern to them. They didn't know that I was receiving dismal grades, or that I was punished for insubordination. That was three-and-a-half years ago, ancient history. To me, the only other reminder of those days is the gym's punching bag that I kept hitting and which gave me a piercing right hook. My best friend, Demir, calls it "deadly."

***

As evening approaches and the sounds of shipping traffic on the Bosporus become muted, more members arrive for dinner on the patio next to the now darker, calmer waters.

Almost none of the people here at the Istanbul Horse Club's Bosporus location rides horses; despite the name, the club is for socializing and playing cards. Riding happens at another place, inland, beyond the hills of the Bosporus. Really, the only ones who go riding are the younger members or the children and grandchildren of members.

I used to ride but no longer do because it's an expensive sport. And it's too dangerous. Once I got caught standing in a corridor connecting the indoor and outdoor rings, my body flattened against the wall as a horse, scared-for-no-clear-reason kicked up, its horseshoes rising within inches of my face. My head was pressed against the wall and turned sideways, the corner of my eye following the path of the hoofs in horror. I could feel the wind of the kick. Since then, I've avoided standing near the rear legs of horses. Mom told me that when she was seven her father's horse bit her cheek and cut it open. So, I avoid standing near their faces, too.

I do not play tennis or ski either, two other popular sports among the club members. They are also too expensive. Basketball is my thing. And soccer.

2

STARE AND LEAVE

I LOOK UP FROM THE BACKGAMMON BOARD AND SEE MY PARENTS walking out of the clubhouse. I watch them move about the patio, stopping every now and again for brief greetings with members. When they finally arrive at their table, I excuse myself from Hammer, thanking him for the games and the food. I greet my parents in the same manner I greet their friends, formally. As I've been taught. We are not an affectionate family.

The group's dinner conversation quickly turns to international politics and military strategies, the Soviet Union's designs for expanding into the Mediterranean, the Communists' grip on power in South Vietnam. And, of course, US politics—which seems to always be a constant favorite topic of conversation.

"They wasted a talent like Nixon, unfairly pushing him out of office," one of my parents' friends says. "The man did great things; he opened up to China to counterbalance the Soviet threat."

"Unlike here, in some countries even the president is held accountable . . ." I begin to mumble.

"What's that?" the man says, turning abruptly in my direction. "Is that the nonsense they teach you at Technical University nowadays?"

"So Adem, how's basketball going?" an older man at the table asks, interrupting. *Thank goodness.*

"I don't play much anymore, sir."

"It got too tough for you?" he says with a chuckle and a wink. I feel my heart pound in sudden anger, wondering if Nixon was a better subject after all.

"Come on, honey, he doesn't have time for silly games anymore," his wife says. She is sitting next to me. Maybe she felt my recoil and decided to come to my rescue. "You know what they say, Technical University is hard to get into but even harder to finish." She turns to me and ruffles my hair. "You're so cute when you sit with us, trying to act like an adult." Hairs on my neck rise; my face turns hot.

Her words hang in the air as I scrape together the last bit of my sorbet. I think about how to respond but to be polite, I hold back and remain silent, pasting a stupid grin on my face instead.

I look around the patio, trying to drown out the voices at the table by counting the other sounds around me—the clinking glasses, the knocking of forks against plates, the specific words I can discern from nearby conversations, when I notice an elderly man at a nearby table motioning for me to come over. I look at my dad, who turns in the man's direction. Dad nods his approval and I excuse myself. Though he's motioned me over, the man, who looks like he's well into his eighties, keeps talking. I don't really know him. Dad briefly introduced us just a few weeks ago. All I know about him is that he's a professor of medicine, well respected, and spent many years working and lecturing in Europe. I stand behind his chair, trying not to stare at his bald spot, unsure of what to do.

Finally he wraps up his story and, sweeping his arm across the table, asks, "Does everyone know Adem? I would like you all to meet this promising young man—Adem Bayer. Adem, meet everyone. Please, please, have a seat." There are no free chairs. He snaps his fingers, and a waiter appears with a chair and places it next to the professor at the corner of the table. People I don't know shift their seats; there's a whole lot of scuffing and huffing and the nuisance I've caused embarrasses me. The professor turns toward me decisively. "Good, Adem. Good of you to join us. This fall, you will begin your third year at Technical University, yes?"

I nod politely. "Yes, sir."

"Once you finish, you can go to America and become a first-class human being," he says, looking at the others at the table. He points to one person after another with an arthritic finger. "You can be like those among us who went to America or Europe, went to graduate school, worked hard, gained experience, then returned home with valuable skills. Those are the kind of people our country needs."

I smile out of politeness. He has more confidence in me than I do. I'm still trying to figure out how I gained entry to the hardest university in Istanbul. But he's right about one thing. I *do* want to go to America. Going to the "land of opportunity" has been my dream since I was nine, when Demir and his parents moved to Washington, DC. My parents took me to the airport to see them off. I think my dad was just as sad as I was to see them go. While my family jokes that Demir and I were best friends before we were even born, my dad and Demir's father, Colonel Zeki Toros, have been friends even longer, since the 1930s, when they met at the military academy. I can still recall that sinking feeling as I watched their plane ascend into the clouds. How I wanted to be on that plane.

Demir lived in the US for eight years. He went to middle and high school there; Zeki worked at NATO. While Demir was away, he wrote me letters about America. He told me that people in America were different from people in Turkey. There were letters about how adults hear what kids have to say: "They listen to you, they trust you, even if you're a kid, even if they don't agree." There were letters about war protesters: "Students led the protest against the Vietnam War. War veterans responded, throwing away their medals outside of the Capitol Building." And there were letters about freedom of expression: "Half a million people marched in DC and they made change happen."

I've never told anyone about my dream to leave Istanbul and go to America. It's such an impossible dream, and an implausible one. I've kept it to myself to avoid ridicule. But here's the professor suggesting it to me. *Is it possible? Could I really go to America, to get an advanced degree in mechanical engineering?*

No. It would be for rock 'n' roll. The blues. I find myself smiling. *I could buy a 1970 Dodge Challenger.*

These people don't really know me and ridiculously exaggerate my abilities. If I go to America, nobody there will know me either. Maybe I can have a fresh start there.

The people who mock at my parents' table won't be in America; my parents, who never seem to have confidence in me, won't be there. Savas Kartal, who wants to kill me, won't be there. Could I possibly . . .

A cold, harsh voice muscles its way into my brain. *With what money? You need money to leave Istanbul. You need money to live in America. You need to speak English to earn money in America.* I must get it through my head, all I have of America is my dreams. I need to learn to be satisfied with dreams. But still, I would trade places with a homeless man in America right now.

"You can spend some time with Suzan and Mira here," I hear the professor's wife say, her voice piercing my thoughts. "They're nice girls, your age. Suzan is my niece. You know her, right? Didn't you used to ride with her?" She flashes a smile at me and tucks her short curly hair behind her ear. I smile and nod. I want to be polite. *So this was why they called me over—to play matchmaker?*

They are all talking about me, but they are making things up about what I would or could or should be. Why don't they just ask me? Why are they making my life into a bad game of "telephone?" If someone said, "Adem is average," it would turn into "Adem will be an astronaut" and next, "Adem is the first Turkish astronaut accepted into NASA's training program!" And then, "Adem is the youngest astronaut in space!" I chuckle out loud. No one hears me. I don't think anyone really sees me either.

Yet, part of me wishes my parents were at the table, hearing the way these people are talking about me. Not that my parents' opinion of me would change, but it would be funny to see how they reacted. They'd have to be polite. I'd bet Mom would say, "Oh, his aspirations are so lofty," with her infamous sarcasm. "You know, his big dream is to be a garbage man." She would say it in the present tense, failing to mention that it was a four-year-old's dream. Then she would continue, "And he pooped on the carpet in the dining room. Then he came into the living room, with his naked bottom, and announced to me, and all my guests, 'Dropped it, dropped it!' pointing back to the dining room." I was two years old then.

It's confusing, these diametrically opposed opinions people have of me. It kind of messes with my brain. I don't know if I'm smart. I do know I'm lazy. At least that's my parents' propaganda. I feel like I simply muddle through school and life. But, I also know I'm not a give-up-type. I stick with things, most things, until eventually I find my stride. Eventually. Okay, most of the time, I guess. There may be fits and starts, I do fail, a lot. But eventually I get *somewhere*, even if it's not my intended goal. And, isn't that okay? Shouldn't that be okay? Shouldn't it be okay to change course? My parents make it seem like re-routing is wrong. But do I have a choice? I am, after all, a student at the most demanding university in Istanbul. They don't let just anyone in. So, doesn't it mean I'm smart? Why then is it, stuff I'm studying at school is making my head explode—3-D visualization, kinetics, fluid mechanics, and thermodynamics? There are students in my class who just seem to naturally "get it." But I haven't mastered even one of those subjects yet. And, if I don't figure it out soon, I will be expelled from school. The shame that would result; it's . . . it's . . . unfathomable. My parents would be . . . I can't even think about what it would do to them. My parents and my two older sisters already think I'm a . . . well . . . a disappointment. They've witnessed my consistently mediocre performance at life. My opinions aren't taken seriously and worse, they're mocked. To avoid being mocked, the older I've gotten, the quieter I've become, and that seems to reinforce their opinion. I do talk when I'm around my friends, but around my family, I've learned to be silent.

I've been silent about Savas Kartal and his Nationalist gang. Savas thinks I'm a Communist. Yep, a *Communist*. He wants to kill me. Actually kill me. The fact is, he wants to kill all Communists. Rumor has it, Savas has killed before. And, more than once. But what's confusing is that Savas pointed right at me, stared me in the eye, and announced, "I will kill you." I've never done a thing that I know of to incite such ire, to provoke such a violent pronouncement. I don't know Savas Kartal other than by reputation and I certainly don't know much about Marxist or Leninist doctrine. But I was not about to buckle down before this bully either. So I decided not to fear him. Fear is never a remedy against fate anyway. I stood my ground and stared at him until he looked away.

Why doesn't anyone just let me be? Why *are* there so many conflicting perceptions about me? Why is there *any* perception of me? Why can't I just be an average kid who likes to dream, just a teenager who wants to fall in love, who wants to no longer struggle in school?

I just want to run away from this life of misinformation, misdiagnosis, misunderstanding, danger. I think what I really want is to leave Istanbul for a simpler life. Couldn't I do that? Couldn't I go to America, get a minimum wage job, save up enough to buy myself a Dodge Challenger? Couldn't that be my American dream?

The clatter of dishes brings me back to reality. A waiter has dropped a tray. I look around the professor's table. The conversation buzzes around me. I'm no longer the topic of conversation. I wait for a lull in the dialogue and then start to excuse myself. The professor grabs my hand and repeats his great expectations of me. I nod, smile awkwardly, then thank everyone for their company. With my head down, ignoring suspected glances, I walk over to my parents' table to tell them I'm going home.

As I walk back along the flower-lined path to the gates that lead back to the real world, my heart skips a beat. Savas Kartal. He wants to kill me. *Kill* me, know-nothing do-nothing Adem Bayer? I can't let him succeed. I either have to kill him or get away from here.

When I get home, I go right to bed, but I don't close my eyes. I stare at the ceiling thinking about America. *Perhaps . . . perhaps I should start somewhere closer, somewhere that doesn't seem so unreachable. Like a Greek island—maybe the one where Dad was born. I could drop out of everything and go, it's only a half-hour ferry ride. I could grow vegetables, earn enough money to buy a fishing boat, live in peace.*

I fall into a troubled sleep.

***

Redbuds are in full bloom, hydrangeas are budding, leaves on sycamore trees are getting larger, their shadows on the streets wider and deeper; pine trees have light-green shoots on the tips of their branches. Parks are full of picnickers; outdoor cafés are packed.

The summer vibe inside the gates at the club is not just about the temperature. It's that light feeling that comes with summer vacations and being outside all day. The warmth breeds a kind of peaceful feeling. I try to absorb it, breathe it in.

I change into my bathing suit and walk to the patio. It's such a clear day that on the passing Soviet cargo ship, I can see sailors walking around on the deck.

I jump in. Heading north against the current, I swim hard. I think of what it would be like if I hadn't been born. If Mom had been successful in losing me from jumping off a two-meter wall. Or, if she'd gone up another notch and tried a higher wall. Or, if she'd gone to the hospital for the procedure. Would I be better off? I mean, I wouldn't be here. So that's a stupid question. Would my parents have been better off? If I weren't here, there'd be no son and all his failures; no basketball games to miss, no failing grades to scold me about.

My baby brother isn't here. Is *he* better off? "He was taken away," my sister Eliz told me. She was ten. "At the hospital, they took him away," Ela said. She was twelve. "Mom and Dad couldn't afford a fourth child," they both told me.

I'm not that far from the patio. I've probably been swimming for only ten minutes, but I'm exhausted. I realize I'm holding my breath. I let myself sink for a moment, closing my eyes against the baby brother I never knew. *Where is he?*

I rise back up and turn around to swim back, swimming even faster, counting as loud as I can in my brain to suffocate all the questions.

I pull myself out of the water to walk toward the changing room. At the far end of the patio I catch sight of a girl I have never seen before. She's willowy and the wind plays with her long dark hair. In a long, sheer white dress that reveals a white bikini underneath, she is facing me but appears to be staring past me to the strait. I can't look away. As the dress billows in the breeze, transparent high-heeled sandals are revealed. The white soles match the frames of her sunglasses, which dangle from her right hand. When I get closer, my heart traps my feet. I can't move. She is beautiful. Exquisite. I manage to turn my head away and take a moment to compose myself. Then I steal another glance, and, as I do, she looks right at me. I have no time to look away. Our eyes meet. I hear my heartbeats in my water-clogged ears.

We both look away. My brain is screaming at me to leave the area. But my heart won't let me move. The headwaiter waves me over to him. When I don't move, he rushes over to me, blocking my sightline. "Can you do this Tuesday? 2:00 p.m., okay? Even every other Tuesday would be good."

I can't say no. He can't afford a professional tutor to guide his son. I had been planning to tell him that I didn't want to tutor over the summer after all, but I cannot carry on the conversation right now. My brain doesn't seem to be working properly.

"Yeah. Sure," I say.

I walk a few steps with the waiter in the direction of the girl. I keep her in sight out of the corner of my eye. She hasn't moved. I turn my head to glance at her again. She catches me. This time I'm closer. She has hazel eyes. And, she looks like money. A rich girl is a big mistake. "Danger zone," Demir calls it. He learned the phrase in America.

Peeling my eyes away from her, I hit the changing room. I need a cold shower. Within minutes, I am on my way out of the club, proud of myself for leaving. It's good, my self-control. But I can't deny it—I'm hoping to see her again.

I arrive at the club at nine the next morning. There are only a few people around. It's still fairly early for the club crowd to start arriving. I walk to the edge of the patio and jump in for a long swim. Thirty minutes out and, with the help of the current, fifteen minutes back. I wish my life were more like swimming—a nice reward after an investment of hard work. *Is there a life force, a current that will ever push me forward?*

When I climb out, there she is. That same girl. This time she is wearing a one-piece blue swimsuit. The frames of her sunglasses match.

So I didn't exaggerate her in my mind. She really is that beautiful.

Our eyes meet. She smiles.

Flustered, I grab my clothes from the changing room and leave the club, without a shower.

***

I return to the club the next morning, early again.

As I walk to the edge of the patio for my dip, I look around even though the club is still empty. Maybe she won't even be here today. But if she is, I need a plan, I tell myself. I jump in the water. Today, instead of timing my swim, I count my strokes. I've planned to go to five hundred and then turn around, but I keep thinking of that girl and losing my count. I persevere, swim through the distractions in my head, swim faster. When I finally get to five hundred, which could really be eight hundred or three hundred, I turn around.

The second I climb out of the water, I look down the length of the patio to where I saw her yesterday and the day before. She's not there.

I'm both disappointed and relieved.

I hit the showers, change, and grab a copy of the *Nation's Daily* sitting on a table in the men's locker room, left out for the guests. I find a chaise lounge and flip to the international news headlines, which I always read first: *America is 200: Bicentennial Celebrations Underway; Boston Celtics Win the NBA Championship; Uprising in Soweto; Concorde Flights between London and Washington, DC, Commence.*

Which one travels faster, the Concorde or a bullet? I read about how fast the Concorde travels and then do a quick calculation: the bullet wins, but not by much, with 760 meters per second versus 700 for the Concorde. Just as I'm wondering what it would feel like, being in a tube in the air moving almost as fast as a bullet, a flash of red catches my eye. I glance up and drop the newspaper. There she is, standing a few meters away in a flowing red dress. Again, the frames of her sunglasses match her outfit. She is out of my league, I know it. I smile at her. She catches my smile but doesn't return it.

What am I thinking? She wasn't even looking at me. Maybe she didn't smile at me yesterday. Maybe she was smiling at someone behind me.

"Dark love." Oh no! Is that what this is? I've heard the stories: People were confined to their bedroom or even committed to a mental institution for most of their lives after falling victim to unrequited love. "Dark love." It's what the locals call it. Until this moment, I've laughed at the thought that a person might never get over a failed attachment, could go insane from the intensity of their feelings. I can feel this girl boring her way into my heart. I quickly consider my own fate, then shudder. I wait for her to turn away from me. And I continue to wait. One minute, two minutes. She's still looking my way. I put down the paper and walk out of the club. "What is this?" I ask myself as I walk through the iron gates. Am I going to do this each time I see her—stare and leave, stare and leave?

Fear and embarrassment follow me like twin shadows all the way home.

3

THE DINNER

I FIND MY MOTHER SITTING AT THE KITCHEN TABLE READING A magazine. I walk past her to grab some juice from the refrigerator.

"Have you been to the club?" she asks.

"Just this morning, for a swim," I say, pulling out a chair to sit down.

"A new girl is visiting," she says. "Did you see her?" There's a tone of excitement in her voice.

"What girl?"

"A beauty. Slender, pretty. Long hair . . ." I give Mom a sudden look and she stops mid-sentence. She raises her hand to her collarbone and says, "What?"

"Nothing," I say, clearing my throat. "I just think I saw the girl you're describing."

"Ah," she says, shifting in her chair. "I play cards with her grandmother—her father's mother. Very friendly woman. Francesca—is the girl's name. Truly a beauty."

Francesca. I let the name roll off my tongue.

"A beauty. I met her. She is lovely," my mother says. "Ethereal."

"Interesting," I say, trying to sound casual. "How. I mean, who?" I ask, jabbering, failing miserably to keep a poker face. My mother doesn't seem to notice. "She didn't look Turkish to me," I finally sputter out.

"Yes. Yes, I thought the same thing. She's part Italian," Mom says, leaning toward me, as if she's telling me a secret. "Her father is Turkish, her mother Italian. Her parents are divorced. Her grandmother told me Francesca was born in Florence and has lived there almost all her life."

"So what's she doing here?" I say, taking another sip of juice and concentrating on not choking. My stomach feels tight and full of butterflies.

As Mom launches into an entire story about Francesca, it occurs to me that I've never, ever before listened to her so intently. "After the divorce, her father moved back to Istanbul. He remarried here. The mother stayed in Florence and remarried there. A wealthy man, Francesca's grandmother said. In fact, her stepfather's gift for her fifteenth birthday was a yacht, named *Francesca*, which they keep at their summer house on the island of Elba."

I listen. Patiently, I wait for Mom to answer my original question.

"So, Francesca comes to Istanbul to visit her father and grandmother every summer. And this year, her parents decided that she's old enough to join her grandmother at the club."

Francesca. I repeat the name under my breath, to savor the taste of it on my tongue. It is the perfect name.

***

That evening, I join my parents for dinner at the club.

While they are ordering drinks, the headwaiter comes to stand behind my dad. Bending forward slightly, he speaks quietly but loud enough for me to hear. "Sir, the young lady over there is asking your permission to have dinner with your son."

The waiter angles his head to the left and I turn my head, expecting to see Suzan or Mira. It's Francesca. My heart thumps. My face heats up. My knees begin to twitch. There she is, alone at a two-person table next to the water, overlooking the strait. She is looking at the water, away from me, and I steal the moment to stare unabashedly at her. Her neck is long. Her back is straight. Her slender, elegant arms lie softly at her side. Her head remains fixed, facing the water. *She is inviting me to dine with her?*

Dad doesn't even bother to look round, he simply nods. Has he even heard what the waiter is asking? *Dad, this girl, this beauty, wants to dine with me, your son!* His eyes never leave the menu. I shake it off. *Why would I expect anything other than your dismissiveness? I don't need to care about your opinions. Your permissions! I've been summoned by this beauty to dine with her.* I carefully push my chair out and stand up. I smooth down my hair and adjust my shirt collar. Three days. Three days I've been thinking about this girl that I was too scared to speak to. And now, I'm going to dine with her? I push my chair in. I begin to walk toward her. Toward *Francesca.* My body feels heavy. I feel like I'm in a trance.

As I get closer to the white-clothed, candlelit table, two feet from the waters of the Bosporus, I see her face up close for the first time. She is even lovelier than I had believed. My heart thuds.

I smooth down my hair again, bow slightly and greet her. "Buona sera," I manage.

Francesca looks up at me. "Iyi aksamlar," she replies, looking me right in the eyes.

We dine politely while exchanging some quiet conversation. She tells me about her life in Italy. I listen. I hear her words but not their meaning. I watch her face and how the words form on her lips before they leap from her mouth and into my ear, caressing me. She speaks slowly, softly but confidently. Her demeanor is calm, her voice is soft, her Italian accent is musical. She is romance. She appears totally unaware of her beauty. Has she never looked at the mirror? Has nobody ever told her?

I'm fascinated by the way she thinks and speaks.

"What are you doing with your free time this summer?" I ask, trying to reel in my thoughts and hold up my part of the conversation.

"I have science lessons. And piano lessons." *I must focus on her words.* I nod. I smile. "I also have writing and speech lessons, and English diction."

"I mean, how about, for fun . . . after those things are finished?"

"I've just arrived; I have a few friends in town from last year, maybe I'll see them. My stepmother thought that I should visit with my grandmother at the club; she thought I'd like it. My parents don't come here."

She's only sixteen, I find out, and already knows, definitively, that she wants to be a TV journalist. She asks me questions and I realize she is smarter than I am. It deepens my attraction.

"What do *you* do for fun? I know you swim," she says. *She's been watching me?* "You play backgammon too." *She's been watching me!* My heart. It's going to explode. I am unable to suppress a smile.

We talk until late into the evening. My parents, her grandmother, and the other diners have moved from the dining patio into the clubhouse to play cards. The candle on the table melts into a small pile of wax and shudders. The waiters leave us alone.

"I played basketball. Five years. I quit a few months ago. Wintertime I go to school, university, and tutor; summertime I go to different beach towns with friends. I play soccer too."

Just past midnight, Francesca turns her head toward the clubhouse. "My grandmother . . ." I see a woman standing in front of the sliding glass doors. "I need to go now. I didn't realize it was so late."

We make plans to meet the next day at the club. Rising from my seat, I walk around the table and pull her chair out for her. *Should I kiss her?* I want to. But I can't, not with her grandmother watching.

Together, we walk over to where her grandmother is standing. Francesca introduces me. We make some small talk, but I'm not listening at all. I'm high, drunk without a drop of alcohol. I smile, but I barely speak. I forget to thank them for dinner.

***

At home, in bed, I can't fall asleep. *What's happening?* I'm not used to this . . . this feeling. Happiness. I'm happy! I just had a candlelight dinner with a girl I wouldn't ever dream I could dine with. And, she wants to see me again tomorrow. I close my eyes, thinking about our dinner together, counting and recounting every detail I can think of until, eventually, I fall asleep.

***

In the morning, I get in an early swim at the club. My adrenaline is pumping. I can't believe I have a second date with the most beautiful girl I've ever seen.

We spend the rest of the morning together, talking, walking. For miles. For hours. It feels like five minutes. We amble along the Bosporus, unaware of where we are or where we are headed. I notice nothing other than Francesca. We exist in a bubble.

At 2:00 p.m. we say goodbye, making plans to see each other after dinner. She goes home for a piano lesson; I tutor the headwaiter's son. It occurs to me about halfway through the lesson that I'm not concentrating; but it's easy to work with a smart kid and I don't think he realizes how unfocused I am. I think about the evening ahead. At 8:00 p.m., I will pick Francesca up at her house. Maybe I will kiss her. I begin to calculate the minutes until I can see her again. The longest 360 minutes of my life. I wonder if her fingers are tripping over the piano keys.

I arrive at her house seven minutes early, still counting the minutes.

I recognize the place immediately. Her father's house overlooks the Bosporus. My dad was the construction manager for this development six years ago. I used to play ball on the terrace while he was working. I wonder what my twelve-year-old self would think of me, now, back here to pick up a beautiful girl for a date.

At exactly 8:00 p.m., the door opens. I watch as she floats down the stairs. My Lord, she is pure grace. I jump out of the car to greet her.

"You look beautiful," I say, the words coming out before I can stop myself. And then, embarrassed that I have absolutely no filter, I introduce her to my car. "This is Duldul," I say, touching the hood of the car. *Why did I say that? What is wrong with me?*

"Hello Duldul," she says. "Hello, you."

You are spectacular.

"I think she likes you," I say, as I open the passenger door for her. She smiles at me. My heart skips about twenty beats and falls into my stomach and then gets swarmed by hundreds of butterflies that have been awakened. *This better not be a dream.*

We drive along the strait. My right hand holds her left. I don't want to let go, so I drive with my knee and awkwardly change gears with my left hand. I just can't let go. I think, I hope, she feels the same way. We go north toward the Black Sea and pull over at the crest of a hill. I lean in to kiss her. She doesn't stop me.

Her head rests on my shoulder as we watch the sparse lights twinkle on across on the Asian side. At 11:00 p.m., we drive back to her house.

I spend the next three days straight with Francesca. Every morning at 9:00 a.m. we meet at the club. Every night, I bring her home before her 11:30 curfew. When I say goodnight, my heart hurts. I can feel the pain. I imagine my heart curling in on itself, becoming smaller so there is less surface area on which the pain can live. Then in the morning when I see her, my heart opens up again, expanding, unfolding, rejoicing. I want to be with her always. I cannot imagine how I lived and breathed without knowing her.

I help increase her Turkish vocabulary and she tries to teach me Italian. Together, we come up with funny combinations of meanings and pronunciations. I ask her where she would like to go tonight, she mispronounces the name, Poplar Hill, and says "Bald head." I try to correct her, in Italian, tell her that she's saying, "bald man's head," but apparently, I say something like "old man's testicles." Our antics make us giggle and our conversation turns into a laughing crisis.

"I want to buy a Vespa, but my mother won't let me. She thinks it's too dangerous," Francesca says.

"You like motorcycles?" I ask, surprised. "I like motorcycles! Do you want to ride with me?"

"Only the scooters, I've never ridden on a motorcycle. Do you have a motorcycle?"

"My friend Demir does. He's my best friend. I can borrow his motorcycle. We can ride it. Tomorrow. I'll bring it to the club."

As I say good night to Francesca, standing on her doorstep with her, my hands gently caressing hers, I think about how she will wrap her arms around my waist tomorrow. I nearly lose my breath imagining it.

***

The following morning when I arrive at Demir's to borrow his Kawasaki, it looks like it was dumped in a mud pit then rolled in grease. I grab a rag and start cleaning it off. It's a lot of work. *Is it better to show up late with a clean bike or on time with a filthy one?* I don't know the answer, so I scrub for another five minutes and head over to the club. Francesca doesn't complain about the dirty bike. She hugs me, right there, in the club parking lot, in front of several members. My face reddens.

I take her for a ride along the winding road of the Bosporus. As she screams into my ear to slow down, she hugs me tighter around my stomach and her breasts press against my back. I twist the throttle all the way and keep raising the gear to go faster. Her grip tightens. Her breasts feel so warm and soft against my back. I shiver.

I stop when we arrive at the crest of the hill at a pine grove on the side of the road. She shakes out her long hair and I can't pull my eyes away. "I thought we were going to fly into the water!" she says, with a lilt in her voice that is begging me to kiss her. I pull her toward me.

I kiss her soft and long. "I love it," she whispers. "Let's do it again." I grab her jaw in my hand and kiss her again, harder this time, and longer.

"I meant the ride!" she says, laughing. I pull back, embarrassed. She tips her head to the side as if she's reading my expression. "That too," she says, pulling me in and kissing me.

"If my mother knew I was doing this," she says, rubbing her cheek against mine, "I'd be in big trouble."

I don't know if she's referring to the bike ride or the kissing.

4

LOVE AND LEAP

For a seventh morning in a row, Francesca and I meet at the club. But instead of having the early hours to ourselves, we are ambushed by Demir and my other friend Izzy.

"So, this is why we never see you anymore?" Demir says, smiling at Francesca and extending his hand. "Hi, I'm Adem's brother, Demir. Not his real brother, of course. He is a very bad friend for keeping you from us."

"And I'm his other brother, Izzy. Nice to meet you."

Francesca greets them warmly and my cheeks start aching from smiling while watching her. We sit around and chat over tea and melted cheese on toast. We talk about what it's like living in Italy and her summers in Turkey. Though I've hidden her from them, now that they've met her, I'm curious what they think. I don't know what the looks behind their smiles mean.

The second Francesca gets up to go to the ladies' room, I lean across the table.

"What do you think?" I ask. "Do you like her?"

Izzy looks at Demir, then turns to me. "Consider this your summer fun, Adem. Enjoy it while you can. Enjoy her while you can."

"What? What does that mean? You don't like her?" I ask, shocked.

Disappointed. I feel like he's punched me in the gut.

"We . . . no, it's not that," Demir says, looking at Izzy, then back at me. "It's just, Adem, we just don't want you to get hurt. Danger zone, remember?"

"Why would I get hurt? She likes me. I think she really likes me."

"She doesn't even live here," Izzy says. "What're you gonna do—move to Italy? It's a summer thing, a summer fling."

"Adem. We like her. I mean, look at her. She's beautiful. She's nice. I mean, you're actually smiling. But, like Izzy said, you don't even live in the same country. What are you gonna do? Marry her? Can you even keep up with her? With her expectations?"

"Are you talking about money? You're saying I don't have the money."

"Yes, that's what we're saying. It sounds cruel but we just don't want you to get serious with her. Just have fun. Probably that's what *she is* doing."

Suzan walks over to our table. Mira is close behind her but stops to talk with someone else.

"Hi Adem," Suzan says.

"Hi," I say, my voice deflated.

"How's Ranger doing?" she asks Demir.

"Good, good, thank you," Demir says. "His tendon has healed. One more week, then I can ride him again, the vet says."

Until I had my horse incident, I used to ride with Suzan and Demir. Izzy has never admitted it, and probably never will, but he is scared of horses, too.

"Adem, why you don't come over to ride anymore?" Suzan asks. "You can ride Bandit. He'd be a good horse for you."

"I'd like to, but . . ."

"He's scared," Demir interrupts, and chomps down on a big piece of his toast.

"Oh, no he isn't. You're not scared of horses, are you, Adem?" She doesn't wait for me to answer. "Well, even if you don't ride, we'll have lunch. You have to join us, Adem! It would be so much fun!" She looks at her watch. "Oops. Gotta run. We'll make a plan. See ya."

Suzan leaves as quickly as she arrived.

"What's wrong with *her*?" Izzy asks as we all watch her walk away. "Why not her?"

"She likes you, man," Demir chimes in. "Didn't you see how she looked at you? She begged you to come for lunch."

"If they both come from money, Suzan and Francesca, why is one a 'danger zone' and the other isn't?" I ask, throwing Demir's warning words back at him. "Why is Suzan okay but Francesca isn't?"

"Um. Obviously, it's because she *lives here*. Boy, you're not thinking clearly, at all," Izzy says. "You gotta come back down to earth."

I shake my head at them. I'm enjoying it up in the clouds with Francesca. *They're wrong. This is not a summer fling. Then again, I haven't thought about what will happen at the end of the summer.*

When Francesca gets back to the table, I stand up to pull out her chair. Demir and Izzy soon excuse themselves and exchange nice-to-meet-yous and goodbyes with Francesca.

I watch her smile at them and wave goodbye. I study the graceful way her hands move. *My boys are wrong.* I grab her hand.

"Let's go swim," I say.

"Yes! Let's," Francesca agrees.

"But let's go somewhere else, not here," I say, getting up from the table. "Let's go to Lovers' Leap."

We walk out of the club, holding hands. I try to quiet Izzy's and Demir's voices in my head.

"Why is it called that?" Francesca asks once we're in the car.

"Huh?" I say, turning to her, unable to shake the guys' comments out of my head. "What's called what?"

"Why is it called Lovers' Leap?" She asks the question softly, yet with such authority, that I am pulled back into her orbit. I look at her and pause before answering her question. *Izzy is wrong. This is not a fling. I'm in love. And I think she loves me, too.*

"Well, legend has it that a long time ago a couple committed suicide there. Their parents didn't approve of their relationship. So, they jumped off together one night, in the dark. They were caught up swept out by the currents."

"What a sad story," she says.

"It's one of the narrowest points at the Bosporus, with the heaviest currents," I say, changing the subject, worried that maybe the same way Demir and Izzy don't approve of her, Francesca's parents don't approve of me.

"I didn't know that," Francesca says, looking out the window at the water below as I pull up and park.

We get out and walk down the sidewalk just a few steps to the end. The concrete stops abruptly right at the edge of the sidewalk. There's no guard wall. We stand there, silently, looking down the two-meter drop to the deep, dark waters swirling rapidly in whirlpools below. Francesca grabs onto my arm. Her nails dig into my skin, but all I feel is a hot current rush through my veins. The sound of the whirlpool below drowns out the thumping of my heart.

"Let's jump," I say.

"What?"

"Let's jump!" I say, louder.

"When you said 'swim,' this wasn't exactly what I had in mind," Francesca says, stepping back from the edge. "I don't want to die. My stomach is doing flips just thinking about it."

"We won't die. We're just going to float and glide on the current and get off a couple hundred meters downstream. I've done it before. It's safe in the daytime. It'll be fun."

I take off my shirt and jump before she can respond. The cold, swirling water, with all its volume and power, pushes me south toward the Marmara Sea. Before the current grabs me, I swim back to the wall and grab hold of it.

I look up. "Jump!" I shout, closing one eye against the sun behind her. She looks like an angel standing above me, her silhouette outlined with a halo.

"No way!"

"Don't make me come up there."

"We'll die!"

"We won't die. Just relax and jump in. I'll save you if you have trouble."

"Have you ever saved anyone?"

"Yes! Just jump."

Francesca pulls off her sundress, tossing it behind her, and then, without waiting, jumps in, right over my head, screaming as she falls, "Ti odio, ti odio!" *You hate me? What happened to Ti amo?* She splashes into the water, her hair flying straight over her head.

And then she is gone. Three seconds, five seconds, seven seconds. *Too long. Francesca! What have I done?*

And then, in a burst, she emerges from the water shrieking. Her words bounce off the shore's walls and get absorbed by the echo chamber of water; I don't know what she's saying. I swim over to her and grab her hand, pulling her hand to kiss it. Lying on our backs, we let the violent torrent of water take us. We float down to a more peaceful part of the strait, to the concrete stairs that lead right out of the water onto the bank above. We climb up and stand under the sun to dry.

"My God, that was so much fun!" Francesca says, screaming. "We almost died!"

"You jumped right in, like a pro," I say. "One minute you were scared and the next minute you were in the air. It was amazing."

"It was glorious," she says, kissing me. "I'll never forget it."

We start walking back toward the car.

"Ooh, ooh, ouch," Francesca says, jumping from one foot to the other. "Ouch, hot. I can't walk on this concrete barefoot."

"Why not?"

"It's too hot; hurts my feet."

"Okay, hop on my back."

"Really?"

"Really!"

"My hero," she says, kissing me. I bend down a little and she hops on. Her legs wrap around my waist and her arms wrap around my chest. *Is this what heaven would be like?*

The precious cargo on my back, I walk on and off the grassy areas to cool my feet. She kisses my neck.

"Did you really save someone from drowning? Was it a girl?"

"Yes. No, it was a man. A stranger."

"When was that?" she asks, kissing my neck and my cheek again.

"Three years ago."

"That means you were only fifteen years old! How did you know what to do?"

"We learned water rescue at the navy high school, when I was a cadet."

"Do you think he would have died if it hadn't been for you?" she asks, sounding genuinely impressed.

"Yes," I say matter-of-factly. "He almost died even after I got him back to the shore." Her breasts press more closely against my back. I feel strong carrying her. Confident. A man taking care of a woman. I don't know why, but this moment, this event, makes me feel somehow secure. I never thought I could be so happy, that any human being could be so happy.

"Wow!" she says. "That means you really are a hero!"

"What do you like about me?" I ask, stepping onto a grassy patch.

A woman with a basket of flowers walks toward us and stops. "May your belly-buttons come together for life," she says in a heavy, northwestern Turkish accent. It's a lewd comment that many of the flower peddlers make. I blush, hoping that Francesca doesn't understand the nuance, the intention of the comment. "A rose, sir, for this special lady on your back?" she asks.

"I don't have any money on me," I say. She begins to walk next to us.

"What did she say?" Francesca asks, whispering in my ear.

"She wants to know if I want to buy you a rose."

"No, not that part. I understood that. The other part, about our belly buttons."

"May your belly-buttons come together for life," the woman says again.

I feel the heat on my face as Francesca's breasts push against my back. It's almost too much to take.

"What do you like about me?" I ask again, veering away from the flower peddler.

"Your smile," she says, kissing me again. "You're handsome. And smart." She hugs me with both her arms and legs. Her breasts . . . *May your breasts push against me for life.* I feel lightheaded and exhilarated. "What do you like about me?" she asks in turn.

"A rose, for the lady," the flower lady asks again, catching up to us. She pulls a rose out of her basket. "I don't know," I say, hesitating. The flower lady is making it difficult for me to concentrate. But the truth is, I *don't* know because it's not one thing. It's everything. Everything. *Your eyes, your lips, your smile, your breasts, your belly, your legs, your feet. Your voice, your accent, your mind, the way you walk, the way you smell, the way you kiss, the way you seem to love life.* "You're smart, you're handsome—I mean beautiful—you're beautiful, and I love your smile," I say instead, repeating her words.

She kisses my neck again. The flower lady keeps pace and remains at our side.

"Here's our car," I say to the flower lady as I put Francesca back down on the ground. "One rose, please." I grab my wallet out of the glove compartment and pay the peddler.

"For the lovely lady," I say, bowing to Francesca and handing her the rose.

"My prince," she says with a curtsy and we both laugh.

Our hair has dried stiff with salt. My skin tingles and itches. Francesca holds the rose up to her nose and breathes in the smell. I take a picture of her in my mind.

I love you.

5

THE PARENTS

I want to tell her I love her.

"I'm hungry," she says.

I shake the word *love* out of my head.

"Hungry. Yes!" I say. "Hungry. Let's get some fish sandwiches."

We drive up to one of my favorite lunch places. It's a shack overlooking the Bosporus.

"Hey Adem, the usual?" the owner, Rasim, asks as we walk up to order. He winks at me.

I look at Francesca and back to Rasim, "One clam, two fish. Thanks Rasim."

Rasim throws two skewers of clams in bubbling hot oil. "And who's the young lady?" he asks.

"This is Francesca, my . . . friend."

"Out swimming, I see?"

"We jumped off Lovers' Leap!" Francesca blurts. I close my eyes for just a second and I can see her flying through the air like an angel. She grabs my hand and presses her breast against my arm. She has no idea what she does to me. I want to kiss her. I want to wrap my body around hers. I do a quick series of calculations to calm myself down.

When Rasim serves up the fried clam sandwich, it's still sizzling.

"Here," I say, holding the sandwich out to Francesca. "Taste this." Her eyes grow big as she takes a bite and then bigger still as she begins to chew. The tartar sauce runs down her chin. "So good, right?" I ask. She nods and I think I hear her moan softly. I've never witnessed such perfection. "Oh my goodness. That is delicious!" she says, still chewing, one hand covering her mouth demurely.

"Shall we get another one of those?" I ask, laughing. She nods again, smiling.

"Another clam," I say, ordering for her as she takes yet another bite. By the time I've turned back, she's almost finished my sandwich. "Did you like *my* sandwich?" I ask, laughing, pretending to try to grab it from her. She kisses me on the cheek, right in front of Rasim. "Yes!" she declares. "And I like you too!"

***

The next day Francesca tells me her father wants to meet me over dinner. At their house. It will be me, Francesca, her grandmother, her stepmother, and her father. I smile and accept the invitation. She jumps up and down and hugs me. "He's going to like you, don't worry," she says.

"I'm not worried," I say, *because I'm terrified.*

I'm used to being around rich people at the club. But this is different. I'm not just going to be around rich people. I'm going to be on display for rich people. On display so they can judge me.

That evening I put on my nice suit, my only suit, and slick back my unruly hair. The two ties that I have look too ordinary; I ask Dad for one of his. Neither he nor Mom asks why I'm dressing up; neither one asks where I'm going.

I arrive early and pull Duldul over on the side of the road, waiting until exactly 6:53 p.m. to pull into the driveway. To calm myself, I count to three hundred then check my watch. It's 7:00.

I park the car, then walk up the steps to the front door. My forehead feels clammy. My hands, too. I can't shake hands like this. I quickly reach for my handkerchief and wipe my face and dry my palms. I take a deep breath, then ring the bell. I begin to count to calm myself; after nineteen seconds the door opens.

"Good evening, sir," the butler says. "Please, come in." It's not like I was expecting Francesca to answer the door, but a *butler?* I follow him through the vast vestibule. Halfway down the hall, he stops and holds his hand out to the left. I step into a large parlor where Francesca's family is gathered.

"Mr. Bayer, sir," the butler announces.

Francesca's father stands to shake my hand, then introduces me to his mother and his wife.

"And I believe you know Francesca," he says with a smile I can't quite decipher. *Was that a "beware, I know your intentions" smile?*

We all move to the back terrace, which overlooks the Bosporus. It's breathtaking. I can almost make out Lovers' Leap from this vantage point. I silently debate mentioning being here as a child when their castle, ripe with groutless travertine floors and glass walls, was just a slab on the ground. I say nothing.

Uniformed maids—I count at least five of them, one for each of us, it looks like—circulate with trays of drinks and hors d'oeuvres. I am tense, my shoulders riding high by my ears. I want to look at Francesca, I want to look into her eyes so she can calm me, but I don't want her father to see—to see how intimate we've become. I feel like two hundred pairs of eyes are on me, analyzing, assessing. I am sure I look as out of place as I feel. I try to make myself small by making small movements, creating less mass for everyone's eyes to inspect. I've been here only five minutes and already have a headache. I want this, need this, to end now. It's going to be a long evening.

I fortify myself by thinking about Francesca. If I want to be with her, I need to prove that I'm worthy.

After thirty minutes of small talk on the terrace, the butler comes outside, positioning himself at a ninety-degree angle from our little crowd. "Sir. Madam," he says, bowing twice, first in the direction of Francesca's father, then toward her stepmother. "Dinner is served. Please follow me." He leads us to the dining room. There are place cards at the table. I am seated next to Francesca's father who is at the head of the table, across from her stepmother and next to the grandmother. Francesca is across the table, diagonal from me. As far away as they could seat her, I notice.

I stand behind my chair, waiting for the women to sit. The table in front of me is laid with ornate, gold-rimmed china. Next to each plate, in multiples, different-size forks are lined up on the left; knives and spoons on the right. Crystal goblets sit off to the top left of each place setting. It makes dining at the club look like a paper-plate picnic.

Someone comes over and pulls my chair out for me. I sit down and grip the edges of my seat. *Calm down,* I tell myself. I unclench my fingers and place my napkin on my lap.

I speak only when spoken to and, when asked a question, I keep my comments brief, while at the same time trying not to be monosyllabic. I am terrified of using the wrong utensil, or spilling my food, or making an awkward sound. I eat slowly, taking tiny bites, to make sure not to choke on my food. This is so nerve-racking, I don't even know what I'm eating or how it tastes.

"Adem . . ." Francesca's grandmother says. Putting on a smile, I turn my head in her direction, catching a glimpse of Francesca. She looks pale, despite her tan. She's not smiling. I think my hands are shaking.

"Your mother told me that when you were four years old, you used plastic letters of the alphabet to spell out words," she says. "During a visit by your father's commander, his wife asked you to spell her name, and you spelled it out without hesitation on the coffee table." I don't know if this is a question.

"Yes, ma'am," I say, putting down my fork to concentrate.

I don't move my head. I look only at the grandmother because I don't want to see, to know, that everyone is looking at me. It's enough, too much, to even assume that they are.

"The commander's wife was astonished," Francesca's grandmother continues, looking around the table as if her family is an audience and she is on-stage. "She then asked whether Adem could read the newspaper headlines—the large print. His mother said that he could read even the small print. He then read excerpts from John F. Kennedy's speech—the one that said they would put a man on the moon by the end of the decade."

I don't know if I should smile, nod, or say something. I keep looking at the grandmother.

" 'This boy is brilliant,' the commander's wife said, 'A child prodigy!'" The grandmother dips her head, as if taking a bow. She looks delighted by her story. *Ahem. My story.*

"So, why did you want to be a garbage man when you grew up?" Francesca's father asks, with a bit of a chuckle. I cough on a bite of food. Why would he ask me this question? It's true. I did want to be a garbage man. I'm sure my mother told the grandmother in passing. But why would the father ask me that? I was a little boy. *He's mocking me. I must be careful with my response.* I want to look at Francesca, but I can't. *Careful, Adem.* I clear my throat and attempt a smile.

"Because they rode hanging off the back of a truck and wore cool yellow slickers," I say, trying to sound honest but not snarky. "I believe I made that declarative statement when I was four years old, sir. I've greater aspirations now."

"Ahh," the father says, with a possible smirk. I am having trouble reading him, understanding the look on his face. I am not sure what kind of answer he is seeking. I don't know if I've satisfied him. "Mmmm. So, greater aspirations now. Such as sidewalk engineer. Street loiterer?"

"Daddy!" Francesca says. "Please be nice."

I do not look in Francesca's direction, though I am grateful she has come to my defense. Her father is testing me. I'm walking a tightrope. I need to be strong in my conviction, show I'm a man, without being rude or disrespectful. "No sir. I attend Technical University, which doesn't offer those disciplines." My eyes are on the father, but I hear a few chuckles, I think from Francesca and her stepmother. "I plan to be a mechanical engineer, sir. I graduate in two years."

"Two years? I thought you were eighteen."

"Yes sir. I am. I skipped two grades."

Francesca's stepmother places her elbow on the table, rests her chin on her cupped hand, looks me in the eye, and asks, "And, what are your intentions with our beautiful Francesca?"

That startles me. "I'm sorry?" I say, clearing my throat.

I want to marry your daughter, sir, ma'am. I want to hold her, forever. I want to sink my body into hers and never let go.

Panic sets in. I reach for my water, but accidentally knock my hand against the glass. Water splashes on the table. I recoil, then shoot my hand forward to stop it from falling over, but I miss. The glass falls over and bangs on the table. Water spills out, winding like a river around the numerous plates, glasses, and pieces of silverware. Mortified, I pull my hand back and, in the process, my left forearm accidentally hits the edge of my plate, catapulting my knife up in the air. The thoughts in my mind now are moving at the speed of light; time slows. I watch the air-borne knife flip, splatter bits of food on the table, clang off the edge, and land finally on the massive oriental carpet underfoot. I hear a chuckle coming from Francesca's father's direction.

"Oh, no worries," Francesca's stepmother intercepts, hardly missing a beat. "It happens all the time." The maids rush in to clean up. Everyone is looking at me. I'm burning with humiliation. I feel my face grow hotter. "So, you were saying, you want to be a mechanical engineer?" She has changed the subject for me. Francesca's stepmother has saved me.

I clear my throat, again. "Yes. Ma'am. Yes. Mechanical engineer," I say, stuttering. "And I am sorry about that," I say, "about making a mess."

She ignores my apology.

"So, where will you work?" the grandmother presses. *If I get kicked out of school, I'll work on a fishing boat off a Greek island.*

I shake the thought out of my head and clear my throat again. *They are going to think I have a cold.*

"I would like to go to America for graduate school."

I don't know why but I'm glad I've said that, even if it's not going to happen.

The stepmother turns her face slightly away, maintaining eye contact with me. A strange silence falls over the table.

Francesca breaks the silence. "America!" she says, a little too loudly, her usually melodious voice piercing the air sharply. I can't tell whether she is vexed or excited. "Sure, Adem could go to America. Right, Daddy? Couldn't he?"

Grandmother responds, "Of course he could."

They think I could do it?

Francesca's father says nothing. Instead, he begins to talk about sports. I'm grateful to him for steering the conversation away from me, though I doubt he's done it *for* me but rather because he's *bored of me.* Slowly, the awkwardness begins to dissipate, and I ease into the evening, able to enjoy the steamed vegetables, pasta, and blue fish.

I get the feeling that Francesca's parents have chosen to politely disguise their disapproval of me. Maybe this is how rich people behave when they're terrified by their daughter's choice.

"Enough with sports," the stepmother says, as we begin the dessert course. She looks at Francesca. "Remember, dear, we need to go shopping. There isn't much time left. You need another suitcase."

A suitcase? Why does she need a suitcase? I feel perspiration forming on my upper lip. *Is she leaving?* My heart drops. *Is she going back to Italy? Already?*

***

I don't really know how I survived the dinner with Francesca's parents. I don't know if I should ask her directly what her father and stepmother thought of me. I don't even know if I should care. The fact is I'm focused on my fear that there's already a plan underfoot for Francesca to return to Italy. How am I going to breathe without her? How will I exist? I am in love. I know it's love. Nothing else in the world matters.

***

On my way to the club to meet Francesca the next morning, I resolve to tell her I love her and that I don't care if her father doesn't approve of me.

When I pull into the club parking lot, she's there, waiting for me. As with each time I see her, I gasp. She's breathtaking. My mother called her ethereal. She is right.

"Let's go to Sedef Island today," she says, clapping her hands together. "We have a summer house there. It's been a long time since I've been. I miss it. Go with me?"

I've never been on Sedef, but I know of it, of course. It's a small, semi-private island with a population of only a few hundred wealthy people and their staff. Sedef sits in the Marmara Sea which connects the Bosporus and Dardanelles Straits; together they connect the Black Sea to the Aegean. When I was at the navy high school, we practiced our rowing skills around the island. That's the closest I've ever come to it.

"Okay. Yes. I will go with you." *I will go anywhere with you, my love.*

We drive twenty minutes to the Golden Horn and hop on the commuter boat that transports mostly staff to the island; the rich folks have private boats that they use to come and go to the mainland. At ten thirty in the morning, the boat is nearly empty. We sit outdoors for the forty-five-minute ride. The boat glides on the Marmara Sea. The perpetual hum and vibration of the engines is calming. I breathe in the cool saltwater mist and watch the particles dance in the air, in and out of the streaks of the sun's rays. Francesca lies down on her back and rests her head in my lap. I pet her head, ears, and cheeks until I feel her breathing slow into a sleep-filled cadence.

When we arrive on the island, Francesca leads us to a little market for cheese-and-salami sandwiches and Coca-Cola. Then we hike to the island's highest point. "That's our house, the one with the pool," Francesca says, taking a bite of her sandwich and pointing. I follow the arc of her arm down to the tip of her finger. My eyes linger on her appendages; I have less interest in looking at the house. Finally, I pull my eyes away. "I don't want to go in because the house staff would have to tell Daddy I was there . . . with you," she says. I nod as I take in the expanse of the house—the compound, really—below, with tiered gardens, pool, and guest house.

"That's okay. I like it up here, just the two of us," I say, taking her hand.

"I like it up here with just you, too," she says, smiling. And then she turns her head in the direction of her father's house, again. "Does it bother you that my parents are wealthy?"

"Um . . . I don't know. Maybe. But, maybe not. I know a number of wealthy people," I say, not quite answering her question.

She looks down at her tanned legs. I do too. The fabric of her short navy-blue dress caresses her thighs. I start counting. She repeats, "Does it bother you? I need to know."

"No," I say, definitive in my lie. I'm not sure why I can't tell her it worries me, that I think about it all the time.

"Does it bother *you*?" I ask.

"Yes."

"Why?" I ask, surprised. *Maybe I should have told her how much I think about it. And, about Demir and Izzy's warnings, too.*

She looks up. Then she turns to face me. "I don't know if people are being nice to me just because my family has money. They always want to talk to me and try to be around me. But, you didn't do that."

"I was scared to talk to you."

"Why?"

"Look at you. You are so beautiful. So perfect. And, look at me."

"But I smiled at you first. Didn't that mean something to you? Didn't you get that I liked you looking at me?"

"No. I don't know. I'm sorry. I didn't know. I thought maybe, I don't know, that you are beautiful and nice and just smile at people."

"I was so upset. I told my grandmother that I saw a handsome boy but that he wouldn't talk to me. She was the one who arranged our dinner. At first I was angry with her. Embarrassed. I thought I was having dinner with her, but then she left, telling me she would send you to me. I was so nervous."

"Nervous? But look! We're here right now because of your grandmother. I am so grateful to your grandmother. I didn't understand that you liked me. I'm not good at reading people's faces," I say. "Or, being with a girl."

"Am I your first girlfriend?"

"Yes."

"You're my first boyfriend."

I smile. And then I kiss her. I cannot let go of her. I don't want to let go.

And then I remember her stepmother's voice. The suitcases. She's leaving me.

"Can I ask you about your suitcases?"

"My *suitcases*?"

"What your stepmother said, about needing more suitcases. Are you leaving?" Just saying the words out loud makes my hands tremble. I think I can actually feel pain in my heart.

"I'm not going to buy more suitcases," she says. "I've asked Daddy if I can transfer here and go to the Italian high school in Istanbul."

What? You want to stay? "For me? For us?" I ask, in disbelief. "What did he say?" I ask, not daring to breathe.

"He said he'll think about it. He'll talk to Mom. She has to agree." I nod. I reach for her hand. "I don't want to leave. I don't want to leave you. You can finish university; I can finish high school. Then you can come home with me to Florence. Or, we can go to London together. Or, America!" she says. "But, I told Daddy it's because I want to stay with him." I look down at her. "I had to say that. You understand, yes?"

"Yes. I do. He would have said 'no' immediately otherwise."

I can't believe Francesca wants to stay in Istanbul to be with me. "Do you think your mom will agree?"

"I don't know. But, Daddy can't tell my mother that I want to stay so I can be with him. So, he has to be strategic in what he tells her. Honestly, I wish I were eighteen so I could make my own decisions. I don't like to lie. It's not natural for me. But I also know I can't go back. I can't leave you. Do you want me to stay?"

"I want you to stay. I'm so happy. I don't think I ever knew happiness before. I cannot imagine not being with you. I worried all night about the suitcases. *Suitcases.* I don't think I've ever worried about suitcases before in my life," I say, and we both start laughing. "I'm happy. I have never been happier in my life." *I am in love. I love you.*

We lie down on the overgrown grass, side by side. I reach for her hand, bring it to my lips and hold it there, kissing it. I turn my head and rest my cheek on her hair. I want this to never end.

6

KISS AND LEAVE

IT'S BEEN FOUR WEEKS AND FRANCESCA AND I NEED SOME PRIVACY other than a hilltop. We plan a day at my parents' apartment when Mom is at the club and Dad is at work. "I'll drop Mom at the club at nine and then I'll drive right to your house to pick you up," I say. "A flawless plan. Then, at three I can take you home for your lessons and pick up my mother."

"It's a wonderful plan," she says, giving me a look that I like.

When we arrive at my apartment, I give her a tour, trying not to apologize for the size. She doesn't like being rich. But I don't like *not* being rich. I want to get a feel for her attitude about money. I'm constantly hearing Demir and Izzy whispering their warnings in my ear, about the "Danger Zone." I look to see if she rolls her eyes or furrows her brow. I listen for any changes in her voice. I don't notice anything, but then again, I'm pretty bad at reading people.

I end my short tour at the door to my tiny bedroom. Then I step inside and walk over to the bed, sit down. She hesitates at the door. *Is she nervous? Repulsed?* I watch her gaze as she takes in the single bed, a small desk with a study lamp, a chair, and a small oriental carpet. My clothes are folded and piled up in the niche behind the door. I don't have a dresser. A narrow window opens up to the apartment's small, enclosed courtyard. Despite a ray of sunlight coming through the curtains, the room is fairly dark.

"Let's listen to the radio," I say, reaching over to my desk for the transistor radio and flicking it on without getting up. I pat the spot next to me and she comes over. Her back is straight, her scent is intoxicating. "Diorissimo," she had told me when I finally asked. I pause, gently touching her hair and breathing in her fragrance. I want to touch her cheeks, burrow my face in her neck. Her hair with sun-stroked highlights, her eyes, her nose, her silky-smooth tanned skin, her arms and legs, their shapeliness and proportion, her clothing, her voice, her brain, each one is enough to take my breath away.

I lie down and ask her to join me. "We'll just lie here," I say. But, my body knows I'm lying. Francesca takes off her shoes and lies back slowly and, as she does, I turn in her direction. I touch her face. I touch her hair. I lean in and kiss her. I feel her resistance. I try to slow down, but my body overrides my brain. My hands move down her face, to her chest, to her stomach, in between her thighs, they linger at the button on her pants. My brain knows these are places I should not be going. But, I don't stop. I lift up her shirt and begin to kiss her stomach. I forget she is only sixteen.

I'm confused by her intonation. Her words are "Please don't" but it sounds like she means "Please do."

Then, something in my head snaps and I pull my hand away.

"Why did you . . .?" she whispers, and I cut her off, kissing her forehead, then her nose and I pull back again, looking into her eyes. *What does she want?* This battle between my brain and my body is confusing. She is confusing.

Then, she kisses me on the lips, pulling my head closer, pulling my body closer. I kiss her back.

I feel drunk. High. I want to feel her naked body against mine.

On the radio, the Stones sing, *You can't always get what you want.*

Our clothes stay on. But we spend the rest of the morning kissing and touching. It's painful how I ache for her.

We emerge from my room at about one thirty, so I can take her home for her piano lesson—or was it English diction today? Traffic is light, so I decide to go the long way and show her Technical University. Francesca "oohs" and "aahs" a little; she's not wrong, it's a beautiful school with majestic, elegant buildings, even though I've read that some of the finest architecture in the world is in Florence.

"I hope we hit every red light between the university and your house so we have more time before having to say goodbye," I say, smiling at her when the first light we hit turns yellow, and the car in front of us slows down and then stops. "Oh well," I say, "looks like we have to stop," shrugging my shoulders and faking a complaint. I lean over to kiss Francesca. I don't mind that people in the cars all around us might see. As our lips meet, something catches my attention. I pull back, squinting to focus on a group of men standing on the sidewalk. "What's wrong?" Francesca asks. It's Savas Kartal standing on the corner talking with several of his goons. He's looking directly at us. I look away, terrified, and check the traffic light. Still red.

"What's wrong?" Francesca asks, again. I don't answer. My hands grip the steering wheel.

The light isn't changing, I look straight ahead, turning my eyes just enough to keep Savas in sight. His right hand is holding onto his jacket's pocket flap.

"What's going on?" Francesca asks, pleadingly, pulling at my arm. I turn to look at her, to explain, but my mind is blank. *What can I say? What could I possibly say?* I shift my eyes an inch and Savas and I make eye contact. His body responds in one swift movement. I watch as he pulls out his gun. I let my foot off the brake. Duldul rolls back as I throw it into first gear. I hit the gas pedal and release the clutch. The wheels squeal and the car begins to vibrate as the tires look for traction. We jerk forward. I swing right around the car in front of me, and the front wheel on Francesca's side smacks against the curb cut and pops up onto the sidewalk, the rear wheel follows. I hear a single gunshot and a simultaneous shattering of glass. The side window behind Francesca is blown out. I feel shards of glass hit the back of my head; pieces land on our laps. I race through the red light, almost hitting a car at the intersection; I swerve around two other cars and make a sharp turn onto a narrow street, hitting a garbage can, then continue to the next street where I finally slow down.

"What's happening!?" Francesca screams. The wind is blowing in through the smashed back window. I can smell the burnt rubber.

"Sorry, I got confused," I say, trying to downplay what just happened. "Club . . . I'll take you to the club."

"I'll take you to the club? Adem, what is going on?"

"I told you, I got confused for a minute. Home . . . Piano. I'll take you home."

"Adem, that was not confusion. Tell me what just happened!"

I'm silent.

"What is going on, Adem? Adem! You have to tell me! You nearly got us killed, the way you were driving! Was it those men on the sidewalk?" She's yelling and I can't keep up with her questions. "Adem, talk to me," she says, putting her hand on my arm. I jump. "Did those men shoot at us?"

I stare straight ahead, driving slowly and concentrating on the road. I remain silent.

"Take me home. Right now. I want to go home."

"Yes, yes. Home."

I turn us around and head toward her house and we ride in silence. When she finally speaks again, I jump.

"Did those men shoot at you, Adem?"

I don't answer. What am I going to say?

"Let me out of the car," she says. "Now!" she yells. "Stop the car!" she screams even louder. I don't know how she will get home. I can't speak. I try, but words won't come out. She starts opening the door and I slow the car and pull over.

I watch her get out of the car. I watch her walk away. I let her walk away.

I sit there, on the side of the road. I sit there until she disappears. She never turns to look back.

It starts to rain.

My body begins to shake, uncontrollably.

***

I'm on autopilot when I take the car to the repair shop the next day. Afterward, for days, I walk around like a zombie, unfocused. Other than getting the car fixed and chauffeuring my mother to the club, I stay in my room. I can't eat. No one seems to notice. No one asks why, suddenly, I'm hanging around the apartment so much.

I haven't called her. I can't even say her name. I don't want to have to talk to her father or stepmother. I don't think she would get on the phone with me, anyway. But if by some miracle she did, I don't even know what I would say.

I replay the scene over and over in my mind until I almost go mad with the memory. I see Francesca's loving, trusting face, I see Savas, I see the car in front of me, the men on the sidewalk, the red light, Savas's hand on his jacket pocket, the shards of glass flying, the curb, her changed face, my silence, the garbage can, the yelling, her hand on the door, my silence. Her back as she walks away . . . away from me. The rain.

"You know that beautiful girl you had dinner with once? Francesca?" my mom says when I pick her up from the club a week after the "the Savas Incident," as I've started calling it in my head. "Well, she has left Istanbul. She has returned to Florence, early."

"What?" I cry, unable to stop myself.

"Why are you yelling, dear?"

"I was reacting to the car in front of me. Please. Go on. What happened? Some girl moved to Italy?" I ask.

"Francesca. You dined with her at the club? Remember?"

"Yes." I nod. My knuckles have turned white on the wheel.

"Her grandmother is devastated. Apparently, they were all set to move her here permanently."

My mom appears unaware of my reaction or my pain. She has no idea Francesca has left behind a broken heart. *Is that your broken heart or her broken heart? You wretched creature. You did this to her.* "I feel so sorry for her grandmother," Mom says. "She told me she was so surprised that Francesca left so early. And so suddenly. Apparently, Francesca had been looking to move to Istanbul but suddenly changed her mind and left. She had tears in her eyes, Adem, when she told me. That poor grandmother. She won't see Francesca until next summer." *Will I ever see Francesca again?*

When I finally tell Demir and Izzy that Francesca has left, they drag me out of the house. They know nothing about Savas Kartal, they think that Francesca left me because she is as shallow as they had predicted. They take me island-hopping to distract me, extricate me from my misery. We go from island to island, beach town to beach town. We sleep on the sand, in tents, in the car, and, when we're fortunate, in someone's summer house.

***

Weeks later, when I return, I go to the Bosporus. I sit on a bench and watch the water—eight hundred meters wide, one hundred meters deep—and look across at the green hills of Asia. I fix my stinging eyes on a cargo ship. It looks like it's standing still.

The water is getting choppy and, dark. Scary. As the autumn winds pick up it will grow choppier. Dangerous. Everything around me looks gray. Smoky. Blurry.

Dark love.

7

ALL IN

SUMMER IS GONE; THE 1976 FALL SEMESTER IS IN FULL SWING. I hope that a change in scenery and routine will help with my desolate feelings. Without Francesca, nothing matters. Demir broke up with his girlfriend, four weeks later he was over it. Izzy did too, and it was the same, he was over it within four weeks. Their girlfriends? They moved on even faster. Why am I still grieving? Why can't I be like them and just forget about Francesca? *No wonder people are so afraid of dark love.*

And school? Only my fear of imminent expulsion from school stands strong against my grief. Soon, all those who called me a genius, predicting I would be an astronaut, will gather around, picking at my carcass, crowing with incredulity and surprise, "He never was a genius!"

Technical University has been the crown jewel of Turkish higher education since the eighteenth century, producing scientists, engineers, and leaders who make our country stronger, better. I was supposed to be one of them once, but now . . .

I'm looking down at the dirty dishes piled in the sink of the townhouse

I've shared with classmates for the past two years. There are six of us. Another half dozen stop by every so often to study and socialize. My roommates took me under their wing as a kid not even shaving yet, and they watched with wonder and humor as I grew taller. I'm still not shaving, but now I'm the second tallest in the house. The group formed a revolutionary gang, along with others that sprouted up at Technical University, dabbling in Communist thoughts and ideologies, earning for the school the nickname, Castle of Communists. They've brought me into their group even though I've told them I am apolitical.

This week, it's my turn to do the dishes. The chore list was created following a simple mantra: "From each, according to his abilities." And I, since I cannot cook, am a dishwasher. I believe those who say they can cook do so to avoid doing the dishes, because the food is always lousy.

"The water heater is down again," Polat says as he walks into the kitchen, startling me from my thoughts. "It's going to be cold water for you." Polat is three years older than I am. During registration at Technical University, we met when he asked if I'd lost my way to high school and ended up in the wrong building. When I told him I was a student at the school, just younger than most, he told me he was looking for one more roommate for his group house and asked me to come over and meet the other roommates. He also suggested that I needed protection from the Nationalist gangs of City University across town. When I moved in a week later Savas Kartal hadn't yet threatened to kill me. I'd never even heard his name before. I didn't know he was the leader of the Nationalist gang. I didn't know who Nationalists were.

I heat a large pot of water on the stove and pour it into a plastic tub with a little detergent. I soak and wash the dirty dishes in the hot tub then rinse them with cold water from the tap. The frigid water numbs my hands. *As numb as my mind*, I think, as I struggle to push Francesca out of my thoughts, replacing her with calculations about my courses and how close I am to failing out. It's been nine weeks and four days and the pain of losing Francesca remains almost unbearable.

***

The dread in my life has returned from its vacation since Francesca left. My memory of dread goes back to when I was six years old. Mom and Dad, under pressure from the commander's wife and others who had declared me a "child prodigy," sent me to school two years early.

The process began a year before I was slated to start first grade, when Dad took me to the local elementary school to be evaluated. My parents weren't as convinced as others that I was so brilliant, especially Dad; a test, he said, would determine if he was right—I was average—or if the others were right. I've never understood why believing in me is so difficult for Dad.

It didn't start off as dread. Actually, when the panel of three teachers gave me a few reading and writing tasks, I remember thinking it was a game because they were so easy. There were also math questions; those were even easier. When the teachers walked out with me to tell Dad the news, I kept my eyes fixed on his face. They hadn't said anything to me other than "good, good," and "that's right," and "how do you know that?"—a question I didn't know if I should answer. So, as the head teacher started speaking to Dad, the corners of his lips curled up into a smile, which rarely happened. His eyes grew big. His eyebrows danced up. I vaguely understood it was because of something I'd done, but I didn't know what it was. I learned that I would skip first grade and go directly and immediately to second grade with the eight-year-olds. I've never forgotten what he said, standing there, outside the school office. "I am proud of you, Adem." He looked happy. I, six-year-old Adem, had made my dad proud.

But it wasn't pride. That's what I didn't understand at the time. It took years for me to figure it out. I came to understand that what my dad called pride was actually relief. At that moment at the school my dad believed I could accomplish all of *his* unrealized dreams. For my dad to get an education, the kind of education he now saw I could get, he had to join the army as a cadet. He was fourteen and it was the only way he could afford to go to school, because in the army, education was free; he had food, shelter, and clothes, plus a monthly allowance. But his son, little six-year-old me, was so smart that he would be able to circumvent the army, remain a civilian, and become an engineer. I was my dad's second chance, and I was already two years ahead of my peers. And, the icing on the cake, which took me even longer to figure out, was that I would be self-sufficient two years earlier. The earlier, the better.

***

Dad wanted to be the one to walk me to school the first day. But he had to be at the army base. So, Mom walked me to school. And that was the first day that dread came to live with me. I still wonder if it would have been different if Dad had taken me.

I was the third child Mom was taking for the first day of school and I remember feeling that walking me to school was more of an annoyance for her than anything. She walked two paces ahead of me the entire way, and each time I ran to catch up with her, to grab her hand, she sped up. She had a piece of paper with a number on it and, when we arrived at the school, she walked me to the classroom that had the matching number. The room was filled with children. "Go sit at that empty desk," Mom said. We were standing in the hallway in front of the open door. I looked up at her imploringly, but she didn't look down at me. She seemed oblivious to me and my fear. I tried to reach for her hand, but she'd lifted it up to point at the desk. "Go, Adem. What are you waiting for?" she asked, pushing me.

I wanted to cry.

"Can't you stay?" I asked, quietly.

"No, I'm leaving."

Another nudge from my mother made me stumble as I crossed the threshold and the children laughed. Even sitting down, they looked so much bigger than me. I trudged to the empty desk with my head lowered. When I sat and looked back at the door, Mom was gone.

And then the dread implanted itself in my brain, in my body.

For starters, I didn't understand that there were rules. No one told me that there were rules to learn in school. So, during class that first day, when I felt like eating, I took out my sandwich from home and began to eat. How would a six-year-old know that was the wrong thing to do? The other students, their eyes and mouths wide open, stared at me. "What's wrong with him?" I heard some kids murmur before they started a quiet chant: "Ayy, the new boy, such a cheat. He's gonna be a slab o' dead meat."

When the teacher turned around to shush the children, she walked over to my desk and loomed over me. "Adem, go out and look at the clock in the hallway and tell us what time it is."

I put down my sandwich and went out to the hallway. On the wall was a big clock. I realized I didn't know how to tell time by looking at a clock. I was terrified of failure.

Down the hall, I saw a janitor pushing a mop. I asked, "Excuse me, sir, could you tell me the time?"

"The clock is there on the wall, look! Can't you tell?"

"No, sir. I can't tell."

"It is eight minutes to eleven."

I walked back into my classroom.

"It is eight minutes to eleven," I repeated what the janitor had said.

"Good," the teacher said. "So you understand now, Adem?"

Understand? "Yes, ma'am." *Understand what?*

The girl sitting next to me whispered, "We eat at twelve, or during class breaks. Never during class."

"Oh," I said. I took one last bite of my sandwich and wrapped it up.

***

That afternoon when I arrived home, I immediately asked my sisters to teach me how to read a clock. They were playing the Beatles' *A Hard Day's Night* on their portable turntable and dancing. They grudgingly complied. It took me an hour to figure out the difference between the big hand and the small hand. But just as I thought I had figured it out, Ela grabbed her wristwatch. There the big hand and the small hand looked the same size. We had to start all over again.

***

On the morning of the second day of school, dressed and ready to go, I walked to the door and turned around to look for Mom.

"What are you waiting for, you're going to be late," she said sternly.

"Aren't you coming with me?" I asked, surprised, feeling a burn in the back of my eyes.

"No. That was only for the first day. Now you know how to get there," she said, handing me my sandwich wrapped in paper.

I walked out the door of the apartment building and looked both ways. I couldn't remember how we had gotten there yesterday. I hadn't paid attention. I hadn't known to. I chose to turn left, because I had two choices and I liked the idea of walking past the field where I sometimes played soccer. Once I'd passed the field and buildings sprouted up again, I saw two parents with their children ahead of me and decided to follow them. They made a left at the grocery store, went up the hill, and then turned right. I turned the corner just behind them, and there were the school gates. I remember being surprised that I had been able to figure it out on my own.

At school, I waited to be told I could eat, but I didn't know what to do about going to the bathroom. So I waited. And waited. And then I really had to go. During the class break, I asked the girl sitting next to me, the one who'd told me about the eating rule, where the bathrooms were.

"Downstairs, right there, you'll see them," she told me.

I went down the stairs. But I didn't see them. "Bathrooms?" I asked a girl in the hallway. She ignored me and ran away. I turned around and walked the other way. "Bathrooms?" I asked a boy. He pointed vaguely down the hallway, and I ran in that direction. But still, I didn't see a bathroom. I took a turn down another corridor, running up and down the large hallway, but the doors were all classrooms. "Bathrooms?" I asked a boy having a cookie.

"That corridor," the boy said. "In there."

But it was too late. I couldn't hold it anymore. Urine trickled down my pants until it puddled by my feet. The boy pointed at my crotch and started laughing. I ran down the hallway and just kept running, running from corridor to corridor until I saw a beam of light. The main door. I ran out and didn't stop until I was back at home.

My pants were almost dry by the time I arrived home. My sisters were home, dancing to a song on the radio I'd never heard before.

"Why are you so early?" Eliz asked. "Mom's shopping."

I didn't answer. I stepped into their room.

"Pee-yew, you!" Ela said. "You stink."

"Adem. What happened? Eliz asked, more kindly. But before I could tell her, her voice grew stern. "Go directly to the bathroom and take a shower."

I walked into the bathroom and peeled off my pants. As I stepped into the shower, Ela knocked on the door. "I left some clean pants for you outside the door." I couldn't tell if she was angry.

When I finished, I went back to my sisters' room and stood in the doorway. Quietly, as heat rose up and into my face, and I held back tears, I asked, "What do I do with my pants?"

"We can't let Mom find out," Ela said. "You'll be in trouble." She went to the bathroom and picked up my dirty clothes and put them in the laundry bag. "We won't say anything."

"I couldn't find the bathroom," I said, answering her question from before.

Ela ripped a piece of paper from a notebook. "Where is your classroom? What's the number on the door?" she asked.

"Um. It's 221."

"Okay. So, here is your classroom." She wrote 221 in a rectangle. "Here is the hallway," she drew a line, "and here are the stairs. At the bottom of the stairs, turn right, and then turn right again. And that's where the bathroom is." She handed me the piece of paper. "Fold it up and go pick out the pants you are going to wear tomorrow. Then put it in the pocket in case you get lost again. When you come back, we can go over how to tell time again," she said.

***

As I rinse the last plate, I realize just how long I've been struggling to keep up with my classmates and my friends. I've come from behind my whole life. Francesca was really the only person in my world who was younger than me. She made me feel like a man. I didn't need to prove to her that I was something that I wasn't. When it was me and Francesca alone, I never felt like I was struggling to keep up. I just *was*.

The plate cracks in my hand. I let out a little laugh, then shake my head at how pathetic I am. And then I wonder if it's a sign. *It must be. It must be a sign. Yup. It's a sign you are broken, Adem.*

I throw out the bits of broken plate and move on to the pots and pans, heating a second pot of water on the stove for the next load of dishes.

It's been six months since the day Savas Kartal and five of his Nationalist gang members came to the Technical University, looking for trouble. That was the day he threatened to kill me. Even before that day, Savas was known as an enemy of the revolutionaries. My roommates had schooled me about him. He is twenty-eight years old, from Oren, a village on the Aegean coast some 360 kilometers south of Istanbul. His father was a policeman, killed during a gunfight with revolutionaries near their hometown. Ever since, word is that he's sworn to eradicate the revolutionaries, "Communist sell-outs," he calls them, from the country. It's also said that he carries two pistols in the side pockets of the jacket that he always wears no matter the weather. He worked as a courier for the Nationalist Party while leading the gangs at City University. I'd seen Savas and his gang half a dozen times before the day they made their way into our school. They would come to the university and watch the students from outside the gates. I'd noticed that Savas would compulsively touch, straighten, and smooth the flaps of his jacket pockets; checking his guns, I supposed.

The day Savas came through the gates and entered the school grounds had started out pretty routinely. Polat and I and a few of our roommates had walked out of our Differential Equations class in the Mechanical Engineering Building. We were chatting about the goal Hammer had scored with the National Team against Greece. As we emerged from the stairwell into the building's main hallway—a marble-floored, basketball court-size space stretched between walls of windows—there stood Savas Kartal and five members of his Nationalist gang. They were at the far end of the hallway in front of the exit. They didn't belong inside the building and I wasn't sure how they had entered.

"Death to Communism!" Savas yelled, pumping his fist in the air as his men spread out blocking our path. I looked at Polat and then one of our other roommates, Pars. I knew at least three of the guys in our group packed guns, including Polat, though I didn't know for certain if anyone was armed that day. I had been offered a gun when I moved in with them but had declined.

"Fascist dogs, go back to your doghouse and obey your masters!" Pars yelled back. But, instead of retreating, they inched forward, stepping in tandem.

One, two, three. I counted. Four, five, six. And then, suddenly, Savas stopped.

His eyes locked on me. "I will kill you!" Savas said, pointing directly at me, grabbing his left side pocket. Then, swaggering over to a stack of wrought-iron chairs, he grabbed one and heaved it toward me. I stood there; immobile. Not out of bravery, but rather outrage. I didn't move; I didn't retreat, and I didn't look at the flying chair. It landed with a crash and skidded toward me, coming to a screeching stop just about a meter away from me. I didn't say anything. I was too angry, staring at Savas even after he'd turned away. He patted his jacket flap. "We're done here!" he announced. And just as quickly as they had blocked our way, Savas and his gang turned around and walked out of the building.

***

I finish washing the dishes.

Pulling my reddened hands from the wet chill, I think about how Francesca used to hold these hands, now chapped, cold; hands retired from romance and reduced to housework. Francesca. My love. My dark love. Being with her was like a glimpse of heaven; I saw it, touched it, lived it, and when the visit was over, I returned to earth, to dread.

I grab a dish towel, stained brown with flecks of food, trying to remember who's on laundry duty.

I walk into the living room and sit down on a low stool next to the coffee table. Grabbing my notepad, I flip open my textbook to Bernoulli's Equation. I seem to be able to understand the math, but I'm lost in using the principle to solve problems. I cannot figure out how to apply the formula to the contour on an aircraft wing or a jet engine blade. We've been working on this concept for more than a week in my Fluid Mechanics class, but I just can't seem to think in three dimensions, an elementary exercise for a mechanical engineer. Part of the problem is that I'm not learning anything in class from the professor. I can't understand him. It's not just the material I don't understand, it's his actual words. He mumbles; he sounds like an old, crazy man muttering to himself. I don't know what it is about Technical University, but several other professors are like that. Yet, no one seems to complain or talk about it—or even mention it—and they are all passing the courses. So, it's gotta be me. *What the hell is wrong with me?*

As I give it yet another try, try to visualize a problem, a group of Polat's gang members walk into the room. They throw themselves down on the two daybeds that decorate the common space. Pars, Kenan, and Taner sit on one bed. Polat enters last and joins Cengiz on the other bed.

They're a tight bunch. They all went to the same high school, one of the top schools in the country, the one I couldn't get into when I took the entrance exam in sixth grade. As they pull out their guns and start cleaning them, they launch into a conversation about Marx and Lenin and their teachings, another subject that goes over my head. "Supremacy of the proletariat" and "the legitimacy of collateral damage." *What the hell does that even mean?* "Innocent people killed during a revolution is collateral damage, unavoidable, and legitimate," Polat declares, putting down the rag he's cleaning his Barracuda revolver with; he slides a bullet into the chamber. Taner, whom I've noticed is very particular about how he cleans his 9 mm Beretta, grabs Polat's rag and keeps shining up his pistol.

I try to ignore them and concentrate while every few pages clearing my throat, subtly trying to send them a message. But they grow louder and louder and I clench my book harder and harder until I burst. I slam my book shut and shout, "Can't you shut up, for just one night?"

"Whoa. Baby Adem. You got a knot in your diapers? What the hell is wrong with you?" asks Polat, as he slides a second bullet into his revolver.

"Nothing!" I yell in response. "What's wrong with *you*? Marx and Lenin, the fools, have spawned a generation of clowns like you and I can't—" Before I finish, Polat springs up from his seat and shuts the revolver's drum. He swiftly launches the gun's cold barrel to the back of my head. He holds it to the left of my right ear.

I don't move. I can't move. I don't want to move.

My shoulders drop. I feel an intense sense of relief. This is what I need. This. An end. I am tired of living. Polat can put me out of my misery. *This is the solution, Adem. Sure, it's the weak way out. You won't have to jump off Lovers' Leap or the Bosporus Bridge. Let Polat kill you. He'll be a murderer and you'll be the brave kid who stood up to him. It'll be better for everyone. Mom and Dad won't need to suffer from the embarrassment of your failures anymore. Will Francesca cry when she hears the news?*

I take a deep, calm breath. *Death, please, come get me.*

I hear the click of the hammer being cocked. I smile. Death, I finally understand, is the formula for life.

"Take your words back or I will pull the trigger," Polat says.

"Be a man, Polat. Pull the damn trigger." I hear the poise in my voice. "Death," I say to myself, again. "Come get me."

With the hammer cocked, Polat doesn't even have to pull the trigger. A simple touch or bump, even a slight twitch of clumsiness could release the bullet in the drum. Pop! It would take one ten-thousandth of a second for the bullet to travel twelve centimeters before it lodges in my brain. *I came into this world by accident; I'll leave the same way. Easy come, easy go. Do it, Polat. End it for me.*

"Everybody has a guardian angel," my grandmother used to say. "You Adem, you have two guardian angels."

Every Sunday morning I'd sit at the window with intense expectation that Grandma would arrive and hand me my favorite chocolate bars, white inside. As I savored them, she'd tell me her stories. If Mom and Dad went away for the weekend, she'd stay with us. Several times she stayed with us an entire week, which meant more chocolate bars and more stories.

Grandma wasn't an overly religious woman, but she lived where the word *Christian* was used for the first time, in Antioch. Her city was where the first Christian church was built, and the only place where Jews, Christians, and Muslims lived together without conflict since the founding of each faith. "Because you were born despite all the odds," she would answer each time I asked what she meant, a response I only understood after my mom told me how she and my dad never wanted me. "You have needed your guardian angels since before you were born, and you have kept them busy ever since."

I wonder if Grandma's guardian angels are hovering around me right now. If I want to die, will they help me? Or is their job to keep me alive? Are they even there?

"The opposite of fear is not bravery," Grandma would tell me. This was one of the things she learned from visiting evangelical Christians whom she and others in Antioch would host during pilgrimages to their town. "It is faith. One can be fearful and brave at the same time. They do not oppose each other. It is faith which opposes fear. The opposite of fear is faith."

Pull the trigger, Polat. I am not afraid.

"But, if you have no faith, you live in fear all the time. Faith is not a feeling; it's a decision." As Polat holds the gun steady against my head, it occurs to me that Grandma's musings can be represented as mathematical formulas: if my spiritual force is a total of one hundred and I have fifty units of faith, it means I have fifty units of fear. If I have no fear right now, do I have 100 percent faith?

What are you waiting for, Polat? Do it. I'm not afraid. With two bullets in the chamber, there's a 33 percent chance that it could work. But is it 33 percent? Did he put the two bullets next to each other in the chamber? If he'd left one empty slot in between, would the probability rise? As I contemplate the question, I feel the gun move ever so slightly. *No.*

Though my eyes are focused on one spot in the middle of the room, I can see almost everyone in the group. Taner is frozen, holding an unlit cigarette in his mouth and a lighter in his hand. Cengiz, who was eating a candy bar, has stopped chewing. Pars is holding a bottle of orange soda to his mouth. Kenan has turned his head away and is looking out the window; maybe he's bored with the drama, or, maybe I misread Kenan and he's really not as tough as I thought. Maybe he can't stomach what's about to happen to me, my brains exploding all over the room, but he's too afraid to be the one to stop it. They all just sit there. No one tries to stop Polat. No one stands up for me.

"Take your words back, or I will pull the trigger," Polat repeats.

I say nothing.

Francesca. What would you think of me now? Would you leave me a second time? Would you think I'm crazy? Would you pity me? Would you tell me you love me and give me a reason to live again?

I close my eyes against the tears that sting the back of my eyes. *I will never taste your lips again, never touch your hair, never smell your skin, never feel your breasts pressing against me, never look into your eyes again.* I take a deep breath. *My life ended when you left me. Do you know that? Do you?*

If the gun goes off the pain will be instantaneous. But then, my heart would cease to ache.

I hear a click, the two pieces of metal hitting each other rings in my ear. I feel the spring of the trigger, a vibration.

There's a buzzing in my ears. *Am I dead? Is it over?*

I can see the mouths on my roommates faces moving, I can see their eyes widen in shock. *You are not dead, Adem.*

No one moves. Including me.

The gun remains against my head.

Pull the trigger again, Polat. Let's go!

Polat engages the hammer again. Two bullets in five slots. My death formula now is $2/5 = 0.4$; now we're at 40 percent. *Pull the trigger.*

Nothing is happening.

I am not going to give in, Polat. I'm not going to cave. Pull the damn trigger.

I remain still. Quiet.

Polat pulls the trigger again. I feel the slight movement of the nozzle; I hear the click again, a ping, then resonance, and then silence. I feel no blood oozing down my neck. I see no brains splattered on the walls or the couches or my roommates.

Polat immediately cocks the hammer again.

"Take your words back, or I will pull the trigger," he says for the third time. Now we're closer. There are four slots left, and two bullets. It's now 50-50.

"Go ahead," I say, "pull the trigger."

Taner stands up from the daybed and walks past me. I feel Polat step back. I don't move. The gun barrel grazes slowly against the back of my head until the pressure is gone, until the gun is no longer there. I don't move. Taner walks back into my view. He's holding Polat's revolver.

Cengiz clears his throat. "Bread. Adem go . . . buy bread . . . breakfast . . . money's in the key bowl." Cengiz's words echo in my buzzing ears, muting some of what he's saying. I look at him, trying to read his lips. His face is pale. He goes back to chewing his candy bar.

I ignore the key bowl and leave the house.

I should be dead right now.

8

THE VALUE OF LIFE

I KNEW EARLY ON THAT I WAS NO CHILD PRODIGY. I SPENT EVERY day listening to and watching my older sisters study. My mother plopped me in their room while they were studying. I watched how they learned, and I learned to read and write by age four. It was that simple. One does not have to be a genius to do that.

Admittedly, it took me a while to believe the commander's wife had it wrong. I wanted to be a genius. I wanted to get by without studying. I tested out my "genius hypothesis" for far too long, which put me behind even more than I already was. I studied just enough to earn Cs and Ds. Later, it became a strategy. I'd complete enough of the answers during a test to pass, then stop, and turn in my exam. The more my dad pressured me to study, the less I did and the poorer the grades I got. My senior year in high school, at the end of the first semester, I had the worst report card the school had ever seen: ten failing courses out of fifteen, including gym. The teacher was mean and I didn't feel like climbing the rope. During the second semester, I increased my effort just enough to graduate. I knew my school grades weren't important, that it would all come down to the national university entrance exam. That was my focus. I'd been preparing on my own for two years. I'd told no one. I liked having my own strategy. I liked how I resisted my dad with my school performance while knowing I had my own plan.

I didn't find the studying hard at all, especially the math. I like numbers. Memorizing them, using them, calculating with them. I know the tag numbers of neighbors' cars, the cabstand's cars, even some city busses. I memorize numbers aimlessly. I've memorized my classmates' ID numbers. I've memorized the populations and GDPs of countries as listed on the cards that came out of chewing gum wrappers. When I'm on a city bus, I calculate how many basketballs would fit in it, then how many soccer balls, then how many ping-pong balls. I estimate how many decks of cards would need to be piled on top of one another to reach the top of a building. Sometimes, I time myself on how many seconds it takes me to solve a problem. I've counted out the world's capitals, listing them in my head. I've also memorized the fifty US states and their populations.

I find myself standing in front of the bakery. I wasn't planning on following Cengiz's order to buy bread. But I'm here. I point to a round loaf on the shelf that I think the gang won't like. It's my favorite. "Five loaves. That kind," I say.

I head back to the house and enter a smoke-filled, dead-quiet room. Everyone looks at me as I walk through the living room into the kitchen. The floor is freshly mopped, dishes dried, counter tidied, trash taken out. I leave the bag of bread on the counter then trace my steps back through the living room, ignoring the stares. Without saying anything, I walk back out the door and head to my parents' apartment for the night.

***

In the morning, when I arrive at school, there's a small crowd gathered on the sidewalk near the front doors of the main building. A few members of Polat's gang are off to the side. Taner catches my eye and walks over to me immediately, grabbing my arm, "Cengiz and Kenan have been shot!"

"What?"

"Cengiz and Kenan have been shot. They've been taken to the hospital."

"What?" I say, shaking my head. That's when I notice the blood. It's splattered all over the sidewalk and the wall. "What happened?" I ask, trying to pull my eyes away from the blood.

"It was Savas Kartal and two others. I saw them. I saw it happen. Savas yelled, 'Death to Communists!' and began to shoot. Kenan was yelling back at them, 'Low-life dogs, go to hell!' "

I feel nauseous.

"Polat ran after them, there were gunshots."

I can't form any words.

"We're marching to Taksim Square, to the hospital to protest," says Taner. "The police must provide more security around the school. It's our demand. Just now they arrived without sirens, they didn't do anything, they didn't even ask for statements from witnesses. When I tried to tell them what I saw and who did it, they told me to go away."

I join the march. As the group shifts away from the school door and toward the hospital, we spread out past the sidewalk and into the street, blocking traffic. Cars and trucks start honking at us in support which adds to the escalating energy of the group as more students arrive and the crowd swells. "Revolutionists never die!" someone shouts. "Down with the fascists!" screams another. The energy is palpable, a buzzing. A vibration. The crowd breaks into song, "At the end of the darkness is a glorious dawn." By the time we arrive at the hospital, about two miles from the school, our crowd of a few dozen has grown exponentially. I turn around to see just how large. A sea of faces reaches back four or five blocks. I walk backward as I scan the crowd, counting. There are more than a thousand people. The police stop us at the entrance of the hospital and tell us to back off. The gang presses them for an update on Cengiz and Kenan's condition. They ignore our demands. When Cengiz and Kenan were shot, the police presence was weak; but here, dozens, maybe even a hundred strong have shown up to stop us from protesting the shooting of two innocent students.

I see Taner move away from the crowd. Somehow he makes his way behind the police line. I watch as he stands near the doors of the hospital, looking aloof, looking like a confused citizen who just exited the hospital. Then, he backs through the doors and disappears into the building.

Pars jumps up onto a wall in front of the hospital. He starts shouting with his hands cupped. "This is the work of a murderer! Savas Kartal is a murderer! He has killed before and he will kill again! If either one of these men dies, I will kill Savas Kartal!"

After a few minutes a megaphone is passed up to the front of the crowd and handed to Pars. "Revolutionaries never die!" he screams and the crowd cheers in response.

"Democracy and freedom are out the door. These fascist thugs are killing us, and the police are doing nothing. Just look at them, the police, just standing there, against us. The murderers walked away. Will anybody arrest Savas Kartal? No. The entire government is on their side, protecting them. That's why we will bring down this government and its rotten, corrupt system. The revolution is near. At the end of this darkness is a glorious dawn."

Taner comes rushing out the doors, jumps up the wall. I watch him as he says something to Pars. Pars almost drops the megaphone. Taner grabs it before it falls and holds it up.

"Cengiz has died," Taner announces. "Cengiz is dead. Murdered by Savas Kartal. Cengiz is dead." "Down with the fascists!" the crowd screams. "Cengiz lives!"

Cengiz is dead?

I start backing away from the crowd.

Cengiz is dead.

Frantically, I push and shove my way through the throng until I am free from the crowd. Then I break into a run. *Cengiz is dead. It should have been me.*

I arrive at the town house about two hours later. Polat, Taner, Pars, and six other members of Polat's gang are sitting in silence. They look up and their somber faces turn into surprised ones when they see me.

"Cengiz is dead," Polat says.

"Yes, I heard. You chase them down?"

"They all got away, in different directions. I almost got Savas."

"Kenan is in the hospital still," Taner says. "He was hit in the thigh. The bullet missed the bone and exited his body. They say he'll be okay."

"That's good," I say, not knowing what else to say.

"Cengiz had no chance. He was hit in the torso. Multiple times. One bullet pierced his heart."

I nod, then sit with them. *What will happen next? Will Polat's gang remain part of the revolutionary movement in theory only, or will they rise up physically? They are not thugs, they are intellectuals, students whose friend was murdered for being a student. He was a student! Murdered for being a student.* I can't wrap my head around this. *Is this my country—students getting murdered because someone has decided that Technical University is the Castle of Communists? What will Polat's gang do—rise up against hit-and-run assassins who shoot freely without any concern of law enforcement, who have the police on their side as well as the government, businesspeople, and Nationalist Party?*

Polat breaks the silence. "This is not the end of our struggle; this is the beginning. There will be more casualties. The fascist gangs work to preserve the status quo, to protect the imperialists. Don't expect the police to arrest the murderers. If you choose to join in the armed struggle, be prepared to be jailed, tortured, shot, or killed. Even those who don't rise up and join the fight may be attacked merely for being a student. We're in the midst of a revolution. Cengiz is a hero."

It's decided unanimously that none of us will go to the funeral service or burial. It's just too risky. Anyone other than close family at the funeral would be an easy target for Savas and his gang.

We listen to the news of Cengiz's murder on the radio. The reporter doesn't use the word "murdered." He doesn't even say that the police are actively looking for the shooter. In fact, the report is completely misleading, twisting the truth and leaving out the facts, the cause. What the public learns is that the cause of Cengiz's murder is a student uprising and protest at Technical University that left one dead and, as a result, the Ministry of the Interior advises Technical University's governing board to close the school until "further notice."

"Just like I said," Polat says, getting up to turn off the radio, "don't expect the police to arrest the murderers."

***

I use the school closure to take a break from the growing unrest, to clear my head, to try to understand what is happening in my country, and to figure out where I fit in.

You're not a fighter, Adem. But, your friend is dead. And your other friend is in the hospital. Savas has threatened to kill you. Savas is the enemy. Is he your enemy, Adem?

I want to belong; I just don't know where I belong. Savas almost killed me and Francesca. I don't have Francesca because of him. I do understand, I'm ultimately at fault. I could have explained to her the bizarre danger I was in. But, yes, maybe Savas is my enemy. But do I live with him as my enemy? Or, do I try to stop him? Do I offer myself up for a suicide mission and save those who want to live? I don't mind dying, it's the possibility of surviving that scares me. Getting caught, being sent to jail.

Torture.

9

THE DISCO

THE STRATEGY I SETTLE ON IS TO MOVE BACK INTO MY PARENTS'
apartment and bury my head in the sand like an ostrich, ignoring calls from
Polat to "man up" and "fight." I realize that by doing this, I will be living
exactly like my parents do—ignoring the real world around me, the rising
violence, the hate, the politics, and focusing on my own small world.

I visit Demir at his school to try to escape the conversation, but it's
everywhere. Although Demir belongs to the upper-middle class—rich with
the trappings of the wealthy, like a horse, a motorcycle, and an American stereo
system—the older he gets, the more he sympathizes with the revolutionaries.
Izzy sides with the government.

During an afternoon tea at Demir's apartment just two days after Cengiz's
murder, the conversation turns political.

"The government is no longer a center-right-nationalist coalition, it is
outright fascist," says Demir. "As it weakens, it becomes more oppressive."

"That's because the revolutionaries are resorting to violence," Izzy retorts.

"The police are biased. When it comes to murders and other crimes
committed by Nationalist gang members, they look the other way and make

no arrests. Yet, they are intensely pursuing the revolutionaries for everything."

I watch them. Back and forth, like a tennis match. I listen but say nothing. I have nothing to contribute. The discussion is endless, the conflict unresolvable. My friend remains dead.

"The revolutionaries want to topple the government by force. They have no respect for democracy or elections. Who does the conflict actually help?" Izzy asks, looking at me. I can't tell if he's being rhetorical. I shrug. They don't seem to notice that I'm not part of their debate. Izzy looks back at Demir and continues his tirade. "Maybe there's some foreign involvement here. I overheard someone in the coffee house actually saying, 'Let the two gangs kill each other. When there are enough deaths on both sides, they'll get tired of it and will stop.' They don't even care."

"Somebody has to care!" Demir says, straightening in his chair and shaking his head. He's agitated. I know he's tearing himself up for justice.

"New manufacturing technologies have made workers more productive and increased profits for the factory owners but they're not sharing the profits with the workers. Inequality is bound to lead to conflict and—"

"The revolutionaries want to confiscate those profits from factory owners," Izzy interrupts. "They want to take the money and redistribute the wealth. Then what happens to the free markets?" I watch him take a sip from his tea and wonder what Demir is going to say.

"There is no free market and you know it. It is all rigged for large corporations and multinationals, which then feed the politicians, and the rich get richer."

"Labor unions always have the right to strike and negotiate higher pay. Why don't they do that?" asks Izzy. "The capitalists are the ones who invest their money and take risks. They should profit as much as free-market forces allow them to. The capitalists are the ones who provide the opportunity for the labor force to earn money. The laborers can become capitalists themselves if they save and invest. No one's stopping them. And what happens when a factory goes bankrupt? The capitalist owner loses his entire investment, but the laborer simply changes jobs."

"Adem, say something," Demir says, jabbing at my arm. He looks at Izzy, who jabs my other arm.

"I don't understand it," I reply. What I want to say is that things are more complicated than just left and right. People have their own versions of socialism or capitalism, their own versions of everything, even the truth.

The doorbell rings.

"Saved by the bell," Izzy says, looking at me.

"The girls are here," Demir says, walking to the door. I look at Izzy, not understanding.

"Demir and I decided you needed to get out. We know you're still depressed about Francesca, and now also, what's going on with the violence at your school; your roommate's death."

"Murder. He was murdered."

Into the house dance five young women.

"I brought my brother Galip," one of the girls says as a tall man walks in, her spitting image. She grabs my hand, pulling me up from the couch and twirling.

"Let's eat and then go dancing!"

"Let's go to the Bosporus—to the Corner Tavern for fish and raki!" another shouts.

And as quickly as they arrived, we're all out the door, two of the women grabbing my hands and pulling me and a third pushing me. The mood is lively; the group splits into two cars. Everyone is singing. The car windows are down and the music blaring. *You are an ostrich, Adem. Enjoy the evening. Just let go.* Their enthusiasm ends up being contagious. I laugh as I watch them sing—it's more like yelling.

We grab a table outside on the deck, next to the water. We start with olive-oiled dishes, fried eggplants, fried hot green peppers, fried potatoes, eggplant salad, red beet salad, crushed walnuts in pepper paste, crushed tomatoes in hot sauce, green beans, red beans, stuffed grape leaves, and stuffed green peppers. Then a little lentil soup, and some cheese, olives, and melons, some calamari, clams, shrimp, and bluefish. Then, some fresh almonds on ice, freshly cut fruits, and crème caramel. And lots of beer, wine, and raki.

An accordion player serenades us. I feel the heat of the alcohol warm my blood as the food fills my empty stomach. After four hours and what amounts to two back-to-back meals at the same table, we're all sated and drunk. We decide to go to Module, a disco near Taksim Square, about fifteen kilometers away. On the way over, I join the chorus, singing and yelling out the open car windows. I give in to the buzz, let the raki do its thing. I let the wind whip away the pain.

Next thing I know, someone is tugging on my arm.

"Wake up, sleepy head. Wake up!" I open my eyes to one of the women kissing me. "You're cute. Let's go dance!" she slurs, pulling me out of the car and wrapping my arm around her waist. Gently disentangling myself, I accompany Galip to the bar to order drinks while the rest of the group rushes out to the dance floor. We find a U-shaped booth that's big enough to hold all of us. As we sit and watch the dancers, we begin to chat about basketball. Galip says he's heard from Izzy and Demir that I used to play. The waiter comes over and sets our drinks down on the large coffee table circled by the booth. As he walks away, a man I don't know approaches our table and, to my surprise, sits down, without hesitation, next to Galip. I wait for Galip to introduce me to his friend, but instead, he looks at me and shrugs. "Hello?" I say in a polite voice meant to sound like one part question, one part welcome. Shouting over the music in a hoarse voice, the man says, "I can come to your table anytime I want, just like this, and sit down, and drink your drinks." His diction is sloppy. He reaches for one of the cocktails and takes a sip. Galip and I look at each other. I clench my teeth and then my fists. Galip looks at me again. "Please don't do anything, Adem," he says as I set my jaw. I don't respond. He hits my knee with his own then bumps my knee harder, and when I don't respond again, he covers his mouth with his hand and leans in close to my ear. "The man is obviously drunk. He's just a drunk idiot."

I can feel my fingers closing into my palms. I'm angry, but I know I must stay focused. "I'm Galip," Galip says, holding out his hand for a shake. The man swipes Galip's hand away and grabs another drink.

ABBA's new hit "Dancing Queen" starts blaring from the speakers. The bar erupts with a buzz of excitement; people seated on either side of us rush to the dance floor; "Young and sweet, only seventeen . . . Dancing Queen!" The disco lights flash, splashing all the white clothing with dizzying hues of purple. What flashes before my eyes is Francesca. She's seventeen and she's dancing, and Savas is shooting at us, and Francesca is leaving. I look at the man sitting at our table, drinking our drinks. It's Savas. I see Savas.

I stand up, taking a step away from the coffee table. "You are not welcome here, please leave," I say in an even tone, sweeping my arm out in a non-combative gesture meant to convey "Get up; leave."

He stands up. He has a full head on me. "Your friend here invited me to drink with you, asshole. I'm not leaving."

I don't move. I just keep my eyes locked on him. "Go. Leave. Now."

The man stares at me, looming over me. I can't tell if he is surprised by my response or merely drunk. The purple lights flash across his face. I fix my stance and harden my fists; but, still, I'm not prepared for his next move. He jumps up onto the coffee table and, in one swift motion, dives, airborne, toward me. He lands a headbutt between my eyes and nose.

My head jerks back, but I remain standing. All I can see are stars that turn purple in the disco lights. I feel warm blood in my throat. The man grabs my shirt at the chest with both hands.

I swing up my arms to dislodge myself from his grip and throw a right hook. And as I do, I see the smug face of every kid who ever bullied me, like a slideshow of my childhood. The final image is Savas. The punch lands between the man's eyebrows. He flies back over the coffee table, hits the floor with a crash, then slides to the edge of the dance floor before coming to a stop. I look around to make sure the man doesn't have any friends lurking.

Galip pumps his fist in the air dramatically, as if he's watching a boxing match, "Knock-down! Yes, ladies and gentlemen! It is a knock-down!" he yells. He gets up and walks over to the man, leaning over gingerly, as if afraid the man will jump up and beat him to a pulp. Then, assured that the man is thoroughly immobilized, Galip steps backward to me, still looking at the man on the floor. He grabs my wrist and lifts my arm up like a referee. "No. It's a knock-out, folks," he says in an announcer's voice. Then he puts down my arm and says, "You knocked him out, man! Wow! In one punch, Adem."

I look over at the man lying there on the side of the dance floor. The disco lights flash over his bloodied face like a scene in a horror flick.

You're a teaser, you turn 'em on, ABBA sings. *Leave them burning and then you're gone . . . Looking out for another.*

I step out of the disco and walk over to lean against the car. My head is throbbing from the liquor and the headbutt. My fist is aching from the punch. I start thinking about Francesca. *What would she think of me now; how would she have reacted to what I just did? Would she have been mortified and embarrassed by my behavior or proud and impressed? It's been seventy-six days since she stormed out of my car. How long am I going to have to live with her memory? With dark love?*

I wake up the next morning in my parents' apartment. The clock on my nightstand reads 11:07 a.m. I have no recollection of how I got here. I'm still wearing my slacks and shirt. My head is killing me. My hand aches. I close my eyes and try to remember what happened. The last thing I can recall is standing in front of the car. I roll over and go back to sleep.

***

Three weeks pass and school remains closed. No Francesca, no dating, and no school. I have no focus, nothing to aspire to, nothing to look forward to, really nothing to live for. The only thing I do have is simply constant pain. Emotional pain becomes physical pain; physical pain becomes psychological pain. Back and forth and back and forth, bombarding me. I can't sleep.

I begin to smoke and drink. I visit nearby gambling houses at night, alone. I go to places hidden away, unlicensed, some in the backs of billiard halls, others in coffeehouses; they open after their fronting business closes. I count well, and fast. I know by calculation that eventually everyone loses, that the gambling house is the guaranteed winner, pulling in a half percent of every pot. The longer one plays, the more one loses. My knowledge enables me to slow down the inevitable, allows me to lose less and play more. I mostly play for myself and spend my tutoring income. Sometimes, though, I play at the higher stakes table for a rich man whose son I had tutored. He finances the bets I make for him.

I can stop, of course. I'm trained for it. The navy high school trained me for it. I'm trained not to fall for an addiction, a woman, drugs, alcohol, gambling, anything; against any dependence, I'm trained. How to leave a burning vessel, how to shoot (though I never was good at it), how to survive in the wilderness, how to save a drowning person. I was trained when I was a navy cadet.

Now all that is out the door; I'm experimenting with life's dregs and misery, and I don't care what happens because it feels like the things I want, the things I care for, I don't have. And worse, it feels like many things I don't care for, I have. Is that the formula to life? I want something, I don't have. I have something, I don't want. That's not a formula, that's a fact . . . That's the fact of my life. Is this how everyone feels?

I've developed a routine. I leave the gambling place around 5:00 a.m. to go to an all-night diner that's popular with neighborhood kids; I watch them, drunk or high, or both, on raki, marijuana, or hashish, while warming my alcohol-filled stomach with intestine or goat-feet soup. At 6:00 a.m. I walk home, slowing down to play with the neighborhood's pack of stray dogs; I feed them my leftovers. Sometimes they follow me home and I raid the fridge then come back out to feed them more. It feels good to be noticed, loved, touched, even if it's by a pack of wild dogs.

I sleep until noon, then start all over again in the evening. My parents either don't notice or don't care. They ask me no questions. Don't ask, don't tell reigns. The cycle continues until Technical University reopens after a two-month hiatus. Then cold turkey, I stop smoking, drinking, and gambling. I go back to school with a renewed sense of urgency laced with a little bit of fear.

Police officers are deployed and stand at the doors now, with ID checks and full pat downs. They even have a metal detector. I don't believe for a minute it's going to stop Savas Kartal from hitting his targets. All he and his gang have to do is lie in wait outside the school.

And then it happens.

We've been back in class for a few days. It's a Thursday morning and I'm in the middle of my twenty-minute walk to school. My head is down, but I know the path well. Without looking up, I can see the trees lining the road, feel the width of the sidewalk underfoot, visualize the cuts of architecture on the apartment buildings attached to each other for seventy years or longer, their gargoyles and slanted roofs, most only five stories high, some six. I'm in front of the cabstand near the dried fruits store, waiting to cross the street, when a student comes running in my direction through the red light, dodging cars and almost getting hit by a truck.

"Shots were fired!" he screams, "shots! At the school!" he repeats, without slowing down, yelling to anyone who will listen. I look around. I don't know who I'm looking for or what I expect to see. The second the light turns green, I run toward the school. As I get closer, the swell of people increases. Most are running away from the school. A block away, I have to elbow my way through, almost getting pushed over in the stampede of people going the other way. I put my head down and barrel through, stopping right in front of the door to the schoolyard. I can see the new blood splatter. Polat comes up behind me, startling me. "Pars," he says. "Pars."

"What? What happened?"

"Savas Kartal and his men, eyewitnesses said. They were over there across the street," Polat says, pointing, "and Savas shot him, shot Pars, and they all walked away. Just walked away. Police didn't do anything. A good Samaritan drove Pars to the hospital, right before I got here."

Within an hour, more than a thousand students have gathered and we begin to march toward the hospital in protest. This time, I'm in front with Polat and Taner.

"I'll try the back door," Taner says, and I watch him walk behind the hospital.

From megaphones, student leaders speak to the crowd. They call for unity in the revolutionary cause, vow to bring down the government and avenge the victim's blood. As the speeches continue, Taner emerges from the front doors of the hospital. "Pars is dead," he says. "Multiple gunshot wounds." Nine weeks ago it was Pars who spoke from a megaphone, promising revenge. Now he's dead, too. I feel my blood run cold. Who will be next?

Back at the house, it's a déjà vu moment, with an extra empty chair. We sit in silence as we did after Cengiz was killed. "This . . . what happened to Pars, what happened to Cengiz, this is the struggle," Polat says, reaching toward the coffee table and picking up the pack of Camel cigarettes that belonged to Pars. Next to the pack of cigarettes is a plate with the leftovers from Pars's breakfast, bits of bread fried in margarine, a piece of cheese, and a teaspoon of sour cherry jam. The hot tea that he burned his tongue on this morning, ice cold by now. "There will be even more casualties. I may be next, or you, Adem," Polat says, handing me the pack. I take one, accepting a light from Taner. "The fascist gangs will continue to work to preserve the status quo, to protect the imperialists," Polat says, pausing to take a long draw. "No one has been named in Cengiz's murder, more than two months later. No one will be named in Pars's either. Mark my words. Pars is a hero. Cengiz is a hero. And Kenan, even though he has left us to go back home to Antalya, is a hero."

By late afternoon the next day, all of Pars's cigarettes have been smoked. Once again, we're sitting in the living room, silent with our thoughts. There's a gentle knocking on the front door. Though it's barely audible, I jump. I think I see Taner jump too. I point to the door and Polat reaches for his gun. There are three more raps, a little louder this time. Taner grabs his gun, too, then slips into the kitchen. Polat crouches behind the couch. Once he's in place, his gun cocked, Polat gives me a nod to open the door.

10

KING OF THE FOREST

THERE ARE FOUR MORE KNOCKS.

"Who is it?" I ask, while moving toward the door, stopping behind a structural column.

"Nail Ozkan," a voice comes from outside the door. "Pars's father."

I look at Polat. He nods. I open the door. A man in a white shirt with bloodshot eyes and Pars's face stares back at me. Next to him is a boy, maybe six years old, holding a ball. There's an empty crate on the stoop next to them.

"I'm coming from the field," the man says, looking down at the boy, then looking back up at me. It takes a second for me to understand that he's saying he came from the cemetery. They buried Pars today. He doesn't want to say it in front of the boy. We made the choice, as we had done with Cengiz, not to go to the funeral.

"I came to pick up his belongings," the man says, then looks down at the kid again. "This is Aslan, his brother."

"Please come in," I say, opening the door all the way. The man picks up the crate and walks in. I shake his hand and extend my sympathies. Polat comes out from the behind the couch and Taner, too. I feel awkward. I don't know what to say other than "I'm sorry for your loss." I don't know how much the little boy knows. I'm relieved when Polat says he will show Pars's father to his room.

Polat stops in the hallway and turns to me. "Maybe you and Aslan can kick the ball around. Outside. Would you do that?"

I nod at Pars's father, then look down at Aslan. "Wanna go out and play?"

Without answering me, the boy silently turns and opens the door. I take his actions as a "yes," and follow him outside. "Pars is gone, Pars is gone," he starts saying over and over, clutching the ball and walking in circles.

"Aslan—do you want to kick the ball to me? I'll kick it back to you."

"Pars is gone."

"Where did Pars go?" I ask, trying to get him to talk. I wonder what his parents told him about his big brother.

"Pars is gone."

"Hey, Aslan, do you know what 'Pars' means?"

"It means leopard."

"Do you know what your name means, Aslan?"

"It means lion."

"Yes, you are right. Your big brother is, *was,* a leopard. And you. Well, you are the lion. You know what a lion is?"

"The king of the forest."

"That's right. He isn't scared of anything. He never backs down to anybody." *I wish I were a lion.*

"Even an elephant?"

"Even an elephant. You know what your last name means—Ozkan?"

"No."

"It means like true blood, the essence of blood. It means you're the lion with true blood."

"Okay."

"Do you go to school, Aslan, Aslan Ozkan?"

"Next year."

We sit down on the front stoop. He doesn't want to kick the ball. So we talk. First it's about names. Then I start teaching him some arithmetic. After about a half hour, Pars's father comes outside with the crate filled with the contents of his eldest son's life—clothes, towels, and a few books.

"Goodbye Aslan, King of the Forest! Nice meeting you," I say as Aslan walks away. I wonder what he will remember of his brother. I wonder if his parents will talk about Pars with him. I wonder if they consider Pars a hero.

***

The *Nation's Daily* reports that student violence isn't limited to Technical University or even to Istanbul anymore. Protests and uprisings at universities are spreading quickly through the country from Edirne in the west to Kars in the east, from Black Sea Technical to Adana Cukurova on the Mediterranean. I come to understand that what is happening isn't just about Polat or Savas Kartal or even me anymore; the conflict has grown and is spreading—fast. It's turned from random shootings into planned attacks targeting groups and individuals. The paper reports that the number of students killed has reached one thousand. "Alarming," an editorial calls the violence. Another calls the deaths of so many young people "shocking," especially in a country that has always had low crime rates. A third article reports that the military is watching the conflict closely and has warned the government to put a stop to these "senseless killings."

***

Another four weeks pass, and the Technical University's governing board announces the school will reopen on November 15. I've spent the month smoking and drinking and hitting the gambling rooms late at night to poison myself even more as I try to drown out the strange feelings of guilt I have; Savas threatened *me*, but it's two of my friends who are dead.

On the first morning back, I'm lost in thought, my head down, as I walk to school. I'm looking at the concrete hexagonal pieces of the sidewalk, trying to avoid stepping on their edges. I'm worried about the semester ahead and the relentless schoolwork. I'm not sure I'm going to make it to graduation. I calculate the grades I need to pass each course and if I fail only one more course, how long it will be before I'm expelled.

What would Grandma say about my quandary? "God created the heavens and the earth. To do that, three things are required: power, authority, and wisdom. God's power, authority, and wisdom are endless. God also gave *us* power, authority, and wisdom, but they are limited in strength so that we do not destroy ourselves." Grandma said, "A soldier and a criminal may both have the power to shoot but a criminal doesn't have the authority." I don't feel I have any power or authority or wisdom to speak of, whatsoever.

It smells like roasting almonds. My eyes drift from the sidewalk, and I look up and see that I'm in front of the dried fruits store. I'm nine minutes into my walk to school, I have eleven to go. My timing is perfect. I'll be five minutes early for my 10:00 a.m. class.

Then, as if Grandma is sending me a message, the skies darken. Lightning flares. And, seconds later thunderclaps rumble and it begins to rain. I stop walking and lift my head up to the rain. I stand there, enjoying how the drops feel on my face, how they trickle down my neck and into my open collar. Strangers around me pull umbrellas out of briefcases and bags; others, unprepared for the unexpected rain, run into doorways and buildings. As I watch people disperse, I catch a glimpse of Savas Kartal ahead on my side of the street, his left hand against the flap of his parka's side pocket as he disappears into the alcove of an old townhouse set back a couple meters from the rest of the buildings. It thunders again.

I stand completely still as my heart races. *Was that actually Savas Kartal or am I imagining it? Could it be him? Oh my Lord, what if it is? What will he do? What do I do? What can I do? You can't just stand here, Adem. If it's really Savas Kartal, you are an open target.* I cross the street and continue to walk to school. *Don't turn your head. Don't turn your head, Adem. Just walk. Just keep walking and looking forward.* But, I don't listen to myself; I turn my head. I make eye contact. It *is* Savas Kartal. He and his gang of three, huddled together in an archway suddenly step forward. Exiting their base in a V-formation, they begin to cross the street, slowly but deliberately in my direction. I stop, frozen, watching Savas. He reaches into his parka pocket and in one swift motion pulls out his gun and points it at me. Everything slows down. I watch myself dive face first onto the wet pavement, scraping my cheek as I go down. I see the flame burst out of the gun barrel and I hear a simultaneous pop. The bullet hits the curb and bounces over me, whistling into the stucco wall to my right. *How did he miss me?* The few people still out in the rain begin screaming and running for cover, their umbrellas bobbing behind them. I spring up and begin to run. My cheek is burning. I run to the nearest building. The door is locked. I run to the next building; that one's locked, too. I keep running. I hear three more shots, then footsteps. *How is he missing me?* I continue to run, looking back every few seconds, they're walking, but somehow getting closer. I try the door at the next building. It's unlocked. I swing it open, violently, and run straight up the marble stairs in front of me. Second floor. Third. Fourth. I take the steps two, sometimes three at a time. *Where am I going? What is happening?* I stop on the fourth-floor landing. *What next? Where do I go? What do I do? A plan. I need a plan.* I hear footsteps and voices. I look down the open stairwell and see Savas and two others. Where's the third? I look up. *I can only go up. The roof! I need to get to the roof.* There's one more flight. I quicken my pace. I get to the fifth floor and look around the landing. I see a ladder leaning against the wall and run toward it, hoping it means there's an exit hatch to the roof. I look up at the ceiling, looking for my escape hatch. *And there it is!* I grab the ladder and climb, unlatching and thrusting the hatch open. It squeaks and crashes with a bang on the roof. The rain assaults me as I step up onto the roof. I slam the hatch back down. I can't lock it from the outside. I look around for something to put on top of the hatch to weigh it down, to make it more difficult to open. *The ladder.* I run back to the hatch, open it, grab the ladder and throw it up onto the roof. *That should slow them down.* I look left then right. Both connecting buildings are taller than the one I'm on. *You're going to have to jump up, then pull yourself up and over to get onto the next roof. You have no choice, you need to keep moving.* I know that even without a ladder Savas and his men will figure out a way to get up here. The building to the north looks a little shorter. I walk to the far end of the roof, run to the edge of the building and jump. As my feet hit the air, I see Francesca's lithe body jumping off the Lovers' Leap wall. *Francesca. Would you believe me if I told you that Savas Kartal wants to kill me?*

My body and head slam into the side of the building. My left hand misses the ledge. I catch the top of the wall with four fingers on my right hand and immediately feel my grip slipping. *Is this the day I die?*

I swing my left arm up. I grab the top of the wall, readjust my right hand and with a strength I didn't know I had, pull myself up onto the ledge and fall onto the slanted roof. I hear the hatch bang open behind me. I look down, it is Savas. I stand but can't get a footing on the uneven and slippery tiles. I throw myself down to hide myself from Savas and start sliding down the roof backward, my knees and head banging against the sharp tiles. I can taste warm blood mixing with the cold rain as I try to grip something to slow my backward slide down the wet roof. *I thought it was going to be a gunshot that killed me, but maybe fate has me falling off a roof.* I come to a stop when my foot hits the gutter. I can't see Savas, but I know he's coming. I look down over my shoulder to a terrace one floor below me. *I could drop down onto the terrace, but where do I go then? If the owners are home, they'd call the police. Once the police are involved, I'll be worse off than I am now since they work with Savas and the Nationalist Party. I'm one of the assumed enemies.*

I need to get to the next building. I stand up slowly. Then, as carefully and as quickly as I can, I walk, on the edge of the roof, crouching down, one foot on the tile, one foot on the gutter. I hear the pop of gunfire behind me. At the far side, I jump about two meters down onto the flat roof of the next building. *Just like my mother did when she was trying to get rid of me. Is this some kind of poetic justice from nineteen years ago?* I turn around to see if Savas is coming but can't see him. *I need to get back inside a building. I'm too exposed out here.* I find a metal door, but it's locked. I run across the rooftop to the attached building, heaving myself over another, shorter wall and landing on its tar-covered surface. I turn around again. Savas is on the slanted roof, two houses behind me. Only one of his men is with him. *Where are the other two?* Savas fires at me. I duck my head as I run over to the metal hatch in the middle of the roof. It's unlocked. I throw it open and jump down into a dark hallway. I'm in. There's no time for me to figure out how to shut the hatch. *They're going to know where I am. I've got to get out of this building.* I run down four flights and as I get closer to the front door, I hear a police siren. I look out to the street; three police cars have pulled up, their emergency lights flashing. Suddenly, being inside seems unsafe. *I need to get out of this building. What if they come in and search it? But I can't go outside, either. I have a university ID that says I'm a member of the Castle of Communists. The police are not on my side. You are in this alone, Adem. Figure it out.* I turn around in circles, a stream of water running down my face and into my eyes. Trying to catch my breath, I hear a thump above me. Savas and his men are coming down the stairs. The only way for me to go is down. Down to the basement. I take the stairs, quietly, and enter a dark, narrow hallway. I can hear Savas talking to his men, but the words are unintelligible. I trip over something and fall, holding my breath to stop myself from screaming out in pain. I curse myself and get up, reaching for the wall to use as an anchor. But, my hand falls into emptiness. Where there should be a wall, there is nothing. I lose my balance and fall over, banging my head against the wall. Confused, I blink my eyes so I can adjust to the darkness. My hand has found a crawl space a few feet off the ground. I blink again to see a narrow, dark space filled with blankets. I fold myself up and crawl inside. Inside I can't see at all. I move a few blankets in front of me to cover myself, hide myself even more. I can hear Savas talking, clearly now. They must be right above me in the first-floor entry hall.

"Where'd he go?" a voice asks.

"Don't know," another voice answers.

"Do you think he's here, still in the building?" a different voice asks, in a loud whisper. "I bet he's gone by now. Slipped away."

"I'm gonna check downstairs. Follow me."

I hear their footsteps, getting closer and closer. *Does Savas have the authority to shoot me, Grandma? He sure has the power. I hope he does not have the wisdom to find me here.* I push my back flat against the wall of my hiding place. Between me and my killer are three blankets, and three meters.

"Go . . . and find the custodian," someone says, I think it's Savas. "I'm not leaving 'til we find him. He's the kid from the school of Communists. He was standing there with the Communists. You saw how he defied me, looked right at me with those eyes, with that face that looks like the murderer who killed my father."

It is Savas. This man is crazy.

"Isn't the murderer dead?" someone says.

"It doesn't matter. I know his kind, he's a young Communist. He's got to go. And I'll be the one to do it. I said so; I gave my word. Publicly. Everyone will know that Savas Kartal keeps his word. I don't know how I missed him. I can see his face in my head. I will never forget that face. Right now and right here I promise you, this kid will never get away from me again. First, I will find him. Then, I will kill him."

Are Grandma's angels with me right now in this hole in the basement? Do they see this mad man? Or they're not there at all, like Santa, they're a part of feel-good stories told to comfort children.

"I found the custodian. He's down there shoveling coal to the furnace. He says nobody came downstairs."

"You sure? You checked?"

"Yes, boss. He's not here. He must have slipped out."

"All right, I'll talk with the police, tell them he was shooting at us. Okay? Five or six shots . . . that we escaped into the building for safety. Got it?"

"Got it, boss."

"Don't give too much information. He's mine. Let's go."

Their footsteps fade. After about a minute, I hear the building's front door open and shut.

I start shaking. *What if it's a trick? What if they pretended to leave?* I remain in the crawl space, surrounded by the blankets and darkness. I start counting to calm myself. *I'll count to one thousand, and then I'll leave.*

***

My foot starts cramping and as I stretch, I realize I must have fallen asleep. But this nightmare is real. I don't know how long I've been here. I edge myself out of the crawl space slowly, gingerly, remaining hidden behind a blanket. It's dark in the hallway, but there's enough light to see shadows. *If Savas is waiting down here for me, his eyes will be adjusted to the dark, he'll be able to see me move.* I peer out of the crawl space but can't see anything. I sit there with a blanket wrapped over my head, leaving a little window for my eyes. *It's too risky to go up the stairs and out the front door. I have to find the basement exit. There has to be one. I have a 50-50 chance of running in the correct direction. Grandma, what do I do? Do I go left? Do I go right?* I wait a beat. I get no response but feel my body list to the left. *Left. Okay, Grandma. I'm going left. On three. One, two, three.* I hold my breath, burst out of the crawl space, and run to the left down the narrow corridor. *A door!* I whip it open, anticipating that Savas could be on the other side, lying in wait. The room—the furnace room—appears to be empty. I look around. There are three doors inside the room. A sliver of daylight edges in through a small, grime-covered window. I check my watch; it's 12:43 p.m. I've been here for almost three hours. I open one of the doors and walk into a courtyard filled with pots of wilting daisies and petunias. No one is around. I breathe in the fresh air. My lungs expand and my shoulders fall. It's stopped raining.

I peer out to the left and right, then walk across the courtyard to the next building. I test the door to that building's basement entrance. It's unlocked. I enter and walk through the corridor and up the stairs to the front. I look out the iron-framed glass door to the cobblestone street. Even though I'm now a block away, I'm still afraid that Savas or his men or the police are standing guard outside. I step out the door to the sidewalk and glance both ways. Then glance both ways again. And then, so as not to arouse any suspicion, I saunter into a crowd of people, quickening my pace at the start of each block until I'm walking as fast as I can, my head down, until I'm at the front door of my parents' apartment building.

Was it my angels that saved me, Grandma? I can't see them, but does that mean they don't exist? Do they move as fast as the speed of light and that's why I can't see them? If they slowed down, would I see them? Were they the ones that protected me in the womb from Mom's two-meter jumps? From Polat's gun or Savas's bullets?

I unlock the door. The apartment is quiet. Empty. I head right to the bathroom and turn on the shower, inspecting my face in the mirror as the water heats up.

11

MONEY MATTERS

THE APARTMENT IS STILL EMPTY WHEN I GET OUT OF THE SHOWER. My scraped face hurts. I walk to the kitchen with a limp and grab some food from the refrigerator. I don't even feel hungry. I just need to do something routine, something that is part of everyday life. I tidy up my room and bring my wet clothes to dry on the balcony. I've missed both the morning and afternoon classes today.

I lie down and replay the events of the day over and over until I fall asleep.

It's almost 8:00 p.m. when I wake up. The house is dark. I have no idea if my parents have come home, had dinner and left again for the club, but I assume so. Mom's left a pot of stuffed grape leaves on the stove. I serve myself four, sit down on the couch with my plate, and turn on the TV to watch the national news.

The reception is poor; the screen is snowy. The perpetually serious and somber-looking anchor has bottle-blond hair, stiff with hairspray. The top news story is something about the government being warned by the army to establish law and order. I realize I've tuned out when I hear her say, "and in other developing news, gunfire near Technical University. A man opened fire on several students this morning. According to police, after a chase, the man being sought got away. He is considered armed and dangerous . . ." A video shows the buildings I ran into and out of and empty shells on the street. *Is that me she's talking about? I'm armed and dangerous? I opened fire?* The police have decided to believe Savas Kartal's made-up version of the events and have fed the information to the news media. The anchor shuffles the papers in front of her. "The man was last seen wearing gray pants, a white shirt, and a knit green hat."

My jaw is hanging open, my fork suspended in midair.

I decide to stay at my parents' apartment for the night. I can't imagine going outside even under the cover of darkness. I'm number one on Savas's kill list now, just because I look like the man, the boy, who killed his father. *I'm a murderer because I look like a murderer? That's crazy! That's insane. And, now because of Savas Kartal, I'm a wanted man. Wanted by the police.* I fall asleep trying to figure out how to protect myself from this madman.

But why? Why should I protect myself? It wasn't so long ago that I didn't mind dying. Is it that I'm forgetting Francesca, have a sliver of hope that I could possibly graduate, and my future could in some way be better? No, no, and no. Is it that I don't want to die by Savas's bullets? I don't want Savas to win? Correct.

In the morning, I stash all my gray and white clothing on the bottom of my clothes pile. Those are the colors the gunman was reported to be wearing during the shooting incident yesterday—not the colors I was wearing. Savas doesn't want the police to know he was the shooter, yet he doesn't want me to be caught and arrested either. He wants me to himself, to kill me himself. I wonder if the police can already guess Savas is lying and they will never bother to look for a man in gray and white clothing with a green hat.

Still, I don't want to accidentally grab anything in that color scheme. Best for me to rotate those colors out of my wardrobe for a while. I put on a yellow shirt and blue jeans and grab a baseball cap. I need to be unrecognizable. I curse myself for not being able to grow a beard yet; even a mustache would do.

I leave the apartment, my parents seemingly unaware that I've spent the night. If they know I was there, they didn't bother to say hi. Then again, neither did I. I walk to the bus stop, jogging with a limp to catch the coming bus. Two buses to get to school. It's a good place to hide even if it takes longer than walking. I blend in with the crowd.

As soon as I get off the bus, I overhear someone saying there's been another shooting. A student, killed on the same street where Savas shot at and missed me yesterday. I walk through the crowd until I spot Polat and Taner.

"What happened?" I ask them.

"It was an execution-style murder," Polat says. "We went to the location to talk to the eyewitnesses. We talked with the cab drivers and the boy who was roasting almonds right outside the dried fruits store. They said four men surrounded a student. They all said it looked like they were just talking to him. Then, the student suddenly went down on his knees, like he was begging for his life. And just as suddenly, they heard a shot fired. One bullet, to the head. The killers just walked away and left the body on the sidewalk. It was the eyewitnesses who called the police."

"It happened in the exact location as a shooting yesterday," Taner says.

I look at him quickly. And then my eyes dart to Polat.

"What happened to your face?" Taner asks, pointing.

"Nothing. I fell."

"Yesterday?" Taner asks. "Is that why you didn't show up at class?"

"No."

"No, what?"

"No, falling isn't why I didn't show up to class."

"So what happened to you?"

I feel my left eye start twitching.

"And you didn't come home last night either, did you?" Polat says. "I was going to ask you if you wanted to study."

"You were?"

"Adem. Where were you?" Taner says, redirecting me.

"What happened? How'd you get the cut on your cheek?"

I shake my head at my roommates.

"Wait. Adem. Were they shooting at you?" Polat asks.

"Yes."

"What?" they both shout at the same time.

"Who was it? Who shot at you?" Taner says.

"It was Savas Kartal, wasn't it?" Polat asks.

"Yes."

"Adem! Are you the man the police are on the lookout for? Were you shooting?"

"No."

"So, who was the shooter in the white shirt?"

"There was no shooter in a white shirt. That was Savas's story. He made it up. I listened as he and his gang decided they'd tell the police that they were the victims."

"Savas shot at you and missed you?" Taner asks.

"He was close. I have no idea how he missed me. I haven't been able to figure it out. He was shooting right at me. Chased me over the roofs of five buildings. Kept shooting and kept missing."

"I don't even know what to say," Polat says, shaking his head. He pats me on the back, then pulls me in for a hug. "I'm glad you're alive, kid."

***

This time, the governing board closes the school for only two days. It seems to me that in less than three months, officials have become numb to the increasing violence in and around the campus. Not only at Technical University; there are demonstrations in cities beyond Istanbul, protesting the government's indifference to the increased violence against students, actions of the riot police, and actions taken by university administrators. According to a report in the *Nation's Daily*, in their "casualties" column, "Politics Monster," there are free-lance, hired "provocateurs" who infiltrate large protests and then, at a certain point, pull out their guns and start shooting in the air. The shots create a panic in the crowd, people are crushed in stampedes. Every day, the death toll is higher than the day before.

It's been a week since I moved back into the house with Polat and Taner and classes have been back in session for three days. We all go to and return from school together. I continue to wear a baseball cap just in case the police are still looking for me. All Savas has to do is show them a photo of the kid who killed his father and say, "This is the guy we're looking for." Not likely, but neither it is impossible. If he can't kill me outside, he could try to have me killed in jail.

In the evenings, we hang out in the living room discussing scenarios, debating whether we should stage revenge killings, considering how and whether we will be able to graduate and what Turkey will look like in the future. The air in the living room, thick with smoke, is as clogged as my brain. I find it impossible to concentrate on school, worrying whether any of us even has a future.

I wash the dishes and settle into a low chair next to the coffee table, grab my notepad and open my book to enthalpy and entropy and try to understand the concepts for the fifteenth time. It looks like a sixteenth time will be necessary.

"Do you want me to tell you how that works?" Polat asks as I leaf back through the pages of my book in frustration, trying to make some sense out of the definitions so that I can apply the principles to solve problems.

"Huh?" I ask, looking up at Polat. He's leaning over my shoulder. His proximity reminds me of our standoff earlier in the year and I shiver at the memory.

"Do you need help with that? I can explain how it works," he says, as he reaches for a pack of Samsun cigarettes. I watch as he taps on top of the pack twice and two cigarettes pop out. He takes one, puts it between his lips, and extends the pack toward me. I need one. I take one. He lights up my cigarette, then his own. "Let me show you," he says.

He takes a puff from his cigarette and then spends the next two hours explaining and illustrating the principles.

"Let's make a study plan," Polat says, standing up and stretching as his third cigarette in as many hours hangs from his lips. "Explaining things to you will help me too," he says. "It'll help me understand the material better."

I look at him, not quite trusting his motive.

"Consider it a selfish request on my part. Okay? Plan?" he asks.

"Okay . . . plan," I say, with reluctance.

***

Polat and I have studied for more than two years. I've turned twenty-one. I've begun to shave, once every three days. At the club, lilies of the valley have bloomed twice. Roses too. But, Francesca hasn't returned to Istanbul, as far as I know. At least, she hasn't returned to the club. Each summer for the past two years, I have hoped she would come and visit. I've dreamed that she would return. I've dreamed that she would love me again.

I wish I could let her know that I still love her, that I think about her, still. All the time. That her departure left a hole in my heart. I could say something to Francesca's grandmother, ask about her. I've come close a few times when I've seen her at the club. But I have remained silent on the subject for two years. A perpetual sadness has settled in my soul, even when I smile, even when I laugh.

I'm comforted, somewhat, by the likelihood that it's not me that Francesca is avoiding. Istanbul's unrest has turned into all but a civil war. Violence against students continues to grow; four thousand people have been killed. Annual inflation is running into the triple digits, causing the lira to plummet against the dollar. Businesses cannot afford to pay workers and the unemployment rate rises to 20 percent. The sidewalks are crammed with people standing in long lines outside the unemployment offices. Young men who have given up hope of finding work loiter on street corners. The government has rationed gasoline. Every vehicle is assigned a gas card and is limited to twenty liters of gas per week. The right lanes of streets are backed up with cars for blocks as people wait in long lines for their rations of gas.

The government is drowning in dollar-denominated debt. It's borrowing money just to make interest payments on the outstanding debt, piling up even more debt. To increase revenue, income taxes have been raised. Most businesses can no longer pay their taxes. To survive, they're forced to lay off workers; some businesses shut down altogether.

Demonstrations continue. Provoking agents continue to participate and instigate panic and violence as a strategy to quell the demonstrations. A record number of people are in jail. The government and its supporters have coined a new word for the demonstrators: *terrorists*. Anybody and everybody who opposes the government in any way is a terrorist. By this definition, revolutionaries are terrorists. Sympathizers are safe, as long as they keep quiet.

The continued violence means on and off cancelations of class. In total, we've lost another semester. Polat and I continue studying together. In all the chaos, despite all the missed days, I've learned more studying with Polat than I ever did in classes from a mumbling professor. I've finally caught up on my coursework and I'm pulling in better grades. It looks like I will graduate with a degree in engineering one semester after Polat and Taner.

In May, *Nation's Daily* reports that Savas Kartal, now thirty-one, has graduated from City University, has become a favorite of those on the political right as well as the wealthy whose focus is to protect their money. His profile in the anti-Communist movement is rising and those in charge of the Nationalist Party have taken notice. He's been tapped to start Yavuz Security, which provides bodyguards for the rich and famous. I fear that Savas's new position will make him more powerful and more dangerous. *Does he remember me? Am I still on his hit list?*

Polat and Taner have graduated too and moved out of the town house. Taner has gone back to Eskisehir, his hometown, west of Ankara; he's taken a job as an engineer in a porcelain factory. We've let the rental agreement expire; Polat has moved in with his girlfriend, Selin, who lives closer to the north end of the Bosporus. I've moved back home to my parents' apartment until my graduation.

The death toll from the civil unrest has climbed to five thousand. Most of the dead are students. Many survivors with dreams of an education have had to quit school, fearing for their lives, and gone back home. Still others—revolutionaries opposed to the Nationalist government—have gone underground. According to Polat, they carry out hit-and-run attacks. Nighttime bombings of banks and other prominent capitalist targets have become commonplace. Polat says the goal of the revolutionaries is to instigate a populist uprising.

At the club, inside the protective gates, life appears unchanged. The civil unrest doesn't exist inside the posh confines where the rich play and dine. The privileged remain focused not on government strategies but on bridge and poker strategies. Rather than talking about rations, they're talking about their yachts and Mediterranean cruises, their expensive cars and horses and the toys they've bestowed upon their children. I don't go to the club as often as I used to. While I felt safe there, the contradiction is too much for me to stomach. But I still act as chauffeur for my mom.

"The other day, Suzan was asking about you," Mom says as I pull into the club's parking lot. "Maybe you have time to come into the club today, for a swim or just to reconnect with her and her friends."

She catches me at a moment of extreme weakness. I had been debating my place, my role, in the demise of my country, wondering how my avoidance of the club helps the cause, brings back the dead. Does enjoying a day make me a traitor? *Grandma, what would you say about this?* "Do not die with the dead," she said once, "mourn them and then move on."

I park Duldul and walk through the iron gates with Mom, who heads directly into the clubhouse. I stop to chat with the headwaiter, then notice Suzan lying in the sun with Mira. I haven't seen either of them in years. Suzan waves me over with a big grin.

"We were just talking about driving up the hill for lunch," Suzan says. "Do you want to join us?"

"I'm not sure," I say. "I'm really here for just a short swim. Then I need to go back home and study."

"Oh, come on, Adem. The books will still be there when you get back. Come. Please? We haven't hung out in forever."

"Well . . ."

"Please come," Mira chimes in. The girls look at each other and start chanting. "Come to lunch, come to lunch, come to lunch!"

I can't hold back a smile.

"Look! Teeth! He's smiling!" Suzan says.

"Come, come, come to lunch!" they sing, picking up the pace of their chant.

"Okay! Okay!" I say, with an undertone of anger.

"Yay. What fun! Let's go to Kale! My treat!" Suzan shouts. She grabs her bag and hooks her arm in mine. I'm glad she can't see the shocked look on my face. Kale is one of the most expensive restaurants in Istanbul.

We walk out the iron gates, and she steers me toward her car.

"Let's all go together," Suzan says, letting go of my arm and running over to her car, pointing to a black 600 Mercedes-Benz. The driver, dressed in a black suit with a black tie, jumps out of the car and opens the rear door for us. I climb inside. It smells like wealth.

We drive up the hillside to the restaurant. The valet opens the door for us and calls me "sir," despite being older than I am. Suzan is greeted by the staff, who call her Ms. Yilmaz and appear to know her well. They treat her as if she is royalty and Mira and I, important by association. Nobody cares that I'm in jeans. I guess when you are rich, you are never considered underdressed. The three of us are seated at a white-clothed table in a private gazebo; sheer white curtains move gently in the breeze. We have a view of the Bosporus that I have never seen. There's no menu. We don't order. The waitstaff simply bring small plates of delicacies, asking us if we would like to try them. They've offered me twenty-three different dishes so far.

When they bring dessert, the waiter tells us that the dish is called "The American": warm brownie, vanilla ice cream, whipped cream, and hot chocolate sauce.

The American. America.

With all the turmoil, with all my worry about school, I haven't thought of my dream in a long time. It's been there in my brain for years, but tucked away. *Is it time to resurrect my dream? With graduation on the horizon—I still can't believe it's true, that I will graduate—is it time for me to make a real plan to go to America?*

12

WORK FOR NOTHING

HOW AM I GOING TO DO THAT? WHERE WOULD I EVEN START? HOW much money would I need? I've tutored a lot, but the income barely meets living expenses. I haven't been able to save any money. Even if I had the savings, how would I get a visa? And a passport. I need that, too.

I've calculated that I need $4,000 to travel to America. From what I've read in the paper, airfare will set me back $900. Then there are the monthly expenses—food would probably be about $150, housing, maybe another $150, but that's just a guess. I will need money for contingencies, maybe even for school. $4,000 should be enough for me to live for six months and learn enough English to get a job. With the elementary English I learned in high school, I already know some everyday words and can read slowly using a dictionary. But I can't speak or understand enough to get or hold down a job.

If I work in Istanbul for $110 per month, it will take more than three years to earn that money, if I don't spend any of it, which is unrealistic. I'd be twenty-five years old then. I don't want to wait that long to get to America.

I've heard from other students that in Libya, mechanical engineers make $800 a month, but that's because the working conditions are harsh. I think it would be worth it. If I lived on $130 per month, I'd have that $4,000 in six months. Those savings and a high-paying job would also be strong references to obtain a US visa. In fact, I could possibly go to America directly from Libya.

I decide to reach out to everyone I know about their connections to Libya. I strike out for a good two weeks as names and contact numbers lead to dead end after dead end. My luck turns when I connect with and land a meeting with the owner of Soner Ozenli Architecture and Engineering. Mr. Ozenli, a well-known architect, builds luxury office buildings, condos, and villas for individual and corporate investors. As a child, I remember meeting him when he and Dad worked for Mr. Baris, now a billionaire. Mr. Ozenli was the architect and Dad was the construction manager. Mr. Ozenli still does a lot of business with Mr. Baris and Baris Holding. The company recently won a housing development project in Libya, it's one of the largest Turkish companies there. If I can get a job with Mr. Ozenli, then I'd have the foundation and connections I'd need to apply to Baris Holding. I'd have to push my timeline back a little, work for Mr. Ozenli for a few months first, but it seems the most promising strategy I've come up with at this point.

I get a haircut for the meeting; it exposes the white skin around my sideburns and neck. I look ridiculous. I try to make up for it by shining my shoes for the first time in years; it was a part of my daily routine at the navy high school. My one suit still fits. I choose from one of my two ties.

I meet with Mr. Ozenli in his spacious and elegant office. Oversize curtains puddle on the floor and filter out the light coming from the windows. Brass floor lamps and desk lamps replace the natural light. There's a meeting table, as well as a separate seating area with two chairs, a coffee table, and a couch where Mr. Ozenli motions for me to sit.

"You're a young man now, how time flies by. How old were you when your father and I worked together, Adem? Ten?"

"Twelve, sir."

"How's Colonel Teo doing? I had so much respect for him. Everybody did."

"He's doing well, sir. Thank you."

"What brings you here today?"

"Mr. Ozenli—"

"Please, call me Soner,"

"Yes sir. Mr. Ozenli, Soner, sir. I'm graduating in three months with a degree in mechanical engineering. I have no remaining schoolwork, just the approval of my thesis. So, I would like to begin working . . . here, for you, as a draftsperson. Eventually my plan is to go to Libya as an engineer, maybe on your behalf?"

Soner nods, then apologizes, "I would hire you, Adem, but right now, business is a little slow. I cannot afford you. Maybe . . ."

"I will work for free," I blurt out, interrupting him, immediately regretting the impulse. *What? Where did that come from?* But, I can't take it back. I have to run with it. "I can work for you for free, as an intern, since I'm still a college student, I can do that," I finish, regretting my desperation. *Who works for nothing? How is this going to help me earn the money I need to get to America?*

Soner jumps on my offer. Rising from his chair, he holds out his hand. "Initiative. I like that, Adem."

I shake his hand and try hard not to shake my head at myself.

"I could use another draftsperson, you can do that, yes?"

I nod my head. "Yes, sir. I know how to do that, including system design and calculations. I learned that in school, and from two summer internships."

"I'll need you drawing floor plans, plumbing, and HVAC designs."

"Yes, sir."

"Okay. Start tomorrow morning," he says, smiling. "Let me show you your desk."

He leads me out of his office into a large open area with more than a dozen drawing tables. Most are occupied. He points to an empty table. No one looks up from their workstation. I hope it's because they are trying to look busy in front of the boss, not because they are unfriendly. I immediately think of my first day of school when the other children laughed at me.

He gives me a short tour of the rest of the office.

"Well, that's it. That's the office," Soner says. "So . . . well, okay then. I think that's it. I will see you tomorrow."

"Yes, sir," I say, reaching out and shaking his hand again. "Thank you for the opportunity."

I head home, on the bus debating with myself what I have just done—accepting work without pay, and in this economy. I do some calculations in my head. The income from tutoring should be enough to get by, especially since I'm living with my parents. *Not so bad, if it presents opportunities for the future.* I decide not to tell my parents about my new job. Though I'm graduating from one of Istanbul's best universities, I still feel that they don't have any high expectations for me. If I told them I got a job working for free, I couldn't imagine the ridicule I'd have to endure.

If they notice my new haircut, they don't say anything. During dinner, Mom and Dad chat about the club. I'm simply a fly on the wall.

***

When I arrive at my new job in the morning, Soner introduces me to his employees. "This is Adem, your new colleague, our new mechanical draftsperson. Please welcome him."

They are pleasant and friendly, which is a relief. They come right over to shake my hand; a few of the draftspeople tell me they eat lunch together every day and immediately invite me to join them. I'm not sure when the lunch break is, so as the clock ticks past 12:15, I wait for a cue from my new colleagues. My stomach growls as I draw bathroom fixture and radiator unit placements and lines of clean water and drainage pipes on a floor plan with a stencil while thinking about that first day of school when I pulled out a sandwich at my desk. If I could do it all over again, could I react to their open eyes and hanging jaws by saying, "I'm new here, I don't know the rules, I'm only six. Help me and please bear with me?"

At 12:45, chairs begin to scrape and as if they are a connected team of oxen, the draftspeople stand up in unison and head down to the cafeteria on the first floor. "We eat here every day," one of my new colleagues says. I think her name is Fatma. I get a soup and salad and a cheese sandwich; it costs twenty liras, more than two dollars. It's an expense I won't be able to afford. I will need to start bringing a sandwich from home. I have to believe that lunch here is costing each draftsperson one-third of their salary and I marvel that they choose to spend their money so carelessly.

Once we are seated, the group begins to pepper me with questions. How is school? When will I graduate? Am I caught up in the political turmoil?

"How much is Soner paying you?" Fatma asks. I'd been waiting for that question. Lately, it's become a cultural norm that makes me feel uncomfortable. How is it that things like salaries, savings, and grades are considered public information?

"It's not determined, not yet," I say, responding with the answer I'd worked on. "Maybe I'll go to Libya to work and that will change everything." I know I'm buying time with an answer like that, because eventually payday will come and I'll receive nothing.

At the end of the first month, I watch as Soner's assistant walks from desk to desk, placing stacks of dollar bills on each employee's desk. I try not to stare as she hands out US dollars. It's a convenience that a lot of companies have adopted. As the lira gets devalued, employers don't have to keep raising their employees' salaries. Polat has told me his employer pays in US currency. So has Demir.

I realize they've noticed the assistant passes my desk without leaving any cash.

"Soner doesn't pay you to work?" Raif, the draftsperson who sits next to me, asks.

"It's just temporary." I hesitate. "Because I'm still a student. When I graduate, I'll earn a salary," I say, trying to put some confidence into my voice.

"By then, perhaps you won't be so slow," he says. I can't tell if he's joking or being obnoxious, but I decide it's best to agree with him.

"Yup. It's true. I am slow. I hope to learn a lot from you and increase my pace," I say, pandering to him, hoping I've redirected him away from the salary subject. Still, I suspect the whole issue will be resurrected after I've graduated. I'll have to come up with a new excuse or find a way to get Soner to pay me.

As the countdown to graduation begins, we learn that it will not be a ceremonial event. All pomp and circumstance have been canceled yet again because of the ongoing civil unrest. It's actually a relief. I had been worried about my parents' lack of interest in this rite of passage. Now I don't have to fret about the embarrassment of them not showing up or, if they did, how they would manage congratulating me publicly. And, congratulations are in order. I'm one of the small group of graduates. There are only thirty-two of us who made it to the finish line, graduating with degrees in mechanical engineering. The program began with ninety-seven students.

Now in its fifth year, the political turmoil has left six thousand dead. The victims are no longer only students. The country is on the brink of a civil war. In some regards, life seems to go on as it did before; children still go to school and adults go to work. But, people seem more aware and cautious, no longer lingering in the streets or picnicking in the parks. They have adjusted their lives to avoid any possible eruption of violence. I change my schedule daily and I suspect others do, too; routes to work and home shift daily as well. It's not surprising to see people glancing over their shoulders as they walk around Istanbul; it's become a habit for most residents. I see the unease of riders on the bus where, instead of reading or chatting with strangers, passengers appear distracted, their eyes darting around as people get on and off the bus. My parents' neighborhood and the streets around my work are all relatively safe. But the nightly news reports on the violence that is expanding around us, from the city of Istanbul east toward Agri, south to Izmir, and even all the way to Antalya. Young people continue to protest daily, defying police brutality. I don't know how this will end, or when it will end. The hatred is deep.

As hyperinflation continues to pressure the lira downward, those who receive payment in liras watch their purchasing power decline by the day. Prices on products are handwritten, replaced with increased figures daily. There's a joke about the vegetable stand: "Buy in the morning, because by the afternoon they will raise the prices." Those who survived a lower-middle class lifestyle have fallen into poverty and those already living in poverty are hardly hanging on. Anything imported—medicine, alcohol, cigarettes, coffee, baby formula—is either not available or smuggled into the country and sold at exorbitant prices that only the rich can afford.

After two years of threats, the Turkish military issues an ultimatum to the center-right coalition government to put a stop to the killings or, as the constitution warrants, the military will assume the country's governance and establish martial law to stop the violence. The military doesn't care about a protester's opinion or political leaning. They come in and stop the conflict, by force, whether the violence is caused by the revolutionaries or by Savas Kartal's gangs in the Nationalist Party.

I still have my eyes on America. With graduation swiftly approaching, the dream feels more like reality—more like something I am really going to do, pursue. This is not the mumblings of a teenager but the plan of a college graduate. I decide to obtain a passport. Why not? If I need it, I have it. If I don't need it, it doesn't hurt.

I keep my head down and work. Yalin, my supervisor, is very hands off, spending most of his time out of the office and on site at the projects he oversees. But, he seems pleased with the work I'm doing and the extra time I put in.

Days before my graduation, Yalin quits. I hear about it even before Soner calls me into his office to tell me. Word is, he's leaving not because he is unhappy with his job here, but because he's worried about the civil unrest. He's moving his family north, to the Black Sea coast, and has obtained a position as a mechanical engineer for a large steel factory that is offering double his salary.

"Sit down, Adem," Soner says when I arrive at his door. He points to the couch. "When do you graduate? When will you officially have a degree in mechanical engineering?"

"In two days, sir. I pick up my diploma on Monday."

Soner nods, looking down at a piece of paper. "Yalin is leaving the firm. He handed me his formal resignation this morning."

"Yes, sir."

"I need to hire someone to replace him. He has recommended you."

"Sir?"

"He likes how meticulous you are. He sees the extra hours you put in to finish assignments on time. I agree. I would like to hire you as a mechanical engineer."

"Sir!" I sit up straighter in my chair. "Thank you, sir."

"You will be the responsible engineer for our projects, you will obtain the necessary permits from the city, and you will direct the draftspersons and workers to get the job done."

"I can do that, sir, thank you." *I hope I can.*

"You have proven yourself. You have earned yourself a salary. $100 per month."

"Yes sir, that's very generous of you." *Yalin earned $120 a month for the same position. But, take what you can, Adem, he had a family to feed.*

Soner stands up and shakes my hand. I walk out of the office trying not to smile.

A week later, I move into Yalin's glass-enclosed engineer's office. I cannot believe I've just graduated and have not only a job and a desk but a managerial position and an office. I sit down and tip back in my chair. Then I pinch myself. This dream is real.

I'm arranging paperwork on my desk when Soner walks in. "Grab your hat. We're going to visit some work sites," he says, handing me three paper sandwich bags.

"Sir?" I ask. "This is . . .?"

"Salaries for the workers," he says. "These sandwiches are salaries for the workers. Hand each bag to the construction manager at each site in order." I look at the bags; they are numbered, 1, 2, 3. "Each bag contains anywhere from five to seven thousand dollars. I trust you not to lose them."

"Yes, sir."

"You drive," Soner says, tossing me his keys.

"Yes, sir!" I say, quickly juggling the bags to catch the keys.

When we get to the car, I tuck the bags inside the glove compartment then start the engine. As all eight cylinders gently roar, I try to suppress the ten-year-old inside me who wants to jump up and down. Ever since childhood, I've wanted to drive a big American car, and now I am. Soner's is a Chevrolet, with an automatic transmission and power steering. It's nothing like driving Duldul. The car almost drives itself.

It takes me about a half an hour to relax behind the wheel. It helps that Soner seems to be at ease with my driving. He asks my opinion about some of his projects as we drive, pointing out open pieces of land and asking me what I think of the various locations. His questions get more and more specific and I start to run multiple calculations in my head when he asks how many hectares on a site, how many buildings, floors, and units a site could hold, and what the proceeds would be.

Soner smiles at me each time I respond with an answer. I'm not sure if his smile means he likes the answer or he thinks my answers are foolish and bogus. But, he keeps asking and I keep reporting my calculations, so maybe he's impressed.

At the end of the day when all the sandwich bags have been distributed, I hand Soner back the keys. "Thank you for letting me drive your car, sir," I say, debating whether I should tell him that this was the first time I drove an American car. I decide that less is more and simply go with a compliment. "It's a sweet ride, sir," I say.

"Why thank you, Adem. Let's do it again. In fact, our time together was very useful to me. Let's do this every Wednesday."

"Yes, sir," I say, trying not to smile. If I can keep this up, I might have a shot at making Libya a reality.

"I want you to meet Mr. Baris," Soner says. "Do you know Baris Holding?" *Is he reading my mind?*

"Yes sir."

There's buzz around the office that Soner wants a foothold in Libya, but until I came along, he didn't have anyone suitable or willing to move there. Maybe I'm his way in.

"In fact, tomorrow, I want you to drive me and Mr. Baris to our construction sites. You'll drive. You'll listen. You will not speak unless spoken to. Clear?"

"Clear. Yes sir."

"I'll give you four more bags for the construction managers. You'll hand them out in order just like you did today. They'll be heavier."

"Yes sir."

"When the time is right, I will recommend that Mr. Baris send you to Libya."

"Thank you, sir."

***

When I pull Soner's car up to Baris Holding, I jump out and open the door for Mr. Baris, making sure not to make eye contact. I remember that's how the soldiers would do it when they picked up Dad in his army Jeep. As we drive from site to site, I listen as Soner "makes nice" with the billionaire in the back seat. At each location, I open the door for them then walk over to hand the money to the construction manager.

Between sites, I remain quiet, speaking only when Soner asks me to do a complex calculation, which I do while navigating the directions. I shoot back the answers to Soner's questions in rapid fire almost as quickly as he asks them. Finally, at the last construction site, Soner formally introduces me to Mr. Baris, even directly suggesting that Mr. Baris hire me as a manager for his project in Libya.

"How old are you, son?" Mr. Baris asks, acknowledging my presence for the first time all day.

"Twenty-one sir, almost twenty-two."

"You're too young. Just too young," he says, shaking his head. "The workmen who take on jobs like the one I have going in Libya are a rough bunch. Hoodlums, really. They won't listen to a word you say. They'll laugh at you. When you tell them they can't drink on the job, they'll drink twice as much. When you tell them no women on the site, they'll bring twice as many. They're just a bunch of thugs. If I sent you there, they would chew you up, spit you out. You're too young and inexperienced to manage those workers, son."

"I can manage them, sir," I say, though after listening to that description, he may be right. *Failure is not an option, Adem. Libya is your ticket to America.* "It's not a problem," I say, standing a little taller.

"I'll think about it. Let me think about it. You're smart, I know that. I just don't know how tough you are," he says, turning to Soner. "You gotta toughen him up. Then, maybe, we'll talk." With no warning, Mr. Baris turns to walk back to the car and I run quickly past him to get the door. By the time I've dropped him off at Baris Holding, I've become invisible again; he doesn't say goodbye to me, or even to Soner.

13

HEAD IN THE CLOUDS

BY THE SUMMER OF 1980, I'VE BEEN WORKING FOR SONER FOR almost a year, tutoring on the side and saving money by living with my parents. Though I'm behind with respect to my self-imposed schedule, I've been working round the clock so I can prove to Soner and Mr. Baris that I'm the right man for the Libya project. I've also restarted my punching bag workouts, getting my right hook back just in case I do go to Libya and need to defend myself against that rough bunch of "hoodlums" Mr. Baris employs there.

I forgo a trip to Antalya with Izzy and Demir, who come back from the Mediterranean beach town tanned and relaxed. It's the second such trip in as many months that I have missed. "It was so much fun, you should have been there . . . again," Demir says. Not only do I not want to blow the money I've saved, I feel like I must stay at the office, at my desk, so that I can build the scaffolding I need to prove that I'm the man for the Libya job—my only path to America.

Demir's mother feels bad that I've missed the vacations Demir and Izzy have taken, so she invites me over for a home-cooked dinner, "a vacation at the dining table," she calls it. Mrs. Toros is a force, plain spoken and blunt. When she offers me thirds and I protest that I've already eaten more than my fair share, she says, "Oh, stop being so nice Adem, shut up and just have more," and dishes more meatloaf onto my plate.

Demir's father, I've always thought, is the perfect match for Mrs. Toros. When Zeki enters a room, all eyes lock on him because he has such a presence. It probably helps that he looks like Robert Mitchum, including the hair and the chin dimple. While he's quiet and soft-spoken, he can be quite persuasive. He loves to give me chores to do, although he tells me it's only because he thinks of me as another son. Unlike my own dad, he seems to like having me around.

"Adem, I need to ask a favor," Zeki says as we get up from the dining table and head into the kitchen with our plates. Demir looks at me with a face that says, "You know what's coming, start making up an excuse now," and walks away into the living room. But I don't mind doing chores for Zeki. "Have you driven a Mercedes-Benz before?"

"No, sir."

"Well, this may just be your opportunity. I need your professional opinion, as a mechanical engineer," he says. "I want you to test drive my car, it's an S class, and tell me how it feels. Check out the engine, too. I feel the car isn't performing the way it should. And, while you are assessing the car's inner workings, check out the stereo, too. Try your favorite cassette tape and tell me how the sound system is. Check the sunroof also. Would you do that for me?"

"Yes sir, of course."

"Can you do it tomorrow?"

"Yes sir, tomorrow works for me."

He hands me the keys. "Oh," he says, pulling out his wallet. "And, here is the gas rationing card. While you're doing your test drive, please get gas for me." He hands me a 100-lira bill.

"Yes sir. Happy to do it," I reply, taking the keys and the money, feeling antsy and excited about getting behind the wheel of such a nice car.

"Thank you, Adem," Zeki says, patting me on the shoulder.

"What did my father want you to do for him?" Demir asks, looking up from the TV as I walk in. He's sprawled on the living room couch.

"I'm going to check out how his car runs and get some gas for him too. Want to come?"

"No way," Demir says, adamantly, as the theme music for *Dallas* starts. Demir pretends to dip his cowboy hat like J.R. I plop down next to him.

We act out the scenes and lines, and ooh and ahh at the palatial homes and sleek cars. The hour passes quickly. As the credits begin to roll, I get up and stretch.

"Gotta go."

"Whad'ya mean? You're leaving already?"

"I've gotta wake up early to get your dad gas."

"Just stay for thirty more minutes. I want to watch *Talking Turkey about Dallas.*"

"Okay," I say, falling back onto the couch. Demir knows that I like the spin-off show, where a Turkish host asks people about the American show, even more than the soap opera itself. "But then I'm leaving!" I yell at Demir, punching him.

"I love Bobby, he is such a nice young man," an old lady on the street says, grabbing the host's mic. "I love Pam, too, such a nice girl. J.R. Ewing, no sir, he is evil! I don't like him at all." The host wrangles the microphone away from the woman then looks right into the camera and makes a funny face. Demir and I burst out laughing.

The next victim is a middle-aged man, who also gives insightful answers about the show.

"Do you know where Dallas is?" the host asks, walking down the street next to the man.

"Ummm, no."

"Do you know where Texas is?"

"Ummm, no."

"Do you know where America is?"

"Oh, er. I know. It's far away!"

Demir and I both laugh.

"Man, I want to go back to America!" Demir says. "It's been five years since I came back. That's too long. I want to go back."

"You do? You want to go back to America?" I ask, shocked. Demir only talks about America when I ask him questions, and then he just seems annoyed. He's never once mentioned his interest in returning.

"Yeah, I've been thinking about it for a while," he says. Then, turning down the volume on the set, he turns and looks at me.

"What?" I ask. "You're freaking me out. What?"

"We should go."

"What does that mean?"

"Man. We should go to America. Together! To DC."

"What?"

"Come on, Adem. Let's do it. Let's go together. Really, let's do it. Let's go to America. Let's do it together. It's an adventure man! Girls, cars, rock-and-roll . . ."

"Seriously?"

"Yes. We should do it."

"I don't have enough money."

"Not a problem."

"How is no money not a problem?"

"Are you in or are you out?"

"You want me to decide something like this right now? Don't I even get a night to think about it?"

"No. Adem. Come on. I know, secretly, you've always wanted to go to America."

"You knew that?"

"Oh come on, man. All you ever do is ask me questions about it. You think it's a secret, but I've always known."

"Really?"

"Seriously. Yes. You're not that good an actor. I can see right through you into that brain of yours. So . . . are you in or out?"

"How can I say 'no'?"

"You can't! So . . ."

"I'm in!" I say, getting up from the couch and pulling Demir up with me. Like little kids, we start jumping up and down and hollering like lunatics.

"Shut up out there!" Demir's mother yells from the other room. We break out in silent laughter and do a slow-motion high five.

"Let's not tell anyone until everything is ready. Okay?" I say. "Agreed?"

"Agreed. Okay. So, we have lots to do. First, we make a list of all the things we need to do. I'll need to renew my green card. You'll need to get a visa . . ." The list is long. After thirty minutes, we sit back, exhausted by the arrangements we have to make.

Passport I have. Money I don't have. Visa I don't have. How do you even get a visa? And, what kind of visa would I get—a tourist visa and then just stay there and never come back?

"Adem, you are going to love America," Demir says, wistfully. "Anyone who works hard there can succeed. I mean, not everyone succeeds, but it's not like it is here, where you need to be born into the right family or know someone important or lie, or wheel and deal. I think, maybe we could even get jobs, I don't know, maybe at the French bread factory. I loved working . . ."

While Demir raves about the US, and DC in particular, all the jobs that are available, the cars we'll be able to drive, I close my eyes, imagining it. Imagining my dream. My American dream.

***

I hardly sleep that night, thinking about our plans for America. By 5:00 a.m., I'm in Zeki's car, parked in the gas line listening to the news on the radio. "Iranian students continue to hold the fifty-two Americans hostage at the US Embassy in Tehran. It has been 240 days."

An hour later, it's my turn and by 7:00 a.m. I've dropped Zeki's car back at his house, taken the bus back to my parents' and I'm back in the gas line with Duldul. This time the wait is an hour and a half. "I won't miss the gas lines for sure," I say out loud and realize I'm smiling. I've only gotten three hours of sleep, but I feel energized by my potential American dream. It really feels like it's within reach.

***

That weekend, I join Izzy and his girlfriend, Leyla, at the Bosporus for lunch. We order grilled cheeses and tea.

111

"I'm going to America. With Demir. Demir and I are going to America!" I blurt out, breaking my own promise.

"What?"

"You heard me. I'm going to America. But, don't tell anyone. No one knows. Not even my family."

"Adem. What? That's impossible. Demir, I get. But you? How are you gonna do that?"

"I haven't figured out all the details yet. I'm working on it," I say, surprising myself with how confident I feel.

"Do you have money?" Izzy asks.

"No."

"Do you own any property here?" Leyla asks.

"No. Why? Would I need to own . . .?"

"Or, do you have a rich uncle in America?" Izzy says, interrupting me.

"No."

My head swings back and forth as Izzy and Leyla shoot questions at me.

"Do you speak English?" Izzy asks me in English.

"Huh?" I say, and then I realize what he's asked me. I shake my head, "No."

"It doesn't sound like much of a plan. When you get there, *if* you get there, then what are you gonna do for work? Clean toilets? Flip burgers?"

I shrug. "Sure, if I have to," I say, trying to regain my confidence. "I don't have all the plans worked out. But, I'm going."

"In ten years?

"Very funny," I say, punching him in the arm.

"When you're forty? Izzy says, laughing."

I look at Leyla. She shrugs.

"First of all, my friend," Izzy says in a mocking tone, "they don't just hand out visas. It's not like buying candy. The consulate doesn't give someone a visa just because they ask; just because they are young and stupid and think they can do something just because they want to do it—like go to America." I feel my face reddening. I feel my confidence waning. I wish Demir were here to back me up. To convince Izzy that there is a plan and that we will work it out. "It's not like buying candy," Izzy says again, droning on, poking fun. This is exactly why I made Demir promise to not say anything about America to anyone. I knew it was a bad idea. *Adem, you're an idiot. Without a plan, people will always shoot you down.* "To get a visa," Izzy says, still talking, still putting me in my place, "you have to show assets in Turkey, a hefty bank account, a nice income, and some property. Americans want to make sure you have reasons and means to come back here."

"I think I can get a visa if I tell them it's for my graduate degree."

"Don't be crazy. Stay where you are, here. You have a good job. Good friends. And, what about that girl who is crazy about you—what's her face, Suzan. I know you're still holding out for Francesca, but that's not going to happen, we both know that. Stay in your job, marry Suzan, stop thinking about dreams like Francesca and America. Plant your feet on the earth. Stay in Istanbul. Enjoy Suzan's wealth and have children and live a good, rich life."

"Maybe you're right," I say, wondering why his opinion so starkly contrasts with Demir's.

"Good. Now, let's have more tea and some baklava," Izzy says.

***

After work the next day, I come home to find my sister Ela, a chemical engineer, sitting at the dining room table with my mother. *No one told me she was planning a visit. Don't ask, don't tell.*

"Look how big you are!" I exclaim. How had I forgotten I was going to be an uncle for the first time? In two months. *If I go to America, I'm not going to meet my niece or nephew.* Ela stands up and I give her a hug. Her belly gets in the way and we both laugh as we sit down.

Mom and Ela chat for a while as I listen. Dad isn't home from work yet. *Should I tell them my plans? Is keeping the idea a secret the wrong approach? Perhaps getting other people's opinions is exactly what I need. Maybe I need to float the idea around and see what people think?* As I get lost in my thoughts, drifting in and out of my mother and sister's conversation, I wonder whether I should tell Ela.

"Remember when Adem was little how he was so desperate to play word games at the dinner table, but he could never come up with the words?" Ela says, snickering.

"I was only four!"

"You poor thing," Mom says, patting my hand and getting up to go to the kitchen. "Okay, enough chitchat for me, I need to cook dinner," she says.

I lean in, motioning for Ela to do the same. "I have decided to go to America," I say, whispering, craning my neck to make sure Mom is focused on dinner, tucked away in the kitchen and out of earshot.

"What?" I can't tell if she hasn't heard me or is surprised by what I've said.

"I'm going to America."

"I heard you, Adem. What . . . what are you saying? What are you *thinking?*"

"Keep your voice down. I don't want Mom to know."

Why?" she asks. "Because she'll know that you're out of your mind?"

"What do you mean? People do it. Lots of people go to America."

"Other people, Adem. Not our family, especially not you. That's what it is. Your head, it's always in the clouds."

"I'm going with Demir."

"Oh, that's supposed to make it better?"

"Eliz is planning to move to Germany."

"Adem, she's got a job. And a husband!"

"Demir and I have already started planning."

"Adem. No. You cannot do this. You have always been such a dreamer . . . completely just . . . lost in your thoughts. How long have you been planning this?"

"A few weeks."

"I mean, really planning this? *Thinking* about this."

"For twelve years. Since Demir moved to DC."

"Oh Adem," Ela says, sighing loudly.

"I've saved $200. If I can borrow $3,800 more, it will work."

"Do you hear yourself? Who is going to loan you that kind of money?"

"Actually, I was thinking that maybe . . . I don't know, maybe you could?" I say, tilting my head sideways. It's the move I'd used countless times as a child to earn favor with Ela. It got me extra candy, desserts, the right to use her record player.

"Ha," she says. "That cute face isn't going to work on me." Then, turning her chair in my direction, she looks at me with a serious face, the face I imagine she uses in the lab when she's whipping up potions with the other chemical engineers. "Adem, this is not like going to a candy store." *Why does everyone use that analogy?* "This is ludicrous. It is a ludicrous idea. You are not going to America, we're not having this conversation."

"So, no money from you?" I ask, laughing.

"I'm going to help Mom in the kitchen. This conversation is over."

"Don't tell anyone. Okay?"

"Tell anyone what? That you're crazy? I think they all already know it."

As I watch her walk away, I make a mental note. Ela and Izzy are both in the "no" column. Demir is in the "yes" column. *Does Demir count? Can I count him in the pro column if he's part of the plan?*

14

INITIAL PLAN

The following Saturday, I join Ela and her husband at their bimonthly brunch with their friends.

"I think I was too quick to judge," Ela had said on the phone a day earlier when she called to invite me.

"What do you mean?"

"I mean, maybe you should talk to other people, other professionals, about your plan. Get lots of opinions. Perhaps I'm too close to it. I only have the perspective of a big sister. So, come to brunch and you'll have a lot of people to ask."

I end up getting into an in-depth conversation about education with a forty-year-old CEO named Kaan Unsel. He tells me his opinions about the Turkish education system, "a failed system, a system of learning by rote" he says. I nod my head profusely in agreement. "It doesn't prepare even the brightest students for a successful future."

"I always thought it was just me," I say. "I learned more studying on my own in high school and with my roommates while at university than I did from my mumbling professors or the teachers who beat me every chance they could get."

"You graduated from where?"

"Technical University."

"Ah. A star!"

"Ha!" I laugh. "I almost failed out. Until I started studying with my roommate."

"And now what do you do?"

"I work for a developer. I'm a mechanical engineer. I supervise . . ."

"And he makes all the money, right?"

"Well, I don't know. I . . ."

"You need to leave Turkey!"

"I'm sorry?"

"You need to leave Turkey. If you want to succeed, you need to leave. You need to get an advanced degree that will really take you places. Until then, you'll be stuck where you are," he says.

"Well, I'm planning to go to Libya."

"No. Not Libya. I've been. No. You need to go to Germany, England, the United States, Japan," he says, pointing to people around the table as he names each country. "Almost everyone here has been somewhere."

My eyes widen.

"What are you gentlemen talking about?" Funda, Kaan's wife, asks, pulling up a chair and leaning in closer.

"America!" Kaan says excitedly. I can't tell if he's answering his wife or talking to me. "That's where you should go." *Wait, he's telling me I should go to America?*

I know from stories Ela has told me that he and his wife Funda have been to America.

"Oh yes!" Funda says. "America. I've done some work there, public relations for the consulate in New York and in DC."

"Funny you should say that. So . . . I am planning to move to America. I'm wondering . . . Well, do you really think it's a good idea?"

"Yes! I love it!" Kaan says dramatically, patting me on the shoulder. "Do it. Go. When are you leaving? We'll throw you a party!" he says, looking at Funda, who nods.

"Wow, well. Thank you. I don't need a party. But, I'm surprised, happy actually, to hear your reaction. I've discussed the idea with a few people and most everyone thinks I'm crazy or stupid or wouldn't be successful. But my biggest problem is how to do it. How does one move to America?"

"The 'how' isn't really my forte. Funda and I were transferred to the US, New York City, actually. So, the company made all the arrangements. But, you'll do it. You'll figure it out. I don't know you well, but Ela has told me a little bit about you. And what I think I know about you is this: Turkey is just too small for you. Your eyes are shooting laser beams. You've got to go. You've got to go after your dreams. And if America is your dream, you are going to figure it out and you are going to make it work. Right, Funda?"

"Absolutely!" Funda says, leaning forward even more. "But Adem, *is* America your dream?"

"It is," I say, unenthusiastically, unconvincingly.

Kaan smiles. "You can do this, man. Say it with confidence."

"Yes. Yes! America is my dream!" I say, finding myself grinning just as wide as the night Demir and I decided to move to America. I'm stoked.

"Thank you Kaan. Funda. Thank you for the advice; the kind words."

"It's the truth Adem." Kaan grabs my hand, squeezing hard and patting me on the back again. "Let me know what happens, pal," he says, standing up.

"Stay in touch with us. Let us know how you make out. Okay?" Funda says, kissing me goodbye on the cheek.

Two more people in the "yes" column.

***

Kaan and Funda have inspired me. I go straight from brunch to the library to research how to move to America. After skimming through about ten books, I determine that my inkling was right; one of the best strategies is to apply for a student visa. The problem is, I can't enroll in an American university without learning English. I stare at the books in front of me, trying to figure out a way around the requirement. I get up and pace a little, drawing stares from those around me. I sit down again, and thumb through the books in front of me, hoping for some inspiration. "I've got it!" I shout after getting up and sitting down a few more times. "Language school!"

"Shh!" the librarian hisses at me. I mouth "sorry," and quickly start rifling again through the information laid out on the table. *Maybe I can get a student visa by enrolling in a language school in America.* I keep reading and reading looking for information about learning English as a second language, quickly learning that ESL is the American acronym. There's nothing in the information I read that says I *can't* do that. I pull out my notebook and jot out the first steps in my plan.

Language School:

Find language school

Apply to language school

Get into language school

Visa:

Get visa application

Fill out visa application

Take visa application to US consulate

The following day, I ask Demir to meet me at the library so he can help me find a language school in Washington, DC. We get shushed at least five times and have to run out of the library at one point when we cannot control a particularly hysterical outburst of laughter. After about an hour, we finally focus on our mission and find a fitting language school. Demir drafts a letter for me requesting an application.

I tell my parents nothing about my plan. And, they don't seem to notice that checking the mailbox, which I've never done before, becomes my new, daily routine. Finally, after three weeks, the application arrives. I call Demir and he helps me fill out the forms. I stop by the post office the following day on the way to work and mail the application back to the school. It's a long process. I soon realize that going to America is going to take a lot of patience.

Things are a lot easier for Demir. Having lived in the US for eight years as a little kid, not only does he speak English fluently but he speaks it without a foreign accent. All he needs to do to leave Turkey for America is go to the US consulate to renew his expired green card, which he gets done. It's conditional to his resettling in America.

It's October by the time the ESL school accepts my application and registers me as a student. The good news is, I don't have to pay for classes until the first day. I grab my notebook and check off the first three items: Find language school, Apply to language school, Get into language school. Next on my list, "Visa." I checked off the first item on the list four weeks ago when Demir picked up the student visa application for me when he was at the US consulate to renew his green card. Then two weeks ago, I checked off "fill out application," which Demir did for me. So now I need to go to the consulate. I take a deep breath, thinking about the enormity of what I'm about to do.

I take the form and the school registration papers and walk to the bus stop. I let my usual bus that takes me to work come and go and wait for the bus that takes me to the city's Beyoglu District, where the US consulate is located. The bus drops me on the corner, just past Pera Palas, the historical hotel known to host celebrities who visit Istanbul. I keep my eyes open for anyone famous as I walk from the bus stop, past the hotel, to the large consulate building next door. But what catches my eye isn't a movie star, but the American flag hanging over the front door. It sweeps back and forth in the breeze; the stars and stripes are waving me in.

I wait at the front door until I'm buzzed in and immediately wipe the smile off my face. Behind a glass partition at the guard post is a Marine. I show my passport and my papers and tell him my memorized line that I would like to apply for a visa. He tells me to walk straight through to the doors at the end of the hall. I enter a large, red-carpeted room with only a few people inside. A man standing behind the counter extends his hand for my papers. A few minutes later I am scheduled for an interview for the following Friday. I exhale. I didn't know I'd have to wait; I thought the interview would be that day. I leave the building and jump on the bus to work.

***

Demir and I spend each evening that week working on English phrases I can use, just in case. The key phrase, Demir tells me, is "I would like to go to America to learn English and study for a graduate degree." On the morning of the appointment, I wake up at 5:00 and keep repeating the line over and over—in the shower, while getting dressed, while on the bus.

Once again, a Marine behind the glass partition buzzes me in and once again I show my passport. This time I tell him, with confidence, that I have an interview scheduled. He checks my name on a list and directs me to the same, red-carpeted room. Just as I'm about to sit down, a skinny, tall man standing behind a long counter calls me over.

I am assigned an interpreter, who comes in just seconds later and stands next to the official, who pulls off his glasses and starts paging through my application. I'm caught off guard when the consular officer immediately starts asking me questions about why I want to go to America. I hadn't realized the interview would take place while standing. *Is this an American culture thing—standing interviews?* As I clear my throat and respond with the line Demir and I have prepared, "I want to go to America, er . . . um . . ." my mind goes blank. "I want to go to America . . ." *Adem, come on man, pull it together.* "I want to go to America to learn English, and study for my graduate degree," I finally blurt out. The officer asks me if I ever considered learning English here in Turkey before going to America. I don't know if I'm supposed to respond to the interpreter or the officer, so I try to look at both of them when I answer. I tell them that while I've tried without success, I believe that once I'm in America, I will be forced to learn English, speak only English, in fact, and therefore will learn the language much faster.

Apparently, that was a bad answer. The wrong answer. My application is immediately rejected. On the spot. After only two questions. While still standing. It took less than two minutes for me to fail in my quest to go to America.

I take the bus to work. I can't concentrate on anything that requires thinking; instead, I run the HVAC calculations of an entire building, which normally takes a whole week, repetitive calculations using the same set of formulas. I finish it by 8:00 p.m., then leave the office, stopping to pick up a cheese-and-tomato sandwich before heading home. I can spend my money now, I think; now that I don't need to save it to get to America.

Instead of hopping on the bus, I start walking. And I don't stop. For miles. I walk with my head down, ignoring everyone around me; I don't even look up to make sure the street is safe from violent eruptions by political interrupters. I hardly notice where I'm going as I pass restaurants and shops, cafés and clothing stores. It's almost 10:00 p.m. when I walk past a movie theater and then stop. I turn back around. A dark room where I can get lost in someone else's imagination is exactly what I need. The theater is playing *The Deer Hunter*, an American movie starring actors I've never heard of, Robert De Niro, Meryl Streep, Christopher Walken. According to the movie poster, the film came out in 1978, two years ago. I wonder if the actors have become famous by now, like Clint Eastwood or Charles Bronson. As the movie starts, I try to remember how long it's been since I've seen a movie. All I can come up with is, it's been a long time.

It's well past midnight when I come out of the theater. I begin to walk home on the almost deserted streets, feeling as though I'm the only man wandering around an abandoned town. There is almost no traffic; everything is still, quiet, like in a twilight zone. I feel lightheaded, like I'm floating down the empty sidewalk. I think about the movie, the steel factories in the US, the large trees with their golden leaves, the clay-colored soil.

I want to go to America and walk in the forests with clay colored soil. I want it so badly. But, maybe America is not for me.

The song, "You Can't Always Get What You Want" pops into my head. Perhaps that's the formula for life—you can't always get what you want. I start singing . . .

You can't always get what you want, yeah
You can't always get what you want, ooh yeah, child
You can't always get what you want
But if you try sometimes you just might find
You just might find
You get what you need.

"I need to find another way to get to America," I say out loud. I need a formula for that.

An alley cat jumps out of a can and lands at my feet.

15

FALLBACK PLAN

In the morning, I debate with myself whether to go to Demir's house to tell him in person that I didn't get the visa or make less of a big deal of it by calling him on the phone. In the end, I decide to call; I don't want to see the expression on his face.

He doesn't sound very upset. In fact, he tells me it's a blip in our plans, "a minor roadblock, man. Come over, we'll devise a new plan." I don't know what *his* plan is, but on the way over, I decide my plan is to tell him he should go without me.

I'm immediately sidelined when Zeki answers the door almost in mid-sentence. "I know what you're going to say, Adem."

"Sir?"

"Adem, I've known you for a long time. You were going to come over here tonight to convince Demir to go to America without you."

"Yes, sir."

"Well, Adem, that's not going to happen. Instead I'm going to help you."

"Sir?"

"Demir is not going to go alone. You are going to go with him. I'm going to help you. Monday morning, I'm going to go with you to get your visa."

"But sir, people say . . ."

"I know people say that once you are denied a visa, your name goes onto a blacklist. But there are ways around that. Do you trust me?"

"Yes sir."

"Good. Monday morning. Me and you. Okay?"

"Yes sir. Thank you sir!"

Demir and I end up watching TV together until midnight. After each show ends, I can recall nothing about the episode; I spend most of the time wondering how Zeki plans to save the day, save my day; really, my life.

***

Sunday morning I tell my parents about my plans to move to America. I don't know what inspires me. I wasn't planning to tell them. There was just something about the way they were sitting at the breakfast table, so unaware that I was there, in their apartment, standing in the doorway looking at them. Perhaps it was that I wanted them to notice me, to finally really see me. See who I'd grown up to be.

"I applied for a visa to the US."

Dad lowers his newspaper slightly; Mom places Dad's scrambled eggs down in front of him and then turns her head toward me.

"I was denied on Friday."

They look at each other.

"Zeki is going to take me to the consulate tomorrow," I say, pausing.

Dad looks up.

"To try again. He says he has a plan to get me the visa."

"Zeki won't be able to help," Dad says, then goes back to reading the paper. Mom says nothing.

I look at both of them, then walk out of the room. *Why did I tell them? What was I hoping they would do, get up and hug me and tell me they are proud of me?*

***

On Monday morning, Zeki picks me up in his Mercedes. "Don't worry, Adem. I am going to take care of this for you. I understand how these things work."

I exhale. I realize I've been holding my breath . . . for years. I'm not 100 percent clear what it is about. But, for the first time in a long time, I feel that I'm being taken care of. I don't have to do anything. Somebody is helping me. Somebody who is competent and confident. I don't think he'll be able to get me a visa, but it feels nice not to expend energy, to just sit there and let him strategize.

Instead of being hyper focused on the task at hand, I look around and take in my surroundings. As we drive by Pera Palas, I again look for famous faces among the few people walking out of the hotel. Zeki parks the car and asks me for my passport. "Let's do this," he says, patting me on my back. I try to match his smile and his confidence.

The Marine behind the glass checks our IDs and lets us in. We walk down the hall to the red-carpeted room. This time I notice that the carpet is more of a maroon than a red; it's plush and clean. I look up. The ceiling is high with shadow-box moldings; thick curtains drape tall windows. And, there are two American flags, one on a pole and one framed and hanging on the wall. I look at the fifty stars and the thirteen stripes and I get goose bumps. *We are on American soil.* I hadn't thought of that the other times I was here. *America.* I take a deep breath. There is an unusual but pleasant smell. *Does America smell like this?* I close my eyes, imagining myself walking through the forest of golden leaves and clay soil.

At the doorway, Zeki motions to me to stay put. He walks across the large room to the counter where the same officer who interviewed me the other day is standing. The room is dead quiet. I can hear my heart beating. I watch as Zeki leans forward and places his left elbow on the counter. I watch intently but I can't assess how the conversation is going.

After a few minutes, Zeki turns away from the counter. I swallow what feels like my last breath of air. I can't tell what the expression on Zeki's face means. I wait, worrying as he walks back to me, wishing he would walk faster.

"I left your passport with Officer Norton," Zeki says. "He said you can come back on Thursday morning to pick it up."

I nod but I'm confused.

"You've got your visa," he whispers, putting his arm around my shoulder, turning me around and guiding me out the door.

What?

"I can go to America?" I ask, whispering back. "I'm going to America?" *America!*

Zeki pats my arm.

My brain is screaming inside my head. It takes everything I have to not scream, to not jump into Zeki's arms, to not dance like a lunatic, kiss the American flag, lie down on the American soil of the US consulate and roll on the carpet like a mad dog. I suppress every ecstatic thought I have and do my best to mimic Zeki's calm. I can't risk my lunatic reaction making them change their minds. This is the happiest moment in my life, but I try to act like it's nothing, like it's just another moment, another day. *America. America! I'm going to America! I'm going to America?*

As soon as we get into the car and the doors are shut, I start blubbering my thank you's to Zeki—for a full five minutes. I thank him in every possible way. Finally, he tells me it's enough, patting me on the knee and laughing. "I want this for you, Adem, that's why I did this."

"Sir, what did you tell the consular officer?"

"I asked him why he didn't issue a visa to you last week. He said because you did not have a bank account or any property here in Turkey, so you had no incentive to come back. Also, your lack of English. He believed that since you don't speak English, you'd be less likely to advance academically and would just stay in the US and work low-wage jobs, taking away blue-collar jobs from Americans who need them."

"So, what did you tell him then?"

"I told him, 'This kid is twenty-one years old. He graduated from Technical University. If he went to the US, he could only be useful to you. He would not be a drain on the system. The US was built by people like this kid. How could you deny him entry?' "

I stare at Zeki. I'm speechless. Life is worth living.

***

Thursday morning before work, I go back to the US consulate office to pick up my passport. The narrow hallway, the glass-paneled guard post, the Marine—everything is beginning to feel familiar; less intimidating, even. The Marine looks up then lets me in.

I walk to the counter where I show a consular officer my ID. She pulls out my passport and turns the pages in the empty book until she gets to the visa stamp.

"Here you go, Mr. Bayer. Your passport has been stamped with a single entry."

"Thank you. Thank you, ma'am," I say as she hands me my passport. I can't stop smiling as I look at the stamp. It's beautiful. Powerful. My heart races. I thank her again and walk back down the hallway to the exit. As I walk past the guard booth, I lift up my passport and grin. "Thank you sir!" I say and I keep walking.

"Are you going to America?" the Marine calls after me.

"Yes, sir," I say, turning around.

He smiles, "You're going to like the American girls!" He reaches down on his desk and picks up a magazine. *Playboy*. I watch as he opens the magazine and holds it up against the glass. The *Playboy* centerfold. Miss September.

I don't want to smile, but I do.

***

All day I try to find the time to call Demir to tell him the news. Finally, just as I'm wrapping things up, I steal a moment.

"I got it! It's official, we are going to America! Your dad. He made this possible. He made this happen." I want to scream, but I'm speaking in a low voice so that my colleagues can't hear me. I'm going to have to find a way to tell Soner that I'm resigning.

"Congratulations!" Demir says.

"I can't believe this is happening. It's my dream. Ever since I watched your plane take off to America when I was nine and you were eleven."

"I know. You love that story!"

"It's when I started dreaming the American dream," I say, laughing with him, though I don't tell Demir that I still need $4,000 to make my dream come true. He needs money, too; but all he has to do is ask Zeki for it.

We decide that Demir will leave for America first. He doesn't have a job here and is itching to go. I need extra time to wind down my job with Soner and raise the money I need to move. It's a good plan. Demir will set things up for us—find a place for us to live and scope out some jobs.

I can also use the time to add to my basic English vocabulary. I know 257 words from high school English. And, I can construct a few short sentences, like *I come home, I'm going to the beach.*

"You know," Demir says, "all our friends are betting on how long you can possibly stay in America."

"You told them already? I just picked up my visa."

"I was betting on you getting it," he says, with a chuckle.

"And so?"

"And so, what?"

"What's their bet, on how long I'll stay?"

"Most bets are for thirty days. The longest is six months."

I nod. They're not wrong to think I won't last. There are a lot of American dreamers. They borrow money from friends and family and go, and when their money runs out, simply return. But they're wrong about me. I know they are wrong. The question in my mind isn't how long I will stay in America, but when I can leave Turkey. I need $4,000. *Where in the world am I going to get $4,000?*

I get off the phone with Demir and leave the office.

When I get home, I find Ela at the dining table gobbling up Mom's lamb chops.

"Sorry," she says, looking up, licking her fingers. "I've been craving these."

"When are you going to stop working?" I ask.

"I don't know. I feel good." She lifts her index finger as if to say, "Just a minute," then covers her mouth with the other hand, and says "sorry" again. She pauses, and finishes chewing. "Mom told me you are back on this America kick and you need me to lend you money."

"Huh?" I say, confused. "I didn't tell Mom I wanted to borrow money from you. You already told me you wouldn't."

"Huh."

"I didn't say anything to Mom about money," I say, peering into the kitchen. "She must have been listening in on a conversation I was having with Demir."

"Well, that's typical."

I laugh, mostly from shock that Mom was paying attention.

"Well, here's the good news, Adem. I changed my mind about your American dream. I think you should go. In fact, I want to help you go. So, I'm going to sell my stocks and you can use the money."

"What? Ela! Wow! Thank you."

"You don't have to thank me."

"I'm . . . I don't . . . I *have to* thank you. I'm speechless."

"Okay. Fine. You can thank me. But, you don't have to pay me back until you've made it in America. Not made it *to* America, but *made it*. Became a success."

"What happened to your diatribe? My head in the clouds and all that?"

"I thought about it. And, I was wrong. I'm living my dream. I love my job. I love my husband; I'm having this baby," she says, rubbing her stomach. "And you're my baby brother. You should have your dreams, too. And, I decided it's about time someone in this family bet on you."

"I don't know what to say, Ela."

"I will sell my stocks tomorrow. They're worth about $800."

"Thank you, Ela." I get up and hug her.

"And, I have more good news."

"You're having twins?"

"No . . . God no!" she says, touching her belly again, and laughing. "I'm not that big! No. No. It's not about this kicker or his invisible twin. No. I spoke with Eliz and she is committing another $600. So, if you need money after you get to America, she is willing to send you $600."

"What? Oh my Lord, Ela! You both believe . . . I don't know what to say." I hug her again. "I'm . . . I'm going to go call Eliz. Thank you. Best older sisters ever. I can't believe this. This is huge, Ela. Thank you."

"Make us proud, baby brother."

***

I wake up to the phone ringing in the living room. I look at the clock. It's three o'clock in the morning. I sit up in bed when I hear Dad on the phone, then grab my robe and find Dad cradling the base of the phone and pacing the room as far as the cord will let him, then pacing back in the other direction. He's nodding his head. After a few minutes, he hangs up.

"What's going on?"

He looks up, surprised.

"That was Zeki."

"Is everything okay?"

"The military is staging a coup. They are going to take over the government. The military will be in charge," he says. "Go back to sleep."

"A coup?"

"Yes and a twenty-four-hour curfew. Go back to sleep. There's nothing we can do."

I walk over to the window. Military and police vehicles are speeding down the street. In the distance, I can hear the faint cry of sirens. Then, closer by, some gunshots.

"Do you think the gunshots are resisters protesting the takeover?" I ask.

"Whatever resistance there is, it should end in a few hours. Go back to sleep."

I go back to my room and turn on the radio. There are statements about how the military "didn't want to do this," but they had to "to put a stop to the violence." The anchor reports that the military plans to return the country to general elections as soon as the country is safe and secure.

As the sun rises, the gunshots quiet and the sirens subside, just as Dad predicted. I spend the day at home with my parents. Every few hours, Zeki calls Dad with updates. Their friends, even their former officers, are about to be running the country.

Dad says this is the third time in twenty years that the military has assumed power. I don't really remember the other times. I was too young. But, Dad says there will likely be a lot of changes. If history is any guide, he tells me, the killings will stop and the arrests will start. A lot of people who should be arrested will walk free, and a lot of people who had nothing to do with politics will be detained. Tortured. It reminds me of the "collateral damage" that Polat used to talk about.

The minute the twenty-four-hour curfew ends, I head to the office. Military and police vehicles have blocked major intersections. It takes the bus an extra thirty minutes to get through the blockades. I get off the bus four stops early and walk the rest of the way. At the office, Soner turns the radio on and the few people who have arrived on time sit frozen at their desks, listening instead of working. "Martial law is declared," the reporter announces. "The heads of all political parties are under house arrest for their own 'safety.' The takeover has been completed without incident; the country is calm. Free elections will be reinstated as soon as the political violence ends."

Those in the office continue to listen as the reporters tell us that the military has dissolved the government and the parliament. Colleagues drift in late, looking disheveled, worried, as we digest the information being reported. The generals have assigned a civilian professor as prime minister to form a government of nonelected civilians.

"The new government is a puppet of the military, the media too," someone says, throwing his hat on his drawing table. "They're all puppets of the military."

"Turkey is now living a dictatorship," says another person. "Military rule must end immediately. The democratically elected government must be restored."

"I'm fine with the military rule if it will stop young people from killing each other," someone else says.

Within hours, rumors begin to circulate. The one that worries me the most, I overhear on the bus ride home. "The military will soon begin restricting foreign travel, especially by young people. I hear it's to prevent criminals from leaving the country."

They may not allow me and Demir to go to America.

16

EMPLOYEE DISCOUNT

By the time I get home, I've worked myself up into a state of complete panic. "Ela left something for you," Mom calls from the kitchen. "It's on the dining table."

It's an envelope. I pick it up. It feels like a stack of cash. Slowly, I run my finger over the sealed flap, then pull out my house key to slice it open. I rifle through the green bills. $800 in American cash.

"What is it?" Mom calls from the kitchen.

"Nothing that would concern you," I shoot back. I hear her gasp. I take a deep breath. "Sorry, Mom. I'm sorry. We were listening to the news reports all day at work. The military coup has me riled up."

"It's going to be fine," she says, walking out to the dining room, drying her hands on her apron. "It always works out."

I try to smile. *I wish I could stick my head in the sand the same way you do, Mom.* "So, what did Ela give you?"

I'm thinking quickly about how to evade her question without lying when the phone rings.

"I'll get that," I say, walking into the living room to grab the receiver. I turn around and watch my mother walk back into the kitchen. *In five minutes, she will have completely forgotten about the package.*

"We need to leave for America as soon as possible," Demir says even before I say hello.

"Demir?"

"Adem, listen to me. We have to leave soon. Not just me, both of us. If we don't leave right away, we may not be able to get out for months. Who knows, *years*. Can you leave as soon as Friday?"

"Friday?" I ask, shocked. My heart drops. I'm nowhere near ready to move halfway around the world. "I don't have the money I need, Demir. I just don't have the funds yet. You go. I'll figure something out."

"Man, just ask Zeki, he'll give you the money, we'll leave together."

"I can't do that. You know that. When you find a place, send me your address. Our address. I'll get out. I'll get there. And send me the phone number, too. Go. Get out."

"Adem. No."

"If I can't get out, well, remember what my grandma always said, 'That's what was supposed to happen.' But, it's going to be okay. I'll get out."

He doesn't sound convinced but gets off the phone quickly so he can head over to the Pan Am office and buy his round-trip ticket.

Two days later, I drive Demir to the airport. It's that fast. We do get stopped and searched along the way, but Demir's ticket allows us to get through. Once again, I watch his plane head off into the clouds and, as I stand there watching him jet off to America, I feel myself transforming into nine-year-old me. My face grows hot. Jealousy bubbles up from I don't know where. "It's not fair," I say to no one, even surprising myself when I stomp my foot.

On the way home from the airport, I try to figure out a new plan, now that I've got a ticking clock. While it still may be a rumor that the military is restricting travel, I've come too far to risk that it's actually true. I rattle off the facts in my head. I have $800. Demir's round-trip ticket cost $900, so even Ela's money isn't enough to cover it. Think, Adem. Think! But my mind is racing so fast, I can't concentrate. At a stoplight, I look down to find my knuckles white from gripping the wheel so hard. I try to empty my brain by thinking of unrelated tasks and simple calculations. *Take a breath, Adem.* It'll have to be a one-way ticket.

The next day I call in late to work and head over to the Pan Am office. As I approach the double glass doors, I hear the click of heels behind me. I turn to see a young woman wearing a Pan Am flight attendant's uniform approaching. I pull the door open for her and stand aside to let her in ahead of me.

She smiles, thanks me, and clicks her way behind the counter and into a back office. I walk over to wait behind the only other customer. When the man in front of me is called up to the counter, I take out Ela's money, all my dollar bills, as discreetly as I can, and start counting it, again. I know exactly how much I have, but I can't help counting.

"Are you traveling?" I hear from behind.

Startled from my counting, I whip my head around and see the flight attendant with the clicking heels.

"Yes, ma'am."

"Where are you headed?"

"Washington, DC."

She exclaims, "America! How wonderful. You are buying your ticket, today, yes?"

"Yes. Yes, ma'am."

"Well . . . as a thank you, I would like to get you an employee discount."

"I'm sorry?" I ask, confused.

"You held the door for me. So few people do that these days. And I'd like to thank you by getting a discount for you."

"I . . . I don't know what to say . . ." I stammer. I don't understand why she is offering to help me this way. I was satisfied with her "thank you" at the door.

"Say 'yes,' then," she says simply. "You did something nice for me; I'd like to do something nice for you."

"Oh . . . wow. Yes, of course. That's so kind of you. Sure. Of course."

"The truth is, I was having a difficult morning and you turned things around for me."

"I'm glad. And thank you for helping me." Even though she sounds confident about it, I'm doubtful they'll let her use her "family" discount for a stranger.

A few seconds later it's my turn. The flight attendant steps ahead of me and says to the woman behind the counter, "I would like to purchase a ticket to Washington, DC for . . ." she looks at me, smiling.

"Adem Bayer," I say. "Um . . . For December First. Please. Thank you."

"Your passport, please, sir."

I hand her my passport.

"Round trip is $899; one way is $499. Will that be a round trip or one way, sir?"

"One way, please," I say. I take a deep breath. My heart feels like it's jumping out of my chest. I don't know if it's because I'm actually doing this, buying a ticket to America, my dream, or because I've now committed myself to leaving in three weeks and I'm nowhere near the $4,000 that I need. Or, maybe it's because I'm scared that the next thing the ticket lady is going to tell me is that the airports have shut down and I can't buy a ticket. Or maybe it's just everything. All of it. *Breathe, Adem.*

The flight attendant clears her throat. "And, please add on the employee family discount," she says, passing her ID to the lady at the counter.

"Ahh, yes. Okay. Okay, let's see . . ." she says, tapping on the keyboard. "Okay, that means the total will be $299.40, sir, for your one-way ticket to Washington, DC."

It worked? What? This woman just saved me $200! This stranger. Just because I held the door for her, which I would have done for anyone!

I place $300 on the counter. I suppress the urge to look at the flight attendant, to smile, to thank her. I don't want to jinx this moment. I barely breathe. We stand shoulder to shoulder in silence waiting for the ticket to print out.

"Here is your ID," the ticket lady says, handing it back to the flight attendant. "And, sir, here is your ticket and your passport and your change," she says, pushing the items across the counter in my direction. "You will fly Istanbul–Frankfurt–New York–Washington. The first and third legs are Boeing 737s. The middle leg is a Boeing 747. Have a nice trip."

I turn toward the flight attendant, wanting to speak. I smile. "Thank you . . . I . . . thank," I say, stammering, searching for words.

"Have a wonderful trip!" she says, smiling back, clicking her way out of my life as quickly as she walked into it. *Grandma, was that one of my angels?*

I watch her walk away. *You have an extra $200. That's almost two months of food, Adem. You are going to America!*

My toes do a little dance inside my shoes. I can't believe what's just happened. I tuck my ticket and passport into the inside pocket of my jacket and head back to the bus stop. In three weeks and three days, I'll be boarding a flight to America. America!

Am I dreaming? Is this all a dream?

On the bus I pull out my passport and my ticket booklet, and I look at the printout. December 1, Istanbul to Frankfurt; December 1, Frankfurt to New York; and December 1, New York to Washington, DC. I pinch myself. *Wow!*

***

On the way to work the next day, I decide I need to tell Soner immediately. He's going to be surprised, disappointed even. He thinks my plan is to move to Libya and work for him and Mr. Baris there. I think he's even banking on it—literally. America is going to be like a complete and utter curve ball.

I sit down at my desk with a cup of coffee, trying to figure out what I'm going to say. *Rip off the Band-Aid, Adem. Just tell him. He can't say "No, you can't leave." You don't have a contract with him. So just do it.* I take one more sip of coffee then I walk over to Soner's office, motioning to his secretary that I want to go in; she nods. "Excuse me, sir," I say, poking my head in through the door. "Do you have a minute?"

Soner looks up briefly. "For you, Adem, my favorite employee, always. Please, come in."

Did he just say I'm his favorite employee? I take a deep breath and watch Soner reach for the pencil tucked behind his ear; he scrawls something in the margin of the document he's reading. "Sir . . . I just wanted to let you know . . . I'm leaving for America."

Soner puts the pencil down and looks back up at me. He says nothing. I watch his face but it offers me no clues. He puts his hands behind his head and I watch as he leans back in his leather chair. "America? What happened to Libya, Adem? I've been working hard behind the scenes here to get you to Libya, working to convince Mr. Baris. I'm going to get you to Libya."

"Actually sir, Libya was my short-term plan. But the long-term plan was always America. It was always America. But, now I've found a way to get there, directly. In fact, I have a ticket, already, for December 1. It came about very suddenly. I can work until November 30. Or, I can pack up my desk today, if you prefer."

"No. No. Adem. I'm surprised. Not angry. You can stay as long as you wish," Soner says, lowering his arms. "So, did you get a scholarship to go to America?"

"No, sir, I'm going on my own. I will work and take English classes."

"I have to admit, I admire you, Adem. It takes guts, what you are doing. I have no doubt that you will do well in America. You are a brave man, Adem Bayer."

"That's very nice of you to say sir. I've very much enjoyed working here, working for you. But America has been my dream since I was nine. It's quite remarkable to me that I am making my dream come true."

"It is, indeed. You should be proud of yourself. Your parents should be very proud." *My parents don't even know I'm going, sir.*

"You've been a very important member of my team, Adem. You will be missed."

"Thank you, sir. I have learned so much from you." I clear my throat. "So, I will work until the end of the month. That is okay, sir?" I ask.

Soner nods and I turn to leave.

"One second, Adem. I need to ask . . . You really have been invaluable to me. Hard shoes to fill. You are a hard worker. I want to thank you for your efforts. Or, at least make up for your early efforts."

"Sir?"

"How long did you work for us without pay, Adem?"

"Oh, three months or so, sir." *Three months and seventeen days.*

I watch him lean forward and reach into his back pocket. He pulls out a wad of US dollars, then counts out $300 on his desk. "This is what I owe you," he says, folding up the bills and handing them to me.

"Oh, sir, you don't owe me, I owe *you* for giving me a job."

"Please take it, you deserve it." He rises from his seat.

"Thank you, sir." I take the money and shake Soner's hand. "Thank you. This is very generous of you."

"Come." Soner leads me to the draftspersons area. The chatter stops the second Soner enters the room. "Everyone, Adem is going to America next month. I would like to publicly thank him for his contributions to us. He will make himself well-liked there and succeed."

My colleagues begin to clap and Soner places his hands on my shoulders as I imagine a proud father would. One by one, my co-workers come over to congratulate me. Nearly everyone has a piece of advice—even though they have never been to America.

"Having a visa does not automatically entitle you to enter the US," one of the architects says as he shakes my hand. "You might arrive at the airport and the immigration officer could decide not to let you in. It's up to that one person. His discretion. Be careful. I know many people who have traveled far and at great expense only to be sent back . . ."

"Yes, it's true," Fatma says, interrupting in agreement. "I've heard that during the flight or right after landing in America, some people destroy their passports in a toilet. When you don't have any identification with you, they bring you to a detention center to give you a hearing date. By law they have to give you a hearing date. Afterward, they just release you into the country. Then you go and disappear, until you hopefully become legal someday."

"You're a red flag," Raif says. "Single. A recent college graduate. They're gonna see you and grab you right at the airport and pull you into an interrogation room. You'll be questioned for hours. You'll be lucky if you get a translator. They will try to wear you down. So, here's my advice: If they ask about your plans while in the US, you say 'I would like to learn English and study for an advanced degree here.' Say it in English. Practice it over and over and over. If they ask you whether you want to work, you say that it should not be necessary, my parents will send me money regularly, and that should be enough. And you tell them that after you finish your studies, you plan to return to your country."

My head is reeling. *I'm supposed to lie to get into America?*

"Thank you, all. Very useful advice," I say as my breakfast rises up my throat and indigestion sets in.

Why didn't Demir didn't tell me any of this? Why didn't anyone else tell me any of this?

That evening, just as I'm about to sit down with my parents to watch *Dallas,* the phone rings. "Adem, it's me." Demir is calling from Washington. "I need to make this quick, the call is expensive. If you can change your plans, do it, don't come here. It's awful here. The worst recession since the Second World War. Inflation is 13.5 percent, interest rates are 17 percent, and the unemployment rate is 7.5 percent. I cannot find a real job. I have been delivering pizza since I arrived. I'm an economist in Turkey but a delivery boy in America. I can't even get a job as a bank teller. I'm putting plans together to come home. Don't come."

Don't come? No. No! This is my dream. I'm so close. No, I want to go to America. If I don't go now, I will never have another opportunity.

"I want to go to America. And, I need you there. I need you to stay. I have bought my ticket. Please. Don't leave. I'll be there in twenty-six days. It'll be better, both of us together. I land on December 1. 7:40 p.m. from New York. Just stay. It'll be better together, with me there. You'll see. I need you there, man. I can't *do* America without you."

After another minute of pleading and listing reasons to stay, Demir starts turning a corner. He tells me he'll think about it and will call me back in a day or two.

I hang up and look at my parents. If they were listening, they say nothing. I think they care more about who shot J.R.

I pick up the *Nation's Daily* and walk over to sit at the dining table. The headlines on the international page focus on the election of a former actor as president, his planned armament program, corporate tax cuts, and the American hostage crisis in Iran; it's day 340.

Then I turn to the domestic news and see Savas's name in bold print. *Savas Kartal, head of Yavuz Security, a security guard firm providing businessmen and politicians with armed personnel, has been arrested and convicted of one count of premeditated murder by the military court. He is sentenced to thirty years in prison. He is accused of seven other murders. The trials for those murders are to take place while he is in prison.*

I exhale. This is a huge relief. But within seconds, I realize Savas has men; he can be just as dangerous while in jail.

17

CASH AND CARRY

IT'S BEEN SEVEN WEEKS SINCE THE MILITARY COUP AND THE declaration of martial law in Turkey. The violence and protests have mostly stopped, but the military is wreaking havoc on people's lives. The brother-in-law of one of my colleagues was plucked off the street and has been missing for a month. An artist and lecturer, the man has nothing to do with the Nationalists or Communists. Stories like his are rampant.

Each day, getting to work feels like a chore. Roadblocks and vehicle searches continue to disrupt traffic. My bus often arrives late or not at all and I scramble to get to work on time.

"He wants to see you." I look up to find Soner's secretary in my doorway. "Can you come now," she says, more a statement than a question.

"I need you to go down to the Bosporus," Soner says, launching right in before I've had a chance to sit down. "I need you to go to the IS Bank, the branch on Liman Street. They are expecting you."

"Sir?"

"They will give you a stack of cash, about $800,000. It'll be in a brown bag. I need you to pick it up for me. Take a taxi and I'll reimburse you."

"Yes, sir," I say, trying to sound agreeable even though I don't like this one bit. I don't want to have to leave the office. And, I really don't want to leave the office to carry almost a million dollars in cash. A brown paper bag with $800,000. How much does something like that weigh? Is it all in twenties? Hundreds? In the middle of martial law, this is what Soner wants me to do. What the hell would they do to me if I'm stopped? Almost certainly, they'd throw me in Istanbul Prison. Where Savas Kartal is. That would be the end of me. Or, if someone told them I'm a Communist, they'd send me to Ankara, where I'd be tortured until I revealed my conspiring Communist accomplices, which I don't have. So, that too, would be the end of me. Either way, getting caught with Soner's cash would be a death sentence. *Why are you saying yes, Adem? What the hell! You don't need to be doing this. You're leaving for America in twenty-three days!*

"That's a lot of money, sir."

"Yes, it is, Adem. It's why I'm asking you. I trust you."

"Yes sir. Thank you, sir." *Am I so deprived of compliments that I'll put my life on the line for one?*

I hail a taxi outside the office. Military and police vehicles are in all the major intersections, searching cars for weapons and illegal Communist publications, checking people's IDs. The taxi driver tells me there are bottlenecks throughout the city. I don't know whether to feel safer or more worried. A twenty-one-year-old Technical University graduate with an $800,000 money bag is a red flag, a red Communist conspiracy flag, waving high, shouting out, arrest me!

Should I go back to the office and tell Soner no, I can't do this?

I tell the driver to let me out early. I stand on the street corner looking around. It's not hot but sweat starts forming on my brow. I have a visa to America, and a plane ticket. The military and police are everywhere. What's Soner thinking, sending me out here on this errand? I shouldn't be here.

You've got to do this, Adem. I start walking. I'm only a few blocks from the bank when I pass a vegetable stand. I turn around and buy some lettuce. The grocer hands me the lettuce wrapped in old newspapers. I ask for extra newspapers. And then I head to the bank, the lettuce tucked under my arm like a gun in a holster.

An employee greets me at the door, nodding at me as if he knows who I am. I've never seen him before. He leads me into the manager's office.

"Hello, Adem, how are you?" a woman behind the desk says. I've never seen her before either. The man standing next to her hands me a brown bag; it's open at the top. Without thinking, I peer in. Bundles of wrapped $100 bills are piled on top of each other. If each bundle has one-hundred bills, there should be eighty of them. *Do I count the money? Would it be disrespectful or expected? Soner, you should have told me what to do! Who sends someone out to collect nearly a million in cash without specific instructions! Who? If I don't count the money and they've cheated him, would he assume it was me or would he know these people swiped it? You can't count it, Adem. If you were supposed to count it, Soner would have told you. Just take it. Take it. And, go.*

I pad the cash with the newspapers, put the lettuce on top, thank the people, and leave the building. With the newspapers and lettuce leaves sticking out, it looks like I've gone shopping for vegetables. I walk to the taxi stand with my decoy-topped bag of cash, then rethink my return; a taxi might not be the right way to go. I could have been fortunate not being stopped and searched coming over here. If we're stopped and searched now, it's sayonara Adem. I keep walking, to the bus stop. It'll take longer, but it's less likely to get pulled over and searched.

I wait only a few minutes for the bus to arrive, then walk straight to the back of the bus, the money bag on my lap and the lettuce leaves tickling my face, my legs fidgety.

I begin to daydream about the amount of money on my lap. My calculations are a good distraction. *I have two hundred times more money on my lap than what I need to go to America. I could settle in the US, focus on learning English, get a graduate degree. And with all this money, I could do that not once, but two hundred times. The money is right here, on my lap, in my hands. Right now, it's mine. To make this much money, I would have to work for Soner for more than seven thousand months. That's six hundred years.* I've gone from calming myself to making myself more agitated. "I trust you Adem," I hear Soner saying. *I could get off the bus right now, go home, grab a suitcase, go to the airport, pay cash for a new plane ticket, and leave for America today.* Take the money and run, just like the song. "I trust you, Adem," I hear Soner saying, again and again and again. *But how long would it take for Soner to realize I hadn't come back yet? I could be on a plane before he realizes it.*

As we roll through the city, the bus starts getting crowded. I watch everyone carefully as they enter, making sure that no one's going to snatch my bag of lettuce. I try to stop my leg from jittering.

When I get back to my office, I remove the lettuce and newspapers, set them on my desk, and take the bag of money to Soner's office. "Put it on my desk, son," he says, hardly looking up. I watch as he takes it, thanks me, and, without even bothering to look inside, places it on the floor, underneath his desk. "That'll be all," he says.

Back in my office, I stare at the lettuce on my desk as I run through the events of the last two hours. I could have been mugged or arrested. I could be dead or on my way to prison right now.

I close my eyes and try to breathe. *You are fine. Everything's fine. Focus on work. You are leaving for America in twenty-three days!* I pull a stack of papers from the in-box on my desk and dive into my work.

About an hour later, Soner's secretary is back at my door. "He needs to see you. Immediately," she says, with urgency.

"Bayer, yes, Adem Bayer . . . yes," I hear Soner say to the mouthpiece as I walk in. "He'll be there within half an hour."

He hangs up the phone with one hand and hands me the same brown bag with the other. "I have a delivery for you to make, Adem. This is four hundred thousand. Please deliver it to this person at this address," he says, handing me a piece of paper with a contact name and address. "Take a taxi."

I look at the paper. *I need to say something. I can't do this. I'm still reeling from the $800,000 pickup. Say something Adem. Now!* "Sir, could someone else please do this, please?" I say, shaking my head, fidgeting. "Sir, I don't think I can do this."

"You're the man for the job. You are the only man for the job, in fact it'll be good for your career. It's Mr. Baris's money. If he knows he can trust you, you're one step closer to going to Libya." He hooks two fingers inside his shirt collar, tugging a couple of times to loosen it, then he loosens his necktie, pulls his handkerchief from his pocket, and wipes his forehead. I watch him.

"Sir, I'm going to America in a few weeks. Libya is no longer part of my plan."

He pulls at his collar again. His face is red.

"If not for yourself, then do it for me, to help me," he says, his voice cracking.

What's going on here?

"Okay, sir. I'll do it," I say without much resolve.

I take the bag and walk out of Soner's office. The name on the paper is a Mr. Kaya, no first name; the address is the Nationalist Party district headquarters. I realize that if Savas weren't in jail, he could be there. My hands are clammy. I don't like this at all.

If this is Mr. Baris's money, why is he giving it to the Nationalist Party? Is he even aware where his money is going? And, why is Soner involved?

I decide against a taxi. *Are people looking at me?* Perspiration forms under my nose and I feel my face growing hot despite a chill in the air.

Once I'm on the bus I find myself in a déjà-vu moment, only this time with half the money and no lettuce decoy. *You now have one hundred times the amount you need to settle in America, Adem. You can take the whole $400,000 and go straight to the airport. You don't even need to take all of it. You only need $4,000, even $3,000. Would Mr. Kaya count the money if I shorted it? What if I just took it all? Can I even take all this cash to America? If they found it in Customs, would they take it from me? What if I were to bury it? But how would I do that? If Savas found out I stole the money, he'd have everyone I know killed. Wouldn't he?*

The bus jerks to a stop. I look out the window and see the Nationalist Party headquarters building. I jump up quickly and get off the bus and it pulls away, leaving me standing there. I'm shaking. *Get it together Adem. Get. It. Together.* I walk toward the entrance of the building. A Yavuz Security guard is at the door, standing like a statue in his charcoal-colored uniform with a red badge. I've read that Savas still runs Yavuz Security from behind bars. *That shouldn't be legal.* "I have a delivery for Mr. Kaya," I say. He opens the door for me and I'm stopped by a second security guard wearing the same uniform.

"Room 211? I have a delivery for Mr. Kaya," I say, trying to keep my voice from shaking.

"Name?"

"Adem Bayer. For Mr. Soner Ozenli."

He looks down at a list of names on his desk.

"ID?" *At the bank they gave me $800,000 and didn't check my ID. I am bringing them money and they are checking my ID?* I pull out my ID and hand it to the guard.

"Two flights up, on the left," he says, handing me back my driver's license.

Breathing heavily from the stairs and nerves, I enter room 211. The room is small, with no windows. It smells musty. An overweight, bald man is sitting behind a small desk, flanked by two younger men who are standing. All three are in business suits.

"Name?" the bald man asks.

"Adem Bayer," I say, curtly, trying to sound louder than my heart which is beating so loud in my ears I'm sure everyone can hear it. "And, your name, sir?"

"Kaya."

I hand him the bag of money, he opens it, looks inside, then back at me. He nods, then picks up the phone and dials. "Is the boss there?" he says into the receiver while looking straight at me. I hold his gaze until he looks down and hangs up the phone.

No one says anything. *I should not be here.* I look at the two other men. *Have I seen them before?* They are staring straight ahead. Am I supposed to leave?

I turn toward the door.

"Stay!" Mr. Kaya says.

I turn around, confused, unclear about what is happening. *Who did Mr. Kaya call? What exactly am I waiting for?* I focus on a spot on the desk while trying to keep all three faces in my eyesight. *Who is "the boss" Kaya mentioned? Is it Soner? Is this a test? That's ridiculous, Adem. Two hours ago you were walking around with a million dollars, why would he be testing you now? Is the boss Mr. Baris? Or Mr. Baris thinks he's just contributing to a legitimate political party and his people are arranging where the money goes. Maybe Mr. Baris is contributing to every single political party. Then he's good no matter which one or ones win the elections. Breathe, Adem.* I start counting to calm myself. One minute passes, then two minutes. I try not to turn my head to look at the men standing on either side of Mr. Kaya. But, I can't rid myself of the thought that they look familiar, that I've seen them before, especially the one on the right. *Is it possible I saw them with Savas? At school? Maybe on the street corner when Savas shot at me? Was he one of the men who chased me? I* close my eyes, trying to see the past. *You've seen this man before, Adem. You know it. He was there each time.* I open my eyes. *Is Savas the boss? But he's in prison.*

I start counting again. When I hit five minutes my nerves are more rattled than before. Basketball. That's what I need to think about, my basketball games. I add up my steals and buzzer-beating shots; then I try to recall how many points I scored in those big games.

I've lost count of how long I've been standing. Waiting. What for, I still don't know. I don't want to look at my watch. I don't want to look nervous. I can see Kaya's watch poking out from under his shirt but can't make out the time.

The phone rings and I jump. Someone in the room chuckles. Mr. Kaya picks it up, "Yes, Bayer. He's here. Adem Bayer. Yes, received," says Mr. Kaya to the mouthpiece. He hangs up the phone and looks up at me. "You can go now." I nod and walk out of the room.

I step out of the building and walk over to the bus stop. My right eyelid is twitching. My legs feel weak. I take a deep breath, hold it a few seconds, then exhale loudly, like a braying horse. *I cannot ever do that again; I cannot deliver money like that. I don't like what just happened. I don't even understand what just happened. What was this money for? For whom? Why did I have to hand deliver it?*

The bus comes and I get on, hardly paying attention as I walk to the back. Now that I'm out of there, the questions about what just happened won't stop reeling around in my head. *Who are the players and what are the connections?* I look out the window as I add up all the facts. *Definitely Soner—he's involved; he gave me the money. Definitely the Nationalist Party because that's where I brought the money. Yavuz Security, because those were the guards at the building. Although maybe it's just that they work at the building. Still. Let's see. Is Mr. Baris involved, too? Yes. Because Soner said it's Mr. Baris's money. Is Mr. Baris aware? Is there a connection between Mr. Baris and the Nationalist Party? Okay, let's see. Yavuz Security. Maybe that's it. Yavuz Security provides protection to Turkey's elite, so most likely for Mr. Baris. Savas Kartal runs Yavuz Security, even from prison. So is Savas involved? His security company, his "gangs" are also the fighting arm of the Nationalist Party. Okay, so, if I'm right, those are the players. So now, what's their game?*

The bus pulls up to my stop and I have to muscle my way out of the now-crowded bus to get to the exit. As it pulls away, I'm left staring at the bank across the street. That's it. *That's it! The Communists want to take over the government and confiscate the money of billionaires like Mr. Baris, and even millionaires like Soner. "Transfer the wealth to the revolutionaries and to the labor" is the Communists' political approach. The Nationalist Party is working to defeat the Communists. So, the rich have backed the Nationalists, not necessarily because of their social politics, but because of their financial politics. They all want to preserve the status quo, their money. For the rich, spending a little money, like $400,000, to fund the Nationalists is an inexpensive investment. And they're using cash so nothing is ever recorded as a bank transaction. Cozy-cozy. The Nationalist Party is doing the bidding for the wealthy. And the wealthy have made me their errand boy for this operation. Mr. Baris may know how much money he's contributing but may not know how the money will be used.*

It's all making sense, and I'm not liking it. I walk slowly back to the office, my mind still racing. So, why are they hiding their affiliation? *If this was Mr. Baris's money, as Soner said, then who was that on the phone? Why did Kaya call "the boss" and why did I have to wait for the boss to return the call? And who the hell is "the boss" behind all this?*

18

CHECK-IN CHECK-OUT

"I'VE DELIVERED THE MONEY, SIR," I TELL SONER WHEN I ARRIVE back at the office.

He thanks me and I return to my desk, vowing never to be Soner's money boy again. I take a deep breath and lean back in my chair. In three more weeks I'm going to America.

My mind shifts. America. That's my true worry. The Mr. Baris thing is not my concern. I'm done being an errand boy. Whatever they're doing, they're going to do it. What I really need to focus on is America. I still need $2,600. And what about once I get there? Will the immigration officials let me into the US? And, will I even be able to leave Turkey? Until I'm on American soil, this should be my only worry. Soner and Mr. Baris—not my business, not my worry.

My phone rings.

"They say they haven't received the money," Soner says, before I've even put the receiver against my ear. His voice is loud and agitated.

"Sir?" I say, almost falling backward and off my chair. Alarmed. Confused. "Sir? . . ." *How could that be, I handed them the money.* I slam down the receiver and I spring up from my chair.

"Where's the money, Adem?" Soner says louder, tugging at his shirt collar, as I run into his office.

"Sir, I gave it to Mr. Kaya. I handed it right to him. I handed him the bag. In room 211. There were two others in the room with him." I realize my voice is cracking. I describe the scene to Soner—the phone call, the waiting, the return phone call. As I talk, his face reddens. He keeps tugging at his collar as sweat trickles down his face. "I don't know who was on the other end of the phone, sir, but when the phone rang, after he hung up, Mr. Kaya told me I could leave. I left the bag of money with him, sir. I don't understand why they are saying I didn't."

"Go back and fix this, Adem."

"I'm sorry, sir?"

"Go back and fix this. Take the money back and deliver it, again."

He thinks I stole the money.

"What? Sir. I didn't take the money. *I delivered* it. I handed Mr. Kaya your money, sir. I don't know what's going on here, but I am not going to be accused of doing something I didn't do."

"Just fix this, Adem. You were the last one I saw with the money."

I look at him, sweating in his chair, his face red, then turn and walk out of the office. Without thinking, I run outside and hail a taxi.

"Nationalist Party headquarters," I say to the driver. *Adem, what are you doing?* I'm on autopilot. *Someone stole the money and is setting me up. Who? Why? I thought I had it all figured out.*

My driver is waved through the military roadblocks as the police continue to search cars and seize property. I thought I'd have time to devise a plan, but suddenly this trip back to the Nationalist Party building is a fast one. *What's your plan, Adem? You're going back there to do what exactly?*

I get off at the Nationalist Party building. This time there are no guards at the entrance. I step back to check and see if I'm at the right address. No one stops me when I walk in and go up the stairs, taking them two at a time. I run down the hall to room 211. The door is locked. I look up and down the hallway, looking for someone who can unlock the door for me; then I start running only slowing down when I see a Yavuz Security guard and avoid his gaze as we brush past each other. I find a janitor to open the door. As we head back to room 211, me in front trying to quicken his pace, he tells me 211 is a storage room. "No, you are wrong, that's impossible," I tell him. "I just had a meeting in there, two hours ago," I add, almost trying to convince myself.

He fiddles with four or five keys, before he finds the right one. I push past him and into the room. I'm hit with the same musty smell as before, but this time there is no table or chair. It's just a room filled with boxes.

"What?" I say, out loud.

"I told you, son. A storage room."

What's going on? I was here. I turn around a few times. I walk around the boxes into each corner of the small room. *What's going on?* I thank the janitor and walk back out into the hallway. I stop everyone in a suit to ask if they know where I can find any Mr. Kaya. No one has ever heard of him. *No one has ever heard of him! What's going on?*

I leave the building and jump in a cab. "Sakayik sokak," I tell the cabbie. I can't go back to work. *Adem, you can't go anywhere. There's $400,000 missing and you are being accused of taking it. You are the last person who had it, according to Soner. $400,000! I start having trouble breathing. $400,000 is missing and your boss believes you stole it.*

At home I don't wait for the elevator. I run up the three flights and burst into the apartment; Mom is in the kitchen. She hardly looks up despite my clearly dramatic entrance. *Adem the Invisible.* I go straight to my room. I pace back and forth for several minutes. My head is exploding with thoughts. *Kaya knew my name. He knew my name before I got there. Okay, well, clearly Soner told him my name. That would make sense.* My mind is going in circles. *Okay, what about the phone call? That's key here. That's the one key thing here I don't know. Who did Kaya call? Why did he call first, then wait, then receive a call from, I'm assuming, "the boss"? Who was "the boss"? Not Soner. if it had been Soner, he wouldn't have repeated my name, "Yes, Bayer. He's here, Adem Bayer." That's what he said. "Yes, Bayer. He's here, Adem Bayer." I'm sure of it. He repeated my name. It wouldn't add up that it was Soner. It couldn't have been Soner. I mean, he looked like he was going to have a heart attack. So, Soner is out. Could Kaya have been calling Mr. Baris? No, no. There's no way. Is there? Could it be? But then why would Mr. Baris call Soner to say I didn't deliver the money? It couldn't be Mr. Baris. He hardly knows me. Why would he want to set me up? I'm not important.*

I sit down on my bed and run my fingers through my hair. *Is someone trying to frame me? Me? Why would anyone do that?*

There has to be an answer.

Soner told me to ask for Mr. Kaya. The man in room 211 said he was Mr. Kaya. But it was really a storage room. The first time I went to the building, people knew who Mr. Kaya was. The second time, they didn't. Is there even someone named Mr. Kaya or is that a made-up person? Okay, list the facts Adem. I pull out my notebook:

- I delivered money to Mr. Kaya.

- "Mr. Kaya" called someone on the phone.

- Someone, either the same person or someone else, called "Mr. Kaya" back.

- Someone, either the same person or someone else, called Soner to say they didn't receive the money.

But maybe they did receive the money? So, either the Mr. Kaya I met was an imposter who stole the money or the real Mr. Kaya got the money and is saying he didn't get it. Is it to set me up? That's ludicrous, Adem. Why would they set up a lowly errand boy? Is it to set up Soner?

Why would they get their money but say they didn't and blame me?

I stand up and start pacing my room, again. *They knew me; they knew my name. The person on the phone specifically asked a question about me that prompted Mr. Kaya to say, "Yes, Bayer. He's here, Adem Bayer." Is that the person who set me up—the person on the phone, "the boss"? Soner thinks I stole the money. If I'm caught, I'm going to be sent to jail.*

I stare blankly at the passport on my desk.

Jail, Adem. Jail! Istanbul Prison. Prison! With murderers. I stop pacing. *With Savas Kartal.* I shiver.

I grab my passport and airline ticket booklet from my desk. I look at the numbers until the pages go blurry.

I walk into the kitchen.

"Mom, which suitcase can I take to America?" I ask, my voice cracking. I clear my throat.

She turns to look at me from the sink. "Are you packing already?" she asks, as if it hardly makes a difference to her and she is merely making conversation.

"Can I please have it now?" I say, more sternly than I had intended.

She lets out a heavy sigh and takes off her kitchen gloves. I follow her down the hall to the linen closet. She pulls out a small, cream-colored suitcase, opens it, and begins to empty it. My summer clothes. I stand there impatiently waiting for her to unpack the suitcase, ignoring her mutterings about why I need the suitcase "right now." As soon as she removes the last item, I take the suitcase from her, exhaling loudly. "Thank you," I say, trying to sound a little more congenial. She nods silently as she begins to reorganize the shelves, finding a place for the clothes from the suitcase.

I take the bag to my room. *What am I doing? What is my plan? Pack first, then plan. You only have so much time before someone comes after you. Who? Who would come after you? Soner? Mr. Baris? His security goons? Okay. Breathe. Pack. What are you going to pack? This is not like driving down to the beach. I need clothes to get me through the winter. I'll wear my sheepskin coat and pack my sheepskin fur-lined mittens. I'll wear my suit.* I open a drawer with my sweaters and grab four, and an Angora scarf, a hand-me-down from Eliz's husband, Erman. Shoes—one pair; blue jeans—two pairs; white dress shirt—one. T-shirts—five. Underwear and socks—seven. Toothbrush, toothpaste, razor.

I look at myself in the mirror. I feel like I did the day I left the navy high school, or just before the university entrance exam, or right after Francesca broke up with me—empty, nervous, unsettled. I walk to the bathroom and splash some water on my face. Then, I pace the room some more.

What's going to happen? If I go back to Soner, to tell him what happened, to plead my case, would he believe me? Would he believe that I didn't steal the money? Or, would he think it was part of my con—I show him I'm trustworthy with $800,000 so I can steal $400,000. But would he believe that? I mean, I didn't know there would be a second money delivery. What if he's in on this? What if this is some kind of set up? What if someone got to him and threatened him, and throwing me under the bus is his only way out?

You know what you have to do, Adem.

I take a shower then get dressed in my three-piece suit. I pick up my notebook, my passport, and the ticket booklet, and put all the items in the inside pocket of my suit jacket. I feel them against my chest, above my heart. I walk out into the dining room and look into the kitchen.

"Bye Mom."

"Oh, how handsome you look in that suit!" she says. And then she notices the suitcase. I watch her eyes dart from my suit to my suitcase. I have no idea what she's thinking. *Do this quickly, Adem.*

I grab my coat and kiss her cheek. "Bye Mom. Please, say goodbye to Dad for me." *Leave, Adem, quickly, in case if she asks where you're going; before she asks for an explanation.*

I don't know when I will see her again. Will I ever see her again? I take one last look at my mom. She still looks so young, even at fifty-two. Even with three grown children, two in their thirties. Even though she's about to become a grandmother. I wonder if she will miss me, the child she never wanted. The accident. And look at you now Adem. You are an accident . . . an accident waiting to happen.

"Tell Dad, I will call. No, write. I will write," I say and walk out the door. "My last time in this elevator," I announce to myself. "My last time walking out the door to the apartment building." I'm the emcee of my life. As I walk away from the building, I force myself not to look back. I don't want to know if she's at the window watching me leave. If she's not watching, it'll be too much to take. *Like the first day at school.* If she *is* watching, I might change my mind and stay. *I hope she's not watching.*

I walk two blocks to the cabstand, "*Yesilkoy*, to the airport, please," I tell the driver, looking around me on the street before getting in the taxi.

It's a forty-minute cab ride. But the driver tells me, in a rambling monologue, that he's trying to break his own personal record and make it there in twenty-nine minutes. I hang on to the door with one hand and the seatback in front of me with the other as we whizz by police and army checkpoints. I tell him he has to slow down so he doesn't draw attention to himself. We come close to crashing a couple of times. I imagine how messy a crash investigation led by the army would be. Adem Bayer is on his way to the airport on November 7 with December 1 tickets to America, $400,000 is missing from his office, and his cab, which is rushing him there, crashes.

But, before he can slow down, we get stopped. "Again?" the driver asks, rhetorically. "It's the second time today already."

An army sergeant and a soldier walk over. "Step out of the car," the soldier says to me, knocking on the window and pulling the door handle. The driver steps out; I do too. They don't even look at the driver. It's as if he's just part of the car.

"Do you have a gun on you?" the soldier asks me.

"No. No, sir."

"I ask because, you see, I'm afraid of guns," he says, shifting the G3 army assault weapon he has holstered across his chest.

I grin to honor the soldier's joke, humoring him. A second soldier approaches and together, they search the car, down to the spare tire.

The sergeant leaves us and runs over to his Jeep. I watch him pick up his radio, but I can't hear what he's saying. He's looking at my direction and gesturing with his hands. He keeps looking at me. My eyelid starts twitching.

The soldier pulls my coat out of the back seat and starts digging into the pockets, feeling inside the coat, too, turning it over. He throws it back in the car, then walks over to me. He motions me to put my hands up high and place them on the roof of the cab; I comply. He begins to search my suit pockets. Halfway through the pat-down, his sergeant calls him over to the Jeep and he leaves in a rush over to the sergeant. I remain where I am, my hands on the car, my feet spread. I watch them as they talk; the sergeant continues making hand gestures. The cab driver is rambling on about an upcoming soccer match he's bet on.

I can't control the thoughts racing through my head. *Has Soner reported me? Or Mr. Baris?* I feel weak in the knees.

"Did you see Hammer on Sunday?" the cab driver asks. "Wham, bazooka, the goalie didn't even see the ball."

I close my eyes, trying to tune him out.

After a few more minutes, my arms are still on the car and starting to ache, the sergeant tells us we can go.

"These roadblocks, a waste of time!" the cabbie yells once he's slammed the car door shut. "The military coup is really slowing me down. Can't catch a break trying to set a new record." I don't respond. I don't want to engage with him. I ride in silence. He keeps talking.

A few minutes away from the airport, when we can see planes low in the sky, I unmute myself. "International departures," I say.

"Got it. But it looks like we're stopping here first," the driver says as he's flagged down and slows to pull over at another checkpoint. This time it's the police who stop us.

"Step out of the car, sir."

Is this it? Is this when I get hauled off to jail?

They search me, then the trunk, and my luggage. I was fortunate at the last checkpoint when they didn't ask for my name. If Soner or Mr. Baris reported me to the police—this is it. *Please don't ask for my ID.*

"ID please."

I pull my wallet out slowly and hand him my ID.

"Are you traveling?"

"Yes." *Please don't ask for tickets.*

"Tickets please."

I pull the eight-page ticket booklet out from the inside pocket of my jacket and hand it to the police officer.

As he goes through the details of my three flights, I repeat over and over to myself, *don't look at the departure date, don't look at the departure date.* It says December 1 for all three flights. It's printed on the top of the first page; maybe even every page. If he notices and asks why I'm headed to the airport three weeks early on November 7, what am I going to say? *Think. Be ready.* I watch as he checks the name on the tickets against my ID. He then turns back to the first page and looks directly at the flight date. What are you going to say? *Think man.* He hands everything back to me.

"Go ahead."

I look up at him, surprised, holding my breath. As I step back into the taxi, I exhale loudly. *What just happened?*

Breathe. Is this what it's going to be like for me for the rest of my life? Looking over my shoulder, wondering when I'm going to be grabbed off the street and thrown in jail for stealing money I didn't steal? I look like a criminal. I mean, look at the facts. I don't know that I would even believe me! $400,000 is missing and I just got a visa to America. It looks bad.

Will it happen in the airport? Will they find me in America or will they think I'm hiding out somewhere in Turkey? Did I ever mention DC. to Soner, or did I just say America . . . that I was "going to America"? I don't think I was specific.

Did I ever mention that I was traveling with Zeki's son? Could they track me down that way? If they found me through Zeki, would he and my dad help me? Zeki would help me, definitely. Would Dad believe that I didn't take the money? If Zeki's military pals found out, the people who are currently running the country, the people who sentenced Savas Kartal to thirty years in prison, would they protect me?

I look out the window, at the dusty landscape zooming by.

Soner had to have told Mr. Baris that the money is missing. Or, maybe he hasn't. Maybe Soner has covered his tracks—my tracks—to protect himself. Maybe the $400,000 isn't worth the nightmare and Soner has taken the remaining $400,000 and delivered it himself. Or, maybe this is all a setup to take down Soner. Maybe Mr. Baris was in on the deal with Mr. Kaya. Maybe the money was delivered to whomever it's for and they are pretending it wasn't delivered to ruin Soner's career, his business. Maybe I'm not that important, maybe Mr. Baris created this ploy to destroy Soner. But why? Why would he do that? Soner is a small fish. Baris is a billionaire.

I'm driving myself crazy with all these "maybes."

By the way, this is all happening because I wasn't brave enough to say, "No, I can't do this. I can't deliver illegal, nontraceable money for you." I cannot let this happen again. I must remember this for the rest of my life. If something seems dangerous or risky, it's better to lose a job and keep my dignity and freedom.

"International departures. Here you go brother! Forty-five," the cab driver startles me, bringing me back to reality. I hand him fifty liras. "Thank you. Keep the change."

I get out of the cab, and the driver hands me Mom's cream-colored suitcase.

I have a $300 ticket, $800 cash for America, and a $600 loan commitment from Eliz, if I need it. It's $2,300 less than the 4,000 I had planned on.

19

THE JOURNEY

I HAND MY TICKETS TO THE CLERK BEHIND THE PAN AM COUNTER. "Ma'am, I have these tickets to Washington for December 1. I am wondering if I could fly sooner? Today, maybe?" *Because I'm a fugitive. I'm running from the law, or the military, or the police, or the Nationalist goons. I don't know exactly who I'm running from!* I move slowly, trying to look nonchalant. I fear people are watching me. There are uniformed officers everywhere. I feel that at any moment law enforcement is going to come up behind me and tackle me to the ground. My body shivers and stiffens at the thought. I've got to get on the plane. *Once I'm on the plane I'll be safe.* I lean against the ticket counter. My heart is thudding rapidly. "Calm down, Adem," I whisper to myself. I can't calm down!

"Sorry sir?"

"Oh, nothing." *Just talking to myself like a crazy person. Until I'm on the plane, I'm not safe.*

The ticket clerk smiles at me and takes the ticket booklet. "Let's see what we can do," she says in a sing-songy voice that usually I would find soothing. She starts typing, then pauses, and looks. Types again, then pauses. Type.

Pause. Look. Type. Pause. Look. Over and over and over. I start tapping my foot every time she types, then run my fingers through my hair with each pause. I look at the big clock on the wall behind her. I adjust my watch by half a minute to synchronize. It's been about two minutes, but it feels like thirty.

"Okay," she says.

I lean in.

She taps a few more times on the keyboard. I can't take the not-knowing. I take a deep breath.

"Okay."

I lean in again.

"Okay, Mr. Bayer. I can get you on a flight to Frankfurt tomorrow at 8:15 a.m."

I shake my head. "I need to leave today." *I'm a fugitive.* "It has to be today. Is there anything for today?" I say, trying to keep calm, to keep the edge out of my voice. "Sorry," I tell her, "I don't mean to . . ." I don't want to make her nervous. If she thinks I'm crazy, she'll alert the police. She smiles at me and starts typing again. Type. Pause. Look. Type. Pause. Look. Two soldiers with assault weapons walk behind me.

"Okay!" she says excitedly. "I've found a flight to Frankfurt for this evening at 19:15. But it will mean seventeen hours in Frankfurt, before I can get you to New York."

"That works. How much?" I ask, reaching for my wallet.

She looks up. "There's no charge, sir, for flying earlier," she says. "If you postponed your original flight, there would be a charge of $100." I'm hardly listening. I can't believe there's no charge.

"Would you like to make the change?"

"Yes. Yes," I say, realizing I sound hurried. "Yes. Thank you," I repeat, slower, smiling.

She issues a new set of tickets and boarding passes, checks in my luggage; and I'm done. *Done! I'm going to America. Today!*

"The flight is boarding now. You'll need to hurry," she says. *Hurry is good. Hurry is excellent!* "You'll have to pick up your luggage in New York, Kennedy, and go through the immigration and customs there. Then you move to the domestic terminal to fly to Washington National. Okay sir?"

I look at my watch. The flight leaves in thirty-four minutes.

As I walk quickly over to passport control, I see men in dark suits everywhere. They may simply be men who chose to wear dark suits today; but they are making me nervous. I don't know what I'm worrying about more, the missing money and who might be after me because of it, or the military-backed government that could at any moment impose travel restrictions. Plus, there's still the possibility that once I land in New York, immigration will reject my entry and I'll be forced to come back to exactly what I'm running from. *One worry at a time. I need to get through passport control.* I get into line, look at my watch again, and prepare my poker face and my strategy as I listen to the rhythmic stamping of passports.

If they stop me here and arrest me, I will not resist.

I start humming, *You can't always get what you want,* in harmony with the sound of the officer's rhythmic thump-thumps. The person in front of me turns around and gives me a look. *Man, you can't sing out loud.* I smile apologetically and banish the song from my head. I start counting how long it takes for the nine people in front of me to get through. The line is moving quickly. In less than eight minutes, or an average of fifty-one seconds per person, it's my turn.

Keeping my face bland, I hand the officer my passport. No smile. *Don't say anything. Don't offer information. Answer only the questions asked.*

The officer looks at my passport, then looks at me. He turns through the empty pages of my passport, back and forth. He stops, looks up at me briefly, then looks back down. Thump-thump, pause, thump-thump-thump, pause, thump-ta-thump. I know the rhythm now: *You can't always get what you want.*

And as quickly as that, he hands back my passport. He says nothing. I say nothing, I nod ever so slightly. I walk away exhaling deeply.

I walk through a gate only to find another gate in front of me.

The guard motions for me to stop.

"$100," he says.

"Sir?"

"$100. The exit tax. $100." Darn. *I forgot about the exit tax.* I take out my wallet.

"Your passport?"

I hand over my passport as I open my wallet. The officer looks at my US visa. "No charge," he says. "Student."

"Oh. Okay. Thank you then," I say, surprised, as he hands me back my passport and lets me through. I head for the departure gate, glancing at my watch again.

Eighteen minutes till takeoff. *Do not miss this flight!* I pick up my pace.

I spy the boarding lounge ahead of me in the distance and it's completely empty. *This can't be good.* As I approach, I realize there's a security guard standing next to the ticket agent. *Are they waiting for me? Is this it? Seventeen minutes and thirty meters away from freedom and they capture me? Is this how it ends?*

As I approach, the ticket agent looks down. *She can't bear the sight of my take-down. She knows what's about to happen.*

"Stop there, sir," the security officer says walking toward me. I stop, waiting for him to tell me to turn around so he can cuff me. He waves a metal detector wand up and down my body.

"Thank you. You are good to go."

Good to go? Good to go!

"Thank you," I say, trying not to sound shocked, but it comes out with a cackle, and I sound like a maniac. I rush to the ticketing agent.

"Mr. Bayer?" she asks, almost rhetorically. "We were about to announce your name. You are the last to board. Glad you made it."

"Yes, me too!" I say, smiling for the first time in a while. Days, maybe. "Me too!"

"Your boarding pass please."

"Oh, sorry," I say, as I hand it to her. She separates it into two pieces and hands me back the smaller piece. "Have a nice flight." Once out of her sight, I jog down the ramp to speed up the process.

As I enter the plane and find my seat, I hear the heavy door close behind me. I shove my coat and jacket into an overhead compartment and squeeze into my middle seat.

I stare out the window and a few minutes later, the plane starts backing out before taxiing to the runway.

"Folks, we are second in line for takeoff," the pilot announces first in German, then in English. Then a flight attendant announces it in Turkish. "Sit back and relax, we will be in the air in just a few minutes."

I start to count. I can't relax until we are in the air. Until the wheels are off the ground, we could still be grounded by the government. 207, 208, 209, 210 . . . and then we are off. We are in the air. I stop counting. We're flying. I'm out. I made it. I exhale.

I lean back and close my eyes. *I am off to America. I am off to America! I can't believe I did it. I am going to America. I am going to be in America tomorrow, November 8. I'm going to see Demir. Demir! He doesn't know I'm coming! That's okay. I'll call him when I arrive in New York. It's okay.* "It costs ten cents," he told me. "It's called a dime." I have two twenty-five--cent coins and a dime, the left-over change from my ticket purchase. Calling Washington from New York may cost more than a dime. I'll have to figure it out.

The plane careens to the right as we rise over Istanbul. Flying in a jet plane feels safer than a prop plane. It's the only other plane I've ever been on. I was nine when Mom and I went to visit Dad who was stationed in eastern Turkey. We first took a small twin-engine plane to central Turkey, then changed to a single-engine plane that was even smaller. The plane rocked and rattled with each gust of the wind, free falling when we hit air pockets, making alarming noises. I remember how loud that small plane got as we climbed to six thousand meters, flying over the mountains of eastern Turkey. Mom kept telling me to relax and enjoy the views down below; I could do neither.

The plane turns again, and I look out the window to see Istanbul below. *There's the soccer stadium and the Istanbul Sports Arena where I played basketball. Will I ever see Istanbul again?* The plane straightens out and continues to climb. *What will happen to Mom and Dad if the police come looking for me? Mom wouldn't know how to lie. I can imagine Dad saying, "When you find him, bring him to me first so that I can slap him." Can Mr. Baris send thugs to my parents to find me or recover the missing money? He wouldn't dare. Would he? It's not the way it's done. But rich people have their own rules.*

I strain my neck to see what's below, to get one last glimpse of home. *What if I'm detained in Frankfurt? Can they do that? Can they arrest me in Frankfurt for a crime in Istanbul? Of course they can. It's called Interpol. They'd send me back to Istanbul and to prison. Would I get a fair trial? How would I be able to prove I was framed or used as a pawn for someone else's illegal activity? Would I serve time with Savas Kartal?*

Even if the goons don't threaten my parents, what about the social implications? It would kill my parents. I can only imagine the things people at the club would say. "Poor Meral and Teo. I knew there was something wrong with that child. He stole his company's money and tried to escape to America! You know sometimes it's not the child, but how he was raised."

What if I make it to the US but I'm not admitted? What will happen if I'm turned away by immigration? I couldn't come back to Istanbul; I'm a wanted man there. So, where would I go? Greece, perhaps? Would I have enough money to buy a ticket to Greece? Would I be able to get a visa to live there?

If I do make it past immigration into the US, will I ever see my parents again? My sisters? Friends? Istanbul? Can I ever come home, again?

I try to rid myself of my racing thoughts. *None of this makes sense. How is it possible that there's a missing $400,000 and nobody has reported it? Shouldn't I have been stopped at the airport?*

I can't stop my mind from reeling. Will I ever stop worrying?

I'm so involved in my thoughts and worries that when the pilot comes on with an announcement, I jump. "Guten Abend meine Damen und Herren" he begins. That's all I can understand. Then he switches to English, "Good evening ladies and gentlemen." I catch no more of what he's saying. Finally, the announcement in Turkish, and I understand we're in Bulgarian airspace.

The flight attendant arrives, pushing a cart before her.

"What would you like to drink sir?" she asks in English. I look up. There are drinks on the cart.

I recognize the word *drink*. "Coca-Cola, please," I say, trying to sound confident with my English.

A few minutes later another flight attendant comes with a sandwich cart. I take a cheese sandwich and then also quickly grab a salami sandwich before she moves away.

***

The pilot announces that we are beginning our descent into Frankfurt. My stomach drops and I immediately start worrying again. *Will there be people waiting for me when I deplane? Have Soner or Mr. Baris reported the missing $400,000?* I still don't understand how I've made it this far. Maybe it's less dangerous for them to send thugs after me in another country? Would they have visited my mother? Would she have told them about the suitcase? Would they be able to trace my steps to Frankfurt? They could easily do so. They would just have to call the airlines and ask about all the flights that left for America today and they'd be able to track me down.

I didn't realize how safe it felt to be on the plane.

Now I don't want to land. *I hope we'll crash.*

The landing is smooth and people clap for the pilot. I follow those in front of me and disembark down a set of stairs right on to the tarmac. I realize I'm stepping on foreign soil for the first time in the entire twenty-two years of my life. I take a second, pausing to remember this moment.

I continue to follow the other passengers across the tarmac and board a bus, assuming that if this is what everyone is doing, then this must be the right thing to do. The bus is different from those in Turkey. It's low to the ground. It's quiet as we pull away from the plane. And it moves smoothly, no vibrating or rattling. But it is just as crowded and, when it makes a turn, a few of those standing lose their balance, falling into one another. People apologize to each other in different languages. I bump into the woman standing next to me and apologize in Turkish, frowning and shrugging my shoulders. I realize that when I'm not with Demir, I'm going to be doing a lot of pantomiming. Thank goodness for Demir.

The bus stops in front of a modern looking glass building. One by one, we exit the bus and enter the building through the automatic doors. Immediately, it feels different. *Is it the air? The smell? The people?* The floors are concrete, the walls are glass, the sounds reverberate differently than they do in Istanbul's old buildings. I choose a group of fellow passengers to follow. Some stop in bathrooms, others at restaurants and stores. Suddenly, I find myself all alone.

I peer both ways. I don't know what I'm looking for. I look up to the signs overhead, which I assume are in German; I'm glad to see there are symbols, too. I study the images trying to figure out where everything is and where I should go during my seventeen-hour layover.

When I look down from the signs, I see a man in a black suit heading my way. He's a few meters down the corridor. *This is it. Is he a cop? A thug?* I turn around and look behind me; we're the only two in the corridor. I clench my fists. *If it's a cop I won't fight, if it's a thug I will.* I hold my breath as he approaches. I squeeze my fists harder. And then, he walks right by me, nodding. I follow him peripherally to make sure he doesn't come back to jump me. I unclench my fists and put my hand to my heart. I can't do this for the rest of my life; I can't live this way, fearing every man in a dark suit. The reality is, it could be anyone. I should be afraid of everyone.

The worrying part of my brain is on autopilot. I do a 360-degree turn, see that the coast is clear again and then start walking and wandering trying to find corridors with people. *I may feel more protected in a crowd.*

I find a restaurant selling tomato soup for thirteen deutsche marks. I have to forgo it. The hamburger is eighteen, schnitzel twenty-one, all expensive. I decide not to waste my money on food. I wish I'd asked the stewardess if I could have a few extra sandwiches for my layover. I'll have to remember to do that on my next flight to New York.

I walk around for a couple of hours. I have nothing with me but my coat, my minder notebook, and $800. I sit down at an empty gate, in a seat against a wall so no one can come up behind me, and watch people go to and fro. The people look different here. It's not just the color of their skin or facial features; it's hair style, and clothes too, especially their jeans. I only know a Turkish domestic brand and what I wear, which are Levi's 501s. And Francesca wore some blue jeans I'd never seen before.

Francesca.

It's been four years and 109 days. I wonder what she'd think of me now. I wonder if she thinks of me.

A fast-walking man in a cape goes by. I watch the cape whip up behind him, flicking at his heels as he steps. I wonder what his story is; how he came to own a cape, an odd clothing choice; but maybe not here in Germany. Certainly odd in Turkey. Or maybe he's not from here. Perhaps he's from

Tahiti and is here on business—his cape business? A woman with a fur coat crosses his path. Is she on her way to Paris? New York? I see only a few women as I sit there. I see mostly men in dark suits and neckties. Businessmen. And then I smile. *Do people think I'm a businessman because I'm wearing a suit and necktie? Will they think I'm a businessman while entering the US?*

After an hour of watching people, I get up and walk around some more. The flight to New York is thirteen hours away and things are quieting down in the airport. Shops are closing up for the night, food establishments, too.

I realize I haven't spoken Turkish since the Pan Am counter in Istanbul. I probably won't speak Turkish for a while, except with Demir. *Demir*! I keep forgetting that Demir has no idea I'm on my way to America.

I wander around for a few more minutes, then find a row of seats at another empty gate. I lie down and pull my coat over me. I close my eyes but open them quickly. I'm worried that someone is watching me, waiting for me to fall asleep so they can jump me and haul me off to Istanbul to jail or worse. So, I just lie there, thinking.

Who took the money? Why am I being framed . . . and how are Soner and Mr. Baris involved? I realize that, once again, I'm the patsy. I try so hard to do the right thing, to help people, but in the process I lose.

Does my life equal "I lose"? Is that the formula for my life?

I lose, even if everything starts out promising, like it did with Soner. At the office things were going great. But then, I felt I had to help out a stressed and sweating Soner. Why did I agree to deliver that money? Why couldn't I say "no"? Would another person have said "no"? Do other people have a different formula?

My life is futile. It doesn't matter what I do. I lose.

Just like in the navy high school. I had to drop out because I was trying to help a classmate. At first I was excited that I'd gained entry and especially happy that I would no longer be a financial burden on my parents, for life, basically. I learned how to escape from a burning ship and how to save a drowning victim. I was the only ninth grader who made the navy high school's basketball team. My future looked bright.

Yet, I found a way to screw it up, to lose what I'd gained, by helping a failing, scared, and sweating fellow cadet during his final oral exam in chemistry. He was on the fast track to failing, which meant expulsion. Sitting at a desk near the front of the classroom, I began writing the answers down so he could see them.

He immediately took me up on my help and started getting the answers right; until the teacher caught me and filed cheating charges against me. The other cadet passed the class, denying that he'd used my answers; I admitted my guilt and was punished with a two-week house arrest and a "Number One Haircut" to advertise my guilt, show my fellow cadets that I was a disgrace to the uniform.

But the true punishment was the official record, the resulting stigma that I would carry with me throughout my navy career. While I had been on track to become a warship commander by the time I was twenty-six, I was now branded a cheater. I feared that I would become an officer and then be assigned to a desk job and forgotten about. I'd heard the stories. I needed to quit. It was my only option. My career trajectory had hit a dead end.

I told my parents I needed to leave the navy, they didn't ask why, and I didn't tell. They took the news with no surprise, reacting as if it was just another one of my unsuccessful attempts to do things correctly, forever unsuccessful Adem. They told their friends that I had changed my career goals; they could call me "fickle," rather than a "failure," though the latter was how I am sure they felt.

The bothersome thing is, I never learned my lesson from the experience that ended my navy career and changed my life forever. Even today, I would do the same thing and help that cadet. It's the same trap I walked into with Soner. I helped him and got screwed. And this time, instead of leaving school, I'm leaving my country.

Will I ever learn?

20

TOUCHDOWN

It's only been fifteen hours and I'm homesick already.

Will I ever be able to return to Istanbul?

I'm a thief in Soner's eyes. While it's true that I *thought* about stealing the $400,000, I didn't do it. But I also know my decision not to steal was not honorable. I didn't steal the money because I know it's *wrong* to steal, I didn't steal the money because I didn't know how to get away with it. Does that make me guilty? Regardless, without being exonerated, I don't think I will ever be able to return to Istanbul. How could I? Mr. Baris is a powerful man.

***

I'm staring idly at the ever-changing split-flap display when my flight to New York shows up. I'm well past hungry, I have moved on to nauseous. The flight and its food service cannot come soon enough. I gather my things and head to the gate. About an hour later, without incident, I step from the jet bridge onto the Boeing 747 bound for America.

The flight attendant smiles and greets me in English. I smile back and continue down the aisle.

Well-dressed men and women are busy smiling and making conversation with one another. Not just in English or German. I listen for languages I can recognize, Flemish, Korean, Spanish. It's a wonderful cacophony.

I quietly take my seat next to a passenger who appears to be fast asleep. I take in the activity around me as people settle in. I'm on the same plane as these people, but I feel like I don't belong. I paid for my ticket just like they did, so why do I feel like an outsider, an imposter? Is it because I'm a runaway? A fugitive? Or is it because I'm not good enough?

Soon we are accelerating down the runway. With a loud noise and a strong shudder, the jet begins to climb, rising higher and higher, and faster. I'm pressed back into my seat as the plane soars.

Frankfurt fades away and New York City awaits. I glance at my watch. The new world, my childhood dream, the Promised Land, is only nine hours away. *I am going to work hard. I am going to succeed. I am going to live the American dream.*

By the time the food cart comes down the aisle, my nausea has subsided and I am ravenous. I gobble up my almonds, drink Coca-Cola, scrape up my dinner and dessert plates, and drink more Coca-Cola. I'm still hungry, but I'm too embarrassed to ask for more food. The man beside me wakes up to have his dinner and then goes back to sleep. Other passengers enjoy their after-dinner coffee, some a glass of wine. I don't know why, but I start thinking about Francesca. Maybe it's the proximity of Germany to Italy, maybe it's the international crowd around me. I wonder if she's still in Florence or if she moved to London like she wanted. *It's been more than four years, why am I still thinking about her?* I've built her up in my mind as the perfect woman. *Would we still be together had it not been for Savas? Or were our worlds too different?* I wonder if she ever thinks about me. Was there a way to explain to her the trouble I was in—a way that would have enabled us to stay together? I believe Francesca loved me. But I wonder if she felt it in her heart the way I did. And I wonder if her heart broke the way mine did when she walked away.

"Happy love does not exist." I read that line in a poem once.

Grandma talked about a different kind of love, God's love. God's love, Grandma said, *was* happy love. The poet was wrong, she told me. She told me how God loved us and how pleased He was when we loved Him back.

Everything else was a sideshow that didn't matter. "Rule number one, never sweat the small stuff. Rule number two, everything is small stuff," she said. Unlike my parents, I'm a sweat-the-small-stuff and sweat-the-big-stuff, too, kind of guy.

***

My seatmate is still sleeping. I look around and see that most passengers are sleeping. I close my eyes and immediately, I'm flooded with thoughts and worries, Savas Kartal, Mr. Baris, Soner, my parents, America, Istanbul.

How many years will it be before I swim in the Bosporus again? Will I ever sit on that bench overlooking the strait again? Will I ever see my parents again? My sisters? I'll need to write letters to my friends. When will I see any of them again?

I open my eyes. It's still dark in the plane. I want to think of something bright, like the sun. Like the beach. I close my eyes and tell myself, "You're on the beach, think of the beach, think of the surf, think of the water and the sun. Walking on the beach with Francesca. No, no, don't think about Francesca. Something else. Ah. Our beach vacation to Oren when I was fifteen. Yes. No—Savas Kartal is from Oren. His father was shot and killed there by a Communist rebel. Don't think of Savas. Think of the beach, just the beach and swimming in the cold water."

It was June 1973, I was fifteen years old, had just dropped out of the navy high school. My parents and their friends had arranged a four-week beach vacation in Oren, a small town on the Aegean coast. Each family had rented a villa.

It was a walk down memory lane for my dad. He loved it there. The trip brought him back to the 1930s, when he was an army cadet. "The other cadets and I would hang out at the beach here in Oren on our days off," he told me. "I wasn't much older than you, then. A teenager." We were walking down to the water together. It felt good to have my dad's attention. To have him telling me his stories. "The place feels different now," he said, "not just because it's forty years later, but because I am a father now." I remember looking up at him and smiling. And then he walked away, catching up to Mom and leaving me behind.

On Sundays, the Oren beach would get visitors from nearby towns—mostly young factory or construction workers. So tourists would find other things to do, to avoid going to the beach "to avoid *them*," as my mom put it. But not me. I went every day. That last Sunday before the vacation ended, I decided to go for an extra-long walk on the beach while everyone else went for breakfast.

The water in Oren wasn't really for long distance swimming like the Bosporus. Even when it was thirty-five degrees on the beach and our feet could hardly handle the heat of the sand, the water would remain cold from the cold-water springs on the seafloor. In some spots, it would be downright frigid. I would let myself get so hot that perspiration would be dripping from my forehead into my eyes and sand would stick to my sweat covered legs and then, I would run to the water and jump in. I could almost hear the hiss my hot skin made meeting cold water. I would be able to swim for only a few minutes, moving my arms and legs as fast as I could and I'd still come out shivering, relishing the heat of the sun until it was too hot again and I'd jump back in. I made a game of it. Counting how long it would take until I got too hot, then how long I could last in the water. The longest I could make it in the water was 242 seconds, just over four minutes.

About a half hour into my walk, I noticed my first swimmer of the morning. I started counting to see if he could outlast me. He was far out, a couple of hundred meters away and hard to see. But I kept counting. By the time I got to 242, I was still counting. I squinted against the sun, looking harder; then I walked to the edge of the water to see if I could get a better look. Something seemed off about him. I peered harder and realized he wasn't swimming at all—he was drowning, one hand barely out of the water, asking for help. I looked around to see if anyone else realized there was a man in the water drowning. Down the beach a bit, there were three men standing and pointing at the drowning man. One of them saw me and started toward me, the others following. As they ran toward me, I could hear them shouting. "Help us! Can you help us? Please! It's our friend. We can't swim that far! Can you help him? It's too far. Can you swim? Can you save him?" they shouted at me all at once, out of breath, as they ran toward me.

I threw off my shirt and dove into the cold water. Swimming faster than I knew myself to be capable of, I kept the swimmer in my sightline. When I got closer, I saw a man at least ten years older than me, curly hair, and unshaven.

"Brother, please save me . . ." was all I heard before he was dragged under.

I dove down, my eyes open, kicking hard to grab him as he sank. I got him from behind and pulled him up. Wrapping my arm around his neck to keep his chin and head above the water, I propped my right hip to his lower back, lifting his body up a bit like I'd been taught at navy high school. I swam with my left arm while kicking with my left leg and holding the drowning man in my right arm. It was long and arduous. My body was numb with the cold water. Every few seconds, I looked up at the shore to see how much further, it didn't look like we were getting any closer. He felt dead, not buoyant, as if I were dragging a bronze statue, stiff and heavy. Halfway there, I switched sides, holding him with my left arm and swimming with my right. As we neared the beach the water began to feel warmer.

The man's friends had waded out into the water up to their waists. When I got close enough, they grabbed him from me. I let go of him and watched them heave him up and out of the water onto the shore as I tried to catch my breath, kneeling in the water as the tide pushed me forwards and backwards. Exhausted, I got up and walked up and onto the beach, pausing again to regain my breath.

They laid their friend down, covering him with the hot, dry sand. I overheard them say he was unconscious but breathing.

I stood up and walked over to him.

"Is he okay?" I asked.

They rolled him over to his stomach without answering me and water poured out of his mouth and nose. He began to shake uncontrollably, and his friends grabbed their beach towels and wrapped him up, one towel on top of another. One of them dropped himself onto the sand behind his friend and wrapped him in a bear hug, "to make more heat," the man explained, looking at me.

A few minutes later, the swimmer started coughing. "Looks like he's going to be all right," I said to the men. Then, I looked around for my shirt and moved on.

***

The shades on the plane are still drawn. Everyone around me still seems to be sleeping. I think about my decision to go for a walk on the beach that day, the timing of it all, life's fragility. That's not what I was thinking then, when I was fifteen. After I left the drowning man and his friends, it took me less than a minute to return to my own worries—to resume thinking about the navy, how I had to quit, how hard it was to see men in uniform. If I wasn't going to be a naval officer, what was I going to be? Was I going to be able to enter a decent university? Any university? I'd heard stories of students being driven to suicide because of the stress. At the best universities, there was room for only a few hundred students a year while more than two hundred thousand were applying.

I prepared for the dreaded university entrance exam day and night for two years. I attended two separate preparation courses, in parallel. I took more than a hundred simulation tests. Each year there was only one exam, one which foretold the course of a high school graduate's life. How well a student did in that exam determined his or her future; doing well meant attending a stellar university. Those who did not do well on the exam and could not afford to pay for private college in Turkey or somewhere in Europe were drafted into the military as privates. There were no second chances. It didn't matter that I had pulled Cs and Ds throughout high school. All that mattered were the results of this one test.

On June 10, 1974, I took the test.

I walked out thinking I hadn't done well. I walked out believing I'd failed my parents and my teachers. Hoping for distraction, I threw myself into sports.

About six weeks later, after a basketball game in the Istanbul Sports Arena, while walking home, I received the results—hand delivered by a mailman who seemed to know who I was even though I'd never seen him before. I was a block away from my parents' building when he called out to me from behind, "Adem, I have your university entrance test results." I looked around wondering if there could be another Adem waiting for university results. I couldn't imagine how this man knew who I was.

I turned around. He was smiling.

"It's a big day," he said, "a big week, actually. I have six more of these to deliver today." His excitement bothered me. My fate was literally in his hands, and he knew it. I was still trying to figure out how he knew who I was when he handed me an envelope with perforated edges. It looked like a computer printout. I took a big breath when I saw my name printed on it. Then I thanked him and began to walk away.

The mailman stepped in front of me, blocking my path. "Don't you want to open it?" he said, sounding surprised that I hadn't ripped the envelope open in front of him. "Open it now!"

I ignored him. I didn't want anyone to see my face when I saw in black and white that the life I had hoped for myself was hijacked by my own failures. I didn't want anyone there when I found out I was going to be a private in the navy with my former classmates, now officers, ordering me around.

But the mailman wouldn't move out of my way. Like all the bullies of my life, he stood there, controlling me. He insisted that I open the envelope. I couldn't punch him. He was a government employee. I'd get thrown in jail for that.

"I'd rather not, thank you," I said politely, trying to sidestep him.

"Open it. Go ahead and open it. Now," he said, in a tone that was confident, determined, insistent, arrogant. I thought of walking away. I had the paper in my hands. But I couldn't. He broke my resolve, and I opened the envelope, tearing at the perforation of the computer printout. It felt pathetic to acquiesce, to be forced to give in to a mailman. But I did it, I unfolded the paper. "Technical University—Mechanical Engineering." It was printed in bold right at the top.

I looked up at the mailman. He was looking at me. "So?" he asked.

"For your information, sir," I said, "I just got into Technical University— Mechanical Engineering!" I said, already running to my parents' apartment.

I ran past the elevator to the stairwell taking two steps at a time. I couldn't unlock the door; my hands were shaking too much. I tried again and again. I couldn't put the key in the keyhole. I began to bang on the door like a crazy person.

"Mom. Mom! Open up. Mom!"

"Adem? What are you . . . have you gone mad?" she called from inside. I could hear her coming closer, calling through the door. "What? What happened?"

"Open the door! Open the door!"

"I'm coming, I'm coming."

The moment the door opened, I burst through the door. "Mom, you won't believe it, it's the Technical University!"

"What are you saying, Adem? Stop screaming."

"Mom, I'm saying Technical University!"

"I don't understand, what happened with Technical University?"

"I got in, I got into Technical University!" I screamed and without waiting for her reaction, grabbed the phone to call my dad.

"Dad! It's Technical University. Yes. Yes, it came in. Yes, it is."

It was the happiest moment of my life. The happiest. I was sixteen and was going to attend Turkey's best university.

My hands were still trembling when I got off the phone with Dad. I grabbed my gym bag, throwing it up in the air with excitement. And there it was—my large name tag dangling from the bag: "ADEM BAYER." So stupid. That's how the mailman knew my name.

***

I open my eyes. The flight attendant is serving glasses of water on a tray. I take one. "Thank you," I say it in English. I take another sip of the water.

I pull out my notebook.

"November 8, 1980—American Dream Game Plan," I write at the top.

1. Get into the US (Today)

2. Get a job (Two months)

3. Survive and learn English (Two years)

4. Speak little or no Turkish (Three years)

5. Save money for graduate degree (Three years)

6. Pay off debt to Ela (Three years)

7. Send parents money (Three years)

If I'm admitted to the US, I have to get a job within the first two months. I only have $809, rounded to the nearest dollar. I don't know how long it will last, but not long enough.

I close the notebook and put it in my pocket. I do not fear failure. I fear letting others down, Ela, Eliz, Zeki, Demir, Kaan. My parents?

***

The lights come on, and the flight attendants begin asking the passengers to open their window shades. I see arms going up in the air as people start waking up and stretching. I look at my seatmate, who has been asleep the entire flight except to eat. He doesn't still move. I wish I could sleep that soundly.

In English and German, the pilot makes an announcement I cannot understand. My stomach lurches. I must learn English. To do that I must not speak any Turkish. Not even with Demir. I need to learn quickly, understand everybody the first time they say something, make sure everybody understands me the first time. That's the rule I'm establishing for myself. No "pardon me's," or "say that again's."

A few minutes later, the flight attendants begin another round of food service. *Is this lunch or dinner? Or is it breakfast?* It's a relief that two free meals were included in the ticket price—no, three, if I count the sandwich from Istanbul to Frankfurt.

I eat all the food on my tray, down to the last speck. Scrambled eggs, bread, yogurt, cheese, butter, jam, fruit, a danish. A flight attendant makes another pass with a cart of bread, butter, cheese, and honey; I ask for two rolls and slather them with butter and honey. Although I feel full, I keep eating. I don't know when I'll get my next meal, and eating free food is a good money saver. I'd love to grab a few more rolls and stuff them in my pocket but I can't push myself to do it.

Before I'm done with my second roll, the flight attendants hand out two pages of forms, one for immigration and one for customs. I have difficulty understanding some of the questions but do the best I can to fill them out.

A half hour later, the seatbelt sign goes on and new announcements begin.

"Ladies and gentlemen, New York Kennedy . . ."

It's been twenty-nine hours since I was at the Pan Am counter in Istanbul; thirty hours since I said goodbye to Mom.

ONE WAY PLEASE

PART II – THE PROMISED LAND

A NOVEL

MEHMET TAMAY

CONTENTS

1

WELCOME TO THE US, JR

The Boeing 747 lands at New York City's Kennedy Airport. As we prepare to disembark, my stomach lurches when I once again realize how much less stressful it is, being in the air. I'm about to face reality on the ground. The lady at the ticket counter in Istanbul said I'd go through immigration and customs in New York, then take another plane to Washington. So, it could all end here. It could end if the immigration officer decides I'm not worthy of admission into the US. or it could end if Interpol grabs me and hauls me off for stealing $400,000.

If Soner or Mr. Baris have reported me, why are the police so slow to arrest me? If they haven't reported me to the police, why not?

My brain is a scramble of worries. *Deal with one issue at a time. Okay.* Deep breath. My immediate and looming concern is immigration. I see my chances of entering the US as 50-50. I already have a visa; that's good. But, it's a single-entry visa. So, if for any reason, I leave the US in the future, I will have to go through the visa request process all over again. The immigration officer at the door will know that. It's a sign that I'm a risk, that I'm a potential enter-once stay-forever job grabber. *Will he ask me how much money I have? Will he make me confess to him that my parents won't be sending me any money, which means I'll need to make money, taking a job away from an American citizen during the worst recession since the Second World War? Will he ask me if I plan to settle here? Are there right answers or wrong answers that will let me in or keep me out? If I unwittingly say the wrong thing, will I be sent back?*

I'm more panicked than I've ever been in my life. More panicked, even, than I was taking my university entrance test. I'd trade places in a second with a younger me nervous about having dinner at Francesca's parents. I'd even relive Polat Mardin holding a gun to my head, and each empty pull of the trigger, or Savas shooting at me while I ran across rooftops and yanked at locked doors. I'd redeliver Soner's $800,000 in exchange for this feeling. In thirty minutes, I will face US immigration. My entire future may be based on the mood of an immigration officer who may make a negative split decision about me. *Breathe.*

I get off the plane and enter a vast corridor, following my fellow passengers. *I'm on US soil. I'm in America. Even if I get kicked out and turned back at the border, I got here.* I look around at America.

I go up ramps, and then down ramps, down stairs, then back up different stairs, around corners and down long corridors. Everywhere is rich, plush carpeting. It smells like the consulate office. I'm engrossed by everything around me, from the massive A/C ductwork above me to the huge plate-glass windows overlooking the airfield. People push past me as I walk slowly, looking left then right then up then back down, taking it all in. "Excuse me," I hear, over and over. *Excuse me,* I say to myself, rolling the English words on my Turkish tongue. *Excuse me.*

The crowd ahead of me funnels into a large, open space and I follow until a sign with arrows pointing in opposite directions greets us. A fork in the road: US citizens, right; non-US citizens, riffraff like me, left. I join the latter, in a line that winds and weaves. I look ahead to see a couple dozen cubicles with officers dressed in black sitting inside. Some are female officers. Would a female officer go easier on me? Or would she be tougher? "Who do you think you are, coming into my wonderful country?" I imagine they all are thinking.

The line moves steadily until we get closer to the cubicles, then stops. The man in front of me looks like he's from my part of the world, or maybe even more east, the Middle East or even Pakistan or Afghanistan. I peer over his shoulder to see if I can get a glimpse of his passport, but he's fiddling with it so much I can't get a good look. I want to ask him how he's feeling right now; if he's as nervous as I am. But in what language?

A family with toddlers and two older kids behind me is speaking German, and behind them I hear two women speaking French. Within minutes I will know if I'm being allowed into the US or sent back home for whatever faces me there. I smile and gesture to the German family to go ahead of me. They take up my offer and I step back. I'm sure they think I'm nice to let them ahead of me, but I just need a little more time before I face the immigration officer. *What if they have quotas, a per shift amount of people they let in, and the officer who takes me has already reached his number for the day? What if the officer just found out that an immigrant took his brother's job and now he has to help feed his brother's family? What if something I do or how I move irks him? Or her? Grandma, are your angels watching me? Are they shaking their heads? "Tsk-tsk-tsk, no, no, even we can't help you here."*

It's the Middle Eastern man's turn. He steps up to the booth. I think he can speak English because he seems to be responding to the officer. A minute later the German family is called into the next cubicle where a female officer is stationed. That would have been me if I hadn't let them ahead of me. I'm next.

I watch the whole family walk over. Then I turn back to see the other booth where the Middle Eastern man is. He's not talking with the officer anymore, just standing there. A minute later, another officer walks by me and heads over to that booth. *Changing of the guard.* I watch, trying not to stare, while clearly staring. *What's happening?* The second officer says something to the man, then holds the man's arm gently and leads him away. *Oh my Lord. What's happening?* My eyes follow as the man is led to the far end of this huge room. He and the officer disappear through a door. My heart drops. *Is that going to be me? Is that going to be my fate too? I can't breathe.* My ears clog up. All I hear is my thumping heart.

Oh no! I'm next. It's about to be my turn. My heart drops. *Am I going to end up with the officer who rejects people?*

I feel like I'm going to throw up. *I can't do this. Let me out of here!* I try to take a deep breath; I need oxygen. *What if I faint?* I turn back around and watch the officer lift his head up; the sign over his booth lights up. *Oh no! It's my turn. This is it.* I don't move. I can't move. One of the French women behind me says, "Allez," and then in English, "Go." I hesitate, turning around with a shaky smile. "Allez," she says, motioning. "À votre tour maintenant."

I don't know how to get my feet to move. "Your turn now," the French woman says in English. "Okay?" she says, gesturing me to move forward. My feet disengage and I take one step, then another. I'm slow, moving tentatively, like I did when I walked over to my new desk on that first day of school with the second graders.

With each step I see the movie of my life play out. In the first clip, I'm detained. In the second clip, I'm in a prison in Istanbul. In the third clip, Mr. Baris stands in my prison cell as Savas beats me, my hands tied behind my back.

My hearing remains echoey, clogged. Voices around me sound like a 45 RPM record being played in 33 mode. Moaning sounds come at me from all angles.

I reach the booth; eleven steps. The officer looks at me but doesn't say a word. I don't know what to do. I look back at him trying to soften my face so as not to seem like I'm challenging him. I feel my eye twitch. *Can he see that? Should I smile? Should I try not to blink? What should I do with my hands?*

"Passport," he says in monotone.

I hand over my passport and the two forms I've filled out on the plane, one for immigration and one for customs. The officer opens my passport, turning the pages back and forth, back and forth. He turns to the page with my photo and then looks up at me. He pulls out a small white card, a form, and starts writing on it. *Is that my detention order?* He staples the card on my passport, on the same page with the visa, page seven. I keep my head straight as my eyes glance right then left, looking to see if another officer is on the way over to escort me away through that door at the far end of the room.

I watch, almost catatonic, as I resign myself to my fate. I can almost feel the second officer standing behind me, ready to take me away. The immigration officer flips back to one of the empty pages in my passport and with his other hand grabs a stamp. I listen to the stamp thump and stare at the trail of red it leaves on the page. He takes another stamp and does a second thump. This time, the ink is black. He closes my passport and places it on the tray in front of him.

And then he smiles. *He's smiling. He's smiling!*

"Welcome to the US, JR!"

What?

"That way," he says, extending his arm.

No questions? I'm in? I haven't been turned away? I'm in? I take a step. I'm in America. I'm really in America now. I look at him one more time and then, I start walking away. I count my steps again, this time joyfully: One, two, three, four, five.

"Stop," I hear from behind me. *Oh no. What's happening?* Bile rises up in my throat. *He screwed me. I knew it was too easy, too good to be true. I'm such a fool. He toyed with me, and I fell for it. It's over. You failed.*

I turn around and wait for someone to grab my arms and pull them behind my back.

"Why do you always do something wrong, Adem?" I hear my dad saying. "Why do you constantly fail? It's disappointing."

"Passport," the officer says. I look at him, confused. He points to the tray in front of him where my passport is still sitting.

My legs almost give way under me. *My passport. I forgot my passport.*

"Thank you," I say, my voice dry, the words barely audible. "Thank you," I attempt a little louder, my voice squeaky.

I retrieve my passport and I walk away. *Don't walk too fast. They may still be watching. Keep cool, man. Just walk like a normal person.*

I leave the row of immigration cubicles behind and walk out through a set of doors into a large, carpeted hallway. My heart is slowing to a normal pace but my head is pounding. *Am I done? Am I in? Am I safely in America? Can they still come up from behind me and say they changed their minds?* The hallway funnels me into a larger space filled with dozens of enormous luggage carousels. Everything here seems to be massive. I find my flight number and head over to the conveyor belt, recognizing a few of the people I saw on the plane. My mom's cream-colored suitcase spits out onto the carousel.

"Ronald Reagan is the new president. An actor. Only in America," I hear someone say. "Only in America." It takes me a second to realize they are speaking in Turkish. This is the first time I've heard Turkish in twenty-nine hours.

I grab my mother's bag. And then I take a deep breath. A good breath. Not a breath to calm me. A breath to take it all in. I breathe in the new smells, once again. Is the air different here, too?

I put down my mother's suitcase and open my passport. I turn to the small white form. I-94. *Remember this moment. I'm in America!*

I have two hours until my flight to DC. I start wandering around the airport. When I see a bank of pay phones, eighteen of them, I remember I need to call Demir. In Istanbul, there would be only one telephone, or maybe two. I dig into my pocket for the change from the purchase of my airline ticket back at the Pan Am building seven days ago. I put ten cents in. A *dime*. "If you're in town, just dial the last seven digits. Out of town, dial a one, first, then the entire ten digits, not just the last seven," Demir had instructed me more than two months ago. It feels like two years ago. "If you hear a voice come on the line that's not me, it's probably the operator telling you that you need to add money. Just keep adding coins until you hear the phone start ringing again." A voice comes on. I add more coins and the phone starts ringing. And ringing. I let it ring ten times. No answer.

When I hang up, my money is returned, all sixty cents. I decide to try again in an hour and in the meantime walk over to the ticket counter to check in my suitcase for the DC flight. I combine a lot of pantomiming with the few English words I know, "please," "suitcase," "plane." Then I walk around for another hour, browsing in shops and looking into restaurants. At the newsstands, half the magazines and newspapers have Ronald Reagan's picture on them. *A former actor. Only in America.*

I call Demir again. No answer.

In no time, I'm boarding the flight to Washington, DC. This time with a seat by the window. As we take off, the sun setting on the horizon, I gaze at the New York City landscape below briefly, as we turn south toward Washington. I can't believe how well-lit everything is. When I can no longer see anything out the window, I glance over at the man sitting next to me and then at what he's writing on the notepad in front of him. "Presentation" is the only word he's written that I know and the whole page is filled with words. I turn away. I wonder what he will present and to whom. *I'm so glad Demir is going to be with me to help me get by.*

It's a fast flight and, as we descend into National Airport, I crane my neck once again, looking down at the landscape of the city I'm about to call home. I can see a huge obelisk all lit up; a domed building all lit up, too. *Maybe one day, I'll visit those places. One day, I'll know what those things are.*

When I step off the plane, my heart is pounding, again. *I'm here. I'm in Washington, DC. My new home. I have arrived "home."*

Even before heading to baggage claim, I find a pay phone and call Demir. Still no answer. It's been three hours now. Where is he? I grab my suitcase from the luggage carousel and walk back to the pay phones and try again. Demir's phone just keeps ringing. *What am I supposed to do? Is there anyone to ask?* I look around. *How could I ask someone? Should I try to go to him? That's stupid, the only thing I know is that Demir's apartment is near a place called Rockville.* "Rockville is not in DC," I remember he said during one of our phone calls in which he described our apartment. "Rockville is in Maryland, which is nearby. It's almost like living in DC." I had found it on a map and was surprised that it was just a few miles away.

I start walking around and decide to stay at the airport until I'm kicked out or reach Demir. I saunter into a convenience store, killing time before trying Demir for the fifth time since I've landed. There's a rack of local maps. It occurs to me that if I need to leave the airport, if it closes for the night and I *have* to leave, I need to be prepared to go somewhere. So, I buy a map for two dollars. One side shows DC's streets; the other side covers the surrounding areas. *If I have to find my way to Demir, this map will be my lifeline.* I reason that just like in Istanbul, if I can get to the downtown area, I should then be able to find a bus that takes me to other, nearby places outside of the city.

I try Demir two more times as the shops around me start shuttering for the night. *Do I stay and wait to be told I have to leave? If I wait, will there still be buses left to take?* I can't believe this is the way my first night in America is going to be. *Where in the world are you Demir?* I decide I need to cut my losses and leave the airport before the busses are gone. I'll figure out my next steps later.

I walk outside and I'm hit with a blast of cold air. I look for signs that have a picture of a bus and follow the arrows. There's a bus waiting at the stop. The panel in the front says "16th Street, DC." It costs eight dollars. I've been in the US for less than a day and I'm already overbudget.

Thirty-five minutes later, I'm on Sixteenth Street, in front of a big building, Capital Hilton, the sign says. On either side of the street there are several bus stops and a few posted tables listing bus routes. It takes me a minute to get my bearings. I look at all the tables, trying to find the word *Rockville*, then find the corresponding bus. It costs forty-five cents and leaves in fifteen minutes. I walk over to a pay phone and call Demir again. No answer. I'm starting to get worried about where I'm going to sleep tonight as hunger starts to set in. The last time I ate was on the flight from Frankfurt to New York. *I should have grabbed those extra rolls.*

We pull away from the bus stop with only five people on the bus and they all get off well before the final stop. About an hour later, I thank the bus driver and step out onto the street. It's 10:30 p.m. and a lot colder than it was at the airport. Lots of large buildings, a brick-paved road, and a park surround me. *This must be downtown Rockville.* Down the road, at the far end, I see the golden arches of a McDonald's. I walk toward it and find a phone near the entrance. I dig out the dime and try Demir again. The phone rings and rings. I hang up the phone. *What the hell, Demir. What if I wrote it down wrong? How am I ever going to find Demir?* I walk into the McDonald's for some food and warmth. *Okay. It's okay. I can figure out how to call Zeki and get the right number for Demir. It'll break my budget, but it's a solution.*

A few hamburgers and a cup of coffee later, I head to the bathroom. I wet some paper towels, add soap to half of them, and go into a stall to give myself a paper-towel bath. I also change out of my suit into a pair of jeans, a sweatshirt, and my warmest sweater.

I have no idea where I'm going to be spending the night, especially if I can't reach Demir. I stay at the McDonald's until 1:00 a.m., when it closes and then I'm back out on the streets. I try Demir again. Again, no answer. I debate calling Zeki, but I can't put bills into the pay phone and at this hour, there's no place to get change. *I should have gotten change at the McDonald's. Add another failure to the column.* I look around and then walk toward the largest building, which turns out to be a library. There's a church next door. *Looks like I'll be sleeping on the street tonight, like the hippies in Istanbul.* I open my suitcase and pull out my extra-long cashmere scarf and fur lined gloves and tuck myself in the church's side portico. I'm worried about the $800 in my pocket. Still, I close my eyes. Less than a minute later I open them with a start when I hear the wind howl, sending a chill right to my bones where it settles in for the night.

I don't sleep much. By 9:00 a.m., when the library has opened, my feet and face are numb. I head right for the bathrooms where I try to thaw my hands under the hot water tap. Then I call Demir from a public phone inside the library. There is still no answer.

I check the stacks for an English-Turkish dictionary and look up the words "change" and "phone." Then, I walk over to the librarian. "Change? Phone?" I ask, pushing a ten-dollar bill across the desk.

"No change here, sir," the librarian says, shaking her head.

I take back the money and smile meekly. *What if I have the right number and he's hurt, in the hospital? He doesn't expect me here for three more weeks. What if he's flown back to Istanbul? Is that possible? Would he do that? What if he did, what if he called my parents' house to tell me and I was already gone? What if he's at my parents' right now running down the hallway yelling, "I'm home, Adem! Surprise!" There's no way. No way. But it's possible. Isn't it?*

I resolve to spend the day in the library, eating chips and drinking soda out of the vending machines, which accept dollar bills. I'll go to McDonald's for dinner and get change to call Zeki there when the library closes. That's my twelve-hour plan. "He can't be back in Istanbul. He can't be," I mutter, trying to convince myself.

I find some English as a Second Language (ESL) books. My eyes close a few times as I study. Every hour, I take a break to call Demir. With each call that goes unanswered, my stomach ties into tighter knots. I did ask him for his address. He gave me only his phone number. *What do I do if I can't find him by tonight? I can't go to a hotel; it would probably cost $20 a night. But I can't keep sleeping in the church portico. I'll get sick or freeze to death.*

2

SOCIAL SECURITY

Finally, at 7:30 p.m., just an hour before the library closes, Demir answers the phone. "Where have you been?" I yell. "Man, are you okay? I almost called Zeki. I thought I had the wrong number." I don't know whether to be relieved that he's alive or angry that it took me so long to reach him. "I've been calling you for almost two days."

"Adem! Hey. Whaddya mean, where have I been?"

"Did you not hear what I just said? I've been calling you for almost thirty-six straight hours. Where have you been, man? I need you to pick me up! I slept on the steps of a church last night. I'm hungry and tired."

"What are you talking about?"

"I'm in Rockville. I'm at the library."

"No you're not!"

"You think I'm joking. Do I sound like I'm joking?" I yell, "I've been here since yesterday."

"Damn, what happened to December first? You said you were coming . . ."

"Are you gonna pick me up or what?"

"Okay, okay, give me fifteen. I'll be there. I'm so sorry man."

I slowly gather my belongings and throw on my coat, buttoning up against the cold. A minute or two after I walk outside, I hear a horn honking to the beat of the song, "You Can't Always Get What You Want." I start laughing, even though I'm so angry at Demir for being MIA and leaving me out in the cold.

"Plymouth Fury," he says as he rolls down the window. "Nineteen-seventy-four. 500 bucks. I still miss my sixty-eight Firebird, but this is okay for now." Demir jumps out of the car and gives me a bear hug. "Welcome to America, man! Welcome. Get in, get in!" He gets in himself and rolls up his window.

I toss my suitcase in the back seat and fold myself into the passenger seat. It's a single-piece, vinyl covered bench seat. Demir slaps my left leg hard. He always calls it his pal punch. I call it painful.

"Man, Addo, I'm so happy to see you, man! I can't believe you're here. You are in America, man!" The car swerves as Demir changes lanes. He's driving like crazy; I slide on the slippery seat and slam against the door. Demir is singing along with the cassette tape and laughing.

I can't get no satisfaction.

'Cause I try and I try and I try and I try, I can't get no, I can't get no,

When I'm drivin' in my car . . .

He rolls down his window again and as the breeze hits me, I have a flashback to the night at the disco when we all went dancing. I brace myself against the dashboard as Demir hits a right turn.

"Where the hell were you for two days, man? I kept calling you. I started calling when I landed in New York yesterday morning."

"Man, Addo, I met this girl, she is so cool, you'll like her, man. Why didn't you let me know you were coming early? You could've even told Dad, he would've called me to let me know."

"I didn't have the time."

"Aha! Trouble, my friend? Girl trouble, an accident, perhaps?"

"No, nothing like that. I'll tell you later. I'm here now, and glad that I found you." *I'm going to have to tell him sometime. Then he's going to tell Zeki. What a mess.*

Demir has rented us a studio apartment. "An efficiency," Demir says in

English. It smells like fresh paint and something else. "I think you have a gas leak," I say, putting down my suitcase near the front door. "It smells like gas in here."

"It's natural gas, that's how it smells," Demir says. "They don't use butane or propane over here. That's just for outside grilling."

There are two single foam mattresses on the floor, both looking worn out, ripped along the edges and in the middle, exposing the yellowed sponge underneath. No bedsheets, just blankets and a couple of pillows. In one corner of the room there's a kitchen counter, sink, and refrigerator. Across from the kitchen there are two doors. I walk over and open one, a closet, and then the other, a bathroom.

"Perfect," I say, punching Demir's shoulder. "That's payback for hitting my leg."

"Man, I can't believe you are here! This is going to be the best."

We talk for a good two hours. It feels like home. I may be in America, in Washington, DC, but it feels like one of the countless nights Demir and I lay awake in his house on the twin beds in his room laughing and play-fighting as his parents yelled at us from outside the room to be quiet and go to sleep. "I'm really happy to be here," I say. "I gotta go to sleep," I add, closing my eyes. I don't even wait for Demir to respond.

In the morning, I wake to the smell of coffee. I grab the cup Demir has made for me and walk over to look out the window to see, in the daylight, where I'm living. It's a two-story, garden-style apartment. We're on the ground floor facing a lawn and then woods.

"We need to get you a Social Security card. That's the first priority. You can't work without it. The sooner we get it, the sooner you'll be able to get a job. Plus, I read in the paper that the new president is going to be issuing a policy change and all foreigners will have a distinct set of numbers on their cards, which will state 'Not valid for employment.' We have to get your card before this change happens."

We get dressed and drive back to downtown Rockville, where the government buildings are. I fill out the Social Security form while Demir translates. When I am done, I walk to hand the form to the lady behind the counter. "Why do you need a Social Security card, sir?" she asks, hardly looking up.

I know "why," I know "need," and I know "Social Security." I understand the question. As pre-instructed by Demir, I answer, "To open a bank account."

The lady turns to her coworker and says something. She sounds angry. Demir and I grab my new Social Security card and rush out of the building as if we've just robbed a bank.

"What did she say?" I ask Demir when we get in the car.

"Basically, she's angry that she had to give you the card because it means you're going to take a job away from an American 'cause you'll work cheap and off the books."

"Oh."

"You're nobody in America," Demir says, "until you prove that you are someone. If your uncle was a king in your home country and rich, they wouldn't care. What can *you* accomplish—that's what they care about. You must prove yourself."

I don't know why, but I like that. I hope it's true. I can't claim that my uncle was this or that anyway.

We drive to the bank where Demir has opened an account so I can open one there, too. I deposit $100, which is the smallest amount allowed to open an account.

When we arrive back at the apartment, the phone is ringing. It's the manager of a different bank telling Demir that he's been hired as a teller. Demir had applied for the job two weeks earlier.

"You're my good luck charm, man!" Demir says. "Things are looking up!"

I decide to write my parents a letter telling them the good news about Demir and me without telling them anything specific. I also want them to have our phone number, in case they need to reach me. I don't want to give them my address; I don't want anyone in Istanbul to know where I am.

"Dear Mom and Dad, I hope all is well there," I write. "I'm in America with Demir who just got a job as a bank teller. I will be taking English classes and will soon begin looking for a job. I will write again soon. Regards, Adem."

My English classes aren't set to begin for another month. Demir calls the school to get me enrolled in an earlier class. I need to start learning the language but I'm dreading going back to school. I fear it's going to be as futile and violent as my education was in Istanbul.

In middle school, we were beaten by our teachers. While we were often reprimanded in elementary school, in middle school it was actual corporal punishment. Not just me, every student who disobeyed was a target. We were beaten for our behavior in the classroom, and we were beaten for our behavior outside the classroom. Mr. Halil was particularly brutal and found many reasons to beat his students. In fact, he was a notorious beater. My sisters had warned me about him, telling me he never beat the girls, not because he thought they were fragile or because he feared a parental backlash, but because he saw that they were obedient and smart too. He'd said that outright and my sisters told me. He wasn't wrong; one of my sisters had grown up to be a chemical engineer and the other, a pharmacist.

Someone was always being beaten by Mr. Halil. Sometimes a beating came with a speech. "We are a poor nation, and math is the remedy against poverty," he would say. It was one of his favorite speeches. "You will master it whether you like it or not." If a student struggled to solve a problem on the blackboard or received a failing grade on a test, Mr. Halil would knock the student's skull repeatedly against the blackboard in front of the whole class. It didn't seem to matter to him if the student was a slow learner or not math oriented. "You will go home this afternoon and study until you learn this, understood?" he would say almost every day those three years I had him as a teacher. "Many of my students over the last twenty years have grown up to be successful doctors, lawyers, and engineers. They come back to visit me to thank me for being so hard on them."

I remember the first time Mr. Halil beat a group of us for something that happened outside his classroom. He'd spied us scaling the wall of a private school across the street. The private school had a high stone and stucco wall that closed it off from the rest of the city. Someone had chiseled holes in one little section of the wall, little pockets for our hands and feet, which made it easy to climb the side of the wall and jump over into this private enclave. That spring, almost every day after school, a few friends and I climbed up the wall and jumped down to the other side. We called it the "Promised Land." The soccer fields had real grass and goal nets without holes; the blacktop on the outdoor basketball courts always looked as if it had just been retarred and repainted. It was there that a visiting coach recruited me to the U14 Besiktas basketball team.

Rumor had it Mr. Halil watched us from the window in the teachers' lounge. After a week of jumping over the wall, we arrived at class on a Monday morning to find our names on the blackboard. Mine was first on the list. "You have been playing ball instead of going home to study," Mr. Halil said. I remember thinking how crazy it was that his anger seemed to stem not from the fact that we'd broken the law as trespassers but that we'd chosen to play rather than study.

Mr. Halil pulled out a pair of wooden compasses made for the blackboard and then he called me up to the front of the room. With the compasses, he hit me on my palms, knuckles, arms, shins, and the backs of my knees. My friends and I left school that day bruised and sore, but it didn't hurt any of us enough to stop us from going over the wall again. None of us told our parents about the beatings because they would simply have beaten us, too, for doing whatever it was that the teacher found so egregious. The teacher was always right; that was the collective belief. Those of us whose parents asked said they'd been injured playing a pickup game. My parents never asked me about the huge welts on my body; they looked at me and went on doing whatever they were doing.

It wasn't just Mr. Halil. Once in the English lab in high school, the teacher noticed that I wasn't repeating all of the English sentences that I was listening to on my headphones. The teacher pulled me up by my shirt collar and dragged me out of the lab into an empty classroom. Then, without warning, he started kicking and punching me, even hitting me with karate chops. By the time he was finished, I was huddled in a ball on the floor, brutally beaten. He kept screaming at me to get up. When I tried and couldn't, it seemed to make him more irate. He opened the door to the classroom, then grabbed me by the shirt collar again, almost choking me, and threw me out into the empty corridor. I landed with a thud and a crack on the shiny floor and slid down the hallway until my head crashed into a cast iron radiator. I got up and walked back to the classroom, afraid that if I didn't return to class, he'd have another reason to beat me.

***

The first Monday after arriving in DC, I enter an American classroom for the first time. I spend the day waiting for the English teacher to grow angry and start yelling. I wait every day for two weeks but find the teacher to be nothing but kind and helpful. Within a month, my brain, free for the first time in my life to think and learn instead of worrying that I'll make a mistake that would warrant a beating, begins absorbing the lessons. I'm learning to speak English.

Encouraged now, I study English day and night. The language program cost $110 a month. Each day I travel an hour by bus to the school, taking classes from nine to noon, filling the commute time with studying. I take a reading-speaking class and a writing-grammar class. By New Year's, I've advanced to a class with people who have been in the US a lot longer than I have.

The English classes are the start of my transformation. Now that I can string sentences together, I begin making friends with my classmates. Karla is from Brazil and Roberto is from Bolivia. She's has been in the US six months; he, a year. Their English is much better than mine and often when we go out for coffee, they correct me. It's like an additional conversation class. Roberto, who is two years older than I am, is studying English so he can study marketing in college. He came to the United States "for an adventure" and "to make more money," he says. He has a large family back home and he sends money to his mother. His father died in a construction accident and she can't earn enough money to feed his younger siblings. Karla, who is my age, wants to become a nurse, then marry an American doctor. I tell them my goal is to take the "graduate-level" English classes so I can earn an advanced degree in engineering.

Both Karla and Roberto have more than one job. Roberto works for a hotel-and-office-cleaning company and sells clothing on the side. He buys boxes of unsold clothes from stores and sells them out of the back of his car. He tells me he's really good at sales and tells me if I believe him, that proves it! Karla is a hostess in a Brazilian restaurant. She also babysits.

I'm down to $480. But, I can't get a job until I've improved my English.

I give myself one more month. Demir and I talk about what I could possibly do; busboy and dishwasher are the only two jobs we think I could manage without fluent English. Nighttimes, we also talk about our futures as we lie on our foam mattresses side by side like ten-year-olds having a sleepover.

"You know, I don't think my parents are truly aware that I'm no longer just down the road at the university," I say. "They don't seem to grasp that I'm halfway around the world, in the US."

"Your parents are . . . well, different, Adem."

"Tell me about it."

"Maybe they'll ask you to come home for dinner tomorrow night?"

"Ha!" I say, taking an Oreo out of the bag we're sharing. "I really could go for one of my mother's banquets." I close my eyes and imagine the aromas of meatballs and potatoes in tomato sauce. I fall asleep wondering if I'll ever taste my mother's cooking again.

3

PLAN C

TO CREATE A TRUE ENGLISH IMMERSION ENVIRONMENT FOR myself, Demir stops speaking Turkish to me at my request. With his perfect American accent, he helps me with my pronunciation and grammar. I eat and breathe English, studying when Demir is at work or out with his new girlfriend, and when I'm on the bus to and from my class. At the language school, I stay late after class and use my pocket dictionary to read the news in the *Post*. My teacher says that toddlers can learn up to seventeen new words per day, so that's my goal. Reading the paper is a great way to learn more words. When I pick up the paper on January 21, the day after President Reagan moves into the White House, I learn the words *inaugurated*, *hostages*, and *free*.

On Sundays, Demir and I eat at McDonald's. I love the word *brunch*, both the word itself and the concept. After brunch, we catch the Metro to downtown and walk around the National Mall. On cold days, we run into the free museums that line the Mall to escape the blast of winter. Air and Space and the National Gallery of Art are my favorites so far.

On our way out of the house for a "special brunch," Demir says, "to celebrate my two months as a bank teller," the phone rings. Demir and I look at each other. The phone never rings. Demir answers the phone in English.

I watch Demir as he quickly switches to Turkish then gasps. He nods a lot but doesn't say much. At the end of the call he says, "I'll be home as soon as I can," and then puts down the receiver and turns to me.

"What happened?" I ask.

"My dad is in the hospital. He may have had a heart attack. My mother wants me to come home."

"Is he going to be okay?"

"She doesn't know. But, I think I should go. You'll be okay while I'm gone, right?" he says, more a statement than a question. "I should be back in less than a month."

The thought of being in America alone is shocking. Terrifying. But so is the thought of Zeki being sick.

On Monday I go with Demir to the Pan Am office downtown. He activates the return leg of his open-ended round trip ticket he arrived with from Istanbul. It's free. "I told my boss," Demir says, "but they may not be able to hold my job. I'm gonna sell the car."

"Why?" I ask. "You said you're coming back, aren't you?" *Is he not coming back? He doesn't even have a ticket to come back. He'd have to buy one.*

"I was gonna sell it anyway. If I come back, I'll buy a Firebird."

Two days later, he's sold his car and he's given me his share of the rent for the following month. "Just in case I'm not back by March first," he says. "And just in case you don't get a job right away." The next day, he's gone. It's that fast.

I'm not afraid, but the possibility that Zeki won't be okay and Demir won't or can't return, worries me. I can't afford to stay at this place for $320 per month; where then, would I go? I stay awake all night that first night I'm alone.

I distract myself by throwing myself into studying. Not only has my friend, my lifeline in America, left, I've also lost my best tutor. So, I hunker down. I want to call Istanbul and find out how Zeki is doing, but we're on a strict budget and it's an expensive call. By the end of week two, I'm very worried about Zeki, about Demir, and about how difficult it will be living in America on my own. I hadn't realized what a support system Demir had been. I decide that if Demir hasn't called by the end of the third week, I will call him. I don't know who to worry about more, Zeki or myself.

And then, one week before the rent is due for March, the phone rings.

"I'm not coming back," Demir says. It's the first thing he says. I haven't heard Turkish in almost three weeks, so for a second I think I must have misunderstood him. And then he repeats it. "Did you hear me, Adem? I'm not coming back." It's like a punch in the gut. My heart skips a beat. I feel heat rise up into my face and my stomach fall to my feet. I can't speak. "Dad had to have surgery. Bypass, they said. He will be in the hospital another week, then he'll come home. There's a lot to do here. I'm going to stay at home and help my mother take care of him. I'm not coming back."

I need you to come back, man, I can't do this without you. I'm down to $252, plus Demir's part of next month's rent, another $160. *I need you here, Demir. You are my lifeline.* I take a breath. *You can't tell him that, Adem.*

"Adem, are you there?"

"Yes. Yes, I'm here," I tell him. "Do whatever is necessary. Is Zeki going to be okay?"

"I don't know. I hope so."

"You're fortunate to have a father like Zeki. I hope he'll get well soon. He will. He will get well soon. And when Zeki gets healthy again, you always have a home with me in America."

"Thanks, man," Demir says. "If you want, you can just leave the apartment and use your return ticket to come back to Istanbul."

I don't have a return ticket. And I don't have the money for a return ticket. I don't know if I can do this without Demir, but since I can't get home right now, I have no choice.

"I'll think about it," I say. "Tell Zeki I'm thinking of him."

When I get off the phone with Demir, I stare out the window. *How am I going to do this?*

The following day, after class, I pull Roberto aside and, in broken English, ask him if there are any rooms for rent at his house. I reason that if I can move out before the March rent is due, I'll have some extra cash that I can rely on until I get a job. If I don't pay my $160 and I keep Demir's $160, I'll have $412. Roberto tells me there are no rooms available but that I can sleep at his place since he works an overnight shift, from midnight to eight in the morning. I'm stunned by his generosity, especially when I tell him I can pay him $80 a month and he tells me I don't have to pay anything until I've gotten myself a job.

***

The next day, three days before the March rent is due, I pack up my suitcase and a few of the items Demir had purchased—two coffee cups, an ashtray, some plastic forks and knives and paper plates—and move into Roberto's place in Forest Glen, a free bus transfer from the Metro stop.

"Welcome home!" Roberto says as I enter his room. "You can put your stuff here," he says, pointing to the closet. "I cleared some space for you."

"Thank you," I say, wishing I had more words in my vocabulary to thank him thoroughly. He's a true lifesaver. I'm fairly certain I'd be homeless without him.

As it is, I have to pay $110 for my monthly tuition for the language school this Friday. And, if I don't get a job in March, I'll have to pay my April tuition, too, to ensure that my student visa isn't revoked. That's the smartest approach. That will leave me with $192 for food and transportation. Since I spend $28 a month on the Metro to get to school and I can't cut this expense, I reason that I'll simply need to survive on less food. I'm already living on cheese and bologna sandwiches, but I'm going to have to trim that. Even if I do that and calculate in Roberto's generosity, I have a little more than a month before I run out of money.

Roberto lets me use his phone to call Eliz; I'll pay him back when he gets his phone bill.

"I need some money," I tell Eliz, getting right to the point. "Can you send me the $600 you offered? I don't know if you heard, but Demir moved back home because Zeki is sick, and I don't have enough money to live and I don't have a job yet." I feel pathetic. I feel like a failure. I feel like there's an "I told you so" that's about to hurl through the telephone line and smack me in the face. Instead, Eliz is sympathetic. I give her my bank information so she can wire me the money. She wishes me luck.

I expect the money from Eliz will arrive at my bank account in a week or so. It'll be a lifesaver.

I need to start looking for a job. I have no idea how long it will take to land one. I feel like there's no clear strategy for me. I need to learn enough English, first, to get a job, and second, to *keep* it. If my English is still rough, how can my future employer interview me? If I ask the person to speak slower or to explain what they are saying, I suspect they won't hire me. I wouldn't hire me. Then I worry that even if I get a job but don't understand my boss's instructions properly, I won't be able to do the job properly and I'll get fired.

I really do need to absorb some of Roberto's laid-back attitude. I wonder how much of my approach to life is me and how much is Turkish culture, since it's pretty typical for Turks to look for problems. "And, when we can't find one, we create one for ourselves," I say out loud to myself. "You clearly know that system, Adem. How many problems have you created for yourself?"

***

With the end of March approaching, the people of DC are ready to welcome spring and cherry blossom season—a season I've never heard of. Sometimes after class, I'll find a park bench to study and watch the gray-suited executives walk by on their way to and from lunch. Each day there are more smiles as the cold-weather hustle transitions into a springtime saunter.

As afternoon turns into a chilly evening, I head to the local mall. It's warm, has clean bathrooms, a TV set, a couple of them, actually, and a food court. I can walk, watch TV, eat, and study while Roberto sleeps. At 9:00 p.m., using my free transfer ticket, I take the bus over to Roberto's and by the time I arrive, he's getting ready to go to work. I work on my English conversation with him until he leaves; then, I have his room to myself. In the morning, before Roberto comes home, I get up and go to school early enough to buy my doughnut and coffee and move to the student lounge to do my homework and read the *Post*.

An hour later Roberto joins me in class. After the class ends, he goes home to sleep until 8:00 p.m.

***

I'm slowly making progress with English. For the first few months, it felt like everyone spoke too fast. But lately, I'm understanding more than half of what people say. For the last four months, I have studied English harder than I've studied in my entire life, even harder than I studied for the college entrance exams. I have been doing every single reading or writing exercise in every single ESL textbook I can find, whether I'm at school, at the library, on a bus or train, or at Roberto's. Once a week, I go to the local laundromat with an ESL book and study while I'm waiting. Some days, I study for fourteen hours and sleep for only two to three hours.

***

"I need a job," I tell Roberto. "Where should I go? How do I find a job?"

"I think the best place to start is Georgetown. There are tons of restaurants and bars there. Just walk in and ask if they need a busboy. You can walk there from school," he says, telling me it's only about thirty minutes on foot. "I worked at a place called Pizzeria Uno's for the first six months after I came to America. It's no longer there, otherwise I'd go over with you and tell them to hire you."

Roberto tells me how to walk to Georgetown. "Take M Street, toward west," he says, then pauses. "Or, if you want, we can run cocaine in backpacks across the river from Mexico. It is $20,000 per load. Let me know, and I will go with you. We do it together. Even a single trip will be enough for us to live on for two, three years."

I laugh.

"Not kidding, man. It's an easy $20,000."

I don't even consider it for a minute. I hope he's actually kidding.

After school the next day, the cherry blossoms about to bloom throughout the district, I head over to Georgetown. It's my first time in this part of town. I pass by a convenience store, then stop, walk back to look in the store window. On display is the daily Turkish paper, *Nation's Daily*. From outside the store I can see the top half of the paper. I squint, checking on the date; it's yesterday's news, but it's news from home, nonetheless. Goose bumps tickle my arms and I feel a pressure building up behind my eyes. *Am I homesick?* A price is scribbled in pen next to the date, but I can't read it. "Focus on your mission, Adem," I say out loud to myself in Turkish. "You are in Georgetown for a job." I start walking away, but something tugs me back. "Fine!" I say, exasperated at my lack of willpower. I walk into the store to check on the price, $1.50, way too expensive for my budget. I quickly scan the headlines, flipping over paper for the rest of the news. "You read, you buy," the clerk yells from behind the counter. I put the paper down and run out of the store. *If I get a job in Georgetown, I can read the top stories from Turkey every day while passing by this store.*

When I get to the corner of M Street and Wisconsin Avenue, I'm amazed by how many restaurants and stores there are. And so many people! I hear someone say, "Ugh, tourist season!" as we accidentally bump shoulders on the narrow sidewalk. I turn the corner to walk up Wisconsin and then slow my pace almost to a halt. *Am I really supposed to just walk into a place and ask for a job?*

I turn back to M Street and walk up and down a few times, trying to decide where to start. I don't want to do this. My English isn't good enough and my accent is thick. But I know I have no choice. I step out of the flow of pedestrian traffic and close my eyes for a second to calm myself. *On fifty Adem. Start walking and count to fifty. And, whatever restaurant you are in front of when you hit fifty, that's the one you go into.* I start counting in Turkish, then switch to English. It's good practice, plus it helps delay the inevitable . . . 45, 46, 47, 48, 49, 50. I look up. I find myself in front of a place with purple double doors and a large sign that reads, Crazy Zebra. I recognize the word *zebra* since it's the same as in Turkish. I know *crazy* too. *What a crazy name for a restaurant!* I stand in front of the place trying to figure out what it is—a bar? A restaurant? I take a deep breath. *Go in. Go in now.*

I rehearse my line one final time then push open the doors. It's a big and dark space, and it smells like citrus and beer. It takes several seconds for my eyes to adjust to the dark. At the far end of the room, there's a bar, back lit with a dim purple light. As I get closer, I see a woman cutting limes. She's in a strapless top and skintight trousers.

"We're closed," she says, without looking up, dismissing me without even seeing me.

"Excuse me, ma'am, do you need help? I don't speak English, but I can work hard."

She looks up, then looks me up and down for a few seconds.

"Do you have a Social Security card, honey?"

"Yes."

"Come tomorrow night at seven. Minimum wage. Bus the tables. Set up the bar. Work Friday and Saturday nights, seven to close . . . Bring your Social Security card with you."

I understand her. *Adem, you understood what she just said!*

"Thank you, ma'am. I will come Friday. Seven o'clock."

More than four months of immersion, 24/7 English, and I have carried out my first conversation with a complete stranger. And I've gotten a job! I'm not sure which one I'm happier about. Just like Demir said, a minimum-wage, part-time job requires nothing more than a Social Security card. The job is only sixteen hours a week, which is less than $200 a month. But, it's something; it's a start.

The following night, I grin as I pick up two glasses and wipe a table. I feel like a crazy zebra smiling when I'm cleaning up after people. But I can't help it. It's my first job in the new world. The job is nonstop, but easy. Lots of lifting, not a lot of thinking.

***

On Monday after class, I join some of the other students for a picnic lunch in McPherson Square. It feels so nice to sit on the grass and watch people walk by. "Are you going to join us for soccer this afternoon?" one of the students from Brazil asks.

"No, sorry, not today," I say, disappointed. I have made a commitment to myself to go back to Georgetown and see if I can get another job as a busboy.

As I head north from Dupont Circle to turn west through the park to Georgetown, suddenly there's a bizarre mood shift. Sirens begin wailing, people start running, police cars come speeding down the streets, dozens of them.

"President Reagan was shot! Reagan was shot at the Washington Hilton!" people scream as they run in different directions up and down street, shouting the news to strangers who start pouring out of buildings and restaurants to find out what the commotion is all about. I follow a crowd of people up the hill toward the hotel. The side entrance is cordoned off with yellow tape and in front of it are police vehicles and black sedans with flashing lights on top, fire trucks and ambulances. I get as close as I can with a crowd stretched in front of me. All I can see is a side entrance door to the hotel.

I don't know what to think. While I'm not good at my own country's history, I don't think a prominent politician has ever been assassinated in Turkey. Thousands of sympathizers, but not a key political figure. As I walk away, people continue to run toward the hotel. I see people crying and hugging one another. Every conversation I hear is about the president.

"Is the president dead?"

"They took the president to the university hospital. He may not die."

"Other people were shot too, not just the president."

The farther I get from the scene of the shooting, the less palpable the incident is. By the time I arrive in Georgetown, life seems pretty much normal. I stay on M Street toward Crazy Zebra to check out the restaurant possibilities there.

I notice a small, unassuming place with a big sign. The Blues Saloon. I briefly practice my line and then I walk in, a lot less nervous than I was the day I walked into Crazy Zebra looking for a job.

A young man in a crisp white shirt and khakis is behind the bar. He's pulling glasses out of a green crate, pauses to look up at me. "What can I get you, my friend?" I turn around to see if there is someone behind me, but there's no one there but me. I point to myself, as if to ask, "Are you talking to me?"

"Yes sir, what can I get you?"

"Sir, do you need help? I don't speak English, but I can work hard."

"Oh, sorry. I'm not the owner. I don't make those decisions. Just a bartender here, my friend. But if you write down your name and phone number, I will give it to the boss."

The bartender smiles as he hands me a pen and a paper napkin. I write down my name and Roberto's number, then hand it back to the bartender and thank him for his time. *Next time I need to ask for the owner or the manager, otherwise it's just a waste of time. He's probably already thrown the napkin in the trash.*

By the time I've left the bar, the news about the assassination attempt has made its way to Georgetown. And now, here, it's the only thing everyone is talking about. As I walk back to Dupont Circle to jump on the Metro back to Roberto's, I do a mental check on my goals list. I find it calming somehow. And inspiring too. It helps me realize that I have accomplished something even though I have so much more ahead of me.

Get into the US. Did it.

Get a job. Got one, need another.

Survive. Doing it.

Learn English. Doing it.

The sun goes down, a chill sets in. I think about the president and the others who have been shot, just like my friends in Istanbul, some fighting for their lives, some dying. But quickly, my thoughts shift: What am I going to eat, how much is it going to cost, how am I going to pay for school, how am I going to get a second job. The questions sound trivial by comparison. As my stomach growls, I feel guilty.

I run down the Metro escalators and catch the train seconds before the doors close. Sliding through the closing doors like an expert makes me feel like a local. I grab a seat at the far end of the car and look around. There's only one other person in the train car. Pulling out my notebook, I start going over my list again.

"Excuse me."

I look up to see a tall man wearing a suit and a cowboy hat towering over me. He must be at least 1.95 meters. That's six feet five inches, I calculate quickly. I wonder how long it will be before the American system becomes second nature for me.

"Excuse me," he repeats.

"Yes?" I say, wary.

"Are you a student?"

"Yes."

"What are you studying?" he asks. His accent throws me a little, but I understand him for the most part which makes me feel good.

"English."

He tells me he is a lawyer from Texas, visiting DC on business. I'm not clear on what he wants from me or why he's even talking to me. I smile and look back down at my notebook, hoping I don't appear rude. "And where are you from?"

I look back up.

"Turkey. Istanbul," I say, looking at his tie, which looks like something JR Ewing would wear. I wonder whether he knows where Turkey is on the map. He asks a few more prodding questions, how long have I been here, if I came to America with my whole family. The more he asks, the more wary I get. *Is he Interpol? What if he's an investigator? I've been so consumed with surviving here, I forgot about the $400,000. What do I do? What do I do!*

"Son, you okay?" I hear him saying. *Just answer the questions. Just be polite. Don't say anything more than answering the exact question he asks.*

"Yes sir. Sorry. I didn't hear you."

"Once you learn our language, what you gonna do, then?"

"Graduate degree in engineering," I say, looking down at my book. *Are there others? Will police rush in at the next stop, throw me against the walls of the Metro car and arrest me?* I feel my body stiffening. *It's over, Adem. All this hard work. Over.*

"Oh kid, why did you come here?" he asks. I look up quickly, not sure that I understand what he's just asked. He must see the confused look on my face because he repeats the question. I open my mouth to answer, and he interrupts me.

"I feel for you. You shouldn't have come. There are no jobs here for people like you. Graduate school? Come now. It's impossible." *Is he trying to throw me off? Get my guard down? What is he saying? What's going on?* "Don't you know the US is in its worst recession since the Second World War?" he continues. *Maybe he's killing time, engaging with me until the next stop.* "We don't even have jobs for ourselves here. The American dream is dead. It's over. It's gone and never coming back. There's no way for you to earn money here." *That's it, maybe he's trying to get me to confess that I don't need money. That I* *have $400,000 sitting under my mattress.*

I realize my mouth is hanging open. As the train slows down, I quickly shut my mouth and paste on a smile. I don't know what to say. I don't know what to do.

"Go home, kid," he says, shaking his head. "This country isn't for you. Any of you," he says as the train continues to slow down. I brace myself for the men in dark suits who are about to step into the train car, grab me, manhandle me, cuff me and throw me in a cell. The train stops. I eye the platform, my eyes darting back and forth. I hold my breath. "This is my stop, kid. Go back to where you belong," he says, tipping his hat at me. *What? He's tipping his hat.* The doors open and he walks to the door. I wait for the onslaught.

And then, nothing.

The cowboy leaves, stepping off the train and onto the platform.

No one enters.

The doors shut and the train pulls out of the station.

I exhale. What just happened? I don't know what to think. *What was that all about? If he wasn't the fuzz, why was he talking to me? Telling me to go home?* I run through the conversation again, hearing his words differently now that I understand he was simply a stranger on a train. *Is he right? Is the American dream really dead?* I look down at the list I made in my notebook. *He told me to leave the country. Why would he care? Why would he tell me to leave?* I look around the train car. A few other people have gotten on. I'm the only foreign-looking person. *Was he one of those Americans who hates immigrants? Was he trying to scare me into leaving? Or, does he just believe that it's over and that America will never recover from this economic crisis, from high inflation, high unemployment, and severe recession.* I spend the rest of the ride trying to figure out how I could have played that conversation differently. But, I don't know what I could have done to change his mind.

About fifteen minutes later, the train arrives in Silver Spring, the last station on the Red Line.

I walk straight over to a waiting bus and take a seat in the back, as is my habit. I like being able to see the entire bus while feeling invisible. Before the bus pulls away from the station, a loud group of teenage boys gets on, pushing and shoving one other. They walk toward me.

I hope they don't try to talk to . . .

"Hey man," one says, looking at me. "You got the time?" His grammar is off, but I know what he's saying. It's one of the first phrases we learned in ESL class. I pull up my sleeve and look down at my watch, trying to find the words. But they fail me. I turn my wrist to show him my watch.

He looks at me, then looks at the watch and thanks me. "He is deaf and dumb," he says to his friends, laughing.

"He is not deaf, you dork," one of the other boys says, punching him in the arm. "He obviously heard you, he showed you his watch."

"Fine. Then he's just dumb."

They all laugh, smacking one another. I almost laugh, too.

I miss Demir.

4

HAPPY HOURS

THE MINUTE I OPEN THE DOOR TO ROBERTO'S, EVEN BEFORE HE says hi, he tells me I've received a call. "Some damn guy. He wanted to talk to you about a job. Here. His phone number."

"What's his name?"

"I said, his name is Dan."

"I thought you said, 'Some damn guy.' "

"Ha! No, Dan, like Danny."

It sure sounded like "damn." "Can I call him now?"

"Sure. I'm off to work. See you in the morning."

"See you." *The bartender must have passed my phone number on to his boss. I can't believe it. I really thought it was going to end up in the trash bin.*

Before picking up the phone and dialing, I practice what I'm going to say. I want to use as few words as possible while providing as much information as I think the person who answers will need. I don't want the person on the phone to have to ask me questions that I might not understand. As I try to come up with the right sentence, I realize that for some reason, it's easier to communicate in English in person than on the phone. Maybe because of the hand gestures one can use. *Why are hand gestures universal, but language isn't?*

"Dan, please. My name is Adem Bayer. I return his call," I practice. *No. That's not right.* "I am returning his call." *I need to use the present continuous tense.*

I repeat the phrase then call this Dan person back.

"Dan, please. My name is Adem Bayer. I am returning his call," I say.

"Adem, this is Dan. Can't talk right now. But, come tomorrow, to the bar. Eight o'clock. We'll talk. Busy tonight."

And that's it. I hear a click. *Did he just hang up the phone?*

I replay the conversation in my head, slowing it down. He said come tomorrow at eight o'clock. He didn't say "a.m." or "p.m." Did he mean for me to come in the morning or in the evening? European time makes things so much easier. *Should I show up at eight in the morning? If I go at 8:00 a.m., I'll miss school.* I don't know what to do and I have no one to ask. I walk around Roberto's room for a while trying to figure it out. I can't call Dan back, he said he was busy.

Eventually, I decide to go to school the next day and ask all my friends there. If they say, "he meant morning," it will be a lost opportunity, but I'll know for the next time that I need to ask, clarify. If they say, "He meant 8:00 p.m.," then I'll just show up and hope they were right.

Everyone at school is convinced that he meant 8:00 p.m., so, when I arrive at the Blues Saloon at 7:55 that evening, I feel confident that I'm not showing up twelve hours late. I hope I'll have a chance to thank the bartender before I meet this Dan fellow. But, someone else is behind the bar. When I ask for Dan, she nods then yells for him without moving.

A man with dark, shoulder-length hair and a trimmed beard appears from behind saloon-style, swinging doors. They look like they are right out of an old, American Western, which immediately reminds me of the Texan lawyer on the train. *I need to focus. I need this job.*

Dan is about my height and just as skinny but muscular.

"I'm Dan," he says, holding out his hand while simultaneously patting my right shoulder with his other hand. His handshake is firm. I try to match it.

Dan points to a corner table then motions for me to go first, which feels awkward. I walk to the far chair and stand behind it, waiting for him to sit down first.

"Have a seat, please," he says, his voice forceful, confident.

I pull out my chair, feeling uneasy as I sit down before he does.

"So, you have a Social Security card, right?" he asks. I hand over my card. "Okay. Thanks. Adem. Adem Bayer. That's easy enough." He gives me a crooked grin. "Adem, I'm Dan Sullivan. I'm the owner here. Listen, I don't really care who you are or where you're from. I just care about this card here. I can give you twenty hours a week as a dishwasher. You'll make $3.10 per hour. After taxes you'll clear $2.85. At the end of the year, you apply to the IRS and get some of your taxes back. You can have one free meal per day here, anything from the menu except for steaks or fried cheese. Okay?"

I do a quick calculation. That's another $50 per week. Now I can go to school and possibly rent a cheap room. But it's really not enough.

"I need to work more hours, sir," I tell him.

"Can't do it. I can hardly afford you now, but I need a dishwasher. Start Wednesday at six. We'll see how it goes. Okay?"

"Okay."

"What time did I say?"

"Six. 6:00 p.m.," I say, guessing that's what he meant and hoping I'm right. "On Wednesday, sir."

"Right. Good. Just checking." He stands up and shakes my hand. "Welcome aboard."

"Thank you, sir."

"Lemme show you around." I follow him back to the bar. "Hey Paul, this is the new dishwasher. He speaks English!"

It's the bartender from the other day. "Adem, this is Paul."

He walks over to shake my hand and says, "Paul. Hi. Nice to meet you."

I say, "I'm Adem. Nice to meet you. And thank you, sir, um, Paul. You gave Dan my phone number."

"Oh, don't mention it. Welcome to the Blues Saloon."

****

On Wednesday I walk through the door of the Blues Saloon at 5:55 p.m. Dan takes me into the kitchen and shows me the dishwashing machine, the coffee machine, the espresso machine, the broom, the mop, the garbage cans, and the two walk-in refrigerators—one for food and one for beer kegs. There is a walk-in freezer too. Then he leads me through a back corridor off the kitchen to the door that leads outside to a grassy courtyard and points to a heap of bricks, and says, "Move those bricks from there to here," pointing to the concrete wall on the far side of the courtyard. "Stack them up flush against the wall. Okay?" Before I can respond, he walks away. *Flush. I don't know that word.* I pull out my dictionary and look up the word "flush."

I need to be quick; these are a lot of bricks to move.

Flush: To become red. *Like bricks? Or anger? Is Dan angry with me?*

Flush: Like toilet, water. *Like smooth, flowing? Bricks? No.*

Flush: Like in poker. *No.*

Flush: With money. Rich. *Dan is rich. He has lots of bricks? No. No. No!*

Flush: At the same level as another surface. *Ah. Okay. This one. This must be it. Flush against the wall.*

I look back at the heap of bricks. This is not a dishwasher's job. It's not even a busboy's job. I'm a little confused by my assignment but I start moving the bricks and stack them neatly along the wall. It takes about an hour and when I'm done, I'm really not sure where to go or what to do. So, I walk back into the kitchen. Dan is there talking to someone I haven't yet met.

"Adem. You're done? Excellent. That was fast," he says, speaking quickly. I'm trying not to translate the words but hear them as they are spoken. "This is Raymond, our cook," Dan says. "Raymond, this is Adem, the new dishwasher."

"Nice to meet you, sir," I say to the man who looks to be about my dad's age.

"Nice to meet you too."

"Raymond is going to give you your next assignment," Dan says as he turns to leave. He doesn't say anything about the bricks. *I hope he'll like the way I lined them up, flush with the wall.*

Raymond shows me how to stack the dishwasher crates efficiently. He shows me the microwave, the grill, and a large oven with another, pull-out grill with iron bars.

I bus tables and wash dishes all night long. Occasionally, I sweep the floors in the kitchen. Some waitstaff, as they come into the kitchen to leave food orders with Raymond, introduce themselves. Others just smile and leave.

I'm hungry but too embarrassed to ask Raymond for food, so I go without dinner. I've lost considerable weight since Demir left; and, I really didn't have any extra pounds to lose. But, with only $81 left, and thirteen days until I get a paycheck, I can't spend money on luxuries, like food. I need to reserve that money for transportation so I can get to school.

At 1:30, I hear Dan announce last call to the five or so patrons still at the bar. Then he walks into the kitchen where I am sweeping. "Adem. Come tomorrow at one."

1:00 p.m.? I wish Dan would be more specific.

"Yes, sir. 1:00 p.m.," I say, to confirm, nervous that he's going to say, 1:00 a.m. and think I'm an idiot.

Dan throws his cigarette on the floor and crushes under his foot. Apparently 1:00 p.m. was correct. I wait until he leaves the kitchen, then sweep the cigarette butt off the floor.

At 2:00 a.m., Dan follows the last customers to the door and locks up behind them. "Okay, gather 'round everyone," he says as he walks behind the bar. I look around and watch most members of the staff pull up stools at the bar; a few others sit at the tables closest to the bar. I stand, feeling awkward, hanging back from the bar.

As Dan serves the waitstaff beer, he starts shaking his head.

"Just unbelievable," he says in an angry voice. I'm not sure who he's talking to. "You're students at some of the country's top universities, how could you all be so dumb?"

One by one, he points to members of the waitstaff, shaking his finger at them. I don't understand everything, but I do understand Dan is angry. My empty stomach grows tight while I wait for him to get to me.

"The one bright spot tonight, Adem. Good job on your first day."

Is this a setup? Is he just being nice to me because it's my first day? Do I say thank you to him?

By the time I've decided I should thank him for his kind words, he's dismissed everyone for the evening.

It's 2:30 in the morning when I walk out of the Blues Saloon. I head toward P Street to the Dupont Circle Metro. It's closed. I read the sign posted. "5:30 a.m. to Midnight, Sunday-Thursday. 5:30 a.m. to 2:00 a.m. Friday and Saturday." I can't get home. I have to wait two and a half hours for the first buses and trains to start up at 5:30 a.m.. I'm tired and hungry; I haven't eaten for fourteen hours. I start walking back to the park at Dupont Circle to sit on a bench and, on my way, I see an open 7-Eleven on the other side of the street. I buy a quart of milk and an apple for ninety cents, then continue on to the park in the middle of the circle. I find an empty bench, listen to the chirping of the very early birds, and enjoy my treats. The only other people around me appear to be homeless men—about a half dozen of them. *I'm only a paycheck away from being like them. If Roberto decides to leave like Demir, or kick me out . . . I will be exactly like them.* I shudder at the thought. *I can't let that happen. I have to study harder and work even harder. I have to keep bringing in money.*

With food in my stomach, exhaustion sets in. I lie down on the bench and doze into a dream about the navy high school. The senior cadet on duty keeps poking me on the kidney. "Wake up, get up . . . Come on, get up." The poking gets stronger until it begins to hurt and I grab my stomach. "Ouch," I cry and open my eyes to see a police officer standing over me, poking me with a baton.

"You can sit here, but no lying down. No sleeping here. You understand?"

"Yes, sir, sorry, I'm up. I sit up. I will sit up," I say, correcting myself. "I am up." My mom hit me because I didn't sleep; the officer pokes me because I do sleep. *My formula for life. Wrong + wrong = always wrong.*

I check the time and, with fifteen minutes to go until the Metro starts running, I get up from the bench and start walking slowly back over to the Dupont entrance. On the train, I fall asleep again, nudged awake this time by the conductor at the end of the line in Silver Spring, my stop. By 6:15, I'm off the bus and walking to Roberto's. After a quick shower, I doze off again for an hour before Roberto comes home. Looks like this is my new routine.

***

The following night, I'm alone in the Blues Saloon kitchen washing dishes when one of the waitstaff bursts through the double swinging doors.

"We need silverware! Hurry!"

The doors are still swinging as she turns around and hits the doors with both elbows and runs out.

I don't know what "silverware" is. I reach for my dictionary in my back pocket only to realize I've left it in the cubby in the basement with my jacket. I look around, thinking hard, trying to guess what it could be. The young woman looked distressed. There is an emergency of some kind but that's all I can discern. I look at the fire extinguisher, but I don't smell smoke. I look at the broom, maybe she needs me to mop up a tray of spilled food. I push through the doors and walk quickly to the bar.

"Paul . . . Paul!" I whisper from the end of the bar. He's busy serving drinks. He looks up and nods. "Just a sec," he says, holding up a finger. I tap my foot impatiently until I see him wiping his hands and walking over.

"What is silverware?"

"Forks and knives."

"Forks and knives!" I repeat. "Oh."

I make a mental note to look up and learn all words used in restaurants. *Why haven't I done that already? Rookie mistake. I cannot afford mistakes like that.*

"Thank you! Again."

That's when I notice Dan standing right behind Paul at the bar. "What the fuck, Adem. Silverware. Where's the silverware, man? And, we need beer mugs."

"Yes sir."

"The Miller is out, check the Bud also—the stream is weak, tighten it a bit. Go man, go. Move! We don't have time for idle conversation. Hurry up. Now!" He escalates into a scream, clapping his hands at me.

I see Paul roll his eyes. *Silverware, beer mugs, Miller and Bud, yes, got it. But, stream? Tighten?*

I take the silverware and the beer mugs to the bar area, then go to the basement to the walk-in fridge where the kegs are kept. Miller and Bud are both out; I unhook the empty kegs and take them out of the walk-in box. To get to the full ones in the back, I have to pull out six kegs stacked in front; about 160 pounds each. I lift a full Miller and a full Bud keg onto the shelf and hook them on their respective hoses, which go through the ceiling to the tap at the bar upstairs. My hands are numb from the cold and I still have to put back the kegs I removed. I'm also worried about the dirty dishes piling up in the kitchen; I need to get to them before Dan sees them. I stick my hands under my armpits to warm them, taking a moment to run to the cubby, grab my dictionary and, with my frozen fingers, quickly look up "stream" and "tighten." Ah.

I get the last kegs back into the fridge, then run back up to the kitchen. If it's this busy on a Thursday night, I wonder what this place looks like on a Friday or Saturday night?

By 1:45 a.m., I'm parched and realize I'm famished too. I arrived at 1:00 p.m. and haven't eaten since breakfast. My hunger trumps my fear of asking the chef to make me food. I walk into the kitchen practicing what I'm going to say.

Raymond is scrubbing the grill, singing, "Love So Fine," by Smokey Robinson, I think. My sisters had the album.

"Adem, hey! What's up? You survived day two, huh?" He holds up his hand for a high five.

I smile and slap his hand. I realize he's had a long night, too; I can't ask him to cook for me. I forget the words I've practiced.

"You leaving now?" he asks.

My stomach growls. I really need food. I take a deep breath. "Raymond, I'm sorry, I know you are busy. Can I eat something?"

"Sure, kid. Anything you want, you understand? Anything. You wanna steak? I'll make you a steak. How do you want it cooked?"

"Can I make a sandwich?"

"Sure man, it's all yours—grab what you want, the whole kitchen is yours to eat."

I walk over to the refrigerator and start pulling out slices of bread, cheese, salami, and turkey. My stomach growls. I pile up the meat, taking half of what my hunger is telling me I need. I sit down on a stool in the kitchen and, as I take a bite out of my sandwich, Dan walks in. I freeze in mid chew, feeling like I've been caught stealing. I don't know what to do. I know Dan told me I get one meal a day, but what if he thinks I already had that one meal? *Should I avert my gaze or look at him? What do I say if he asks, "Is this your first meal today?" Calm down. All I need to say is, "Yes sir, first meal, first meal." Raymond knows it too.*

Dan drops his cigarette on the floor and stomps it out, "Be here tomorrow at one."

"Sir?"

"Yes. What? Did you not understand me?"

"No. Yes. I understand. I understood. But, on Friday and Saturday, I work a different job."

"Where? Where do you work?"

"Crazy Zebra."

"Oh. No. No. No," he says. "Not the Crazy Zebra. Don't work there. Quit that job. It's not a nice place. You don't want to work there."

"Sir?"

"They have wet T-shirt contests there. Here, we serve ninety-nine different kinds of beer, twelve on tap. We have live jazz seven nights a week. Best jazz club in town. Mick Jagger, Rod Stewart come here when they're in town. They don't go to Crazy Zebra. You should not work there." I look down at the floor and I see the embers in his cigarette redden.

"I need the hours," I say. I don't know what wet T-shirt contests are. Must be something really bad.

"You are quite the negotiator, Adem. Okay. More hours. I'll give you the hours!" he yells. I can't tell if he's angry, or annoyed, or just loud. "Quit that job."

After he leaves the kitchen, I stomp back down on the cigarette and sweep it up. Then I pull out my pocket dictionary and look up "negotiator."

A few minutes later Paul calls everyone together to the bar. I wrap my sandwich up in a paper towel and join the crew. Dan locks the door as the waitstaff gather and then, just like the night before, he serves up beers. As he hands the last one out, he starts to rant. "Unbelievable! How could anyone!" he yells. I gather this is a nightly ritual.

***

On my way to work Friday afternoon, I stop at Crazy Zebra to quit and collect my paycheck. The manager mumbles something and hands me $120 in cash for two weekends of work. I pocket the money and, as I walk up the street to the Blues Saloon, wonder if I've made a huge mistake. *What if Dan changes his mind again? First he said he couldn't afford me, then two days later he said he'd give me more hours. What if he breaks his promise? Too late, I already quit. I shouldn't have put blind trust in this man I don't know. I did it with Soner and look what happened. When will I learn?*

***

What I do learn, and quickly, is that Dan has anger issues. But he's good for his word. He increases my hours to forty-five a week. I'll be earning $140 a week, which means I can now pay Roberto rent for using his room. *This is good! I've jumped from an initial twenty hours of work to forty-five in just three days!* I'm surprised by a feeling of accomplishment. I don't have much. But I'm . . . happy.

My job is basically doing anything Dan needs done that doesn't fall under anyone else's job description: dishwashing, setting up the stage for live music, troubleshooting the central A/C system, and even fixing the six-foot-tall espresso machine, which breaks often. Every time I fix something, Dan's list for me gets longer. I help carry in the supplies from delivery trucks. I straighten and bus the tables. After closing, I collect all the trash and take it out to the curb for overnight collection. I help Dan put in a brick-and-concrete patio in the courtyard using the bricks I piled "flush" my first day. We add tables and chairs there, and some plants in pots.

***

During class break, I write to my parents. I keep it basic: All is well, I'm learning English, I have a job, here's my address. I give them the address for the Blues Saloon.

After four weeks, I'm averaging sixty-hour workweeks at the Blues Saloon. I'm earning about $750 a month before taxes in salary and another $50 a week from the tip jar. The waitstaff carve out fifteen percent of their tips for the kitchen staff, which I find surprisingly generous.

I start managing the food, drink, and supply inventory. On Sunday nights, I go through the shelves and fridges and mark what Dan should order and how much on a spreadsheet I designed. I drew it on graph paper I got from school and made copies at the school library. Until this spreadsheet, the bar would run out of food, supplies, and liquor by midweek, every week. Once the new system is in place, we run out of nothing.

During bar hours, my main job is dishwasher. Wearing rubber gloves, I scrub Raymond's large pots in a deep double sink. I also load and unload the industrial dishwasher all night long. After a few weeks, I develop a system that allows for speed. Sometimes members of the waitstaff dawdle in the kitchen just to watch how quickly I can load and unload without breaking anything.

Since Dan took so positively to my spreadsheet idea, I decide to make another suggestion: Serve beer in frozen mugs. At the Istanbul Horse Club, they served cold drinks in frozen glasses, and hot drinks, like tea and coffee, in preheated glasses or cups. Apparently, it helps the drinks retain their flavor. It's also good customer service.

Dan likes the idea and implements it immediately. Customer feedback on the frozen mugs is as immediate as Dan's implementation. Everyone loves it. I don't remember if anybody ever took my advice in Istanbul. Except for the kids I tutored. And Francesca. She did almost anything I suggested.

5

WALK IN THE PARK

I continue to think of improvements to the bar. I can't read Dan. He seems to like my ideas—most, he allows me to implement—but I don't think he respects me. While I don't need his respect, it would be nice, since I'm helping him save and make money. That said, I'm grateful I have a job that pays over $900 per month, nine times what I made in Istanbul. Of course, I still can't afford my own apartment because it costs so much to live here.

Most of the ideas I come up with are based on life in Istanbul; they are not original at all. But, since I'm Dan's first Turkish employee, my ideas are apparently brand new to him. Another idea comes to me on the last day of the Cherry Blossom Festival, in mid-April. It's a madhouse at the bar and the situation is further maddened by the lack of a communication system. The bartenders tell waitstaff they need ice at the bar, or beer mugs, or glasses, or silverware. The waitstaff has to stop what they're doing, cut through the crowd, and go into the kitchen to find me to tell me what they need out front and then return to work, even more harried, as they slice back through the crowd to wait on customers.

It occurs to me that the Blues Saloon could use what my parents' apartment building installed for the tenants to call the building's custodian to their unit. They use an electro-mechanical system to easily reach him at the push of a button that's in their apartment. The custodian hears the ring down in his office in the basement, along with the tenant's apartment number, which appears on a split-flap display, kind of like the one airports use to post arrivals and departures.

I spend a few hours designing the system for the bar. Then I spend an hour double-checking my work. I know the idea is a good one, but I'm still nervous. Dan simply makes me nervous. I feel like I'm walking a fine line between helping him with my ideas and offending him. I have several ideas at the ready, but decide to spread them out over time; I'm afraid he might take my ideas as criticism and fire me.

Two days after the craziness of the Cherry Blossom Festival, I grab my designs and knock on Dan's office door.

"Adem! What's up?"

"I have an idea for better communication," I say. "Can I tell you? Is now good?"

"Classic. The guy who can't speak English comes up with a communication system. This oughta be good. Shoot." The first time I heard Dan use this word, I looked it up in my pocket dictionary but was still confused. Raymond had to explain it to me.

"Okay. Well, um," I bumble. *On with it, man!* "Right now, bartender communicates with kitchen staff by sending waitstaff to the kitchen. It's wasted time for staff and bartender." I look at Dan's face. His hand is on his chin, stroking his beard, and he looks bored. I take a breath. Then, I slide the drawing of the design over to him. He moves his elbows and looks down. "I can design system with two light panels, one at bar and other in kitchen— four lights each. Bartender can turn on one or more light switch for fifteen different things. Signal goes to kitchen: ice, mugs, glasses, bring mop and broom, anything. You decide."

"Huh!" Dan says, sounding pleasantly surprised. He looks up from the drawing. "You could build this?"

"I can. I just need electrician to bring supplies and run wires. Man doing wire fix on stage can do. No more than one day to install. This is what I need."

I hand Dan a list of supplies. I am trying to act calm, though I'm shaking.

"Ah, so you came prepared," he says, taking the list. "Getting a little cocky, Adem? You thought I'd say yes."

"Yes sir," I say, though I don't know the word "cocky."

"Okay, let's do it. Make this happen. Now, go back to work."

I grab my papers and walk out of his office. In the hallway, I pull out my dictionary and look up "cocky." *Great, I've just agreed with Dan that I'm conceited.*

A week later, the system is installed. On the inaugural night, I hand out a cheat sheet with the light combinations and their meanings. I've built in nine different requests, including "bring the mop and broom," "clear the tables," "bring ice," and "bring glasses." The new digital system is a hit. At the end of the night, Dan launches into his nightly debriefing, pacing back and forth behind the bar, venting to the waitstaff about all their errors, picking on them, asking each one how they could be in college when they are clearly incredibly dumb. He sounds more agitated than usual. And then, he stops. A smile creeps onto his face. "On a positive note, the only one of the night, maybe even the week, see this marvelous equipment?" he asks, rhetorically, pointing to the box of light-and-switch pairs I designed. I look down, feeling uncomfortable in anticipation of the kudos Dan is about to deliver publicly. He says, "Our electrician Jack came up with this brilliant idea." He bangs his hand on the counter in excitement. "Jack saved us a lot of money and time and your energy by virtually eliminating all those trips back and forth into the kitchen."

My face gets hot as anger bubbles up inside. *What? But . . . why would Dan do that? Clearly, he knows I designed the system. But what can I do? Keep mouth shut. Saying something could cost me my job.* I say nothing.

***

While it's not all good, my routine seems to be working. Every weekday after school, I walk through the park to Georgetown. I keep my head down as I make my way down the brick sidewalks to the Blues Saloon. Pretty much every day, I see the same yellow Volkswagen Bug warning passersby that "The

End Is Near!"—a message that's blasted out through a pair of megaphones fastened to the hood. A sign on the roof reads "Repent and Turn to God." There are also always Hare Krishna, whose bald heads blend in with those of the shaved-head punk kids; together, but separately, they loiter. At night, the noise of drunk college kids mixes in with the religious chants and the beating on upside-down plastic buckets by younger teenagers who sing and recite poetry to the rhythm. "Rap music," people call it. "A new fad."

On weekdays, the Blues Saloon closes at 2:00 a.m., on weekends at 3:00. I continue to wait out the daily reopening of the Metro on a bench in Dupont Circle before heading back to Roberto's for a shower and a quick nap. Night after night, as I try to stay awake, I assess my life. I've learned that sitting on a park bench with my eyes closed is allowed but lying down with eyes closed is not. On the few occasions that I've succumbed to exhaustion, lain down, and dozed off, I've been poked awake by a police officer. I don't know if it's the same officer every time; I apologize regardless.

Sometimes, one well-dressed man or another comes around and asks me to come to his place in one of those upscale residential buildings around the circle. "You can take a shower, I have clothes for you, food and money too," they tell me. Sometimes the offer of money comes first; sometimes it's food. "No sir, thank you," I say each time. While homosexuality is not uncommon in Istanbul, I'm surprised about being solicited; and I'm even more surprised by the different reactions. Some move on with a quick, "Your loss, kid" or "Think about it, I'll be back tomorrow." Others get angry: "I'm trying to help you here, you stupid moron! You deserve to live and die on the streets!"

So, I sit on a bench in the park in the early morning hours, in the silence of the city, and think about my life in America. I'm almost twenty-three, an engineer with a degree from Turkey's premiere university working as a dishwasher, getting solicited by men in a Washington, DC park at three thirty in the morning, trying to stay awake on a bench in Dupont Circle. Is this the American dream I longed for? Why have I come here? To do *this*? What have I done to myself? Nobody in my family attempted such a fool's errand. All my friends, eventually even Demir, told me I shouldn't go to America, that it was a bad idea. They told me I couldn't do it. Is that why I did it, to prove them wrong?

Right now, I should regret that I ever came to America; that would make sense. But I don't regret it. Not because I don't want to accept defeat or I'm too proud to admit it, but because I'm happy here. I was happy the moment I stepped foot in America.

I feel free here. Despite being hungry and tired and poor, I'm happy. No one knows me here, or my troubles. I have created an honest, fresh start. There's no one looking over my shoulder, expecting me to be a certain way. There's no Savas Kartal being released from his prison cell and coming after me.

There are no reminders of Francesca here, either. Not her eyes to look at, nor her hand to hold, nor her neck to smell, nor her legs to put my head on, nor her clothing, her hair, or her grace to think of, nor her lips to kiss. No dinners, no bike rides, no swimming to remember. She is a princess and I'm a pauper. I laugh out loud at my realization and one of the homeless men looks up at me. *Francesca!* That time seems as far away as the stars. *Am I as happy here, living the way I'm living, as I was during our four weeks together?* I think for a minute. Only a minute. *I'm happy.* It's a different kind of happy. I have goals, my own goals.

On the bench I think and try not to sleep. On the train, I sleep and try not to think. Once I went all the way to the train depot and woke up there. The conductor must have shirked his duty and not checked the cars at the end of the line in Silver Spring. When I woke up, still groggy, I was confused about where I was. Outside the train car, as far as my eyes could see, there were trains. I pried open the door, jumped down off the train onto the tracks and walked back to the station. If I hadn't gotten a pebble in my shoe, which I pulled out and put in my pocket, I would have thought it was a dream.

***

At the Blues Saloon, as if to thank me for the new communication system that he'd failed to give me credit for, Dan increases my food allowance. "Three meals a day on me, Addo," Dan says. "It's like a raise, but without the big pinch of the taxman." He's right. While it might not be extra money coming in, it means a lot less money going out. Plus, eating three full meals, not my scrimp-and-save apple-and-quart-of-milk meals, will help me put on some much-needed weight.

"Don't get cocky now, Addo," Dan continues, "you have a ways to go in this new world."

I'm spending so much time at the Blues Saloon that it almost feels like home. But, instead of worrying that my parents will pick on me for my failures, I worry that Dan will make me the focus of one of his tirades. I'm convinced that he's going to fire me for something about which I am fully unaware; or even for something someone else did.

Paul is my favorite person at the bar. I still have difficulty believing he gave that paper napkin with my contact information to Dan. The more I get to know him, however, the more I realize he'd do it again for the next guy; that's just who he is. Raymond tells me Paul is way overqualified to be working as a bartender. He has an economics degree from the University of Pennsylvania. Because he couldn't get a job in his field in New York, or even Philadelphia, he came to DC, hoping to work for the government. His bartending gig at the Blues Saloon was supposed to be temporary. He's been there for more than a year.

After Paul, Raymond is my favorite person at the bar. He teaches me how to cook and plate food. When it's busy, he uses me as his sous-chef. And he's my biggest champion, bragging to anyone who will listen that I have a degree in engineering and I can fix or build anything. I think he knows the communications system was my idea, not the electrician's. I hear him bragging about me to a new member of the waitstaff. "Adem fixed the coffee maker last week and the A/C the week before. Really he can fix anything." I wonder how different my life would have been if Raymond had been my dad.

I don't know if it's because of Raymond's overindulgent compliments, but the girls who work at the Blues Saloon are starting to act interested in me. It's more than even "acting" interested; they are outright asking me out. Coffee, movies, parties, walks, bowling. I've been invited for "sleepovers" by at least three women on the waitstaff. Another two have asked me if they can spend the night at my place. I'm not sure how to explain that I don't have a place, and that I have no extra money to spend, or time to date. It's not that I don't know what to say or how to say it, it's that I'm too embarrassed to tell them why I always say, "No thank you."

After a few weeks and some advice from Raymond, I start hemming and hawing around facts until I finally just tell each girl the reason for turning them down. "I'm a dishwasher trying to get myself established in America," I confess. "I have no time or money to go out on a date." To my astonishment, my honesty makes them *more* interested! They are the opposite of every girl I ever knew in Istanbul, except Francesca. They simply disagree that my reasons are a problem for them. I compromise with them, "I promise, as soon as I have enough money to rent a place, we'll go to the movies." That seems to appease them.

I know I'm missing out by not socializing. But I need to save money. And time is money. A walk doesn't cost anything, but it takes time and I just don't have any to spare. I've never been this focused or directed my entire life. I need $15,000 for graduate school. To earn that, I have to work for more than five thousand hours at my current pay, and that doesn't include what I need to live. Even if I live on half my income, it will take three years to save $15,000—too long already. So, if I went to the movies, I would miss out on three to four hours of work and have to pay for the movie too. The result would be a net loss of $25. I can't stomach an expense like that.

Some mornings, I don't go all the way to Roberto's and this saves me even more money and time. I've left an extra set of clothes at the Blues Saloon for these mornings. After I get off at 2:00 a.m., I wash up in the bathroom and change my clothes. Then I walk to Dupont Circle. I've gotten pretty good at sleeping while sitting up, so the cops won't poke me.

At 6:00 a.m., I walk over to school and wait in the student lounge for the first class to start. I do homework or read the paper, which is provided for free, referring back to my pocket dictionary frequently. I consider reading the paper to be a kind of homework. It helps me learn new words and gets me better acquainted with American culture, issues, and politics.

I'm 100 percent immersed in the English language. Except for the letters I get from Dad and the ones I write back, I don't think about the Turkish language at all. I haven't spoken Turkish since talking to Eliz on the phone after Demir left. I think I've even started dreaming in English, which everyone at the language school says is a sign of proficiency.

My dad sends a letter a week, which I receive at the bar. He's never communicated with me this much in my life. He tells me about Mom and my sisters and Ela's new baby and updates me on the political situation in Turkey. He closes each letter by acknowledging how hard I am working in response to the updates I give him about my schedule. It's quite a switch for me to hear positives from him; I relish his missives. Once a month, I write back, using scrap paper and discarded envelopes I collect from Dan's office garbage bin. An airmail stamp costs thirty-three cents, so it's good that I don't have to buy the paper, too. When Dan finds out that I'm using his discarded mail to write to my father, he gives me a stack of fresh envelopes and paper and a roll of stamps from the post office.

The gesture is so kind that I wonder if I've been too quick to judge Dan. But then, he goes on a screaming rampage and I realize he's Mr. Nice Guy only about 10 percent of the time. The rest of the time, he rages. It seems that every night he chooses another victim to pick on. It doesn't bother me all that much. I've seen worse. Anyone should be able to endure someone like Dan, especially when he's their lifeline, like Dan is for me.

6

SWEET HOME

It's been six months since I arrived in the US and two months since I started at the Blues Saloon. I think I've done okay so far. I have a job. My English is improving. I'm saving money. But I worry about how long it will take to get to the next step, the next level. Can I even get to the next level? I mean, if I were still working at the Blues Saloon ten years from now, that wouldn't be a sign of succeeding at the American dream, would it? Or, maybe it would be. I'd be here, in America. So, who measures what the American dream looks like? Why couldn't that be it? Of course, if that's my only goal, it would mean ten more years of dealing with Dan's mood swings.

I've saved $1,221.23 and it's earning 6.5 percent interest in the bank. As my savings increases, I decide to make a psychological shift, to round the money to the nearest ten. So, on week thirteen of my employment, I announce to myself, "You have $1,220 to your name, Adem Bayer." I toast myself with a cup of tea.

I also decide it's time for me to stop relying on Roberto's kindness and find a place of my own, an inexpensive rental that's near work and school. While it means a big outlay of money, monthly, it will also help me save. If

I can walk to and from work and school, I won't have to pay $1.30 each day on Metro and bus expenses. Having a place of my own that I can walk to would also mean that I could go home and sleep right after work each night rather than sitting in the park, waiting for the rest of the world to wake up. It would help move me forward one small step. It's a minor shift, but I know it's important. Moving forward is important.

I go through the *Post* at school and find a listing for a room in a row house in Adams Morgan. I look at the map I bought in the airport my first night in DC and plot out the routes I would take to work and to school. I calculate the distances and determine it would only be a twenty-minute walk to Georgetown and twenty-five-minute walk to my ESL class. The location is perfect. I make an appointment to see the room.

I arrive five minutes early and find myself standing in front of a majestic, white, three-story row house. It has large windows covered with black iron bars on the first floor. Five brick steps lead to a portico and glass door behind ornate black ironwork.

I use the extra five minutes to walk around the corner to check out the neighborhood. There's a 7-Eleven and two large apartment buildings facing the main road. The rest of the street is lined with colonial-style row houses. I wonder what it would be like to live in this neighborhood.

At exactly 12:30, I ring the bell.

After about a minute, an old lady opens the door.

"Hello ma'am. I am Adem Bayer. We spoke. I am here to see the room for rent." I smile and hold out my hand politely and she ignores my gesture. "Ten bedrooms," she says, as if in answer to a question I haven't asked. "The one available is in the basement."

She turns and walks into the foyer and then continues into a large room. I am still standing on the stoop; the front door is open. She hasn't welcomed me in and I'm not sure what to do. So, I just stand there.

"Come," she says in a scolding voice. I step into the foyer and shut the front door behind me, then walk into the room she's standing in. The space is decorated like a nineteenth-century European parlor, ripe with old carpets and throws. The air in the room feels musty. *Is the whole house going to smell this way?* The windows are draped in long, thick, dark curtains, with sheers behind them. A sliver of light sneaks out between the drawn curtains and dust mites dance. The ceiling is high, the furniture heavy yet fragile looking. It feels and looks like time has frozen inside the four walls.

"I am Mrs. Hardwick," the old lady tells me, breaking the silence. *Oh my how she fits right into her home's decor.* "Follow me," she commands, looking at me over the rims of her eyeglasses. Then, she turns swiftly, her long gray hair and one-piece hippie-style dress flowing behind her. "This room is not for my renters," she says, her abruptness abrasive. I nod in understanding. Despite her demeanor, I decide to like her.

Mrs. Hardwick leads me down a dark stairway to the basement and then down a wide, concrete hallway. The floor is painted dark red. *An odd choice.* She opens a door and we walk through the boiler room and out a door on the far side of the room. "This is the room for rent," she says in a monotone. "You want it?"

"May I look around for a minute, please?" I ask, smiling, hoping to not offend her. I can't tell if she's annoyed. She holds up her hand, motioning me to step in. She stays in the hallway as I peer around the room. It's surprisingly large. The walls are brick but painted cotton-candy pink. The floor is concrete and red here, too. There are two gray carpet runners on the floor on either side of a twin bed. Overhead are a bunch of exposed pipes that look like fuel lines. There is a large dresser, a nice-size coffee table, and a writing desk with a pull-up storage compartment and pigeonholes. Old furniture, but simple and comfortable. There are two windows with pull-down shades, facing a brick wall on the other side of a narrow alley that allows a little light to stream into the room. I peer out the window into the sliver of sun.

Next to the windows is a door. I look back at the woman.

"Open it," she says in response to my glance.

"You can put a chair out there and sit," she says, pointing in the direction of an overgrown garden, fenced in from the houses on either side and an alley at the end. I step outside to look down the alley. "You have no kitchen, but that small fridge," she says, speaking loudly. I come back inside and walk to the fridge, which sits in the corner at an angle. I open it to look inside, wondering if I'll find some old, forgotten food, green with mold and stench. It's empty and has stains but doesn't smell.

She gestures to the opposite corner of the room and points to another door. "Inside that door is the room that has the fuel oil tank. The rooms down here have no heating or air conditioning. On cold days, you may use the natural gas heater," she says, pointing to an uncovered heater propped against the wall next to the patio door. It looks like both a carbon monoxide hazard and a fire hazard.

Basically, the room is between the fuel oil tank and the furnace room and has an open flame gas fireplace.

"I'll take it."

"The rules," she says, counting on her fingers. "One, the rent is non-negotiable $110 per month—cash, upfront, no security deposit. Two, no guests are allowed, whatsoever, ever. Three, you will share the bathroom with the other basement dweller. Four, on the second floor, there's a public pay phone. You may use it until you get your own phone in the room. You need change to place calls. If you need to make an international call, you need a lot of change."

I think about how nice it will be to be able to call my parents once a month.

I hand her $110 in cash, despite my concerns about the fire hazard or dying in my sleep from carbon monoxide poisoning. I can't afford anything more, and from what I saw in the paper, this is by far the cheapest room available. The others start at $200 a month.

The house is in a great location, directly behind the Washington Hilton. My commute to school, then to work and back here—back "home"—will make a perfect triangle.

"You can move in on the first of the month. Or today, if you give me another $30."

"I'll move today," I reply, handing over the additional $30. I don't have much to move, just my suitcase and books.

"Let me introduce you to your neighbor."

We walk back through the furnace room to the neighbor's room. Mrs. Hardwick knocks on the door. "Dr. Tiller?"

"Come in!" comes a voice from the other side of the door.

"Dr. Tiller, this is Mr. Bayer. Mr. Bayer, this is Dr. Tiller."

"Adem," I say. "Nice to meet you, sir." Dr. Tiller is a frail, old man with white hair. He looks at least eighty years old.

"Dr. Tiller, Adem is going to rent the other room down here."

He smiles at me. "Welcome, Adem. Nice to meet you," he says, staying seated.

"Nice to meet you too, sir."

"Call me Harry."

"Okay . . . Harry."

I wonder what kind of a doctor he is. Medical? Or it is a friendly nickname he earned because he knows a lot? I peer past Dr. Tiller into his room. It looks much smaller than my new room and has no windows. His rent must be even cheaper. *Why does he live here?*

***

On my first night in my new home, I return to my room from the Blues Saloon as early as 3:00 a.m., even after Dan's nightly rant and a beer. It takes only twenty minutes, door to door, walking through Dupont Circle without stopping. *No longer will I need to stop myself from falling asleep on a bench in the park while waiting to take the Metro home.* I've taken a step forward.

I'm out of a hot shower and in bed by 4:00 a.m. that first morning, smiling as I stretch my body out on the bed. I fall asleep looking up at the fuel oil pipes, hoping they won't leak, while calculating how much more sleep I'm going to get in my new home.

I sleep for four straight hours despite a metal spring that pops out through a hole in the mattress on the right side. It's the most continuous sleep I've gotten in three months. I head out the door to walk to my ESL class with a smile on my face.

When I get to school Roberto comes and gives me a huge hug. "I missed you this morning, man. I got used to our morning chats."

I hug Roberto back and thank him profusely for letting me sleep in his room, telling him if it hadn't been for him rescuing me, I would have been sleeping on the streets. "I know, it's not been easy, but I do appreciate your letting me stay with you. Thanks, man."

"Sure, man, any time. My room is your room."

That afternoon, I join a group of students from class to have a picnic at

McPherson Square and we play a little soccer after. I haven't lost my touch.

And, I can't stop smiling.

***

On the second morning in my new home, I walk past my neighbor's door on my way out and find it open. I keep my head down, forcibly focusing my eyes at the end of the hallway, so I don't peek in. "Adem!" Dr. Tiller calls out.

"Yes, sir?" I say, stopping just past the door.

"Come here. Come in. And, please, call me Harry."

I look at my watch, then turn around and stand in the doorway, feeling awkward about Dr. Tiller, who is unshaven and sitting in a drab robe in his windowless room. He's surrounded by shopping bags with paper products and other household supplies; there is little room for me to stand.

"Adem, would you go to 7-Eleven for me? It's right around the corner. I just need a few things and my arthritis is acting up this morning. Hurts to move."

I look at my watch again, then realize that's a rude thing to do. "I would be happy to, sir," I say, pretending to be fixing my cuff, not looking at my watch. I'm still not comfortable calling him by his first name. "I am sorry, I cannot do it right now, though," I say with a smile and then a frown. "I go to class now. But, if you can wait, I will come back home at 1:00 p.m. and go shopping."

"Great!" he says, looking up at me from his hunched over position, strands of white hair sticking out all over his head. "I'll see you then."

***

After class I'm invited for another picnic in the park, but I feel the pull of Dr. Tiller waiting for me and my food delivery, so I beg off and head right home.

Dr. Tiller's door is ajar, again, when I return. "Adem," he says, after I knock softly. "Come." I push open the door, slowly.

"Did you have a good class?" he asks. "Did you learn all of the American curse words yet?" I smile. "Nah, I bet they don't teach you that at school. I'll teach you! That'll be *my* job."

"Okay sir."

"Would you be a pal and go to the 7-Eleven and buy a box of Ritz crackers, a bottle of French's mustard, and two hot dog sandwiches . . . Also a bag of potato chips? Get yourself something, too. On me," he says, handing me a few crumpled bills, but mostly change. "Can you stay and eat lunch with me? I'd love the company."

I look at my watch. I have to be at work at two today. "Yes sir. I can stay for thirty minutes, then I go to work."

I order a couple of hot dogs for myself and pick up a box of Entenmann's chocolate chip cookies. I swallow hard at the price of the items as I walk through the aisle. *You can't let that man buy you food, Adem. He might have less money than you.* I find the box of crackers and mustard Dr. Tiller wanted and head to the checkout.

"$9.20, hon," the blond lady behind the cash register says, smiling at me, as she wraps the hot dog sandwiches in aluminum foil. I wonder why Americans shorten and slur so many of their words. "J'eet yet?" and "Just a sec." I can understand it saves a little time. But how much time, really? The shortening of names confounds me even more. Dan has started calling me Addo. Is this about efficiency or affection? Daniel is Dan. William is Bill, sometimes Billy, or Will? Robert is Rob or sometimes even Bob. Elizabeth becomes Liz or Beth. I dig into my back pocket for my wallet, bypassing Dr. Tiller's crumpled bills and change I've stashed in my front pocket, and pull out a $10.

I head back to Dr. Tiller's with the food, then heat up some water on a hot pot I've purchased and return with two mugs of tea. Dr. Tiller pats the rotating bar stool next to him. I sit down, awkwardly trying to make room for my feet among the shopping bags on the floor. There's no room for a real table, so we rest our food on a small table next to the only chair he has in the room. I leave his money on the table. He picks up a hot dog sandwich and, as he's unwrapping the aluminum foil, he looks up and thanks me. I watch as he crushes some crackers onto his hot dog, then tops it off with mustard.

We chat while we eat, his TV flashing in the background, the sound off. I glance at the screen every once in a while, and it reminds me of home—the black-and-white picture switching indiscriminately between reception and snow.

"So Adem, tell me about yourself," Dr. Tiller says. "It's Adem, not Adam, pronounced Adem right?"

"Yes, sir. In Turkish Adem means Adam, and Adam means man."

"What's Bayer mean? Is it German?"

"No. not German. No. It is a different word in Turkish. 'Bay' means mister and 'er' means soldier," I say.

"You mean like 'soldier on'?" Dr. Tiller asks, holding up his fingers like quotation marks.

"What does that mean, sir?"

"It means resolve, determination, tenacity, not giving up. Interesting that your Turkish names have meaning. Interesting." I don't really know what Harry means, but when he laughs, I laugh along with him. "So, did you learn to speak English back home?"

"No sir. I learned it here. I arrived six months ago unable to speak. I knew only a few hundred words."

"Well, your English is mighty good, young man. I'm impressed."

"Thank you sir," I say, smiling.

I tell him about the Blues Saloon and school, giving him abbreviated answers, wanting to save time to learn about him. "And you, Dr. Tiller? What is your story?" I ask, then take a bite of my hot dog.

"Well, let's see, I'm eighty-two years old. I have a PhD in physics, specialized in quantum physics and unification theory. From Princeton and from Berkeley."

"Unification theory?" I ask. I'm slow to digest his words. *Wait. What? Physics, PhD, Princeton, Berkeley. What?*

"Right. Yes," he says.

"Quantum physics? Albert Einstein quantum physics?" I ask, incredulous, sure I must not be understanding his English correctly.

"Yes indeed. Boy, you are a smart fellow. I was a student of Albert Einstein's at Princeton." I stop chewing. *Dr. Tiller was taught by Albert Einstein?* "Then I went on to Berkeley. During the war, I was at Los Alamos. I helped build the bomb."

"*The* bomb?"

"Yes. Did you study World War II in school?"

"Yes sir."

"Well, I bet your history books didn't tell you that the Japanese didn't believe we could build a bomb that would wipe out an entire city."

"No sir. I did not know that."

"Well, so the Americans, we dropped the first bomb. Then, we asked them, again, to stop the war. The Japanese didn't believe we had another one, so they didn't stop. We dropped the second bomb. And we immediately told them that we had a third one."

"Was there a third one?" I ask, trying to remember my history lessons.

"No. The third one was being built, but it was months and months away from being finished. We were bluffing. But, then Japan surrendered."

"Yes sir."

"You know, seven years later, after Hiroshima and Nagasaki, I went to Japan. I'd read so much about the aftermath; I wanted to go and see it. I needed to see it. It was 1952. The remains of destruction were still terrible. The bomb that I helped make; I had done that. After that, I returned to the US and decided not to do physics anymore."

I don't know what to say.

***

On my walk to the Blues Saloon, I can't get Dr. Tiller's story out of my head. *Einstein was his teacher? He helped build the bomb? Did he go mad after visiting Hiroshima, is that why he lives the way he does? Or maybe it's all made up. Maybe he's insane.*

I understand, intellectually, that being smart and being educated doesn't equal being rich. That's not the formula. I know it very well from my dad—smart, educated, but not rich. But how is Dr. Tiller, if he is, indeed, who he says he is, living in a basement room with no windows? How can that be his formula? How can a man who was taught by Albert Einstein, the father of *the* formula, $e = mc2$, be living in basic squalor? I know for certain I don't want to end up like Dr. Tiller. But is being rich what I want? Isn't what my parents have enough? Yet I don't want to be poor and alone in my eighties, that is—if I live that long. I can hardly believe I've made it to twenty-three.

7

GOT A LIGHT?

SEVERAL TIMES A WEEK, IN BETWEEN SCHOOL AND WORK, DR. Tiller and I have tea together. Our conversations are mostly science related. His stories about physics and research provide me with a whole new category of words I don't think I'd ever learn in my conversational English classes. He teaches me physics terms like *distance, velocity, acceleration,* and *derivative,* just in a few seconds.

He helps me with my intonation and pronunciation, like "this" versus "thistle," and has fun trying to explain English idioms. My favorite is "whatnot," which I find to be completely nonsensical. "Every now and then" and "time and again" make a lot more sense to me.

Dr. Tiller also tells me stories about his life. "Two-thirds of my right lung is gone," he says one day, unbuttoning his shirt to show me the scar on his chest. I don't want to see his scar, but I don't want to be rude. He launches into the story of how he got shot at a bar in Texas, seemingly having forgotten that his shirt is unbuttoned. I try to keep my head up because each time I glance at the long, jagged scar, I get dizzy and nauseous. "I drew my gun. Shot and killed him. In the forehead. Didn't even go to jail. Self-defense. Then I started taking pictures of naked women. Started as a hobby and grew into a career. I worked for years full time for a magazine. Got me into a lot of trouble," he says, laughing. I'm not completely clear on what he means by that.

"I traveled the world, taking pictures of naked women. It was fun. Liked it better than physics. I never got married. I have no children, and never saved any money. And I don't regret it."

I come to not only enjoy my time with Dr. Tiller, but relish it, even rely on it.

Once a week, Dr. Tiller asks me to get us hot dogs from 7-Eleven. I come to like the odd combination of flavors—the spicy crunch of the overcooked hot dog, the sweet dryness of the Ritz crackers, and the sourness of the mustard. With each trip, I wonder if our weekly ritual is the only real food Dr. Tiller eats. I wonder if he ever goes outside and sees sunshine.

About a month after our hot dog dates become a sort of ritual, as Dr. Tiller painstakingly counts coins that he's poured out from a jar onto his nightstand, I decide once again to pay for our basement picnic and lift my hand to stop him. "My treat," I say. He smiles and nods but doesn't say a word. "I'll be right back with our picnic!"

When I return to his room, I notice a small TV on the floor in the corner. His room is like a museum; I see something new each time. I look up from the TV and realize Dr. Tiller has caught me staring at it.

"You want it? It's an extra. I don't use it."

"Excuse me, sir?"

"The TV. Do you want the TV? I have two. I don't use that one. It's an Admiral, a good brand. It works, but the knob is broken. You just have to change the channels using these pliers. I will give you the pliers for free. Thirty-five dollars."

"Really?"

"Yes, indeed. I don't need two TV's. You can take it now and pay later—it's okay."

"I can pay now," I say. I walk to my room and grab $35 from my desk drawer, my tip earnings, which I try to live on. My paychecks, I try not to touch; that money goes straight to the bank as savings.

A couple of minutes before my usual one thirty departure, I bring the TV to my room. I place it on the dresser then plug it in and turn it on—just to check it out. A *Love Boat* rerun is on. "Four channels, sometimes five; that's all you'll get using these rabbit ear antennas," Dr. Tiller had said. That's plenty good; in Turkey there was only one channel. As I adjust the rabbit ears, Gopher comes into focus. I turn the TV off and head out to work, looking forward to coming home and watching TV.

***

My afternoon at the Blues Saloon begins with me up on a ladder cleaning the windows. It feels good to be outside in the sunshine rather than in the dark bar where it always feels like it's nighttime, even in the middle of the afternoon. M Street is busy as usual, and the mix of people makes me smile. I watch a Corvette tailgate a laundry truck. "Just like in Istanbul," I think. Except that it would probably be a Lamborghini following a horse-drawn carriage loaded with melons. I chuckle out loud as a Native American man dressed in traditional garb passes a pink-haired punk wearing all black. Neither seems to regard the other as odd or different.

As I climb down the ladder, I first hear then see the yellow Volkswagen Bug parading. "Repent and turn to God. The end is near!" echoes from the speakers. The car turns down a side street, and the haunting chants of the Krishnas replace the fading messages blasting from the "repent car."

I'm about to fold up the ladder when I notice a tall, well-dressed man followed by what looks like a couple of bodyguards in dark suits and sunglasses crossing the street; they turn and head toward me. The man approaches, smiling, holds out his hand, looks me in the eye, "Good afternoon, I'm DC's mayor, Matthew Howard, and I'm running for reelection. Can I count on your vote?"

I can't vote, but can't say that, so I just smile and shake his hand. He thanks me and moves on. I watch as the mayor continues down the street, stopping people and shaking their hands too. *What a country.*

"What's with that goofy grin, Adem?" Paul asks as I walk back into the bar.

"I just met the mayor. The mayor! Came right up to me and shook my

241

hand. Quite a country you have here," I say.

"Ah. Well, you may not be able to vote yet, but as far as I'm concerned, it's your country too. America is home."

I wipe the goofy grin off my face and smile back sincerely. "Yes . . . home. This is my home."

The longer I'm in the US, the more I come to love it. I hope they'll let me stay—whoever "they" is.

***

The evening crowd begins to trickle in at six and a few hours later, the band takes the stage. It's a fairly quiet evening by Blues Saloon standards and the night moves quickly. At 2:00 a.m., I watch Dan gently lead the last remaining patrons to the front door as they beg, "one more drink, one real last one, promise." I grab a gray tub to bus their empty glasses and a few plates with half-eaten appetizers and then head to the kitchen to finish up my nightly routine. I drag the trash cans out from the alley to the street, wash up, have a quick turkey sandwich, and join the rest of the staff, who are already at the bar for the nightly "beer and berating," as some of the waitstaff have started calling it.

It's 3:00 a.m. by the time I begin my walk home across P Street and through the park at Dupont Circle. I'm looking forward to turning on my new, old TV and falling asleep to reruns. The streets are empty, except for a dozen or so homeless men in the park. I keep my head down and don't bother them.

Just past the circle, I notice a man standing under a tree next to the entrance to a small parking lot. He looks to be about my height but is big, like a bouncer. "Hey man, you got a light?" he calls out as I approach.

"Ah. Yes, 'a light,' " I say, walking over to him, holding out my arm to hand him a book of matches from the Blues Saloon. He grabs my forearm and pulls me into a headlock. A second man appears out of nowhere and sucker punches me. The bouncer throws me onto the sidewalk, and someone starts kicking me on the head. I try balling up to protect myself. They kick my head, face, ribs, then my face again. A third man appears.

"Give me all your money," one of them says.

"No money," I moan. "I'm poor."

I don't fight back. One man holds my arms as another digs through my pockets. They fish out my wallet. As they pull out and count the four dollars I have, I see a white car parked on the opposite side of the street. There's a woman sitting in the front seat, watching us through a closed window. We briefly make eye contact, right before I receive another kick in the face. The woman doesn't move, she doesn't even blink. They continue to use my head as a soccer ball until someone yells, "Cops!" and all three run to the car, which swerves into the street and speeds away with screeching tires.

I stand up, surprised that I am still conscious and can get up. I decide to wait for the cops. A few minutes pass but no one comes to help me. I can feel the blood trickling down my forehead, eyebrow, and nose, and my neck. I realize one of the homeless men cried wolf; there are no cops.

Dizzy, I look around, trying to locate my keys and wallet. I find my keys but I don't see my wallet anywhere. I brace myself against the tree. My button-down shirt is torn to pieces, hanging on me by threads and drenched in blood. There is blood on the sidewalk, too. I wonder how I'm still alive.

My watch is still on my wrist, but its face is shattered. I limp back into the park and sit down on one of the empty benches, trying to catch my breath and figure out what happened; I try to remember what the man standing against the tree looked like. *Should I call the cops? Find a hospital?* Without health insurance, it'll cost me more money than I'll be able to make this year at the bar—even the next two years. If I have internal injuries, I'll find out in the next thirty-six hours.

As I debate what to do next, I see a motorcycle cop stop at a light on the outside of the circle. I stand up, limp over to wave at him for help, grabbing my arm in pain. The cop pulls the bike out of the street and up onto the curb of the park. I take a few steps toward him and look down at my leg to assess where the limp is coming from—is it my foot, my leg, my hip? When I look up, I see that the cop is not a he but a she.

"What happened?" she says, sounding sympathetic, as she hangs her helmet on one of the handles. She looks at me, "My God, what have they done to you?"

"Three people, well dressed," I say, panting. I can't seem to catch my breath. "A woman in a car, nice car. Oldsmobile, I think. She sat. Watched while they beat me up. Three men. Someone screamed 'cops.' Men ran to the car. She drove fast," I say, pointing in the direction.

The officer picks up her radio and starts speaking while I use my ripped shirt to wipe the blood out of my eye. She hangs up her radio and then starts asking me questions about what happened. I tell her about walking home from Georgetown, the man asking for a match, how he grabbed me and how the other men showed up out of nowhere. By the time I've finished, two police cruisers have pulled up. The officer walks me over to one of the cruisers and opens the front door. "Go ahead, go in," she says. I sit down on the seat with my feet on the pavement.

The officer in the driver's seat hands me paper napkins so I can wipe away the blood that's still dripping. He asks me questions. Name, address, where I was going and coming. After about five minutes, he asks me to get up and sit in the other cruiser. I get up and limp over to the other car where the police officer asks me the exact same questions using different words. After each question he says, "Do you understand?" I start each answer with "Yes, I understand," and then give him the same answer I gave to the other officer. Then, he asks me what kind of drugs I was buying.

"I do not understand the question, sir."

"What kind of drugs were you buying? Do you not understand the words I am saying?"

"I understand the words, sir; I do not understand the question."

"If you understand the words, you understand the question. Answer the question," he says, sounding impatient, his voice a little louder.

"What's the problem here?" the female police officer says, walking over.

"He won't tell me what kind of drugs he was buying."

"Sir," I say, "I do not disrespect you. There are no drugs. I was not buying drugs. I have no money for drugs. I don't use drugs. Man asked for a match. I gave him match. He grabbed my arm. Big man. Like bouncer. Two men then kick me, then a third man, pull out my wallet. Four dollars. That was in my wallet. They took. Someone from inside the park screams, 'cops!' They leave me on the ground. No drugs. I am poor. I have no money."

"Leave him alone, John. Poor kid has just had the shit beat out of him.

Anyway, it's probably a case of mistaken identity," she says. "They thought you were someone else," she says to me.

"Yes. Thank you. I understand."

"I think you should go to the hospital, get yourself checked out," she says, her voice soft, compassionate. "You could have broken bones, internal injuries."

"Thank you ma'am, I will be okay. I will walk home now. Just fifteen minutes from here."

She tells me to stop by the L Street police station if I think of anything else relevant to the incident. I thank them and resume the walk I started more than an hour ago, this time with a limp. I walk down the middle of the street to avoid the myriad doorways and alleys that line the sidewalk, turning my head in each direction every few seconds to make sure no one is behind me. I'm guessing that it's close to 4:00 a.m. by now; there are a few cars on the street.

When I get home, I go into the bathroom to look in the mirror. It looks as bad as it feels. I take a shower and check the fridge. A red plum. At $3.20 per pound, it's my one gift to myself. I buy three or four plums a week and limit myself to one every other day. I savor it, despite my throbbing jaw.

I climb into bed. *Welcome to the US, JR.*

8

VISA ISSUES

I PRESS THE SNOOZE BUTTON ON MY RADIO ALARM CLOCK. TEN minutes later, another song interrupts my dreams. I just want to stay in bed today, but it's already eight o'clock. After the third snooze, I roll over right onto the loose mattress spring, which pokes me in the kidney. I wince in pain, my whole body still aching from last night. I get out of bed, my eyes still closed. My head hurts, my face hurts, my chest, my right arm, and my left leg, everything hurts. I shuffle to the bathroom. My face looks like how I feel. I brush my teeth; amazingly, all of them are still in place, straight, and white. I take a shower, again, to wake up, gingerly washing my face and body. I feel like I have a hangover and the flu at the same time.

***

When I arrive at class, I'm greeted with alarm. My classmates and teacher see my black eyes, one swollen shut, my puffy face, bruised cheekbone, and swollen, split lips. "Whoa! What happened?" and "Oh my God, are you okay?" everyone in the room shouts at me in unison. The teacher asks me what happened; I describe briefly.

I receive a similar response when I arrive at the Blues Saloon. But the sympathy ends when Dan sees me. "I told you so. It was only a matter of time. You are an idiot, Addo, for not listening to me," I nod, appeasing him, making him believe I agree that I'm an idiot and he's smart. After four months of working for him, I still haven't gotten used to how mean he is and why he always needs to feel like the big, smart guy. As I walk away nodding, I hear Dan mumbling "idiot."

A few minutes later, after I've brought the garbage cans in from the curb, Dan calls me into his office. "Addo, Adem, come here. Sit down."

My heart drops. *Is he going to fire me for getting beaten up?*

"I was thinking about you and your situation. I could let you stay here till the morning, but I'm not going to do that. Because you need to learn your lesson and stop walking home. Get a fucking car already or jump in a taxi." I nod my head, doing a quick calculation of how much either of those choices would cost me. "But, I'm a nice guy and I like you. So, during the day, you're welcome to take a nap, on the cot in the basement, any time. Just let me know in advance. If I need you, I'll send someone down to wake you. Okay? Anytime. Go now, you look like shit. And get the first-aid kit out from under the bar and do something with that face of yours. You're going to scare the customers." I don't understand why he will let me use the cot during the day but not at night so I can walk home when the sun comes up. Is that the difference between a guy who thinks he's nice and a guy who is actually nice? But I thank him anyway and then grab the first-aid kit and go down to the basement.

After dabbing my face with some witch hazel and ointment, I lie down, thinking about the kind of man Dan is. Paul told me that Dan is self-made, starting out in the restaurant business as a busboy and dishwasher. He takes care of his mother as well as a sister and a brother financially. He never went to college but is helping to pay for his brother's college tuition. He's worked seven days a week, sixteen hours a day, for more than fifteen years. He's divorced, and no one really knows about his dating situation. He rents an upstairs apartment two doors down from the bar, doesn't own a car, doesn't travel, and doesn't seem to spend much money on anything other than the bar.

I fall asleep in the damp basement, thinking about Dan's path and calculating how long it's going to be before I can apply to graduate school. I wake up two hours later to a stiff back and wobbly legs and head to the kitchen.

Passing Dan's office, I lean my head in to thank him again. "You still look like shit, Addo," he says, looking up from the paperwork on his desk. "Stay in the back tonight. Don't come out of the kitchen. If the customers see you, they'll lose their appetites," he says looking down again and shaking his head.

"Okay, sir," I say, walking back to the kitchen. Oddly enough, I agree with him.

I'm at the sink, still thinking about when I'll be able to take my next step forward and what that will be. *Will I need to get a better paying job first—with a nicer boss—or will graduate school be the next step?*

"Hola, mi amigo," I hear behind me as the kitchen door to the alley creaks open.

"Jorge, mi amigo," I say. "How is the cooking business at Thira Gyros?"

"Good, mi amigo."

"What did you run out of?" I ask, thinking that I should offer to organize the inventory list at Jorge's, which is right up the street. Dan and the owner of Thira Gyros are friends and lean on each other when they run out of produce, though since I started taking care of Dan's inventory, it's become a one-sided deal.

"Cebollas, por favor," he says.

"Don't tell me," I say, "onions!"

"Muy bien," he says.

The first time I met Jorge, he told me he was a dentist in San Salvador but fled to escape the gang warfare there. After a harrowing journey north through Guatemala then Mexico to the Rio Grande, he crossed into El Paso two years ago. I'm guessing that he moved up to the DC area to join the thousands of Salvadorans who have come here for the same reason. He said he's been working at Thira Gyros for almost two years.

"How many?"

"Una docena."

"Go ahead," I say, grabbing a towel. "Over there," I say, turning around and pointing to a crate of onions in the corner.

"Whoa, amigo, what happened my friend? Your face. You look like me after getting beaten up by the Mara Street gangs."

"Just a fight. Three guys against me. You should see what the other guys look like," I say with a chuckle, using one of the lines Dr. Tiller taught me. Jorge nods.

I grab an empty liquor box. "Here, take this for the onions," I say, handing him the box.

"Thank you. Okay. Be careful out there my friend," Jorge says, hoisting the box of onions and heading out.

I wonder how he gets home at night. I wonder how all these people who work at all these bars and restaurants get home at night. *How can I be the only one walking home from work?*

All day long, as each member of the staff arrives at work and heads into the kitchen to check in with Raymond about the menu changes and to order their free meals, I have to repeat the story of why my face looks like I did five rounds with Sugar Ray Leonard. The reactions vary from concern from the women to obnoxious jokes from the men.

Paul is the only man at the bar who seems genuinely concerned. It's not surprising. Of all the people at work, he's the most caring; he's like that with everyone, in fact. Even Demir didn't treat me with such uncompromising kindness. What does surprise me is that Paul seems to respect me. I'm not sure what I did to earn his respect, but I'm grateful to him for the way he treats me.

When I ask him how he gets around at night, he says he budgets for a taxi. "A few hundred dollars on cab fare versus thousands of dollars in hospital bills if the next group of hoodlums break something," he says. "Or the cost to your family of shipping your body home to bury you," he adds. I don't think he's joking. "Look at it like an investment in your future . . . an investment in *having* a future."

I spend the night thinking about it. $2.45 a night, $3 with a tip. $78 a month. By 2:00 a.m., I've decided he's right and I take my first taxi home that night.

***

Within two weeks my face has returned to normal, for the most part. There's a scar on my left cheek and a vertical line through my right eyebrow where hair no longer grows. "The scars are sexy," a few of the waitstaff tell me. "You remind me of Harrison Ford from that new movie, *Raiders of the Lost Ark*," one says, the rest of them nodding. Even Paul agrees. I'm not familiar with the movie, but I take it as a compliment.

"Addo doesn't come close to looking like Harrison Ford!" Dan says, walking into the room, interrupting, and immediately changing the relaxed mood. It's not only that he's the boss; he pretty much scares everyone with his booming voice and overbearing attitude. "Paychecks for those who agree with me, zero for those who don't," he says, holding out an envelope in my direction. "Say, 'I don't look like Harrison Ford,' Addo." I repeat his line and he relinquishes the check, then leans in and whispers, "I gave you a little extra there, Addo." Then, with a wink, he adds, "Consider it a pity raise. I've bumped you from $3.10 to $3.90 an hour." I'm fairly certain that the raise is not, as he said, "a pity raise," but because my contributions to the bar have helped his bottom line. I'm happy to play along though because the reason doesn't matter at all.

"Thank you, sir," I say, as genuinely as I can. "I appreciate this very much." *That's an extra $8 a day, $48 a week! It more than covers my taxi rides.*

"Glad to see you are taking a taxi home, now. Good that you listened to me."

"Yes, sir. It was good advice."

Two weeks later, after my next paycheck, I decide to put some of my new salary to good use. Earning an extra $196 a month is a difference maker. I find an $11 coffee maker for my room. And, now that I'm down a pair of pants and shirt after the attack, I buy a few new T-shirts, a pair of jeans, and a pair of sneakers, totaling $155. I'm not rich but I am earning.

I am happy.

***

After ten months in the US and six months at the Blues Saloon, my immersion plan is going well and my English has improved considerably. Dr. Tiller continues to teach me technical words I can't learn in class, like "infinitesimal," "congruent," and "binomial." And he helps me with cadence, something the English teacher doesn't really focus on. And, of course, idioms; there are lots of idioms and expressions: "In time," "on time," "out of time," "in the nick of time," "in a jiffy."

My English immersion is interrupted only by Dad's letters. Reading his encouraging letters remains a treat. With each compliment he writes, I remain pleasantly shocked by the 180 I'm witnessing and wonder how different things would have been if he'd been this way when I was growing up. I also wonder why—why is he this way now and why was he not that way then? As a way to thank him for his compliments, I cut out the weekly bridge column from the *Post*, translate it into Turkish, and include it with my reply.

In his most recent letter, Dad asks me if I've applied to postpone my military service, something I can do as a student. I realize it's something that I *need* to do, and soon; I had completely forgotten about it. My Turkish passport was issued for only eighteen months and is due to expire in just about six months. According to the rules Zeki explained to me, to keep my US visa, I must remain a student and have a Turkish passport valid for at least six months; and to extend my Turkish passport, I must be a student.

I look up the location of the Turkish embassy on my map and notice that it's a quick walk from my house. I decide to go the following day after class.

It's a dark-gray stucco building adorned with curved balconies, wrought iron framed doors, and marble floors. I go in through a security door and I'm directed down a long hallway to the visa section, which is quite plain compared to the main building. There are a few framed photos on the walls, but most of the art is posters of Istanbul and Turkey's coastal towns simply thumbtacked to the walls.

I hand the official behind the counter my passport and my school ID. "I'm a student. I'd like to defer my military service and extend my passport, please," I say, in Turkish.

The official looks at me and my school ID. "Attending language school does not count toward student status," he tells me, handing back my passport.

"You cannot defer your military service."

"I'm not sure I understand. I'm a student. It's how I got my visa. The US authorities accept me as a student."

"I don't make the rules, sir. You need to be enrolled in a degree program from an accredited university, not a language school."

"Oh. Okay, thank you for clarifying," I say, not understanding but trying to hide my panic. What does this mean for me? I got here with a student visa for a language school; now that's not good enough for Turkish authorities? The visa Zeki went out of his way to get me, the visa that got me into the US, the visa that I want to keep, I will lose?

I walk out the door and try to catch my breath. *Think. Just stop and think.* I walk to a small park nearby and sit on a bench. I pull out my notebook and start to make a list.

1. I have not completed my mandatory military service.

2. Attending language school qualifies me as a student for US immigration but not for Turkish authorities, so I cannot get an extension on my passport.

3. Without an extension to my Turkish passport, I cannot keep my status with the US Immigration and Naturalization Service as a foreign student studying in America.

4. I cannot go back to Turkey to complete my required military service:

    a) I don't have the money.

    b) I won't have a visa to return to America.

Why didn't I find this out sooner? Why did I leave things to the last minute? *Am I going to have to leave America?*

***

The strategy I finally come up with is basically "hope." I decide to *hope* that the immigration officials will overlook the expiration date. That's it. That's all I can do. I apply for the annual extension for my student visa with my passport valid for only five months. The application is by mail, and the form asks the applicants to enter their passport's expiration date. We are not asked to send in our passports. So, the immigration officials do not check the passports, trusting the date we put down on our visa extension application. It's an honor system. Nearly all the students I've talked to at the language school say they entered bogus dates in their applications and got their visas extended. I don't want to lie, so I enter the actual expiration date, hoping that the immigration officials will overlook the date or give me bonus points for not lying.

They do not. Once again, I'm punished for my honesty.

My US visa is revoked. After eleven months in the US, seven months at the Blues Saloon, I'm "out of status."

"You are now, officially, an illegal alien," I say, looking at the mirror. "Idiot."

***

I know I'm not the only one living in America as an illegal alien. It's not exactly comforting, but it's something. I also know I can't let it stop me from moving forward. If they catch me, they catch me. Until then, I came here with a goal and will continue to pursue it. So, I tweak my daily routine, a bit. Now, almost every day on my way to work, I stop at the library at Washington University to read up on the different graduate schools, their offerings, and how much it will cost me to get a graduate degree in engineering. It may be too little too late to save my student status, but it's not too late to improve my educational prospects. I read up on graduate programs at universities all over the country.

After two weeks, I settle on two schools, one in Maryland, the other in Texas. I write rather than type out my application request letters, even though my friends tell me to use a typewriter because it looks more professional.

Three weeks later, I haven't received any replies. I don't have the time or money to visit either campus.

While I try to figure out my next step, I go about my days acting as if I have a valid visa. Maybe I'm in denial, because it's scary to be illegal. Or, maybe I don't know what else I can do. I live on the brink, wondering if I'll be allowed to stay here, trying to be the perfect citizen and employee so as not to attract any attention.

9

BROKEN GLASS

It's been two years and four months since I set foot in the US and almost two years since the immigration office revoked my visa. Life in America for me has meant pretending I belong here, surviving periodic raids by immigration officers on Georgetown bars and restaurants. Jorge from Thira Gyros introduced me to an underground network of sorts, a group of fellow illegals who somehow receive proactive alerts about the raids.

I've worked on average sixty hours a week at the Blues Saloon along with my ESL classes. My English comprehension, reading, and writing skills are advancing.

Although I've filed my taxes for two years, I have not requested a tax refund. Dan keeps calls me stupid for not doing so. "The IRS and immigration office are two different offices and they do not communicate with each other. You're safe," Dan says. But I don't believe he's right. It doesn't make sense to me to tell the government, "Here I am, working illegally, this is my work address, this is my home address, and now give me some money." Despite not getting my tax refunds, I've saved more than $8,500 plus earned $617 in interest from the bank.

I begin to count my savings rounded to the nearest one hundred: $9,100.

Eliz has been pressuring me to get a telephone. "You don't have to call us," she says. "But what if we need to call you in an emergency?" she asks me on one of our Saturday morning calls. We had been speaking once every two months, but we've been talking more recently over her concerns about our parents. "I have to call several times before I can reach you on your landlady's public phone," she says. She's not wrong. *If* I hear the phone ringing, I have to run up two stories to answer it, it's usually hit or miss.

I finally get a phone in my room; it costs $15 a month. The rent for the phone itself is $3. Calling Istanbul costs $2 per minute, lower than Mrs. Hardwick's phone. I decide to call my parents every other week for five minutes. Eliz's concerns have me worried. I need to hear their voices for myself.

***

My plan for America is going well, and to my surprise, I'm doing better than I had initially projected at first. My initial numbers showed much lower sums for both my income and savings. This positive outcome encourages me to review my plan. I pull out my notebook and a pencil. There are five check marks.

Enter the US √
Get a job √
Learn English √
Speak little or no Turkish √
Save money for graduate school √.

But, I have some biggies ahead of me:

Start graduate school
Pay my debts to Ela and Eliz
Send money to my parents.

I continue to survive in America with no visa. I'm living with my head in the sand, ignoring my biggest problem. "All I need is three horseshoes and a horse. Then I'm all set." It's one of Ela's favorite expressions.

***

I receive an offer through the mail for an American Express credit card. Since it's an opportunity to make myself feel legitimate, I apply. But, I get denied. "You do not have enough credit information on file," they write in the letter I receive at the bar. *Why are you sending me an application form then? Give me credit so that I can have some credit information on file.*

At the Blues Saloon that night, after our shift, I tell Paul. "Would you believe they offered me a credit card and then when I applied, they turned me down? And the reason—I do not have any credit history. I mean, why would they send me the offer in the first place?

He tells me I can establish credit by asking my bank for a passbook loan. "Banks love this," he says, taking a sip of his post-work beer. "You leave in your account the same amount of money you're borrowing, as collateral. That money is locked away until you pay off the loan."

"Okay," I say, trying to process everything Paul is saying.

"Just make sure there is no prepayment penalty in the agreement. You borrow the money and make monthly payments for three months. After that, you pay off the loan. Then wait a month or so until you have established credit. The cost of the loan to you is the interest you are paying minus the interest the bank is paying you for the three months."

"I think I understand," I say, nodding. "Thank you."

"Well, you helped me put my college degree to good use!" he says, clinking my beer bottle.

I take Paul's advice right away and borrow $4,000 dollars at 8.5 percent. The money in my savings account is receiving 6 percent interest. My net cost on the loan is 2.5 percent.

I decide to look into graduate programs again, but this time, as I mull over Paul's situation—an American citizen with a college degree, unable to find a job in his field—I approach my research differently. Rather than continuing automatically as an engineer, I think the smarter strategy is to see what kinds of expertise is in demand. So, on Sundays I buy the *Post* and I sit in my room drinking tea and paging through column after column of want ads. There are thousands of jobs posted. *So much for the worst recession since the Second World War.* I see only two or three engineering jobs available, versus hundreds of computer programming jobs. One week, I count twenty-seven pages of computer-related jobs. *Can I learn computers?* I barely passed a required elementary computer programming course at Technical University. But there are so many jobs in this field, it would be the smart thing to do. I could apply for a graduate degree in computer science, even right here at Washington University in DC. I could just walk in and talk to them face to face.

At the university's library, I look at the computer science curriculum, all the requirements, courses and their abstractions, majors, and minors. I need to take thirty-three graduate credits at $160 per credit hour; it's under $5,500, which I can afford right now. The textbooks, I should be able to afford them too.

After a month of research, the answer is clear. I need to go to school for a degree in computer science. If I'm not accepted, I will start from scratch and apply for a graduate degree in mechanical engineering. If I am accepted, I'll need to cut back my hours at the Blues Saloon, from sixty a week to no more than forty. During summers, I'll work double shifts and won't take summer classes. The plan is contingent on Dan allowing me that kind of flexibility. It's also contingent on my ability to pass a language competency exam. I find out that the TOEFL is required for all international students for admission to graduate school.

I sign up for the test and, since I've been preparing for it with the two years of ESL classes, I don't fret over studying more. I take the test and three weeks later find out that I've gotten a decent but not spectacular score. While I'm disappointed, it's not a deal breaker; I've done well enough to move forward with the next step—transcripts and recommendation letters. To speed up the process, I call Dad and ask him to do the legwork for me since I need to get in touch with old professors and the registrar's office; it's faster than airmail. Dad goes to Technical University for me and requests that my transcripts be sent directly to Washington University and to me at the Blues Saloon's address, in case I apply to another school later. He also contacts three of my former professors and asks them to mail letters of recommendation. Two of them tell him they received their PhDs in the US, which I think is a huge plus.

Dad is very gung ho about helping me and asks if there is anything else he can do, offering to speak to more than three professors. I can't imagine him ever doing something like this for me in my former life in Istanbul. It's revelatory how excited he is.

As Dad is working on his end of my application process, I start working on the essays I need to write to apply for the graduate degree program in computer science.

I work on the application for one full week, then ask Dr. Tiller to proofread my work. He finds a few minor mistakes, which I fix, and he lets me borrow his old typewriter to fill out all the forms and type out my essays.

Three weeks later, I'm accepted. The school officials say that Technical University's reputation is stellar and my transcript is acceptable. But, the acceptance is not without conditions.

First, because my TOEFL test results were not high enough, I have to take advanced English reading and writing courses at $480 each before starting my graduate level courses. Second, because computer science is a branch of electrical engineering, not mechanical, which is what I studied at Technical University, I must take three undergraduate courses in electrical engineering, also before starting my graduate school courses. If I get a B or better in each of these courses, I can begin my graduate schoolwork. These additional requirements raise my total credit hours to fifty-four, and tuition to $8,600, close to my entire savings.

The last requirement has me the most nervous. I need to find a US-based sponsor to act as a guarantor in case I'm unable to pay the tuition. I basically need a signature from a person with money. For a week, I think about who that person could be. I can't ask any of my fellow students, they are all just starting out and most of them don't even have the right papers; I can't ask Paul or Raymond, as from what I surmise, they're not rolling in money; and I can't even consider any of the waitstaff, they are all kids in college. My only option is Dan Sullivan. Every time I tell myself, "No, not Dan, anyone but Dan," I come right back to Dan. It has to be Dan. There is no one else.

I have no idea how to ask him and I spend days trying to find the words, work up a strategy. In the end, I decide Dan's the kind of guy who doesn't like people to stand on ceremony; I have to just ask straight out and hope he's in a good mood.

I come into work a little early and head right for his office.

"Addo, ten minutes early," he says looking at his watch. "What do you want?"

"Sir?"

"The only reason anyone ever comes to work early is because they want something. What do you want? Out with it!"

Just ask directly, quickly, before he really gets angry! "I've saved $9,100 and I've been accepted to Washington University for a graduate degree in computer science. I need a sponsor, a US resident, to sign some papers. And I would like you to be my sponsor, kind of my backup plan, in case I can't pay my tuition. But, if it came to that, which it won't, I would drop out before asking you for money. Would you be my sponsor?"

"You've saved $9,100 huh? Am I paying you too much?"

"Sir?"

"It's a joke Adem. Lighten up, man!" He pauses. *Keep breathing.* "Sure. Good for you. Okay, I'll sign." *What? Did he just say yes?* "Hand them over."

"Sir?"

"You have papers for me to sign? Give 'em to me."

I open my file folder and pull out the papers. "Thank you, sir. Truly."

"Not a problem. I'm impressed you've saved so much money." He leafs through the documents quickly.

"Come with me," Dan says, and I follow him out of the bar, down the street. I have no idea where he is taking me. Abruptly, he stops and walks into his bank. In no time at all, we walk out with a document that shows he keeps an average balance of $20,000 or more in his savings account.

Back at the bar, he signs the papers and staples his documents to the back of the paperwork.

"Here you go Adem," he says, holding the papers out for me to take, but not letting go. "My only caveat. Get all A's. Make me proud."

I am flabbergasted; and, as my jaw starts to drop, I quickly shift my mouth into a smile.

"Thank you, sir. Thank you. I will . . . er, make you . . . proud."

He lets go of the papers.

"Attaboy, Addo."

I don't say anything to anyone in my ESL class about my graduate school acceptance. I keep up with the work as I work up the nerve to tell everyone—my first friends in America. I decide that the morning of registration for my first semester of classes is the time to do it, since the times conflict and I can't stay anyway.

I decide to tell everyone individually to avoid any hoopla or a public announcement. During class break I begin by telling the teacher, and as soon as the class resumes, she announces it to the whole class. I'm not sure how they will react; so, when they break out into applause, my eyes tear up with emotion, exactly the thing I was trying to avoid. One by one, my classmates come up to hug me, shake my hand, pat me on the back. My teachers tell me how proud of me they are. Roberto can't stop grinning. And, he won't stop hugging me.

"You did it, man," he says, his hands holding my arms. "You will be a big executive one day. And once I get my marketing and business administration degree, we will work together. Adem and Roberto, Inc.," he says, laughing.

"That's a plan, Roberto," I say. "It's a perfect plan. But, the name . . . let's agree to disagree on the name," I say, invoking a Dr. Tillerism.

My face still feels warm with embarrassment when I wave goodbye one last time and head over to Washington University. Before registering for classes, I need to go to the international students' office to tell them that I don't have a visa.

***

A gray-haired lady is sitting behind the desk. There are two students ahead of me. After ten minutes of waiting and rehearsing my line in my mind over and over, it's my turn.

"Ma'am, I need to register for my classes this morning. But, I do not have a valid passport or US visa."

The woman looks up at me over her glasses. She doesn't say anything.

"I do have a Social Security card and a driver's license," I say, sounding as positive as I can. "Is there some kind of form I need to fill out?"

She takes off her glasses and smiles at me. "Oh, honey. We are not the immigration office, we are here to *help* and encourage international students, not detain or deter them," she says, looking at me.

"Oh!" I say, surprised.

***

The night before my classes begin, I'm not nervous at all. I think back to the night before starting my ESL class and how worried I was; then, the next day, how surprised I was by how warm, kind, and caring the teacher was. So, I'm excited to start the path to my graduate degree despite being warned by school officials that it's going to be a hefty workload. Three credits in a graduate course, they say, will be equivalent to six credits in an undergraduate course.

I prepare myself for the onslaught. I'm taking the three required "makeup" courses, two in analog and digital circuitry design, and one in assembly language programming. I'm also taking those two advanced courses in English reading and writing.

But, a week in, I actually find it easy.

I feel busy, but the workload is nothing like the crazy amount of studying we had to do at Technical University. The professors speak so clearly that I understand everything they are saying, even though they are teaching complicated concepts and I'm still learning English. *Why didn't I understand a thing during classes at Technical University, in my native language?*

Despite my school workload, with fewer hours at the Blues Saloon, I begin carving out a little free time for myself, fun time. For the first time in seven years, I start playing basketball again. On my nights off, I shoot around with some students from Washington University—sometimes players from the school team even join us. At twenty-six, I've earned the nickname "Old Guy," which I love, the players saying things like, "How could you let the Old Guy score like that" and "The Old Guy—he can't jump, he can't dunk." Despite the smack talk, I feel stronger and faster than I did nearly a decade ago when

I played the game as a teenager in Istanbul; and, I'm shooting better than I ever did.

Now that I'm a student at a real university, I'm hoping that I can get my passport extended at the Turkish consulate, and maybe get a US student visa again.

***

At work, I receive another raise from Dan. I've jumped from $3.90 to $4.30 per hour but I'm working fewer hours, now thirty-five hours a week, because of my new class schedule. I'm happy. I am happy with the way things are going, with where I've gotten so far. On Friday and Saturday nights, Dan has me working the front door, checking IDs. He uses an on-call busboy and a dishwasher on the days I'm off or working at the door. I'd rather stay in the back, but I have to do what he tells me to do. He wasn't moved by my argument about how hypocritical it is for me to check IDs when I'm an illegal alien. "Addo, it's about age, not about legal status. If they are eighteen and in America illegally, let 'em in; if they are seventeen and American and can trace their roots back to the *Mayflower*, turn 'em away. I only care how old they are."

And so, I stand at the front door and play bouncer. Dan calls me "the Doorman," because we're a "peaceful" and "civilized" bar.

During the week, I go back to my job as the bar's jack-of-all-trades, bussing tables, washing dishes, hooking up kegs, sweeping up broken glasses, mopping floors.

One night, I'm in the kitchen washing the dishes when the panel lights up. I grab a mop, broom, and dustpan and head out front. Dan points to the mess with his chin, a broken glass or two, or maybe three. A couple of waitstaff move the table and chairs a bit, as I begin to sweep. As I'm mopping, I look up and see a customer watching me intently. We make eye contact and then just as I'm about to avert my eyes, she smiles at me.

10

LEGAL AFFAIRS

"HI, MY NAME IS BONNIE. BONNIE MORRISON."

I look up from the sink where I'm washing dishes. A woman, who looks to be in her late twenties, is standing in the doorway. She steps forward and extends her hand. She's wearing the waitstaff's white-shirt-black-trousers uniform.

"Hi," I reply, smiling. "I'm Adem." I lift my sudsy hand out of the sink, then stop, midair. "Sorry, can't shake," I say, "Oh, you're . . . you're the lady, the broken glass, last week."

"Broken glass?" she asks, tipping her head sideways inquisitively. "Oh yes," she says a moment later, "clumsy of me," she adds, giving me one of those "I like you" looks.

So, last week she was a clumsy customer and this week she's a waitress?

She exchanges pleasantries with Raymond, whom, it appears, she met on my day off, yesterday.

I watch her. She is pretty, even without any makeup, which I happen to like, a lot; and, she has a mysterious, sexy smile. She turns back to me. "Are you going to be one of those rich engineers someday?"

The question surprises me. Then I realize Raymond must have told her that I have an engineering degree.

I decide to play the game. I haven't flirted in a long time, not that I was ever good at it when I did; but this woman is making it easy. "Yes. I am. An engineer at your service," I say with a bow. She chuckles, then turns to leave the kitchen, shouldering the double doors, all the while keeping her eyes glued to me. I immediately think of the way Francesca looked at me the first time our eyes met.

On Friday and Saturday nights when I work the door, I watch Bonnie work. There's a thing developing between us, though I don't know what that "thing" is. Over the course of her first three weeks at the Blues Saloon, her flirty eyes continue to check me out. I ask Paul if he notices—if it's just me, or if she's like that with everyone. "Oh no, man, she's got it bad for you," he says. Still, when she asks me if she can give me a ride home after work, I decline. I'm not sure why. I haven't been in a relationship since I was eighteen; Francesca still haunts me.

Bonnie and I continue to watch each other. When I'm at the sink, in the back, I look up every time the door springs open and hope that it's Bonnie; when I make myself a sandwich at the end of the night, I hope she'll come over and join me. I even start looking forward to Dan's nightly rants because Bonnie saves me a seat next to her at the bar.

The third time she offers me a ride home, I finally accept, mostly because I've been standing on the corner for fifteen minutes and not one taxi has come by. I'm afraid that taking her up on a ride will somehow advance our "thing" to the next level and I still don't know what that means or what that looks like.

We walk to Bonnie's car, a Volkswagen Golf. During the drive to my place, we talk about work and Dan. About two blocks away, I have a quick debate with myself over whether I should ask her in. By the time Bonnie has pulled up in front of the house, I've resolved to ask her to come in. But, when I turn to look at her, she's staring straight ahead, hands gripping the wheel, looking uninterested. *It's a message. She's not interested. You made it all up in your head, Adem.*

"Thank you," I say, hopping out.

"You're welcome," she says, smiling, turning her head in my direction only slightly. I shut the door and she speeds away.

"Huh," I say out loud, standing alone on the sidewalk in front of the house, watching her car taillights disappear.

***

The next night, as Dan wraps up his rant, Bonnie asks me if I'd like a ride home again. And, while the savings from cab fare she's offering me is in the back of my brain, my first thought this time is maybe she really does like me. *Maybe I misread her last night. Maybe I lost my nerve for nothing?*

"I've had two drinks since closing," she tells me, sounding a little slurry. I look at her and she gives me her flirty eyes back in response. "You drive," she says, tossing me the keys before I even say yes.

I realize as we walk out of the Blues Saloon that if I drive myself to my room in her car, once we get there she won't be able to drive herself home because she's drunk. *She's not planning to go home tonight. She's planning to stay at my house. She wants me.*

It takes Bonnie a few minutes to remember where she parked her car. When we finally find it parked on a steep hill a few blocks away, it's squeezed, inch tight, between two other cars. I haven't driven in three years, but pull out like a pro. *I haven't lost my touch.* I glance in Bonnie's direction to see how impressed she is. Nothing. No reaction. She closes her eyes and tips her head back against the headrest.

It feels good to be behind the wheel of a car. Though I've never driven these streets, I weave in and out like the taxi drivers who spend their lives on these streets. At a stop sign, I look over at Bonnie again. *Is she sleeping?* A few minutes later I pull up in front of my house, shift the gear into neutral, and engage the hand brake. I look over at her; her eyes are still closed. *What now? What do I do now?*

I'm going to have to wake her up. We can't sit here all night. I nudge her shoulder gently. "Bonnie?"

Nothing.

I look around, not sure why. There is no one around. Then I nudge her again. It feels intrusive.

"Oh, yes," she says, looking around. "Not sleeping. I'm not sleeping, just resting my eyes," she says. "Where are we?"

"We're in front of my house," I say, rethinking Bonnie's intentions. "Where's the hazard button?" I ask. She points at the dash and I turn the hazards on. "Thank you," I say, getting out. I walk around to the passenger door and open it for her. "Have a good night, Bonnie—rather, a good morning. The keys are in the ignition. You going to be okay?"

"I think I'm a little too drunk to drive home," she says, looking up at me. "Can I come in for a cup of coffee before I drive home?"

Is this a test? "Sure," I say. "It's probably a good idea to get some coffee in you."

I get back in the car, turn off the hazards, and find a spot several doors down. We both get out of the car and I lock the doors.

"I'm not allowed to have any guests," I whisper in her ear, as we approach the front stoops. "The landlady will kick me out if she catches us." She nods. As I open the door, I turn around and put my index finger to my lips. "Remember, sh," I say quietly.

Bonnie follows me into the house, past the 1850s-decorated, no-one-is-allowed-in-here parlor, to the stairway. As I tiptoe down the steps, I'm less nervous about what "coffee" means than I am about Mrs. Hardwick catching me with a guest. If Mrs. Hardwick kicks me out, I'll lose my $110 room, and I already know that the next cheapest available room in the 'hood is $250 a month. But if "coffee" means sex, it just might be worth the risk. *It's been a while.*

We head down the creaking stairs and then through the furnace room and into my room. *Success. We made it!*

I smile, feeling awkward, and then tell Bonnie I'm going to take a shower. "If you join me, we'll save water," I say, borrowing a lame line from my early teenage years.

"I'm good," she says, lying down on the bed and closing her eyes.

My heart sinks a little. I can't figure her out. I shut the bedroom door and drag myself to the bathroom, disappointed.

"What did you think she was going to do?" I ask myself in the bathroom mirror. "Seriously, Adem, you think she was going to jump into your arms and make love to you? What an ego you have."

I get in the shower thinking about how I must have misread Bonnie. She's probably fast asleep by now.

But, when I get back to the room, Bonnie jumps out of bed. "My turn!" she says. I hope Dr. Tiller doesn't need to use the bathroom at 3:30 a.m. The door doesn't lock, and he's proven that knocking isn't something he's good at. Though somehow, I think Bonnie would handle it with finesse.

Five minutes later, she's standing in my room in a towel, her hair wet and dripping down her shoulders and arms. My eyes don't know where to look first.

And then, she lets the towel drop.

***

"Where are you from originally?" I ask, propping myself on one arm.

"So, now that we've had sex, you want to get to know me?" she says, pushing me. The wayward coil jabs me. "I'm just kidding, Adem. Addo!" she says. "Boy, you should have seen your face! You didn't think I was being serious, did you?"

"I don't know. Maybe? I don't know American girls."

"Women."

"Excuse me?"

"Women. I'm a woman. Not a girl. And, it's fine, Adem. I'm fine. If I hadn't wanted to have sex, we wouldn't have had sex. Trust me. So . . . what was your question, again?"

"Where are you from?" I say, slowly, trying to ingest everything she's saying, trying to understand her tone, her sincerity, her sarcasm.

"I'm from Kansas City, originally. And I went to Missouri State, go Bears! I majored in biology, then went to law school in Wisconsin. After that I landed a job as an aide for a member of congress and moved to DC. That's how I ended up here. I found myself among a bunch of Republicans, which wasn't pleasant, although I could deal with it. But the congressman's longtime aide and I kept clashing. It came to a point where the congressman had to decide between the two of us and I was not the chosen one. So after a year here, I was out of a job. Then one evening, I was hanging out in Georgetown and wandered into the Blues Saloon. I'd been there before several times, with a guy I was dating. That's over now. But I kind of knew Dan from coming in with that guy, who also kind of knew Dan. So, I asked Dan for a job. And, voila, I'm a waitress. And you're an engineer, a dishwasher, and a bouncer."

"Doorman," I reply.

"Excuse me?"

"Dan says we're civilized and peaceful. He calls it *doorman.*"

"Ah. Doorman," she repeats, and we both laugh.

"And, the landlady," she says, "doesn't want you to have any guests, huh?"

"Mrs. Hardick, yes. No, no guests, no exceptions, she said."

"What's her name again—Mrs. what?"

"Hardick," I reply.

Bonnie starts laughing.

"What's so funny?"

"Wait, how do you spell it?"

"Hardick. H-A-R-D-W-I-C-K. Hardick."

She starts to laugh again. "You have to say her name slower. So you need to make sure you pronounce only one *d*. And make sure you do pronounce the *w*. Otherwise you're going to embarrass yourself. It's like two words, *hard* and *wick.*"

"Hard . . . Oh!" I say, and start laughing. The two of us roll around in the bed with the springs poking at us as we muffle our laughter, repeating "Mrs. Harddick" over and over again.

We chat a little more until we can't keep our eyes open anymore. Bonnie falls asleep in my arms, and I fall asleep thinking of Francesca. *Where are you, Francesca? Do you think of me when you're lying in another man's arms?*

"I don't have a driver's license" are the first words out of my mouth when I see Bonnie open her eyes in the morning.

"Good morning to you, too," she says, smiling.

"I drove your car last night without a license. It was stupid. I can't do that again. Ever."

"Let's get you one, then," she says, like it would be the easiest thing in the world. I still can't get used to the "can do" American attitude, the positivity. I grew up hearing mostly, "Forget it, you can't do it."

"It's not that easy. I'm not legal," I reply.

"Let's try," she says. Her optimism encourages me to think that a driver's license might be in my future after all. I feel buoyed as I head to class.

Bonnie recommends that I pick up study materials and also apply for a driver's license test at the police station near the courthouse on C Street, which is a couple Metro stations away. I run over there after class. All I need is my student ID and Social Security card. They give me a pamphlet to study and a date for a written test, a week later.

I head to work feeling a little of that "can do" American attitude.

***

A week later, I go to the Department of Motor Vehicles to take the written test, which is multiple choice and has only twenty questions, which I answer on a computer. I get all of them right.

I don't have that much to be proud of. It was a nine-minute, ridiculously easy test. In Istanbul, it's a forty-five-minute written exam. I remember the first question, alone, on the Turkish driver's exam took me at least five minutes to answer. It asked would-be drivers to list at least nine situations in which a driver must reduce speed. I got eight of them. Another question was about how to make a left turn from a two-lane road to a two-lane road with several different scenarios: with traffic lights, with stop signs, without stop signs, or on a divided highway. I got 72 percent. The minimum passing grade was 50 percent.

Taking the test in English and passing feels good. I credit my time chatting with Dr. Tiller and the college English classes I'm taking as a graduate school prerequisite.

I schedule the driving portion of the test for two weeks from now.

Even before I ask, Bonnie offers to let me use her car for the test. *No problem, we can do it, you can do it.*

I fall asleep that night with Bonnie next to me, the rebellious coil poking me in the back, and, instead of thinking about Francesca, as I do most nights,

I think about how fortunate I am. Zeki persuaded the consulate officer to give me a visa; Ela sold her steel company stocks and loaned me $800; a flight attendant, a stranger, got me an employee discount on my ticket to America; the immigration officer at the airport let me in—no questions asked; Roberto gave me his room; Dan gave me a job and raises; Washington University accepted me without a visa; the city allowed me to apply for a driver's license although I'm not a legal resident; and, Bonnie is letting me use her car to try for that driver's license.

***

Fifteen minutes after Bonnie and I arrive at the testing site, my number is called. With Bonnie's car keys in hand, I walk out a side door and find the testing officer.

I start the car and over the course of the next ten minutes, the tester calls instructions at me in a monotone: "Left, right, switch lanes."

Even though I've been driving for years, she's making me so nervous I question whether I really do know how to drive.

"You've driven before," the tester says. I can't tell if it's a question or a statement. I decide it must be a question.

"Yes, ma'am, but in another country."

She gives me a look I don't understand.

When we return to the parking lot she tells me to pull into a spot between two orange cones.

"Done," she says. I look at her, waiting for more instructions. "You can turn the car off now." I shift into first gear and turn off the engine.

"You've passed," she says, handing me a piece of paper, "Congratulations." I'm shocked. I thought she was going to fail me because I'm a foreigner.

"Thank you," I say, a little wary. "May I . . . can I . . ." I stutter, not sure I should leave, worried there's a last-minute trick awaiting me.

"You are free to go," she says, opening her door. "Just present the paper to the person at booth number one."

I walk back inside to Bonnie with a smile.

"You passed!" she screams. I don't say anything. "Wait, you passed, yes?

That's why you're smiling? Or are you just being weird because you failed?"

"I passed," I say, in the monotone of the tester. Bonnie hits me in the arm and laughs, then, holds her arms open wide and hugs me. Then, she grabs my hands, and kisses me, making a huge congratulatory fuss. I start laughing at how silly she is being until it dawns on me that no one has ever celebrated any of my accomplishments, ever—not when I received the championship trophy after my buzzer-beating half-court shot, not when I gained entry to one of the best universities in Turkey, not even when I graduated. In fact, I remember that my mother specifically told me to stop making such a commotion and calm down when I came running home screaming that I'd gained entry to Technical University. I had no idea how much I'd been missing. I hug Bonnie tight and wonder if I'm falling in love with her or just my life in America.

When I pull away from Bonnie, I look around at the people waiting their turns. Smiles abound. "Congratulations," a few people say. I smile back at them, nodding and saying "thank you," surprised by the outpouring and wondering how different my life in Istanbul would have been if I'd had champions all around me like this. *Would I have ever wanted to move away, to escape to America?*

Bonnie and I get in line to pick up my driver's license. I'm excited to add another ID to my collection. And, a driver's license, no less. Talk about an accomplishment. *Wow! A driver's license.* I'm another step closer to feeling like I belong in America, to actually belonging. I want to be one of those people on the bus going to work in the morning with their brown bag lunch on their lap not worrying about being caught by US Immigration and deported. They just belong. That's how they live. *I want to belong.* Now I'll have a Washington, DC driver's license in my wallet, my school ID, and, the pièce de resistance—another Dr. Tiller expression—my Social Security card. My wallet is bursting and my heart kind of feels the same way. Each new card is another connection point to this new home of mine. Even though it's so different here, even though I love Turkey, I was never quite able to figure out how to succeed there; but, somehow, despite all the barriers in the US, I'm figuring that out here.

"Can I see your test results?" Bonnie says.

I realize I haven't even looked at my results. I hesitate flashing back to the mailman on the street in Istanbul pressuring me to open up my test results for the university entrance exams.

"What's the big deal?" Bonnie asks, as if I'm hiding something. "I want to see them."

"Okay, here. But, hold on. I'd like to take a look at my own results first, if you don't mind."

"Okay, fine!" she says dramatically. I glance at the paper. *Huh.* Then I hand it to Bonnie.

"Oh my God! You got 100 percent!" she whispers. "On both, on both the written *and* the driving tests!"

"So?" I ask, surprised.

"So? Dude, English is our first language and we Americans don't get 100 percent on our driver's tests! That's ridiculous!"

"Well, I studied. And I've been driving for almost ten years. I mean if I hadn't gotten 100 percent, I would have been a little worried."

"Well, I think it's ridiculous. You don't even speak English. Remember Mrs. *Hard-dick*?"

"My English is getting better over time," I say, throwing in one of Dr. Tiller's phrases, though I'm not sure if it's the right way to use it. "Maybe someday I'll even write a book."

"Ha! Now that's funny. Maybe you should try stand-up comedy too."

I laugh a little, though I have no idea what "stand-up comedy" means. How hard would it be to write a book in English? I probably would have to write it in Turkish and translate it. A computer engineering guy writing a book. *Yeah right!*

11

LEGITIMATE CONCERNS

Bonnie and I fall into a relationship of sorts. She gets jealous of me with other girls at work. I shouldn't like it when she accuses me of flirting with the other waitresses, but I do—it makes me feel like she cares. We make love—or maybe it's just sex—and talk until we fall asleep. I think I'm falling for her, may already have fallen for her, in fact, and I'm afraid of doing something stupid and ending up heartbroken again. She's very different from Francesca, yet we hang out together all the time like Francesca and I did. And, while I loved Francesca, we never had sex because I thought it would diminish my love for her. I don't feel that way about Bonnie. Even though we have sex constantly and there's no reason for us to get serious with each other or to respect each other, I'm beginning to care for her, perhaps more than I should, and too soon. If she decides to leave me some day, I have no support mechanism, all alone, it could be hard to cope with. I must keep this light and casual.

"Happy two-week anniversary," I say, handing Bonnie a glass of tea I've brewed in the coffee machine.

"Ah, yes. Happy anno to you too, Addo," she says, laughing and clinking my cup. "I've gotta hand it to you, a coffee maker really does make the best-tasting tea," she says.

"Agreed!"

"A marvel of your engineering brain. Who else would have thought to do that?" she says, kissing me.

After a compliments-free lifetime, the praise she lavishes on me still makes me feel a little uncomfortable. Awkwardly, I change the subject. "I can't believe I've known you, *known* you for two weeks."

"Oh my God! Adem, can't you just say sex? Sex! Just say it. I can't believe it's such a difficult word for you."

"Sex. There, I said it."

"You make me so proud," she says, snorting.

"So, tell me more about you. I feel like I still don't know everything there is to know. Do you have family nearby?"

"I'm going to answer that question, but just so you know, it sounds like a bad pickup line."

"Duly noted," I say, nodding my head, silently toasting Dr. Tiller for that one.

"So, I don't have any family here in DC, unfortunately. My sister lives in Colorado. She's a single mother. My brother is in Missouri and has a wife and two kids. And that's it. I mean, my parents, too. They are still in Kansas City," she says as she takes a sip of her tea. "Just so good! Yum. So, how about you? Anyone else here in the States with you?

"I'm here by myself. But, back home I have two older sisters. Actually, one of them now lives in Frankfurt. I'm the baby. Much younger than my sisters. Ela, the oldest, is ten years older than I am. And the other one who is eight years older, Eliz, she's in Frankfurt. They're both married. My parents are also in Istanbul."

"Are they married?"

"My parents? Yes."

"My parents are divorced. Dad is remarried; Mom doesn't actually believe in divorce because she's a devout Catholic. So, they actually got the marriage annulled after twenty-six years, even though they have three kids. I mean it's a ridiculous concept."

"Are you a devout Catholic?"

"Oh, no. No. I left the church years ago."

"Why?"

"With my lifestyle, it's not possible to stay in the church."

"What does that mean? They have Catholic churches here."

"They kind of don't like women frolicking around in bed with people they are not married to."

"Huh," I say. "I don't really know a lot about it. I'm not religious at all. My parents have some quiet kind of faith. They don't talk about it often. My grandmother wasn't religious either, but she had faith and she knew about the Bible."

"Religion is definitely a personal thing. At least, that's how I feel. I mean, marriage is religious."

"Mmm," I say, not really understanding what she means. "Have you ever thought of marriage?" I ask.

"Yes."

"Have you ever thought about being married to someone like me?" I don't know why I ask that. I don't even know what I mean by "someone like me." Bonnie and I are virtual strangers. I have no idea why I feel the need to know where she stands on the subject of me.

"Yes."

"Would you do it? I mean, if I asked."

"Yes," she says, "as long as you're not actually asking right now."

She squeezes my hand.

I hold on all night.

***

Sometimes, Bonnie and I spend the night at her house. She lives in a part of DC unceremoniously called Upper Northwest. It's farther from work, which is a negative. And she shares the house with three others—a bigger negative, especially since they are not very friendly. Bonnie says that's just how they are, but I take it personally. Despite my worries that Mrs. Hardwick will find out that Bonnie sleeps over and will kick me out for breaking the rules, and despite the fact that Bonnie's place is much nicer, it feels more comfortable at my place. On the few occasions I have seen Mrs. Hardwick in passing, she has said nothing to me about breaking the rules and she hasn't sought me out to reprimand me. I assume Dr. Tiller knows about Bonnie and is keeping my secret safe.

After dating Bonnie for three weeks, it's sheer coincidence that Bonnie doesn't sleep over the night before the rent is due. That morning, as I come up the stairs, my heart drops when I see Mrs. Hardwick sitting in her chair in the parlor near the landing. While it's not a surprise—it's her typical haunt on the first day of the month—I didn't realize it was December 1. This thing with Bonnie has made me lose my focus. Bonnie usually tiptoes out at around 7:00 a.m. before the rest of the boarders start stirring. And on rent day, Mrs. Hardwick takes her place at the door at exactly seven, so she doesn't miss anyone trying to dodge their way out of paying on time.

I run back downstairs to grab my rent money and notice that I never opened two letters I picked up at the Blues Saloon. I can't even remember when Dan gave them to me. *Man! Get it together.* One letter is from Washington University and one is from Demir. I rip open Demir's letter.

Before heading back upstairs, I read it quickly. Izzy's gotten married and he and his wife are expecting their first child in a few months. And, Demir is getting married at the end of the year. *I'm not going to be able to go to my best friend's wedding?* I scribble a quick letter to each of them—asking Demir about Zeki and telling him how sorry I am that I will miss his wedding. I tell them all is well with me, that I'm working on a graduate degree in computer science. I also promise both of them that I'll write more often, once a month if I can. I put both letters in the same envelope so I don't have to spend money on two stamps.

The other letter is a notice from Washington University that my tuition has increased, up from $160 per credit hour to $200. *Is my battle with money problems ever going to end?* I was about to celebrate the end of my first semester after racking up all A's and B's in my pre-requisite courses, including the English classes; but, the news of the tuition increase just spoils it. I'm finally ready to embark on my graduate degree in computer science and now I don't know how I'll afford it. The tuition alone is going to drain all my savings. I don't know if I'll have enough money for books. And now I doubt I'll be able to decrease my work hours at the Blues Saloon, again, to make room for my heavier class schedule. I may have to move forward with my plan to work double shifts over the summer instead of taking summer classes.

Despite my lack of money, my wallet is getting even thicker. Having made the third monthly payment toward my passbook loan, I've established the credit Paul told me I needed and I am now a happy holder of an American Express card. I can't believe it—another ID that ties me to America. I don't know if I'm fooling myself, my illegal self, that I belong here. But, with each new card, with each new piece of official paper I receive, I feel like a regular, mainstream person. That's all I want. To feel like I belong. I pull the card out of my wallet. I look at it, running my fingers over my name. Smiling, I tuck it back in my wallet behind my student ID.

While I feel more legitimate, more confident, Bonnie doesn't see what I feel. She calls me "uptight" and "timid." The first time she said it, we were on the way to her house. It came out of nowhere, as far as I was concerned.

"Uptight and timid? Me? What do you mean? Like how?"

"Oh, I don't know . . . Let's see. Okay, well, at first you kept turning down my offers for a ride home. And, now, well, always actually, you never really talk to my roommates. I don't know if you are shy or aloof."

"I don't think your roommates like me very much, so I'm just trying not to engage with them."

"They don't even know you enough to like or not like you. I think you might just have trouble making friends."

"Really," I say, trying to sound as sarcastic as I can. It's not a tone I use a lot. "So, Dr. Morrison, would you like me to lie down on the couch so you can analyze me?"

"I'm just sayin' . . . I mean, did you have friends in Turkey?"

"Of course I had friends."

"Well, there's something else. Did you have a troubled childhood or something?"

"How do you get from me not chatting with your roommates to me having a troubled childhood?"

"I don't know. I'm just trying to figure you out. I mean . . . Like your body posture, for example. You're hunched over all the time. You just don't look that confident. You don't appear secure."

"Maybe it's because I'm trying to make myself small, unobtrusive. I don't have proper papers. You know, I'm illegal. So, perhaps it's more about trying not to draw too much attention to myself. Maybe I didn't have the greatest childhood but I *do* have friends. Why am I defending myself to you? Americans are overconfident anyway, you know, loud. My people are more deferential."

"Ha! You are not wrong. Maybe I should say that louder? Ha!" she says, and I hold my hands up to my ears. We both laugh. "So, I mean, what happened that you didn't have the greatest childhood? Were you bullied? Beaten?"

"Sure. Like most kids. No big deal."

"Huh. So, did you punch back?"

"Sometimes, but I'd lose the fight anyway because all the kids who picked a fight with me were bigger than me. Always. I skipped two grades, so I was always the runt. But, my friend Demir says I have a pretty mean right hook. I got good at punching at my navy high school. I trained on a punching bag. There was no beating there anyway."

"Who beat you before then?"

"The teachers beat us in middle school, I never fought back. Just balled up to protect myself. You know, the key zones like the kidneys, head, ribs. You know."

"No, I don't know. What do you mean you were beaten up by teachers?"

"What do you mean, 'what do I mean'? I was beaten up by teachers. Like that's what they did when their students disobeyed. They beat the kids."

"What the hell, Adem. That's not normal. That's against the law. I mean, other than in Catholic school."

"Well, it was normal where I grew up."

"Did you tell your parents?"

"There was no point. Parents believed that if a teacher beat up their child, their child must have deserved it."

"Jeez! Honestly Adem. That's horrible. So, um, did your parents hit you?"

"Only my mom; she'd beat only me, not my sisters. But not my dad. He never beat us. Then one day, my mom just stopped beating me. I think it's because I got my appendix taken out."

"What do you mean?"

"I had been complaining one morning that my stomach hurt. I was nine and my mother always thought I lied about everything. I'm not sure why, she just did. So, I had this stomachache and Mom asked me if I'd eaten junk food. When I told her 'No,' which was true, she didn't believe me and hit me for lying. But then, the pain wouldn't stop, and I developed a fever. So, my dad took me in his army jeep to the military hospital. Bouncing down the cobblestone streets was like torture. Sometimes I can feel this sort of phantom pain when I drive on the cobblestone streets in Georgetown. Well, anyway, I had a ruptured appendix. I heard the nurse tell Dad I had nearly died; it wasn't because of the appendix but the infection it had caused. The surgery took nine hours; they kept me in the hospital for six days. After that, my mother never hit me again. I think she felt guilty. I mean, she ignored my pain and because of that, I nearly died."

"And what about the teachers? I mean, did they slap your hands with rulers and stuff like that?"

"It was more like actually being beaten up." I tell Bonnie the story of my language teacher, who kicked and punched me and then threw me down the hallway. "It's probably why I didn't learn English until I moved to America."

"I have no words. That is so . . . I can't believe your parents didn't do anything about it."

"They didn't even notice. I had a black eye and a sliced-open cheek. They said nothing."

"So, did you come here to run away from all of that?"

No one else has ever asked me questions like this before. Not even Francesca.

"Not necessarily. I don't know. Maybe in part. Not every kid was beaten. Only the disobedient ones. And, it's not like I tried to be disobedient. I just didn't always understand all the rules and got in trouble for that. And I didn't know it wasn't normal, you know, the way I grew up. As for America, all I knew was what I saw in the movies and what my best friend from home, Demir, told me. He lived here for eight years, pretty much grew up here. It's why I came to DC, because Demir had lived here. We came here together, but then his father fell ill and he moved back home. Anyway, what I loved about America were basketball, rock 'n' roll, cars, and forests filled with orange, red, and yellow trees."

"Huh."

"And maybe something else . . ."

"What's that?"

"I can't quite explain. It's just a feeling. A feeling of hope, of freedom, of joy, of love. Something drew me here, something strong. I don't know what it was."

***

A few weeks into our relationship, Bonnie's interest in me doesn't escape the attention of her ex-boyfriend, Brooks, who has suddenly become a fairly regular customer of the Blues Saloon again. Over the course of three weeks, I watch his hostility toward me grow. Staring turns into nasty looks and then shoulder bumps. I don't know if that's going to be the extent of it or if it's going to escalate into something more. Working the front door on Friday and Saturday nights, I feel like an open target. I can't shoulder bump him back; I can't punch him or trash talk him; defending myself could mean losing my job.

He's like an animal stalking his prey. He's made it a habit to come in and out several times a night, mocking and harassing me at the door each time, bumping me with his shoulder. He says things like, "Oh, Addo, my doorman," and "Addo, the Wuss." The first few times he says it, I don't realize it's an insult. I'd never heard the term "wuss" before. I also initially assumed that the in and out was a drug thing and that the shoulder bumps were because he was stoned and drunk. Bonnie told me that one of the reasons she broke up with him was because of his cocaine habit.

I try to ignore him, and it works for a short while—until it doesn't. On an uncharacteristically warm Friday night in mid-December, he's been in and out five times, which, by my count, is more than usual. I'm fairly certain he's not going out to enjoy the weather. On his sixth return, I watch as he walks toward me. Standing at the door, I brace myself for another shoulder bump, which will be the eighth of the night. Just as I've turned my body to absorb the blow, he speeds up and throws his head against mine. It feels like a slab of concrete hit my head. My head jerks back against the door and stars dance in front of my eyes. I taste metal in my mouth, and the tang transports my rattled brain back to the disco in Istanbul, when the bully jumped up on our table and flew at me. I'm back in Istanbul, an angry kid tired of being picked on. I throw my right fist at Brooks's face. It's not a reflexive hit, but a punch that carries years of anger jam-packed with rage; I fit it all in between my knuckles.

I watch him as he flies backward from the portico to the sidewalk, hitting the ground like a rag doll. "Canin Cehenneme!" I mumble as blood runs down my face. I begin to go after him on the street, but I feel a hand on my back and whip around, ready to strike. "Adem, Adem. It's okay, stop, stop; he's out," I hear a female voice say. *Francesca?*

"Canin Cehenneme!" I curse again.

"What are you saying?"

"You know what I'm saying. I taught you that phrase, 'go to hell.' Remember?"

"Adem. Adem, are you okay?"

Francesca looks at me, anxiously.

I look back out on the street. Krishnas are singing and dancing across the street. Brooks is lying on the curb, motionless and bleeding, with the top half of his torso out on the street, a couple of people kneeling by him. He looks unconscious.

I turn back to look inside the bar and realize it's Bonnie, not Francesca, who is standing next to me; she's holding a bag of ice against my face.

Dan comes running past me and stands over Brooks for a minute. He looks up and down the street, and then comes to stand right in front of me, stepping into my personal space. He lifts his two hands, then pushes me in my chest, rocking me back. My shoulder hits the wall. "What the fuck, Addo! Can't you handle the door without hitting the customers?"

I hear sirens in the distance.

I push Bonnie's hand away, a little harder than I intend, and the bag of ice falls to the ground. I run to the back of the bar and through the kitchen.

My head feels heavy, my fist is sore. I'm less worried about how I feel than about the cops and immigration. If the police come now, I could be hauled away, even kicked out of the country. The newspaper headline would be clear: An Illegal Worker Flies into a Rage and Attacks an American Citizen in Georgetown: He Remains at Large.

I push the back door open and stand on the back patio. It's not the first time I've done this; immigration drills and actual raids are not unusual at Georgetown bars and restaurants. But this is the first time I'm running from the law for something I've actively done. I jump over the wall and walk around the block. From across the street, I check to see what's happening at the front door of the bar. The sirens are still in the distance.

I walk quickly down a side street and run to grab a taxi that's dropping passengers at the end of the block. The driver looks at me warily in his rearview mirror. I keep my head down for the rest of the ride.

When I get back to my room, I turn on my TV, grab the ice tray from the freezer section of my little fridge, and intermittently hold the cold pack against my head and hand. *Happy Days* is on. I let out a laugh. "Happy day, ha!" I say out loud. "Yeah, right."

I grab some cookies from a half-eaten box of Entenmann's chocolate chip cookies.

I wish Bonnie were here, lying next to me.

12

CAN'T BE RICH

The next day, on the way to the Blues Saloon, I stop by the newsstand to look at the headlines in the *Nation's Daily*. The top story is an article about the formation of a new center-right coalition government. I invest the $1.50 to buy the paper this time. After three years in power, the military-backed government has stepped aside and parliamentary elections have been held. I suspect it's going to be politics as usual, that is, as things were before the military coup, with one key difference: The same men will be running the show, but this time around, since the party heads have been banned from politics, the people of Turkey just won't see their faces or their names in print.

After reading the article, I turn back to the front page and glance at the headlines below the fold. "Retrial for Savas Kartal." My heart drops as I read the thick, black font and scan the sentences below, my eyes jumping around the page, reading the article out of order, trying to absorb it as fast as I can as the blood drains from my face. "Savas Kartal's lawyers are requesting a retrial . . . the military court convicted Kartal of murder without sufficient evidence . . . Kartal is a political figure . . . leader of the Nationalist youth and the anti-Communist movement." Kartal's lawyers argued that the eyewitnesses who were called to testify in his military trial were his enemies, and therefore, he didn't receive a fair trial. If he's not found guilty in the retrial, Savas Kartal, a murderer, will be a free man.

Eight murders. He murdered eight people. He and his lawyers claim Savas was involved in not one of those murders. And what about the additional murders for which he is suspected of being the triggerman? And the attempted murders? What are they thinking? Is this all politics and money? Is it possible that the missing $400,000 went to Savas Kartal's defense team? Is Mr. Baris part of this conspiracy to free this assassin?

The news makes me jumpy. I can't stop worrying about what Savas out of prison might look like and if there would be any implications for me. As I continue toward work, I envision a world with Savas out of prison. By the time I get to work, I'm so worked up about Savas Kartal that I walk right into Paul as I enter the bar.

"Paul! I'm sorry," I say, as I keep walking, my head down, still in thought.

"Adem. You okay, man?"

"Yeah, just . . . you know, a lot on my mind."

"I heard about last night. Jealousy, huh?"

"It's been brewing for quite a while; but, yeah, it was still pretty unexpected."

"He's not a nice guy. Not a good guy at all. I met him a few times when he used to come in with Bonnie."

"I don't think Dan realizes that. I don't think Dan realizes that Brooks attacked me."

I look around for Dan, who isn't visible but could be lurking, one of his new habits. I'm worried he's going to fire me.

"Don't worry about him, about Dan. He's, you know, well, he's Dan."

"Still. I caused a scene. Dan doesn't like 'scenes.' "

"Well, you're right about that. But, trust me, pal, you're good. You'll be fine. I think you're his most valuable employee."

"You really think so?"

"I do," Paul says, handing me some aspirin. "Premedicate. When you start lifting stuff later, you'll thank me."

"Can I thank you now, too?" I ask.

"Good one," Paul says, throwing a towel over his shoulder and picking up a rack of clean glasses. "Wanna help me set up the bar?"

"Absolutely."

We work in silence. It's comfortable. While Dan may be behind a door, waiting to lunge at me, still, it's actually kind of peaceful.

After the bar is set up, I walk down to the basement to make sure the beer kegs are lined up properly, then come back up to add more beer mugs to the stack of crates in the walk-in freezer. I also make sure that the supply of onion rings, fries, mushrooms, zucchini, and cheese sticks is ready for the Saturday night crowd. I check the tables and make sure the condiments are set. I make sure that the stage is set up. I'm not convinced that I'm Dan's most valuable employee. I need to convince both of us that I'm invaluable to Dan.

About an hour later, as I'm checking on the hamburger supply, Dan walks through the kitchen and directly to his office without saying anything. He looks upset, but it's hard to tell if he looks more upset than usual.

I need to say something. I need to keep this job. I need to apologize. I wait a minute, then walk over to his office and knock on the open door.

"Yeah, what?" Dan says, without even looking up.

"I'm sorry about last night," I say, still standing in the doorway. I wait, watching Dan shuffle some papers on his desk.

"It's fine," Dan says, finally, looking up at me from his chair. "Actually, I didn't know you had it in you, Adem. Brooks is an asshole. And I've convinced him not to press charges."

"Maybe I shouldn't work at the door."

"No. No. You've proved to me you can handle it. I want you at the door on weekends."

"Okay. Well. Thank you, Dan. Thanks for talking to Brooks. I'm going to head back to work."

When I return to the kitchen, Bonnie is there.

"Oh my God! Adem, I'm so sorry. I don't . . . I'm just so sorry. You okay?" she whispers.

"Apology accepted."

"I didn't want this to happen."

"I know. But it did. So let's forgive and forget," I say. This was one of Grandma's favorite expressions and I was happy to find out it's one Americans use, too.

Bonnie gives me a hug.

"Done," I say. "It's water under the bridge. We've buried the hatchet. Let's kiss and make up," I say, spouting off my Dr. Tillerisms.

"Okay, let's do that." Bonnie kisses me and we both laugh.

"We're good?" she asks.

"We're good."

***

It ends up being a typical Saturday night. The place is packed, the music is great, and there are no ex-boyfriends loitering and no violent patrons lying in wait.

At the end of the night, after cleaning up in the kitchen and taking out the trash, I walk out to the bar. Paul slides an icy cold bottle of Michelob across the bar top. I catch it and raise the bottle for a salute. I look around for Bonnie.

"You looking for Bonnie?"

"Yeah, I haven't seen her all evening."

"She got fired," Paul says, quietly, shrugging his shoulders.

"What?" I look at Dan, who smiles and raises his beer bottle in my direction.

"Yup. Happened at about eleven o'clock," Paul says.

I down my beer and walk out of the bar, not even waiting for Dan's nightly rant, ignoring him as he shouts at me to come back. I hail a cab and contemplate going straight to Bonnie's, then decide I should go home first. *Was she fired because of me? Why didn't Dan fire me?*

The cab pulls up in front of my house and as he pulls away, I see Bonnie's VW Golf parked across the street.

When she gets out of the car, I nod at her. Together, we tiptoe down the stairs to my room and remain silent even once we've arrived at my room. Bonnie sits down on the bed as I make some tea.

After a few minutes, I break the silence. "Why were you fired?"

"I don't want to talk about it."

"What's that supposed to mean? You don't want to talk about it. Did you get fired because I punched Brooks?"

"No. Not because of that. Please, I don't want to talk about it right now."

"Okay. But . . . I mean, what are you going to do now, for work?"

"I don't know . . . I haven't thought about it yet. It just happened; I don't have a plan yet. I guess I'll start thinking about it tomorrow."

"You mean, you don't have a fallback plan?"

"What do you mean?"

"I mean, what's your backup plan? Like for me, if Dan fires me from the Blues Saloon, my backup plan is to go back to Crazy Zebra to ask for work. If they say no, I start asking other places. So, what's *your* backup plan?"

"I don't have one. I didn't expect to get fired."

"What do you mean, you don't have a plan? You always have to have a plan. Things don't just work out. You have to be ready for a setback. And, you need a backup plan for your fallback plan . . ."

"You sound like you're talking about football, American football," she says, laughing. "It's idiotic."

"I'm serious, Bonnie. If plan A doesn't work out, you have another one at the ready. Otherwise, you can end up on the street, homeless, and hungry."

"Lord, Adem. Wow. You are seriously dramatic. I'm not going to go hungry because I lost my job. I'll be fine. I have some money saved. I have no debt; my car is paid for. I'm not going to be homeless. My place costs $200 a month. Plus, I have unemployment benefits. I'm fine."

"Don't you think you should change your approach and focus on a real job now, use your education . . . your biology and law degrees?"

I walk over to the dresser, pick up last Sunday's *Post,* and turn to the employment section. I plop down next to Bonnie. "Look here, a librarian at the Library of Congress. A paralegal. A real estate attorney. A patent attorney. By tomorrow, you could apply for a dozen jobs. All you need is one of them to accept you."

"Put down the paper and make love to me," Bonnie says.

***

When I wake up the next morning, Bonnie is gone. I've slept well past my usual 7:00 a.m. alarm, which I apparently forgot to set. *Please don't break my heart, Bonnie.*

***

Later, at the bar, the liquor truck is parked in front when I arrive. I help the driver unload four dozen boxes of liquor and beer that Dan has ordered. Realizing that I'm not going to see Bonnie at work today and without any clear plan on the next time we're going to see each other, I'm feeling a little rattled. As I make my way into the kitchen, I drop a case of wine. White wine drains out of the box and pools by my feet. When I open the box, I find more than half the bottles are cracked. *Was that a bad box or was it me?*

"What the fuck happened now?" I hear Dan yell out to me from his office.

"Nothing. All good," I call back. Then, as I begin pulling the broken bottles out, one by one, I see Dan's feet. He's standing in the puddle of wine.

"Nothing? Really, Adem?"

Dan pulls out one of the intact bottles. "The inexpensive stuff. You are a lucky man, my friend. You would never have been able to afford to pay me back for the Chivas Regal and Hennessy."

He smirks at me. I'm not sure if he's serious about me paying him for the broken bottles. "Some engineer you are," he says, twisting the word *engineer* on his tongue so it comes out in a mocking tone. It's the first time I've dropped anything in the three years I've worked for him, but I simply nod in agreement then quickly decide that I should get out in front of the situation and offer to pay for the damaged bottles.

"You're a good man, Addo. Clumsy as fuck, but a good man," Dan says, patting me on the back. "Let's call it even at sixty bucks."

That's more than half my rent!

When Dan leaves, Raymond walks over to me, looking over his shoulder a few times then, and in a low voice, says, "You didn't need to pay him for those broken bottles, man. Dan's not out any money; doesn't have to pay a dime.

The liquor supplier has insurance.”

“Seriously?”

“Seriously.”

“Huh,” I say, because I haven’t a clue what Dan is up to.

***

After another busy night, the staff gathers at the bar for our nightly scolding. But, for only the third time in as many years, there is none. All Dan says is, “When I was your age, anytime I made a mistake, I’d go home and kick myself. Drink up. Go home. Get out of here.”

I watch as everyone looks around at each other, stunned. “Is this a test?” I hear one of the waitstaff ask in a whisper. The rest of the group just stands there, shrugging.

“I said get out of here!” Dan yells, and as if in a practiced choreography, the staff members slam down their beer mugs and half-run, half-walk out of the bar.

I don’t move.

The waitstaff disperse and Dan walks over to where I’m sitting. He puts his hand on my shoulder, pressing it down with his weight, and, despite the fact that we have the room to ourselves, whispers to me, “You know Addo, you can never be rich.”

Oh Lord, here we go. “And why is that, sir?”

“Because you don’t steal.”

“Excuse me?”

“That’s the way to get rich. Steal. Tactfully.”

“You sound like my dad.”

“Your father is a smart man, Addo.”

“How do you know I don’t steal?” I really don’t want to engage with him, but I have to be careful not to make him angry with me.

“Not only do I know you do not steal, but I also know who does steal and how much.”

“How do you know that?” I ask, suddenly genuinely interested.

“Come along, I’ll show you,” he says walking over to the bar. I follow him with dread. "You see these open bottles?" he asks, pointing, then pulling one off the shelf. "I always remember the liquor level in each of them when I leave the bar area. When I come back later, I check the liquor levels again, the cash amount in the cash register, and the credit card transactions to compare what we've made with what's left. Because I rotate and mix the staff continuously and I know which ones do cash-and-carry instead of running a tab, it gives me a good idea about which employee is doing what. And I keep an extra eye on my thief."

"That's quite a process, sir. May I ask, why do you keep them if they steal from you?"

"It's the cost of doing business. Like all the bottles you drop and break. For those who steal from me, I allow a certain amount to be stolen; everybody has an allowance level. Once they exceed that level, Addo, they are fired." He looks me right in the eyes, then winks and nods.

Is that why Bonnie was fired?

13

LIONS' DEN

Between Dan and the news back home—the missing $400,000 may have gone to Savas Kartal and his defense—and worrying about Bonnie, I'm on edge. Plus there are rumors the university is getting ready for another tuition increase, from $200 to $300 per credit hour, beginning in the fall. That means my tuition will increase from $10,000 to $14,000 and my budget shortfall will bump up to $4,000.

On the way to work, after two nights of not sleeping, I stop at the newsstand. I pick up the *Nation's Daily* and look at the stories at the top of the fold. There's a small photo on the left side of the page and I lean forward, squinting to see if I recognize anyone. I flip the paper to read the caption. "Osman Baris with His Project Team." I look back at the photo and pick out Mr. Baris.

"Buy, no read. Buy!" the man behind the counter yells at me.

I buy the paper, $1.50, then walk over to a nearby bench. I scan the article quickly, taking a break every now and again to look at the photo.

The article says Mr. Baris is planning to construct a fifty-thousand-capacity, high-rise residential and commercial neighborhood on the outskirts of Istanbul. He'll be traveling to New York to meet with some bankers to obtain loan guarantees totaling a billion dollars.

I turn back to the first page and look carefully at the photo, again, curious to see if I recognize anyone else. When I get to the man standing just left of Mr. Baris, I pause. "Oh my Lord," I say out loud in Turkish, surprising myself. *It's the man I handed the $400,000 to. What was his name? Mr. K . . . Kaya? Mr. Kaya.* "Kaya!" I say out loud. *That's his name.* I read the caption again. No names other than Mr. Baris's are given. I'm not sure why, but I'm convinced that Kaya isn't this man's real name.

It's been three and a half years since that day I delivered the money at the Nationalist Party's district headquarters. "Mr. Kaya," I say out loud, again, almost to remind myself not to forget his name, even if it's fake. My heart skips a beat as I remember how I stormed breathlessly into the room where I had handed him the money only to find it set up as a storage room, wiping out the history of the transaction entirely.

I get up and continue on my way to work.

So, Kaya is a member of Mr. Baris's team. I wonder if he was a member of Mr. Baris's team on the day the money went "missing." If he's still a member of Mr. Baris's team, that means he couldn't have been the man who stole the $400,000. If Kaya wasn't the final destination, then who was? Who did he give the money to? The Nationalist Party? Yavuz Security? Savas? Perhaps all of the above. When I delivered the money, who did Kaya call to confirm? Obviously not Soner. Could it have been Mr. Baris, like I thought? If Kaya works for Mr. Baris, then maybe. But Kaya said, "Yes, Bayer. He's here. Adem Bayer. Yes, received." Mr. Baris wouldn't give a hoot who delivered the money. Did Kaya call Savas? Could Kaya have called Savas? Maybe. I think back to all the Turkish movies I've seen, which is my only point of reference for how jails work. Inmates call out from a regular, token-operated public phone. Just like we did in the navy high school. Once a week, cadets would line up outside the phone booth and make their allotted five-minute calls—except me; I didn't call anyone because I had no one to call, not even my parents. One could only dial out; pay phones didn't receive calls.

So, if Kaya was calling Savas in jail, he wouldn't have been able to reach Savas directly. He would have had to call someone else first. I suspect someone in an office, maybe some jail employee who supported Savas or who was being paid off. Hmm. So then that person would tell Savas, who would call back as soon as he could. I could just be overthinking this, but I think Savas had a strategy. He was trying to frame me so I'd get nabbed, then thrown in jail where he could kill me to prove to his followers and my "Communist associates" that he keeps his word. When Kaya confirmed to Savas the delivery boy was "Adem Bayer," he had Kaya report that I'd never delivered the money. That way, Soner or Mr. Baris, or Kaya, even, would report me to the police.

But, where Savas's strategy failed, the loophole in his scheme, that is, is that it was illegal money, therefore could not come directly through the legitimate Nationalist Party, so it had to be a covert political contribution supporting thugs and murderers, and therefore had to remain in cash and off the record. There was no proof. Even in his crooked circles, there was no way for Savas to implicate me. He could only hope Mr. Baris or Soner would do so, but they could not do it either, because they too would have implicated themselves.

So, I had never needed to be afraid that the police or Interpol were after me. I wish I had figured this all out three years ago. I wonder if once Savas found out that I wouldn't be joining him in jail, he acknowledged the money was received, and blamed it on a mix-up in communication.

I want to call Soner.

I'm distracted at work again; I've burned french fries and overcooked some hamburgers while working as Raymond's sous chef. I can't think of anything other than what I'm going to say to Soner. It's been three and a half years, how ludicrous it is to call him. But I have to. Shouldn't Soner know who he is working with?

"You know what, let me do that," Raymond says, carefully taking the knife and onions from me. "I don't need you losing any fingers today."

"Sure," I say, still distracted. I trip on the stairs on the way down to the basement to check the levels on the beer kegs, then limp my way back to the walk-in fridge to grab some frozen beer mugs. Crap, I didn't restock them. I take a couple crates with warm mugs to Paul and apologize, then go back to stock the freezer and slide in some new beer mugs. My mishaps continue, one after another, until the end of the evening.

As I walk over for Dan's beer bashing at the bar, I have no doubt my indiscretions will lead off the evening's rampage, and I just don't want to hear it. As Dan starts lighting into me, I chug my beer, then nod my head with a confidence I didn't know I had, and I walk out the door.

It's 3:30 a.m. by the time I pick up the phone; it's 10:30 a.m. in Istanbul. I dial Soner, then hang up before it starts ringing. "Let sleeping dogs lie," Dr. Tiller taught me. "Don't poke the bear." It's a bad idea to call Soner. It's not my job to protect him or do his dirty work for him anymore. As far as I know, he's one of the bad guys too.

I shower and sleep fitfully, again, for three hours, before heading out for the day.

***

That night, when I finish my shift at 2:30 a.m., Bonnie is standing on the sidewalk outside the Blues Saloon.

"You want a ride home?" she asks without saying hello.

"Do I have a choice?" I say in a mocking, sarcastic tone, smiling, playing along.

"Funny guy, a regular stand-up comic!" she says back with a laugh. I still don't get the joke but smile. I have to remember to ask Dr. Tiller about it.

As I follow her toward her car, I hear someone calling out to me. "Hey, Addo!" Turning around, I see Jorge waving his arms in the air. He's standing in front of Thira Gyros.

"Hey Jorge! Are you working hard or hardly working?" I ask, using a Dr. Tiller expression.

"Nah, it's slow now; was busy before. Hey Addo, your cousin found you?" Jorge asks.

"What?"

"Yeah man, your two cousins were here. Nice fellows. They asked if you still work at the Blues Saloon."

I'm wondering who these men could be when Jorge adds, "They told me, 'don't tell him.' They wanted to surprise you, I think."

"Are you sure they were looking for me, not someone else?"

"No man—it was you. Two men. They showed me your picture. They know your last name."

"What did they say my last name was?"

"Bayer, like medicine—you know?"

"What kind of picture did they show you?"

"Old, like, passport picture. Did I do something wrong, amigo?"

I smile. "No, man, it's all good. Maybe they'll still find me later," I say, trying to appease Jorge's concern, if not my own.

Jorge smiles, looking relieved.

"When did they come by?" I ask, looking around for anyone suspicious.

"I dunno. Two days before?" Jorge fixes his eyes on Bonnie. He grins at her, then pulls a sad face. "Bye Bonnie, you said you come to see me. Why you don't? Makes Jorge sad."

Bonnie blows Jorge a kiss. "I'll be by soon to visit, Jorge, I promise."

I tune out their flirting. My mind is reeling, furiously. *Who are these men? My only cousin is twelve or thirteen. Even Jorge would describe him as a boy. Maybe it was Demir and Izzy? But no. No, no way. They would have called me. Or, could it be Roberto, maybe, and a friend of his? What I don't get is two men who know that I work at the Blues Saloon but have to ask around to verify it first. But, if they came to find me two days ago, why didn't they come back?* I can't calm my mind. *Could they be Mr. Baris's men? That's ridiculous, Adem. Why would Mr. Baris send men from Turkey to find me in America more than three years after money went missing?* I can't slow down my thoughts. My heart is racing. *Could it be Savas? Savas? Really? I'm off my rocker. While he's in prison? His men though, maybe? How would he know I'm here? And why would he spend money to track me down in America?* I'm grasping for anything, trying to figure this out. *Maybe they came to New York with Mr. Baris. But Savas wouldn't know where I work. Would he? Nobody in Turkey knows where I work, except Dad, and I guess Technical University too, which mailed my transcripts. Maybe Jorge got it wrong. His English isn't so good. Maybe he just wanted to make conversation in front of Bonnie, impress her.*

"Adem . . . Earth to Adem, earth to Adem," I hear. I look up and see that Bonnie is a few steps ahead of me. She's turned around and has her hands cupped to her mouth like a loudspeaker. "Earth to Adem."

"I'm here. Sorry. Trying to figure out which cousins came to visit me," I say, lying, trying to get myself out of my head. I jog up to where she is standing, waiting for me.

She tosses me the keys as she asks, "Wanna drive?" They almost hit me in the face. "Mr. One Hundred Percent," she grouses loud enough for me to hear, as we get in. I see a flash of Francesca sitting in the passenger seat of my car when Savas shoots at us. Remembering how I lied to protect her, how I remained silent when she demanded an explanation. *Why is my first thought to lie and evade in the face of danger?*

"I wanted you to be the first one to know, I got a job!" Bonnie says as I pull out onto the street.

"Good! Congratulations. Well done! What kind of a job?" I ask, trying to concentrate on Bonnie while half of my brain is focused on teasing out every possible person these "cousins" could be.

"I'm training to be a police officer."

"Wow!" I say, wondering if she'll need to confess to stealing from Dan before she becomes a full-fledged officer. I want to ask her about getting fired, but I figure if she wanted me to know, she'd tell me.

"Well, I'll be like a police officer. An officer without a uniform."

"Like, an undercover cop?" I ask, looking over at her, seeing Francesca, again. *You're in DC, Adem, in Bonnie's car. Get it together, man.* I shake my head, trying to shake away memories from Istanbul.

"Something like that," Bonnie says. "I'll actually be working for the federal government, not for DC. I'll be in training for one month. I'll have a partner, a senior agent."

"Oh. So . . . FBI?"

"No, it's the other one," she says.

I don't know what that means. But, I congratulate her.

"Let's celebrate at your place," she says. "I can stay over, right?"

"Sure." She could be the distraction I need.

I find a parking spot about halfway down the block from the house. As we walk up the hill to the front door, Bonnie grabs my hand and swings it—like a happy kid. Then, practiced in our steps, we tiptoe to my room.

***

The following night, I finish my shift at the Blues Saloon and head outside, looking for Bonnie. When I don't see her, I'm disappointed.

"Ding, ding, ding," the yellow Volkswagen drives by its megaphones blasting, "Repent and Turn to God. The End is Near!"

As the car passes, I see Jorge in front of Thira's. "Hey man," I yell in his direction. "Have you seen Bonnie?" He shakes his head and I shrug. "Women!" I shout back with a chuckle, trying to make light of it, then step out into the street to hail a cab.

As the cab pulls up in front of the house to drop me off, I notice a cream-colored Volkswagen Golf parked across the street, a few houses down. *Bonnie's here!* I find myself smiling as I pay the driver. I get out of the cab and head her way, making out the silhouette of her face through the windshield in the light of the streetlamp. I laugh out loud, thinking of what she's going to say, in the girlish, flirty lilt she has that I realize I've grown quite fond of. "May I please come in and sleep—"

Something crashes down on my head and neck. My knees give way. In some out-of-body moment, I watch myself fall, in slow motion. I hit the sidewalk.

***

I open my eyes to darkness. I hear a moaning sound and quickly realize that the sound is my own. I realize my head is covered. I try to move my arms so I can remove the cover, but I find that I can't. *What is happening? What happened? Where am I?* My body falls sideways and then back the other way. My head hurts. I try to move my arms, again, to brace myself, but I still can't. *What is going on?* I feel around with my hands and discover they are tied behind my back. I tip to the side again. *Am I in a car?* I listen for a second. *Yes, I'm in a car.* There are no sounds other than my breathing . . . and car sounds. And an occasional moan that I emit without the means to control myself. *Is that a distant siren, a honking car horn?* I list to the right again and, this time, I'm stopped by something that feels cold. *A door? A window? I feel what's behind me with my hands. Cold, and maybe leathery, vinyl? Okay. Yes.*

I'm definitely in a car. I list to the left and feel my body lean into something else. On this side, there is something softer. *Is it a person? Am I in the backseat of a car with a person? Is it . . . What is her name? Man, for Lord's sake, you are sleeping with her.* My head is pounding. *What is her name?*

I take a slow breath in through my nose. My neck is stiff. I slowly try to move my feet and discover that my ankles have been crossed and tied together, too. All I can smell is wool, or whatever it is that's over my head, a bag, a hat, a coat.

Why can't I think, what is wrong with my brain? What is her name? Though I can see nothing, I close my eyes to concentrate.

Bonnie? Bonnie. Yes, that's it. Bonnie. Could it be Bonnie's car? Am I in Bonnie's car? Is she sitting next to me? Is she driving? I'm about to open my mouth and call Bonnie's name, but I stop myself. Something tells me, some sixth sense, not to speak. *Wait, it doesn't feel like Bonnie's car.* I'm not sure why, it just doesn't. *Okay, so it's not Bonnie's car. But I'm in a car.*

What's going on? Think. I let out another groan. It hurts to think. I try to concentrate and immediately see Bonnie's VW in my mind. *Bonnie's car was the last thing I saw. Where was I? On Wisconsin Avenue? No, wait, I was home. She didn't pick me up from work. I took a cab from the Blues Saloon. Okay, good. What else? I got out of the cab and . . . what happened when you got out of the cab, Adem? Think! I hit rewind in my head. I paid the driver, got out and . . . and . . . and what, I see Bonnie's car. Okay, good Adem. What else? I am standing in front of Mrs. Hardwick's house and I see Bonnie's car. Was she in the car? I replay it in my mind again. Bonnie was there. I can see Bonnie in the car, the lamppost silhouetting her face. Did she see me getting hit? Did she say, "Watch out"?*

"Ne kadar daha var?" I hear someone say. For a second, I'm confused. *Wait, was that Turkish? It can't be Turkish, Adem. You were hit over the head. Maybe you have a concussion. Maybe you're dreaming.*

"Ne kadar daha var?" I hear the same voice say again, this time, louder, angrier. *It is Turkish. This is not my brain playing tricks on me. This is Turkish. Okay, so that means it's me and at least two other people, men, in a car going to a specific place but at least one of them doesn't know how long it will be until we get there, which means he isn't familiar with the area. So where are we?*

"Bu dogru adam mi?"

"Resme bak gor. Bence o."

They have my picture, they want to make sure I'm the right man—now, after kidnapping me?

Then, as if they know I've regained consciousness, the men start whispering. I hear only "the boss" and "he says." The cover on my head makes it hard to decipher what they are saying. *Who are these men? What do they want?* "The boss's jet," I hear, then "flight attendant" and "nice legs." *Who is "the boss"? What is happening? Are these the men who were looking for me the other day? The ones Jorge was talking about. My "cousins"? Have three and a half years finally caught up with me? Are they going to kill me? Is this the night I die?*

My body lists right and then we come to a stop. I hold my breath. Are they going to toss me out of the car? Are they going to kill me here, wherever we are? The car starts moving again, turning left, then making another left and then stops again. I hold my breath. *This is it. This is where it happens.* I brace myself. And then the car takes a right. We've gone from moving constantly to stopping and starting. *Maybe we were on a highway and now we are on side roads?*

And then it occurs to me that Bonnie could be following the car. *She must have seen what happened. But, if she saw it, why didn't she stop the men? Didn't she say she's a cop? An undercover cop? No, she said she was training to be a cop, not cop . . . not FBI but something else. But that's absurd, Adem; if there are two or three men in this car, how could she, alone, stop them? Maybe she called the police for back up. But if she stopped to call, she couldn't follow us. I've never seen a police radio in her car. Maybe she's following me and will find a way to call for help when we get wherever we're going, if there is an actual place.*

The car slows down. *This is it.* Then it makes a slow turn up an incline and rolls to a stop. I notice then the sound changes; it sounds hollow. *Are we in a garage?* The engine cuts off and doors start to open. *This . . . this is it.* I'm dragged out of the back seat by what feels like two people. I sink into my body to create dead weight. Once inside, I'm thrown onto a soft chair, maybe a couch.

After a minute I feel one of the men poke me. "Wake up!" someone yells at me in Turkish, kicking me in the shin. I cry out in pain. I don't want to; it just happens, I can't stop myself.

And then, nothing happens.

I take a deep breath and try to recall how I felt the day Polat held a gun to my head. I wanted to die that day; I wanted him to kill me. I felt no fear. *Perhaps that's why I lived? If I don't fear these men, maybe they won't kill me?* I take another deep breath, trying to remember how distraught I was when Francesca left me, trying to feel the despair, trying to find that despondence I felt, my desire to die. My shoulders relax, my stomach settles.

And still, nothing happens.

I remain seated, dozing off under the head cover. "Wake up!" someone yells at me in Turkish, kicking me again. I try not to make a sound but sit up straight to show to them I'm awake, just like I had to do for the cops in Dupont Circle.

I listen as the men walk in and out of the room mumbling things to each other that I cannot understand, all but ignoring me. I can also hear a clock ticking but I have no idea what time it is. It feels like we've been sitting here for twenty minutes, maybe. If they abducted me at 2:45 a.m., it's at least 3:15, but I don't know how long I was "out" or how long we were driving. I'm hoping Bonnie is working on a plan. I hope that she followed me here, called in reinforcements, and is parked outside somewhere down the street, waiting to bust down the door and rescue me.

"Are you Adem Bayer?" one of the men asks loudly in Turkish, kicking me again.

I shrug my shoulders, pantomiming that I don't understand the question, that I don't speak Turkish. I take a deep breath, remembering the despair I felt after Francesca left me. "I want to die. I want to die," I chant to myself, trying to believe it, trying not to care.

"Ayaga kaldir," one of the thugs says.

The next thing I know, I'm being yanked to my feet. I feel someone pulling my wallet from my back pocket. Still blindfolded and with my feet and hands still bound, I almost fall over. I can hear them rifling through the contents of my wallet.

"I will ask you again, are you Adem Bayer?" the same voice asks.

"I'm Adem, yes," I respond in English.

"Oturt sunu," he tells his men, and they throw me back down onto the chair.

I hear some fumbling and then the sound of numbers being punched on a phone. I count fifteen digits. Then I hear the sound of a phone being hung up. *Hmm. What's that about?* A few seconds later, there's a punching of numbers, again. And, once again, fifteen digits. "We're ready," someone says. "Yes, we're ready." And then the sound of the phone hanging up.

"You're going to speak Turkish, bastard," one of the men says, kicking me yet again. *Since he's the voice I keep hearing, he must be the head thug.* I nod. "We'll receive a phone call. You'll talk to the boss. Be respectful—understand?"

This phone situation seems eerily similar to the situation the day I delivered the $400,000 to Mr. Kaya. A call was made, then a brief conversation, and then waiting. *What's with this code or system they have: call, hang up, call, speak, wait for a call back? Who are they calling? Is it the same person Kaya dialed at the Nationalist Party headquarters? Is there a connection? Could these be the same men?* I feel myself getting agitated as the questions race through my head. *Is it possible that one of the thugs, here in America, these men who kidnapped me tonight, is one of them Mr. Kaya? Could that be? Is that possible? It can't be. It's been almost four years. That would be insane. Or would it?*

I take a deep breath as I continue to parse out all the possibilities, though I have absolutely nothing to go on. As far as I know, I have crossed no one in America. *Dan doesn't like me, but I don't think he'd kidnap me. He's the only person I regularly piss off but I think he'd just fire me rather than go through this elaborate ... Okay, that's just stupid, Adem. Dan doesn't speak Turkish!*

I hear the screeching of a chair and then footsteps

It has to be related to something that happened in Turkey. And that means it's something that happened more than three years ago ... almost four years ago. And the only thing that happened, the only thing I can think of, is the missing $400,000 and Savas Kartal's promise to kill me. That's it. That's all I've got.

I hear footsteps and the clattering of a teacup.

Could Savas be connected to the $400,000? I've still never figured that out. There are so many unanswered questions, including—Are these men going to kill me?

I take another deep breath. The head thug, I decide, is Mr. Kaya. Maybe he's in America as part of Mr. Baris's investment trip. And the boss . . . who's the boss? I can only come up with two possibilities. If thug one is Mr. Kaya then the boss is either Mr. Baris in New York or Savas Kartal in jail in Istanbul. Ten digits would be a call to New York. But he dialed fifteen digits, which means he was dialing overseas. I run through a list of possibilities in my head as we wait: *Did he call Savas Kartal in jail?*

14

TELECONFERENCE

THE PHONE RINGS AND I JUMP. ONE OF THE MEN LAUGHS, THEN kicks me. On the fourth ring, just like at the Nationalist Party headquarters, someone picks up the phone. "One second, boss," someone says. Then, there's a click.

"Is he there?" I hear a voice ask in Turkish. It sounds like the voice is in the room, though there's a crackle of static. It's a speakerphone. "Is the traitor there?"

"Yes, boss."

"What's your name?" the man on the phone asks in Turkish.

"You know my name. What's your name?" I say, responding in Turkish, trying to conjure up the feeling of indifference I felt as Polat's gun rubbed up against my head.

Someone kicks me. "Be respectful to the boss, you Communist coward."

"My name is Adem Bayer," I say in Turkish. "And you are . . ." I say, taking a deep breath, "Savas Kartal." Though I'm not completely sure, I say it as a statement. A smack nearly sends me off the couch and, as I try to anchor myself, my feet hit the table. I hear the clatter of items hitting the ground.

"Tunc, control your prisoner," the man on the phone says.

Tunc. It's not Mr. Kaya. I was wrong. So, maybe it's not Savas Kartal on the phone. Maybe the man on the phone is Mr. Kaya. What is going on? But, maybe it is Mr. Kaya. Maybe his first name is Tunc. "Mr. Kaya" could be a made-up name anyway.

I pull myself back up.

"You were supposed to join me here, but you got lucky."

"Yes," I say, trying to figure out what he means. *If it's Savas, does he mean to join him in prison?*

"America cannot protect you. As you can see. I can capture you anywhere in the world."

Maybe it is Savas. So does that mean it was Savas on the phone when I made the $400,000 delivery?

"Take off the blindfold. I want him to know when the end is coming. I want him to fear it."

My eyes are closed when one of them removes my head cover. "Open your eyes," the same voice orders, kicking me again. I open my eyes slowly, trying to adjust to the light in the room. There are two people in the room, their heads covered with ski masks. *Are these the "cousins" who were looking for me the other day? And, wait, wasn't there a third man tonight? I thought I heard three different voices.*

I look around the room for the third man.

"Answer the question, traitor!" one of the men yells, lifting the handle of the phone and making a motion to hit me with it.

"I don't . . . I didn't hear the question," I say, trying to take in my surroundings, noticing a small slit in the drawn curtains. I can see it's still dark outside.

"A bullet or hands?"

"I don't understand."

"How do you want to die? Gun or hands?"

Just as I am about to answer, the third man comes walking out of the kitchen, takes one look at me and drops his teacup.

"What's going on in there," Savas asks through the speakerphone.

The man walks closer to me. I flinch, thinking he's going to strike me. He just walks around me, looking at me from all sides. "What is your name?" the man asks, taking off his mask.

"What's going on!" Savas asks again through the phone.

"Adem Bayer," I say, confused, wondering why he's asking me, again; why he's looking at me.

He walks over to the other men, whispers something to them, then picks up the phone, disconnecting it from the speaker. He grabs the phone from the coffee table and stretches the cord as he walks back into the kitchen. I can't hear the conversation and the two other men look agitated as they stand still, watching me, their hands resting on their guns.

A minute later he returns to the living room and he puts the call back on speaker.

"My name is Timur. This is my house. I am friends with Savas from home. But, I live in America now." I nod, though what he has said has given me no clarity.

I look at the other two men. Their hands are resting by their sides now, no longer gripping their guns.

"Adem Bayer, hmm," he says, pacing a little. "Where did you spend your summers when you lived in Turkey?"

"Excuse me?"

"Where did you spend your summers?"

"Um. I don't know—in Istanbul, I guess," I say, thoroughly confused.

"Where else? Anywhere else?"

"Some of the beaches, sometimes. The Princess Islands, I think, maybe two times?"

"How about specifically in 1973—the summer of '73; where would you have been?"

"1973?"

"Yes. 1973. Where were you that summer?"

"Sir, I don't remember."

"Think. It's important."

"My head hurts," I say, groaning, shifting myself on the couch. "It's making it hard to think."

"Untie him," Timur says, looking at the other men.

The men don't move.

"Untie him!" he yells.

"Untie him," Savas says through the phone.

One of the thugs pulls out a knife and cuts my wrists free. I twist them, stretching my hands. He leaves my ankles bound.

"Do you want some tea?" Timur asks me.

"Yes, thank you. I would."

"Get him tea. Now!" Timur yells, and one of the men quickly heads into the kitchen.

"Try to remember, if you can. It's important," Timur says, coming over and sitting on the coffee table in front of me.

'73? I was fifteen. I became a senior in high school that year. "I think I was on the Aegean Coast that year, with my parents, some family and friends, too."

"Where on the Aegean? I mean the town."

"Oren is where we would go. It was probably Oren."

"What happened there?"

"What do you mean?"

"Did you swim?"

"Did I swim?"

"Yes. Did you swim?"

"Probably." Then I reconsider. "But actually, not that much, the water can be quite frigid over there."

"But, did you go to the beach?"

"Sure. Yeah, sure. Every day, pretty much. I went for walks on the beach, usually by myself."

"And, when you were walking, did you ever swim?"

He's being very specific about this swimming question, but he's being so cryptic, I'm not clear why. *He says this is important. So I must think. Think. Did I swim?* I shift myself on the couch a little more. My wrists are aching. "I do remember . . . yes. I did swim. But it was more dipping than swimming. The water was too cold to swim. I remember I would get in the water for a dip when it got hot. I'd jump in for about thirty seconds and then, freezing, I'd get out and keep walking."

"Was it crowded on the beach?"

"Sir?"

"When you walked on the beach, was it crowded? Were there a lot of people?"

"Sure. Yes. It was summertime. It was crowded."

"And, how about on the weekends?"

"The weekends?"

"Yes. Did you go to the beach on the weekend? Was it crowded on the weekends?"

I think back, visualizing the empty beach. "I don't know. I'm not sure. I'm having trouble remembering things. My head is hurting."

"You've got to try to remember."

"Okay. Okay. Right. Most of the vacationing families did not go to the beach on Sundays. I believe that's when the laborers from nearby came to the beach. I remember my father telling me there was some unwritten rule about that. So, we didn't go on the weekends. I don't know if it was crowded."

"So you never went to the beach on the weekends. Think. Please. This is important."

I think back. Closing my eyes, I think back and I see the empty beach. "Wait. Yes. I did go to the beach on the weekend, actually. I remember going. By myself. That last day before we were leaving to go home. It was a Sunday. I took a walk on the beach while my family was doing other things. It was not crowded."

"So, did you see anyone swimming?"

"I don't know. Maybe?" I say, completely unsure.

"Do you remember anything specific happening; anything out of the ordinary?"

"What do you mean?"

"On Sunday, walking on the beach, do you remember seeing anything unusual? Did anything eventful, noteworthy, significant happen? Again, anything."

"Um," I say, thinking back to that day on the beach, the last day before we went home. "Wait! Yes." *How could I have forgotten that?* "Yes. There was a man drowning."

"What?"

"There was a drowning man and I saved him."

"You saved a drowning man?"

"Yes. Wow. It's coming back to me now. I was walking on the beach, I saw a man flailing in the water. Then several men came running over to me. They said the drowning man was their friend. I remember asking them why they were standing there watching him drown, not helping him."

"What'd they say?"

"They said they couldn't swim that far."

"So what happened?

"Well, the man was drowning. I jumped in the water, swam as fast as I could, grabbed him as he went under and swam back with him."

"You rescued him?"

"Yes."

One of the thugs walks out of the kitchen with a cup of tea and hands it to me.

"Thank you," I say, as he hands it to me, eyeing me.

"And?" Timur asks, as I take a sip.

"And? And, the men on the beach grabbed him from me when I got to the shallow water, carried him up to the warm sand, and covered him in towels and blankets. I left when he started throwing up, when he regained consciousness."

"So you swam to him?"

"Yes."

"Can you explain again what happened then on the beach, when the men took him from you?"

"Well, like I said, the man was shivering, then lost consciousness; they wrapped him in a blanket. Then I think I walked away."

"Savas?"

There's silence in the room. on the other end.

"Savas!" Timur shouts.

"Shut up, Timur, I'm thinking."

"Savas, this is the kid . . ."

"I said shut up."

I look at Timur. Then I look at the two other men. Their arms have gone slack. I look back at Timur.

"Savas," Timur says, again, this time, his voice is quiet; resigned.

I don't know what's going on.

"Savas. Come on," Timur says.

The other two men pull off their masks.

"I was one of the men on the beach," Timur says.

"What?"

"I was one of the men on the beach."

"It was your friend who was drowning?"

"Yes."

Timur stares at me.

I look up at the two other men. One is now sitting at the edge of the couch. I look back at Timur.

"Savas?" I say. "Wait. Was it Savas? Savas, were you the drowning man?"

The room is silent again.

"Was that you, Savas?"

"Tunc, Volkan, let him go," Savas says.

I look at the men. I look at Timur.

"Let him go. Now. Go back to New York, to the team. And hang up the phone, now."

Tunc kills the line.

Volkan cuts the tape from my ankles

"Get up. Leave," Volkan says. I try to get up, but I can't. My legs are cramping. I stretch them and try again. Timur holds out his arm and pulls me up onto wobbly legs.

"Thanks, man."

I look around the house, then walk over to one of the windows near the front door. I pull the curtain back very slowly, only about a quarter of an inch, enough to look out onto the street in front of the house. There's a white van on the street and a tent. *Bonnie set up a rescue effort. How did she pull that off—the rookie cop?*

"Where's the back door?" I ask Timur. He points to the kitchen and hands me my wallet and ID cards. I have seventeen dollars, an American Express card, a Washington University student ID, and a driver's license.

I can't go out the front door to Bonnie's people, the cops. I'm in the US illegally and she knows me. They all will know that. That's trouble for both of us. She may be fired; I may be deported.

I walk out the back door, opening it slowly, quietly. I put my hands up in surrender in case the whole house is surrounded, then quickly look back once through the kitchen to make sure the men aren't following me. *I saved Savas Kartal? Savas Kartal was the man drowning on the beach?* From the back of the house, I can't see any cops. I pull my arms down and, crouching, I run away from the house, through the backyard, then jump over the fence to the neighbor's yard. I throw myself down on the ground and wait, listening to make sure there is no one around me, behind me, in front of me, before running across the lawn to the next street. I'm walking fast, my legs, arms and head aching. *I saved Savas Kartal's life.* My eyes dart back and forth, and I turn around every few seconds to make sure there's no one following me. I feel like I'm trapped in a suburban labyrinth of cul-de-sac after cul-de-sac with no way out.

As the sun starts rising above the street, illuminating the endless-looking array of houses I'm trying to escape, I exit the maze. I suspect I've walked a few miles when I reach a small shopping center. McDonald's! I feel like I've found civilization. I go in to use the bathroom and, like too many times before, check the damage to myself in the mirror. "Savas Kartal was the drowning man," I say to myself in the mirror. "You saved Savas Kartal's life." I've got a couple bruises on my face, but I've seen worse staring back at me in the mirror. I move my hand to feel the back of my head and find a walnut-size bump with a cut running in the middle, forming a scab under my hair. I wash my face in the dirty sink and wipe my head and neck off with some wet paper towels then go out and order myself some food.

"What's the address here?" I ask the young woman behind the counter.

"What's your order?" she asks in reply.

"Can you first give me the address of this place, then I'll order."

"Like the address, address?"

"I am not sure what you mean by that question. I just need to know the name of the street we are on, and the town."

"Oh yeah. Okay. Old Black Mill Road, Springfield," she responds in a bored voice. "Do you need the zip?"

"Excuse me?"

"Do you need the zip? The zip code?"

"Oh. No . . . no, that's fine. Thank you. But, um, what state is Springfield in?"

"What state?"

"Yes, what state?"

"Virginia," she says and then, without missing a beat, "are you going to order?"

"Yes, I'll have two egg McMuffins, please. And a small coffee please."

I don't know how far Springfield, Virginia, is from DC. And, I'm not sure how I'll get home or if I have enough money to get home. After breakfast, I have thirteen dollars left in my wallet. I hope it's enough to get to DC by bus. *I should have thought of that before buying myself food. What if the bus ticket is $17?*

I down my breakfast in a minute, eating like I haven't eaten in months despite having trouble chewing. My jaw is stiff. My arms and wrists hurt. And then, I have a delayed epiphany. *I'm free. I'm free of the fear of Savas Kartal that I've been carrying around with me for years; not just the four years that I've been in America. Since he spotted me in the hallway at Technical University. Seven years.* Seven years of worry is gone!

My elation is hardly dampened by my situation: thirteen bucks in my pocket and no clear way home after being beaten and abducted. I have no idea where the bus station is but think better of asking the cashier, who hardly knew where she worked. I want to dance! I get up from the table, speed up my steps and skip a couple times as I head to the trash can to leave my tray. I make a ball with my napkin and throw a one-handed shot at the trash can, and it lands on top of the trays. People stare at me as I mock-cheer the game-winning point at the buzzer. I've survived Savas Kartal. He's never going to come after me again. I can't believe it. *Freedom!* I leave the restaurant to what I imagine are sighs of relief from the breakfast crowd over my erratic, ecstatic behavior.

Stepping off the curb and into the parking lot, I have no idea which way to turn. I look around for someone who can give me directions to the bus station, someone who hasn't witnessed my McDonald's dance. My wounded face may still be enough to scare people off, but I need to find out where the bus station is.

I spy a woman on the far side of the parking lot. She's headed in my direction. As she approaches, I ask her if she knows the way to the bus station. Without stopping, she points and walks quickly into the McDonald's. I thank her and head off in that direction with a limp. *That'll teach you not to skip after you've been beaten up!* I imagine I'm quite the spectacle.

Five minutes into my walk, I turn around to see a car slowing down, then stopping. The driver leans over, reaching across to the passenger window, and cranks it open. It's the woman from the entrance of McDonald's. "Hop in," she says, "I'll drive you to the bus station."

By the time I've arrived home it's 9:30 in the morning. I'm exhausted and hurting all over and already late for class. I need to sleep before my shift at the Blues Saloon. And, I'm still hungry. There is a gallon of milk in the fridge, half-full, and two red plums. I eat my second breakfast. I don't know where Bonnie is now. She wouldn't be home and I don't have her work number.

15

AGENTS AND ANGELS

ON MY WAY TO WORK, FEELING A LITTLE RESTED AFTER A TWO-hour nap, I stop by the newsstand. The *Nation's Daily* has Savas's name as a small headline. I buy the paper. $1.50.

"Savas Kartal to Be Retried," reads the headline. *He was granted a retrial?* I scan the article quickly. Savas's attorneys convinced the judge that the military court unjustly sentenced him. A new trial in a civilian court granted.

It worked. Their strategy worked. $400,000 worked.

And then I feel it. Relief I haven't felt in a long time. I don't ever have to worry about headlines like these again. Savas Kartal no longer wants to kill me!

I keep reading, recoiling as I see how the Nationalist newspapers glorify his image. And the more I read, the more I am sure that Savas has—and had—the full backing not only of the Nationalist Party, which helped him start Yavuz Security, but of the country's billionaires. Acutely aware of Savas Kartal's value to them, they helped stage a PR campaign to portray him as an unjustly jailed folk hero. Now it's clear to me. Mr. Baris was directly involved. He, along with his rich pals, covertly supported Savas for years. And, it's taken me years to figure it out. Savas fought, and continues to fight, even from jail, to preserve the existing system, a system that enabled men like Mr. Baris to become billionaires; a system that will preserve their wealth and power in the future. The billionaires chose to support Savas and the Nationalist Party to prevent a revolution that would change their status quo; a Communist regime, they knew, would confiscate their money on behalf of the "working class."

I continue on to work.

"Bonnie!" I say out loud, stopping short at a corner as a car speeds up to catch a green light. *What do I tell her? She watched me get hit, taken. Then she followed me. She must have, to know where to send backup and set up an operation to save me. Do I tell her that I knew the man who abducted me? Do I tell her about the $400,000 and the crooked way the rich people in my country do business with thugs to keep their money? I suspect they do that in many places, maybe even here in America.*

When my shift that night ends, after a beer and a rant, I step out into the dark, quiet streets of Georgetown. After ten minutes and no taxis, I resign myself to the long walk home. But, as I start up the hill, I see Bonnie's car heading down the street in my direction. I feel nervous, still haven't decided what to tell her. She rolls down the window and unlocks the passenger door.

"Want a lift?" she asks.

"Sure. Thanks," I say, wondering if I should smile. *Why am I so nervous?* I get in the car.

We don't talk the entire way home or even when I get out of the car. I'm a little surprised when Bonnie gets out, too, but I say nothing. Like practiced thieves, we tiptoe down the steps, skipping the ones that creak.

"Tea?" I ask, breaking the silence as I walk over to the coffee maker. She doesn't respond. I can feel her watching me.

"Who is Savas Kartal?"

I spill water on the dresser. "What?" I say, little too loud, without turning around.

"I said, who is Savas Kartal?"

"Sounds like a Turkish name," I say, immediately aware of how idiotic I sound. But, I can't stop myself. "Savas means war, and Kartal means eagle. War-Eagle."

"Do you know him?"

"I've heard of him." *Please don't ask any more.*

Bonnie hands me two pictures and a piece of paper. "Are these the men who hit you over the head and kidnapped you?"

I turn around and look at the pictures without making eye contact with Bonnie. Below their photos are their names, Tunc Solak and Volkan Aytekin. "Yes. Those men were there."

It's over now, please don't ask me any questions.

Bonnie clenches her teeth and walks over to me. "Those two men were detained yesterday. In Virginia. They were armed."

I don't say anything.

Bonnie raises her hand. For a split second I think she's going to hit me, a thought I don't understand at all. Instead, her hand gently pushes aside my shirt collar, and she runs her hand over the welt on my shoulder. I pull away from her. "What's this?" she says, less combatively, moving closer. Her fingers climb up to the bump on the back of my head. "Oh, dear," she says, almost lovingly. "And that bruise on your cheek, what'd you tell Dan, that you did something clumsy?"

"Nothing. He didn't notice. You arrested them?" I ask.

"We questioned them overnight."

"How about the third man?"

"We questioned him too. He's clean. They were only using his house. He didn't abduct you, though he did aid and abet, so there will be different charges brought up against him."

And then, my floodgates open. I need to know what she saw and what she did. "So, what happened? I mean, you saw me get hit over the head. I remember seeing you, in your car then . . ."

"Yeah, I saw the men appear and hit you over the head. It happened so fast. I think they were hiding behind a parked car."

"So you saw them?"

"Yes. I watched the whole thing from my car. I grabbed for my police radio, but it wasn't working, so—"

"Wait, you have a police radio in your car?"

"Yes."

"I've never seen it."

"I keep it in the glove compartment."

She keeps her police radio in the glove compartment?

"Do you want to hear the rest of the story or do you want to put me on the stand and question me?"

"I don't know what that means," I say. "Go on."

"So I couldn't call for back up. So, I decided to follow you until I figured out where you were and then find a pay phone to call it in. I had to stay far behind since there were so few cars on the road. When they got off the highway, I had to drive with my headlights off."

I watch her as she tells me the story. She put her own life in jeopardy for me.

"Then, when they pulled into the garage, I had to assume they pulled you out of the car and brought you into the house. I took down the address and drove off immediately to find a pay phone. I had no idea if once I left they would take you somewhere else, but I had to start somewhere."

She continues, "Then I returned and stopped near the house, hoping that you were still in there. It takes a while to get everything set up. They don't just storm into a house. There's paperwork, a court order. And, they needed to make sure you were safe before engaging . . . It's just part of the protocol."

"I saw the tent," I say, "and the cars parked out front when I left in the morning."

"Right, that's part of the system they set up."

I nod.

"Okay, now it's time for me to ask you a question," Bonnie says.

"Okay."

"Who is Savas Kartal?"

I say nothing.

"Fine. Then I'll tell you who he is. Savas Kartal owns a security firm in Turkey. Yavuz Security. Those two men who abducted you work for him." She begins to pace up and down the room, balling her fists. "They are professionals. They could have killed you."

"But they didn't." I look up at Bonnie. She's angry, but there's another expression I can't quite make out. Fear? *Is she scared?*

"But they could have!"

"No, they couldn't have. Because I have two . . ."

"What? Guns? You had guns on you?"

"No. Angels."

"Excuse me?"

"Angels."

"What in the world are you talking about, Adem?"

"Angels. Everybody has a guardian angel, but I have two," I say, setting out two cups with saucers—properly, like my mom always did. I pour us each some tea.

"What?"

"Yes, my grandmother told me that."

"Jeez, Adem. You need to grow up. How old were you when she said that?"

"Five, or something, I think."

"Dear Lord. What are you, Peter Pan?" She moves her face closer to mine and looks me in the eye.

I shrug.

"Wait!" I say, "How do you know all this? You've only been an officer for a week."

Bonnie looks right at me. I look away.

"Bonnie, I asked you a ques . . ." And, then I realize. It's been more than a week. She's been a police officer, or whatever she is, for longer than a week.

I force myself to look her right in the eyes. It's not natural for me. I don't know that I've ever done it before. I can feel the heat in my face.

"You were always an officer, weren't you? You *lied* to me."

"I was on assignment."

"You did. You lied to me! You've always been a cop. You were a cop from the get-go. Your family, your school, that you were fired from Congress. They were all lies."

"They were true."

"Is your name even Bonnie Morrison?"

"No."

I laugh. "So let me get this straight. You, whatever your name is . . ."

"Megan Hayes, that's my name. Special agent. People call me Bonnie."

"So you, Megan Bonnie, got a job at the Blues Saloon to investigate who—Dan? Paul? Did Dan evade taxes? That would be funny."

Bonnie is silent.

"No," I say. "Not Dan." And then it hits me. I feel my head reel back. There I am, in the bar in Istanbul, being punched by a drunk stranger; there I am in Dupont Circle, being beaten silly by thugs; there I am watching the door at the Blues Saloon, being attacked by Bonnie's ex, or was it? But this—*this* hurts more. Worse than Polat holding a gun to my head, or being abducted in the middle of the night. This is a woman I loved. Love.

"Me. You were investigating me. Me? You . . ." I stand up and start pacing the room. I taste bile in the back of my throat. I want to curse. I want to curse and never stop. But I hold myself. "Never curse and you will never have to," Grandma always said. "Power of the tongue. Negative thoughts will come to your mind, that's okay. Just don't speak them. Either remain silent or speak faith-filled words. Speak victory."

"Bunu nasil goremedim?"

"Adem? English. I don't know what you are saying."

"Beni takip ediyormus. Sasirmis bu insanlar."

"What are you saying?" Bonnie asks, imploring.

I shake my head.

"English, Adem, please."

"Me? You were investigating me? I'm a poor man trying to make a living."

Bonnie looks down at the floor. "I thought, the agency that is, thought that you could be a Communist agent."

"What?"

"An engineer, smart, handsome, illegal, working as a dishwasher? Come on, please. Don't you think it's suspicious?"

"No. I don't think it's suspicious at all. Boy are you out of touch. That's half the immigrants in America!" I say, trying not to shout. My voice catches in the back of my throat. "You have no idea, no idea, what it's like," I say, turning away from her, raking my hand through my hair. "You have no idea."

"Tell me. Tell me what it's like. Please. You're right. I have no idea. What is it like?"

I turn around, slowly, surprised by her tone. "You really want to know?"

"I do. I want to know."

"Well. First, it's a ridiculous, monumental task to even get a visa. Then even if you are fortunate enough to get a visa, it doesn't mean you will actually be able to enter the US. So, you come here, you arrive not knowing if they'll turn you away at the airport. You save money and you borrow money and you get here and you may have to turn around and go home. Which means, you need to spend money you may not have on a ticket back. So, you worry then about what to do if that happens. You may have a language problem. Those who have family or friends to help them out, help them get on their feet, it's a huge help. Because if you don't, when your money runs out, what do you eat, where do you sleep? If you don't have the proper papers, how do you get a job? If you can't get a job, how do you live? If you get a job with broken English, how do you keep that job? If you don't understand something your boss tells you to do, quickly, in a rush, and you do it wrong, you could get fired. What if your boss is abusive? You have to keep the job, because if you quit, you don't know whether anyone else would hire you. And that means no food and possibly losing your room or your bed or the floor you sleep on. What if you get involved in some fight and the police show up to find out you're illegal? What if you get wounded or sick, will a hospital take you? If they take you and you are illegal, will they call the police? And, without health insurance, how do you pay your hospital bills on your dishwasher salary? And, what if you are sent back home for any of those reasons and there are people at home who don't like you, who want to kill you? Every time you see a cop car or hear a siren, you worry whether it's for you. You're constantly on guard, waiting for immigration raids. You want to remain invisible yet you feel everyone is watching you. You always have to be ready to run out the back door of any place you are in. Yet you don't complain. You don't complain because it's much worse if you go back. In fact, you're happy here. You're happy because you have hope. Hope that tomorrow will be better than today."

"I didn't know," Bonnie says, "I guess Americans can never really know, even when our parents and grandparents were immigrants. You can't know unless you live it."

"It could be different for everyone. My friend Roberto crossed the river to get here. Jorge was running from warring drug gangs."

"I had no idea."

"I'm sure your grandparents had their issues, too."

"Well, if I could change the subject a little—it might make you feel better to know that I turned in my report at the end of the first week," she says. "I found no evidence that you were a Communist agent who had stolen money. Again, that's how the file came in. You had been reported to us as a possible Communist agent with some missing money. No evidence was submitted as part of the case."

"Missing money?"

"Yep."

"And, I was reported? Who reported me?"

"I really can't talk about it. I'm not allowed to answer questions like that until it's declassified, and that's years after the investigation is closed. I can tell you one day. But right now what's important is you're alive; you should be glad you're alive."

"Let me guess," I say, "Savas belongs to the Nationalist Party, which has connections to Turkish intelligence, which Savas manipulated, and made them alert you, the US, an ally. And you the ally country must investigate whether you like it or not. And the men of Yavuz Security, which Savas owns, accompanied their billionaire client to New York City, and while at it, why not drive down to DC to abduct me and dump my body into the Potomac River?"

I get up and pace the room for a minute.

"And wait a second," I say, interrupting my own thoughts. "Let's go back to something. Why did you continue to work at the Blues Saloon after that? After you were done with me . . . I mean, the investigation. It lasted one week, you said."

"I wanted more."

"From the Blues Saloon?"

"No."

"From . . . me?"

"Yes." *She was investigating me. She thought I was a bad actor. She lied to me. But she stayed because she liked me. Likes me. I don't know what to do with this information, these facts. I don't know how to reconcile this. She's a liar. Our entire relationship is based on a lie. I lied to Francesca to save her life and she wouldn't forgive me. Bonnie lied to me because she had plans to put me behind bars.* I can't compute all this. I don't know how to balance this in my head. I change the subject.

"How did you conclude I wasn't an agent?"

"You worked sixty hours a week and went to school. For three years. Spies and thieves are lazy. You wouldn't work long hours or go to school if you had money stashed away somewhere. How much was it?"

"$400,000."

"Who took the money?"

"Savas Kartal."

"But, I thought you said he was in jail at the time?"

"He *was* in jail; his people took the money."

"And they said you took it?"

"Yes. I believe Savas wanted me in the same jail with him."

"He wanted you in jail with him? Why?"

"I think it was his plan. He vowed to kill all Communists. He wouldn't threaten people; he'd just kill. He hated me so much that he threatened to kill me publicly, putting himself into a bind. Then he wanted to show everyone that he kept his word. He's a bit of a lunatic. I overheard him telling his gang one time when I was hiding from him as he chased me, shot at me. His father was a police officer. A Communist rebel shot and killed his father and he vowed to avenge his father. It wasn't me. I didn't kill his father, but apparently I just looked like the guy who did and I triggered him. And he knew I didn't kill his father, but he believed he had cause since he believed I'm a Communist."

"And you're not?"

"A Communist? No, some of my roommates in college were sympathizers."

"Oh. But . . ."

"I didn't really understand politics. So . . . those guys, my gang, they were just people who were in my class. And, they ended up being my roommates."

"Huh."

"Can I ask you a question?"

"Sure."

"So. Um, did you steal from Dan? Is that why he fired you?"

"I had to get fired. I had to continue acting like I was a waitress. I watched Dan intently during the time I was working at the bar. I understood his system. So, I purposely stole liquor to get fired. I didn't drink it. I was on duty. I poured it down the drain."

I serve us another round of tea, open up a box of chocolate chip cookies, and ask, "How about Paul, Raymond—are they informants? Jorge? He likes you. Is he an informant?"

Bonnie shakes her head. "I can't talk about it. I wish I could, but I can't."

Then she changes the subject. "I'm going to go shower. Would you like to join me? It'll save water," she adds with a wink.

16

DOWNTIME

Cherry blossom season has come and gone; it's the fourth year in a row that I've missed all the excitement, including the weeklong festival and parade. I've seen a few blooming trees on the way to school and work, they are all over the District. But every year, almost everyone I know tells me, "You've got to see them around the Tidal Basin. The entire area gets clothed in white and pink." My reply to them is a broken record, "Next year." This year, Bonnie tells me I have to take an hour out of my day. "We'll go at sunrise, before all the tourists wake up. It'll be beautiful. You just have to!" I agree. But, we have to cancel our plans because a huge storm rolls in. I wonder, briefly, if it's a sign.

***

My spring semester has gone well. I expect to receive A's and B's again, but I'm dreading the fall semester because the tuition hike to $300 per credit hour proved to be true. When I budgeted for my degree, I didn't plan on the school's constant tuition hikes. Last semester each credit hour rose $40 to

$200. That was hard. But another $100 per credit hour means I'm going to have a $4,000 budget shortfall.

To beat the rate increase, I register for a three-credit summer course, Computer Architecture, that meets in the morning. It's the only required course that works with my schedule and if I take it before the fall tuition bump, I'll save $300. I had been planning to work sixty hours a week at the Blues Saloon to make ends meet; but now, that'll be hard to do.

***

Computer Architecture turns out to be a fast-moving class—accelerated to cover an entire semester in seven weeks. Nevertheless, after the first week, I find it to be relatively easy.

Most of the students in the class keep to themselves, except for a bearded fellow who sat down next to me on the first day and has made a habit of sitting next to me every day since. He wears glasses, and I've noticed that his sideburns are graying. My guesstimate, a Dr. Tiller word I've become quite fond of, is that he's Izzy's age—at least six years older than I am. He makes small talk with me before class but never talks during the lecture, which I appreciate.

"Hi, I'm Trip," he says, extending his hand at the end of the first week of classes, "Trip Cullen."

"Adem Bayer, like the aspirin," I reply, shaking his hand.

"Good one. Like the aspirin. Clever," he says. I'll have to remember to tell Dr. Tiller. It was his idea to say that to people.

"So, Trip. As in 'have a nice trip,' or 'trip and fall'? Or 'trip a circuit'?" I ask.

"Ha! Never thought about it," Trip says. "So, I guess it could mean clumsy. But I prefer to think of myself as tripping, in a charming way. Like the saying, 'you're a trip.' "

I smile even though I'm confused. Since he doesn't seem offended by all my questions, I keep asking. "So, Trip. That's a name?"

He laughs again, which is a relief. I genuinely don't want to offend him, but I've become very curious about American names. "It's a nickname," he says. "My grandfather was William, my father became Bill, and since I was the third William in a row, my parents nicknamed me Trip. I think for Triple, you know, like I'm the third William."

"Oh. I get it!"

He smiles.

"Actually, if I'm telling it like it is, I think it was so my mother could yell at my father and I wouldn't think she was yelling at me," he says, laughing, "and vice versa, so my mother could yell at me and my father wouldn't think he was in trouble," he adds. I laugh with him.

He's quite congenial and, over the course of the following week, I come to look forward to our preclass banter. After a particularly fast-paced class Trip catches up to me in the hallway. "Hey, hey, Adem. You have a sec?" I stop walking. "You seem to be keeping up in this class, like, you understand what's going on. At least that's what it looks like."

"It's been clear enough, so far," I reply.

"Do you have a minute? Could I ask you a question?"

"Sure. I need to get to work in a bit, but I have a few minutes."

"Thanks, man." Trip pulls out his textbook right there in the hallway and points to a problem the professor just assigned to us as homework. "I just don't understand this one. Do you understand it? Could you explain it to me?"

"Yes. Sure. Let's go back to the classroom so we can sit down," I say, turning around.

We sit down in the front row of the classroom and I pull out some paper. I solve the problem quickly. It's not that difficult, in fact. "Wow. That was fast! Can you show me how you did that? And, I mean, explain it to me while you go?"

I show him how to do the problem and then another from last week's class that he's still having trouble with.

"That's amazing. I get it now! You explained both better than the professor!" he shouts, quite dramatically, patting me on my back.

"I'm glad," I say, almost shyly, trying to defuse some of his excitement.

"Hey man, do you think we could study together? And, by that I mean, can you help me study?"

I laugh. He's a little over the top, but I do like him and he makes me feel confident in a way I haven't felt since I tutored back in Istanbul. We plan to meet after class in the engineering students' lounge twice a week before my shift starts at the Blues Saloon.

***

I come to find out that Trip is, indeed, Izzy's age, thirty-two, and has a graduate degree in geology from Southern California. Until a round of layoffs a year ago, he was working in New Orleans for Gulf Oil.

"I was making some good dough then," he says as we walk from the classroom.

I nod, not sure what to say, sitting down in the lounge, eager to get started with our studying. I like him, but he is quite a talker.

"I came back to my parents' house here in Arlington. Then I decided to switch to computer science and get another graduate degree. Electronics is my hobby anyway, so I thought, why not?"

"Where do you work with electronics?" I ask, curious, then immediately regret extending the conversation.

"I have a workshop in my parents' house, so I've always worked on electronic equipment in one way or another."

"Your parents are engineers?" I can't stop myself. The more he talks, the more I like him and his story.

Trip smiles. "No, my father is a retired international banker. Mom's always been a housewife. Both are from small towns in Pennsylvania, near Susquehanna. Kind of rural, lots of farms, you know?" I don't know, but I'm remembering *The Deer Hunter*, envisioning walking in the forests and talking with the locals. "My uncle owns a farm in Pennsylvania, actually. He never left. My mother's brother," Trip says.

Trip and I begin studying together every day after class, and then end up having coffee together a few times until it becomes a regular part of our schedules, too. While he needs help in math and computer programming, he teaches me about politics, laws, taxes, the stock market, cars, archaeology— things I'm clueless about. I tell him he's a walking encyclopedia, like my dad.

One of the vending machines in the lounge dispenses coffee, tea, hot chocolate, and chicken soup, all from the same machine; it looks like even the same spigot, which is disgusting. It's watered down, stale, and chemical tasting, but it's only five cents. All the other vending machines we've found have been upgraded to cost a quarter. After finding two dimes on the ground one day, I get one of each—on a lark—and do a taste test. Each is as bad as the other.

Turns out, Trip is even more budget conscious than I am. He has a pocket notebook in which he pencils in his every expense down to the penny. "I've kept it since I lost my job," he tells me, adding up his out-of-pocket food expenses for the day. "A dollar forty above budget," he announces. "I need to cut back tomorrow."

He confesses that he's been depressed after losing his job and being forced to move back in with his parents. I can understand how demoralizing it must be, just imagining myself returning from America a failure, my mother cooking my meals for me once again. I don't know that I'd ever be able to smile again.

Sometimes when I solve a tough problem, Trip gets up and does a dance, laughing and celebrating. He looks so happy and it makes me crack up; I'm inspired to join him just to keep him smiling even longer.

After one of his more inspired dances, he asks me to come to his parents' house for dinner for a home-cooked meal. I don't even pretend to turn down the invitation, to show that I'm polite. I jump right at the opportunity. I haven't had a real meal in four years; I think that final meal was Mom's lentil soup, green beans, and meatballs with potatoes in tomato sauce. My mouth waters just thinking about it.

The following Monday, my only day off, we leave straight from class in Trip's Datsun 280Z, which he says he can't bring himself to sell even after losing his job. As we drive over the bridge—over the Potomac River—to Arlington, it occurs to me that I haven't been out of the District since moving into Mrs. Hardwick's house, except for the night Savas's people kidnapped me and took me to Virginia. I turn around to look at the Washington Monument behind us and remember seeing it from the sky as I landed at National Airport, worried and lost when Demir didn't pick me up and clueless about what that pencil structure even was. I can speak English now, I have a job, I have a home,

I have school, I have money in the bank, I have friends. And today, I'm being welcomed into an American home.

Trip's mother, a slender, gray-haired woman, prepares dinner while we chat with his father, a big and tall man. His mother joins in on the conversation from the kitchen. They treat me like I'm one of them, like a friend, like I belong, like I'm smart. Over and over, they commend me on my command of the English language.

While his mother finishes preparing dinner, Trip's father invites me to his garage so he can show off his new car. "Voila. My muscle car, Adem, a Chrysler Cordoba V8, two door." He says he learned all about cars from his father and taught Trip everything he knows.

"Yep, taught me everything I know," Trip says.

"We're as good at maintaining cars as any mechanic, son," he says, patting my shoulder. "Trip and I have always bought used cars. We fix them up ourselves."

"Impressive," I say, truly impressed.

"Tell you what, when you buy a car, we'll fix it up for you," Trip's father says, patting me on the shoulder.

"Oh, sir I can't afford a car," I say knowing I still have to figure out how to make up my $4,000 tuition shortfall.

"Okay. Maybe not today. But I can tell, you'll be able to one day. And, sooner than you think. I can tell these things. There's no doubt in my mind, son."

"Thank you sir. That's very kind." *He called me "son." He has welcomed me, an immigrant, into his home and called me son.*

"So, here . . . let me teach you a few things now. Important things to know," he says, handing me a wrench. And for the next hour, I get my first lesson in car maintenance and wonder what life would have been like if Mr. Cullen had been my dad.

When we finally go inside to wash up for dinner, I'm shocked by all the food on the table for only four of us. It reminds me of one of my mother's banquets. Mrs. Cullen is standing at the table with a huge smile on her face. "Okay dear," she says, coming to stand next to me. "We have homemade macaroni and cheese, lamb chops, garlic bread, salad, green beans and," she says, turning and pointing to a small table behind us, "apple pie and homemade chocolate chip cookies for dessert."

"It's an incredible spread, Mrs. Cullen. Thank you," I say as we sit down. My stomach growls and everyone laughs.

***

On the way home from dinner, a "doggie bag" in my lap and a new term in my vocabulary, Trip tells me he has a longtime girlfriend named Melanie who lives in Northern California. She wants to get married, he says, but Trip is so nervous about his financial situation that he hasn't asked her yet and she's getting impatient—in fact, she's given him an ultimatum. " 'Now or never,' that's what she told me. I need to make up my mind by next week. She's coming to visit. I've got to shit or get off the pot."

"What's that mean?" I ask.

"You are literally so smart, I forget that some of the bizarre sayings we have are new to you. Let's see, it means . . . well, it pretty much means, I need to ask her already."

"Oh," I say as we cross back over the Potomac, driving toward the monument, now all lit up. "What are you going to do? Are you going to ask her?"

"I don't know. I just, I mean . . . Wait, do you want to meet her?" he asks. And then, more excitedly, "Would you? Would you come to meet her? She's lovely. She's a nurse. First, actually, she was going to be a nun, but left the convent. Not because of me, though," he says, glancing at me. "She's a good person. I think you would like her. I need to know if you like her. We'll do dinner at my parents' house."

"Sure," I say, relishing another meal.

"Do you think I should tell her that I'm worried about my financial situation?"

"Well . . . I'm not really . . ."

"Oh," Trip says, interrupting me. "I forgot to tell you, I got a job as an assistant at the university's computer lab. It's twenty hours a week, $5.50 per hour. It's better than nothing."

"Man, good, that's really good. Congrats," I say, glad that I don't have to answer Trip's question. I'm not the right person to give advice about women or love. *Francesca.* I sigh, silently.

By the time Trip pulls up in front of Mrs. Hardwick's, we've made a plan for the following Monday, for me to meet Melanie. I thank Trip for the ride home and find myself still smiling as I enter my room. Even though I had a funeral for my ego a long time ago, today felt good. Great, in fact. His parents welcomed me into their home like I was an equal. I'm not sure I've ever had that feeling before.

I switch on the TV and a rerun of *Happy Days* is on. "It's finally not ironic," I say out loud.

When I meet Melanie, I like her immediately. Trip takes it as a sign. On Tuesday, he asks Melanie to marry him and she says yes. Then, for a guy who's been dragging his heels, he starts moving at warp speed. A week later, after Melanie has returned to California, Trip sells his Datsun Z for $5,000 and buys a $600 Ford Pinto. Then he buys a small, one-story house with a basement in Virginia for $99,000 and begins renovating it right away. "You find a good neighborhood and buy the smallest, most run-down house on a big lot," Trip says, explaining his strategy to me when I come to help him out.

While installing a new dishwasher, he asks me to drive with him to his uncle's farm the following weekend to pick up some furniture he's been storing there since losing his job with Gulf Oil. The furniture "is the final touch," Trip says.

"It's going to take three or four trips to bring everything back," he says, and I laugh.

"What's so funny?"

"Is it going to take three or four of you?" I ask, "or are you going to have to drive back and forth three or four times?" I think it's the first joke I've ever told in English.

"Oh, so now you're a stand-up comedian?" he asks, laughing.

"I keep hearing that expression. What's it mean?"

"Ha. It means, so you think you're a funny guy . . . you could tell jokes for a living."

"Oh!" I exclaim, happy to finally get it. "People can make a living telling jokes?"

"Yep!"

"Only in America!" I say and hope I'll be invited for the other trips.

***

The following Saturday, we hitch a trailer to Trip's Ford Pinto and set out for the six-hour drive. Once we veer off the highway onto side roads that take us into the forests of Pennsylvania, the trees arch over us. In a couple of months, the leaves will turn gold and orange, Trip tells me. Bright green grass leads into red-tinted soil, darker and brighter than that in Istanbul. We drive through little towns that seem sleepy, even ghostlike. Stores are shuttered; those that remain open look to be badly in need of repair. "Steel factories are under pressure; cheap imports are forcing them to close," says Trip, almost reading my thoughts. "Young people have moved to larger cities like Harrisburg or Philadelphia to find work." I see a stray dog wandering down the street, alone. "They are slowly recovering here though," Trip adds, looking at me and smiling, as if he's willing it to happen.

In the next town, old buildings and businesses look healthier, but for-sale signs abound. "These go for about $26K," Trip says, pointing to a row of nice colonial houses with porches. Parked in front of some of the houses are cars for sale, too. Chevys, Chryslers, or Fords available for a few hundred dollars. Trip tells me if I want to buy a car, he'll drive out here with me. He still doesn't know I'm short $4,000 in tuition.

We stop at a small family owned candy shop near Susquehanna. Trip says he's stopped at the shop during each trip to visit his uncle and cousins for decades, since he was a kid. The candy store itself is the front room of a brick house; the family lives in the back. The house reminds me of the movie *Deer Hunter*, the house right after the wedding scene. Trip buys some candy for the ride and some for his cousins, as well.

We pull up in front of Trip's uncle's farm at about two in the afternoon. The land around the house is green and lush. Farther out, it turns tan. They grow "seed corn," Trip says, grabbing the bag of candy and opening his door.

"My uncle sells it to other farmers to grow regular corn. Seed corn sells for up to six times the price of regular corn," Trip explains. "He was smart when he decided to get into the seed business even though everyone was telling him not to."

Trip's arrival looks like the arrival of a king. Men and women and kids come running to greet us, Trip's four cousins and their spouses and at least half a dozen children ranging in age from six months to fifteen years, elbow each other for a turn to hug him. They all live near the farm, Trip explained on our way up, when he "warned" me, that I was about to meet a lot of people. He also told me that since they haven't met many foreigners before, I'll be quite a novelty for them. I immediately realize how right he is. It seems they are not sure what to make of me. They speak to me slowly and loudly and I don't know if I should be offended or find it funny.

"He speaks English fluently and tutors me in my calculus and computer programming classes. And you don't need to yell at him; he can hear fine," Trip says, almost unable to breathe, he's laughing so hard. "Just treat him like a normal person, he's not an alien." *Actually, Trip, I am an alien, an illegal one.*

"I promise, I won't bite," I say, smiling, "That's an expression I learned from my eighty-two-year-old neighbor who teaches me Americanisms." A few of the adults chuckle. "Ah, I've broken the ice, it's another good one, right?" I say, laughing, and suddenly everyone is laughing. They ask me about some of my favorite idioms and teach me a few more. Soon they are walking and talking with me as if they've known me for a long time.

"Let's give him a tour of the place," says one of Trip's cousins, a guy who looks to be around my age. "Ever shoot a gun?" he asks me.

"Yes. But I have to warn you, I'm not very good at it."

They lead me to "the gun room." An actual room filled with rifles and shotguns, handguns too. The guns line the cabinets that line the walls. I have never seen anything like it. Even before I've had a chance to take it all in, locks are being opened at a rapid pace as the cousins pull out weapons from their cases.

"Shoot with this one—it's great."

"No. No. Don't listen to him. Shoot with that one, it's mine."

With guns in their hands, I'm grabbed and prodded as each cousin offers me a weapon. "Everyone, back away," Trip says, breaking up the commotion and grabbing a rifle from the shelf. "Use this one."

"Thanks."

"Boy, are you Mr. Popular," he says, grabbing a rifle for himself.

With guns in hands and rifles on shoulders, we walk out into the backyard and cross into a field set up with all kinds of targets, including soda bottles and cans. We take turns shooting. Then one of the cousins hands me a shotgun. "That was shooting 101. Now, it's time for skeet shooting," he says. I don't know the word "skeet," but figure it out quickly when a clay pigeon shoots into the air. I shoot and discover I'm a lot better than I thought I would be. "Not bad, not bad for a city boy," Trip's uncle says, patting me on the back.

A single stray crow flies overhead, and the cousins scream at me to shoot it. I know they are harmful to the crops and the farmers hate them, but I just can't do it. I lower my gun to groans from the family and Trip tells me not to worry about it. He redirects everyone to the archery range, where we begin shooting arrows. I scrape up my forearm, but I'm surprised to find out I'm good at this, too.

"Okay, everyone, Adem and I have some work to do now," Trip says after about two hours of fun and games. He pulls his car up next to the farm's storage building and we start loading up the trailer. In no time, we are on the road back to Virginia.

***

Though I walk in the door of Mrs. Hardwick's house at 2:00 a.m., I feel oddly refreshed . . . and happy. I can hardly believe I've been to *The Deer Hunter* country, with steel factories and forests with red-tinted soil. For the first time in a long time, I remember that in life, there are things other than work or school or money. I fall asleep smiling.

***

By July 1984, I'm earning $4.50 an hour at the Blues Saloon, a twenty-cent bump and my third raise after working there for three years.

Some weekend nights Trip stops by the Blues Saloon for a beer and hangs with me while I work the door. He tells me his wedding will be in California; I tell him I can't afford to go. He understands completely and says he expected that I wouldn't be able to attend. Neither one of us has any room in our budgets for any "frivolous expense," which is why he's also made a "no wedding gifts" rule. My gift, he's reassured me over and over, was helping him with his home renovation and the three round trips to *The Deer Hunter* country—one of which he scheduled in the fall so I could see the mix of yellow, orange, and red leaves as they arched over the small country roads that lead to his family's farm.

***

In August, about a month after Trip returns from his honeymoon, he gets hired full time by a computer manufacturing company. "Time for me to quit school," he tells me after class one day. "I really don't need a second graduate degree. It's time for me to save money, not spend it."

Before leaving his assistant job at the university, Trip puts in a good word for me with his supervisor. And, when I tell him I don't have proper papers or a visa, he doesn't even bat an eye. "Not an issue for me, Adem," he says. "As far as I'm concerned, the job is yours. Just go to the accounting office and fill out some forms so they can pay you. I don't think it'll be a problem for them either, but let me know," he says, sending me off to speak with someone named Ms. Jennings.

"Oh, we don't care," she says, shuffling papers on her desk. "All we need is your Social Security number, contact information and a few signatures and you will be good to go," she says, pushing a few pieces of paper in my direction. "Sign this . . . excellent. Now, just stop by the international students' office to sign one more form and you'll be all set to start working in the computer lab. Good luck," she says, shaking my hand.

Five minutes later, the final form is signed, and I have Trip's former job. I'll be working twenty hours a week at $5.50 an hour helping students with their homework assignments.

I reduce my hours at the Blues Saloon to twenty a week and Dan is okay with it. "School is the priority; just let me know—don't burn yourself out," he's told me a couple of times already. "Don't worry about me." Dan says. "I'll be fine. Get an education and you'll go places," he says.

I don't know what to say other than "Thank you." How such a stonehearted man can turn into a supportive one when it counts continues to amaze me.

I finish out the summer with two jobs, totaling forty hours per week. While I'm earning $800 per month, with fewer hours at the Blues Saloon, I'm getting fewer free meals. The added food expense plus the cost of textbooks means now I can only save $200 per month. But I know the job at the computer center is going to be a good move in the long run.

17

BUDGET CRUNCH

I start the fall semester without having paid for the three computer science classes I'm taking. I only have three days left to pay the $2,700 tuition. But, with only $1,200 in the bank, I'm $1,500 short. And once I find that money, I'm going to need another $2,700 for the following semester.

I have no idea where I'm going to get the money. Ela and Eliz have their own families and I already owe them both money; Trip's money is tied up in his new house and his wedding expenses; I cannot possibly ask Dan, since he's already gone out on a limb for me and signed my sponsorship papers and, on top of that, has given me three raises—though I think I deserved them, if I'm being honest. Plus, if I'm really being honest, I'm just too proud.

Three months ago when they announced the tuition increase, I was confident that I would be able to save the money. And a month ago, when I started realizing I wouldn't, I was so paralyzed by my fear that I wouldn't be able to afford my tuition, that I never did anything about it. Dr. Tiller calls that "paralysis by analysis." I call it hoping for a miracle.

With no other place to turn and three days left, I give in and decide to call

Eliz. It's 3:00 a.m. and I haven't been able to fall asleep for two hours. Though Bonnie and I still haven't figured out where our relationship is headed, we're still sleeping together. I have to whisper my entire phone conversation so I don't wake Bonnie, who's curled up facing the wall. Eliz agrees to send me the $1,500. But, the international transfer will take at least five business days.

"Why don't you ask for an extension?"

I turn around and see that Bonnie is sitting up in bed.

"I'm sorry. I didn't mean to wake you."

"That's okay, I was having trouble sleeping with this coil in my back," she says, twisting on the bed. "If you don't have your tuition money, why don't you ask the school to give you another week?" Bonnie says.

I really don't like the idea. My dad would have been all over me for even considering asking for special treatment. But Bonnie may be right. If I plead my case, perhaps the school could make an exception. It makes my stomach churn. But, what's the alternative? Quit school, permanently? Temporarily? How long would temporary be?

I decide to try Bonnie's strategy. On Wednesday, after class, I make a beeline for the door and hurry down the hall. *If you don't do it right now, you are going to find an excuse not to go.* Deep in thought, I walk down the hallway practicing what I'm going to say.

"Ooof. Ouch, hey man, look where you're going!"

"I'm sorry," I say, looking up, startled.

"Adem! Hey man, you okay?"

"Oh hey, Liban. So sorry. I was . . . sorry, thinking."

"No problem," Liban says, shaking my hand. "Hey, you know . . . I was going to call you tonight, man. You saved me a call."

"What's up?" I say, tempted by the excuse to delay my visit to the bursar.

"Do you remember the lady in our class last semester—very pretty?" Liban asks.

"There was a lady in our class?"

"Yes, there were two, actually. How did you not notice them, man?"

"What can I tell you?" I say, laughing. *If Francesca were in my class, would I have noticed her? Would I have noticed Bonnie?*

"Well, anyway, one of them, her name is Joy," Liban says, "her son was sick, and she fell behind on her coursework and then ended up with an incomplete in the class. The professor has given her an extension, but she needs to complete all of the homework assignments by next week and pass the final test. She called me and asked me to tutor her. But I barely passed the course, so there's no way I can help her. It's your area. Would you be able to help her?"

"Uh, sure. I guess," I say, feeling more confident now about my own extension needs; *maybe this means I'll be able to get an extension on my tuition payment.* "Yes, actually. I'll be working at the computer lab tomorrow."

"She works during the day. Can she come after 6:00 p.m.? Once you see her, you'll recognize her; she is really good looking."

"Yes, okay. I'm there until 9:00 p.m. Joy, you said? I'll look out for her."

I continue on to the bursar's office, which is empty, except for a man sitting at a desk. I stand in the doorway, delaying the inevitable.

"Can I help you?" the man behind the desk shouts in my direction.

"Um. Well," I say hesitantly as I walk slowly in his direction. "Good morning, sir. Um, I'm here to ask for a one-week extension to pay my tuition?"

"I'm sorry, we don't give extensions beyond the one-week grace period we already provide. Unfortunately, you have only until tomorrow to pay," he says. "We're completely computerized. So, if the tuition is not deposited into your account before 5:00 p.m. Friday, the system will automatically remove you from your classes."

"Oh," I say, feeling perspiration form on my upper lip.

"What if I can pay half?"

"Then you can take only one course, three credits."

"I see," I say, nodding, even though I know I need at least nine credit hours a semester to keep my full-time student status, which enables me to also keep my job in the computer lab. "Okay. Thank you."

"I'm very sorry. Perhaps you can borrow temporarily from someone, perhaps your bank?"

"I'll try. Yes. Thank you." *Adem, you have only yourself to blame. You did this to yourself.*

I come home from school that afternoon to find Dr. Tiller's door open. I try to slide by without him seeing me; I just don't have it in me to hang out with him when I'm about to get kicked out of school for nonpayment. But the second I step past his room, I hear him calling my name.

"Hi, Harry, how are you today?" I say as I turn around.

"How does a hot dog and Ritz cracker picnic sound to you?" he asks. He's looking rather tired and frail. I wonder if he's had anything else to eat today.

"Absolutely!" I say with extra enthusiasm, hoping to liven the mood in the room and change my own. "I have about thirty minutes to spare and I'd love to spend it with you. I'll be right back."

I run around the corner to the 7-Eleven, trying to remember the last time Harry and I spent some quality time together. It's been weeks. *You're so involved in your own affairs Adem, that you've neglected this old man who needs you.*

The blond lady at the register—"Hon" I've nicknamed her in my mind— wraps up four hot dogs for me. "$2.97, hon!" she says. "Haven't seen you in a while. Everything good?"

"Yes. Thank you. Nice to see you as well," I say, pulling out three singles. I wonder if I'll always think of Dr. Tiller when I walk into 7-Eleven. Or eat a hot dog? With Ritz crackers. *Such a strange combination*, I think as I pay, adding in a box of chocolate chip cookies to my purchase at the last second, thinking it will be a nice treat for Dr. Tiller.

Back at the house, I drop off the hot dogs with Dr. Tiller and tell him I'll be right back with some tea, my culture's contribution to this wacky culinary concept. Before I even sit down, he asks me to report to him about my classes. Mentioning nothing about the tuition, I spend the next twenty minutes telling him all the details I can think of, impressing upon him how well the professors explain the material, and how much his own tutoring continues to help me.

I leave his room and head off for work at the Blues Saloon with no solution to my tuition issue.

***

The computer lab is unusually empty the next day, which means I have the unfortunate luxury of time to worry about how I'm going to come up with my full tuition in the next twenty-three hours. 6:00 p.m. has come and gone,

Joy has not yet arrived, and I'm feeling agitated.

At 6:45 p.m., a woman in posh-looking clothes and rather heavy makeup walks hurriedly into the lab, shaking her head from side to side rapidly. I can't tell if she's just harried, looking for me, or simply fixing her long hair. She spots me in the office and rushes in my direction. I get up to greet her and reel back a bit from the strong smell of her perfume. Pretty, but way too much.

"Hi, I'm so sorry . . . Adem? I'm so sorry I'm late. I'm Joy."

"Nice to meet you, Joy. No problem," I say, smiling and shaking her hand. *I do not remember this woman from class, at all. And, boy, do Liban and I have very different tastes in women.* "So, Liban says you need some help catching up in Algorithm Development?"

"Yes, I do," she says, throwing her hair back with her palm this time. "My company reimburses me for the advanced courses I take, but only if I pass the course. If I don't, they don't pay. My son has been sick, and I was behind in both coursework and homework," Joy says, slightly out of breath. "So, I got an incomplete. I have one week to finish the course and get a passing grade."

"I'm happy to help you."

"Excellent, thank you."

We move to a mainframe terminal, where we work on writing the programs, debugging, and testing them, and printing the inputs and outputs.

At 9:45, three hours after she arrived and forty-five minutes after I was supposed to lock up the doors for the night, Joy sits back and sighs. I look over at her; she is smiling. First time all night. "Adem, I cannot thank you enough. You just saved me!" she says, looking like she wants to hug me.

"You did really well. I believe you will pass this class."

"I don't think I'll be able to do it without you. Can we set up another tutoring session, perhaps for tomorrow?"

We make a plan for another tutoring session and walk out of the building together. As we say good night, Joy grabs both my hands. "Thank you so much, Adem. Truly. Thank you."

When I get home, I call Bonnie to tell her the bursar's office rejected my extension request, but there's no answer. Feeling desperate to speak with her, I try her house a few times. With no answer, I try unsuccessfully to study, wondering where Bonnie could be at ten thirty on a Thursday night. I finally give up and turn on the TV, changing the channel with the pliers until I settle on *Laverne and Shirley*. Adjusting the rabbit ear antennas, I try to forget that I still haven't solved my $1,500 tuition shortfall. I resign myself to the fact that I'll be taking only one course this semester and I'll have to figure out all the rest another time. I fall asleep trying to decide which class I'll keep.

The tuition countdown resumes the minute I wake up. I have ten hours to come up with $1,500. I know it's impossible, but I resolve not to give up until the clock strikes five.

I have trouble focusing on my two Friday morning classes and remain unfocused that afternoon at the computer lab.

At around one o'clock, Bonnie walks in the lab.

"Hi," she says.

"Hey, what are you doing here?" I ask, surprised. "Such a nice treat, seeing you in the middle of the day."

"Well I'm glad you think it's a nice treat," she says, smiling.

"I called you last night. A couple of times. Where were you?" I say, trying to sound like it's not a big deal, but realizing it sounds kind of accusatory.

"Oh, yeah. Sorry. I was out. A work thing. Can't talk about it. How'd it go with the bursar?"

"Rejected," I say, trying to remember how much Bonnie "disappeared" before I knew she was a criminal investigator—or whatever she is.

"So, you still don't have the tuition?"

"Nope."

"And Eliz's loan?"

"Won't get here until the Tuesday after next at the earliest. Seven business days."

"I'm sorry, Adem."

"It's okay. I'll take one class and figure out all the other stuff, the legal stuff with my student visa, later."

"Well, I've got something for you," she says, holding out a picnic basket. "I brought you lunch. Just in case you needed cheering up."

"Wow," I say, leaning in to kiss her. "That's so nice."

"Open it up," she says, putting it down on my desk. "See what I've packed for us."

I look at her.

"Truly, this is so nice," I say, smiling, hesitating.

"Seriously, Adem? Open the picnic basket."

I open the picnic basket. There's an envelope on top of a red and white checkered tablecloth.

"What's this?"

"Open it."

"Is it for me?"

"No, Adem. It's for the pope!"

I look at her, confused. "What is it?"

"Open the damn envelope, Adem, and you'll find out. Jeez!"

I open it carefully and pull out a cashier's check for $1,500. I look up at her. She is smiling and looking me in the eye. I look back at the check. "What is this?"

"It's your tuition payment, dummy! You can pay me back whenever in installments if you want. No interest."

"I can't believe this," I say, running my fingers over the numbers. "But . . . why?"

"Because I could."

"But . . ."

"I wanted to help you. And I know you are going to pay me back."

"Thank you, Bonnie. I just . . . Thank you so much. You've just saved my semester," I say, hugging her. "I can't believe you did this for me. And not just the money . . . I mean even doing a whole elaborate picnic as a ruse. That's the right word, right?"

"Yes," she says, smiling. "The picnic basket was my decoy. But, there's actually food in there for a picnic if you have time," she says.

"Oh! Ha," I say laughing, so focused on the money that I never looked past the envelope. "Wow, you're incredible."

We take the picnic outside. She's packed some of my favorites, including a salami and cheese sandwich. I think about my picnic with Francesca at the top of Sedef Island.

"Penny for your thoughts," Bonnie says, interrupting my memory.

For just a second, but only a second, I consider telling Bonnie about

Francesca and the island and then quickly change my mind. "I was just thinking about how absolutely crazy and amazing it is that you did this for me."

After the picnic, Bonnie walks with me to the bursar's office. I hand over her $1,500 and my $1,200 cashier's check I got from my bank last week. Tuition paid. And, with three hours to spare.

***

The following day I arrive at the Blues Saloon for my double shift singing to myself.

You can't always get what you want,
But if you try sometimes, oh you just might find
You get what you need.
And I get to stay in school, I add. *I get to stay in school!*

I can almost taste a future that doesn't include lugging beer kegs and kicking out unruly patrons from the bar. This past month, Saturday nights have been rife with rowdy guests. Tonight, I have my eye on four men whose haircuts give me pause—soldiers in civilian clothes, I decide. As the night wears on, I notice the soldiers razzing a couple sitting next to them.

I look over at Dan, who's working behind the bar. I wait for him to look in my direction, then motion to him about the soldiers. "What are you looking at? Get them out of here!" he yells. It's loud, but I can read his lips.

I walk over to them and, shouting over the music, in a polite but commanding manner, tell them they need to leave. "Gentlemen," one of the soldiers says, mimicking me, "I'm afraid I am going to have to ask you to leave. You are bothering the other patrons."

One of them pushes his chair back as if to leave and then, with a swing I don't even see coming, lands a punch square on my jaw. I stagger back on my feet as he takes a congratulatory bow. Then just as he straightens up, I plant one back right between his eyes. I expect him to fall over backward but his body hardly sways. His friends laugh as I grab him and shove him out onto the street. He barely resists. "Stay there," I say, knowing that if he wanted to, he could beat up everyone at the bar and trash the place in minutes, just by himself.

I walk back into the bar and grab another one of the soldiers, who's doubled over with laughter and booze. He's so stoned he doesn't even resist as I toss him outside. I get back in and head to the table for soldier number three. The music has stopped, an eerie quiet has descended on the bar. I hear someone behind me and turn quickly to find a man with his hand high in the air holding a bottle. He swings the bottle down, but I'm able to dodge my head to the right and the bottle comes crashing down on my shoulder, breaking in half. The man stands still, staring at me, holding half of a Steinlager bottle, the neck now a real weapon with its jagged glass edges. He turns the bottle on its side and, holding it like a sword, tries to stab me with it. I quickly jump out of the way and he lurches forward, crashing into an empty table.

"Okay, you're out too, mister," I say, grabbing him and throwing him to the curb with the rest of the soldiers.

"Damn it, Adem! What's the point of a doorman if you can't do your job?" Dan yells at me from behind the bar, as I walk back inside to see that Paul and Raymond have corralled the two remaining soldiers and are escorting them to the curb.

"Thanks man," I say to each of them.

I ignore Dan's comment.

The busboys sweep and mop up. I help them right the fallen tables and chairs as the music starts up again.

Then I go back to the door, my shoulder and jaw aching. Two hours to closing.

***

At 3:00 a.m. the staff start to gather at the bar and tables as usual. I slip in and sit down at a table close to the kitchen. Dan paces behind the bar and looks ready to launch into his nightly rant. I think he surprises us all when he walks out from behind the bar, pulls a chair up to my table, leans toward me, and asks, "How you doing there, Adem?" To the rest of the staff, I imagine it appears that Dan is reaching out to me with kind concern. But it's all a facade. He places his hand on my injured shoulder and presses down, hard. I try not to flinch in pain. He continues in a cutting tone, "I see that you are not only a lousy dishwasher, you're also an incompetent doorman. You have no idea how to work the damned door."

"I quit," I say, blandly, almost surprising myself. I'm not angry. I'm not sad either. I'm tired of being treated poorly. I'm tired of being mocked and I'm certainly tired of Dan's nonsense, his game, whatever it is that this is.

He draws back. I'm not sure if he's surprised by what I've said or that I've said it out loud.

"That's the stupidest thing you've ever said, Addo."

"I will not be back here tomorrow to work. Or ever," I say, looking him right in the eye.

"You are upset right now, Addo. Go home now. In the morning, you'll see this all with fresh eyes," he says, pulling out his wallet and handing me a ten-dollar bill. "Take a taxi home, on me. Get a good night's sleep, be fired up and ready for a new day tomorrow. Okay, Adem?" he asks, sounding unsure and using my real name for the first time in months, if not years. When I don't reach for the money, Dan lays the bill down on the table. "Come to your senses. You know you can't work anywhere else. Nobody else is going to take the risk like I did and hire you. Tell you what—don't come in at eleven, sleep an extra hour, come in at noon."

I get up from the table without touching Dan's peace offering and walk out the door. I take a cab home. "Goodbye Blues Saloon. Three and a half years of Dan's insults is enough," I mumble to myself, resolute in my decision.

Enough is enough. I came to America for a peaceful life.

18

DOWNHILL

It's 3:45 a.m. by the time I arrive home. I head directly into the shower, avoiding the mirror. I can't even face myself right now.

My shoulder and jaw are aching and my head, too. I lie down on the bed, debating with myself what tomorrow will look like. I just quit the Blues Saloon without a backup plan. Maybe I should just return to the bar, like a runaway dog returning home hungry, tail tucked between his legs. No. I can't. I can't go back. I'm not going to lick my own spit off the ground. My stomach turns.

I spend Sunday morning watching TV from my bed, falling in and out of sleep until the afternoon. I call Bonnie, tell her I've quit my job, silently wishing she were in bed beside me. She's sympathetic but doesn't offer to come over and I don't ask. I'm too proud. She thinks I'm strong. I fall asleep again, wishing she had wanted to be with me.

I call Roberto, just to chat. I apologize to him for not reaching out more often. He understands, he tells me. He's almost never home, working hard on his version of the American dream. I don't tell him about my financial woes, but instead listen to him and congratulate him on his success, how he transitioned from buffing office floors to marketing and distributing foodstuffs to Hispanic grocery stores. He's also moved out of his rental room to a one-bedroom apartment. "It's an old building but warm enough during winter and cool enough during summer, and things work," he says. "And you're always welcome to stay here, not just overnight hours but twenty-four-seven," he says, as if he senses I'm in financial trouble.

***

Between my body aches and money worries, I haven't slept well. I still have a $2,700 school tuition deficit for the next semester, which will be here before I know it. But this time, I have half the income. And I can't work any more hours at the school's computer lab; twenty hours a week is the maximum allowed for a full-time student.

***

On Monday the lab is slow; only two students have come in. I stay in the back office alternately wallowing in self-pity and scanning the want ads from yesterday's paper looking for anything from waitstaff to draftsperson, trying to find a business that will hire an undocumented alien. I check my watch so often that my wrist begins to hurt from twisting. I want to go home and climb into bed, numb myself with TV reruns.

About thirty minutes before my shift ends, I look up to find Bonnie standing in the doorway of the lab. "I need to talk to you," she says, without any formalities—or even a simple "hello." Her voice is hushed, ominous sounding. This is the second time in two weeks that she's shown up at work. I look to see if she's carrying another picnic basket.

"Can you close up shop early? It's important," she says, tapping her foot. "I need to talk to you."

"You okay?" I ask, standing up, sounding too loud against her quiet.

"I'm fine, I just . . . we need to talk."

"You're not pregnant, are you?" I yell-whisper. "Please tell me you are not pregnant. If you are . . . I'll . . . I'll . . . we'll get married."

347

"Oh my God, Adem! No, I'm not pregnant, you idiot. I'm thinking of moving," she blurts out.

"Jeez, Bonnie. Is that all?" My relief is embarrassing. *Would I really have married her?* "Good for you. I think it's a great idea to leave your roommates behind. They never liked me, anyway."

"No, Adem, this is not about you, for God's sake. I'm moving, moving."

"What does that mean, 'moving, moving'?"

"I'm moving . . . away. Away from DC to Colorado."

"What?"

"I got a job there."

"You got a job there? In Colorado? You didn't even tell me you were looking! You just got a job here. Oh, wait. That's right. It's not a new job, you've had that job the whole time. You lied to me about getting a new job. So, this is what it's like with you?"

"Come on, Adem, I thought you were over that?"

"Well, apparently I'm not. You lied to me and said nothing about looking for a job elsewhere."

"It's not a lie. There was no reason to say anything if it didn't happen."

"But it did happen. And now you're leaving without any warning."

"Well, there was no reason to tell you until it was final. And now it's happening, so now I'm telling you."

"Oh really? That's your approach?"

"Adem. Please. This . . . what we have, it's a dead end. It's not going anywhere. I need some . . . stability. I need to be around my family again."

"But . . ."

"My sister lives in Colorado."

"So, that's it? You're leaving. I get no say?"

"It's *my* life, Adem."

"But what about *us*? Don't I get a vote? What if I don't agree? What if I don't think we're a dead end?" *Don't leave. I need you. I need you here, with me. I love you.*

"I don't think it . . . I don't know . . . I don't think what *you* want matters. My mother used to say, 'No wins.' I'm saying 'No,' you don't get a vote and I'm leaving."

I throw up my hands. I can't sit here and listen to this, to Bonnie. "I can't do this right now. I . . . I guess . . . Well, since it doesn't matter what I think, goodbye, Bonnie. That's all I can say." I grab my jacket and head for the door.

"Last one out, please shut the door behind you!" I call to the two people in the lab.

"My God, Adem. You are so dramatic!" Bonnie yells at my back. "I'm not leaving for four weeks. We have four weeks!"

***

I'm in a daze. *What's happening in my life, Bonnie, work, America? Was this all a mistake?* I walk home on autopilot, not paying attention to the lights or the cars or the people. "Watch out!" I hear, as an arm is flung across my chest and I jump back onto the curb; the sound of screeching brakes rings in my ears. I don't look back, just give a thumbs up to thank whoever just saved my life, too embarrassed to say anything.

When I finally get to my street, I see Mrs. Hardwick standing at the front door. "Adem," she calls to me before I even reach the outside stairs. "I need to talk to you." *She's waiting for me? It's not the first day of the month, is it? I need to get it together. Oh my Lord, what if she's discovered I've been sneaking Bonnie into my room and she's kicking me out?* "It's Dr. Tiller," she says. "They took him . . . they . . . Dr. Tiller is in the hospital. They took him this morning," she says, choking on her words.

"Oh no," I say, shocked, surprised that I feel a pinch of tears behind my eyes. "What happened?"

"He was having difficulty breathing. You know he only has one fully functioning lung."

"Yes ma'am."

"I wanted you to know because he says you're very kind to him."

"Thank you for saying that, ma'am. He's been wonderful to me, too. He's helped me immensely with my English." She nods. "Where is he? Which hospital? I'd like to visit him." *Maybe I could bring him his hot dogs and crackers.*

349

"I'll get you the information, yes. That would be nice. I'm sure he would like that."

She turns and goes back inside. I follow her through the door and head down to my room. Then I remember the other gut-wrenching news of the day—Bonnie is leaving me. I grab the pliers and spend the rest of the afternoon in bed watching reruns.

***

The following day, the money from Eliz arrives in my bank account. I am relieved to be able to repay Bonnie. I call Eliz to thank her. She sloughs it off and immediately changes the subject.

"We need to talk about Mom and Dad . . . They're fine," she says, interrupting herself, clarifying. "Except there's been a bit of news that's, well . . . it's not so good. They're about to lose their apartment."

"What? What happened?"

"Well, the story is a little confusing, but it seems that the landlord wants to give the apartment to his daughter because she's getting married. And he didn't exactly give them a lot of warning. They have to move out in three months."

"Three months? They have to pack up their lifetime, *our* lifetime, and find a new place and move in three months? We've lived there for . . . what, my whole life. Almost your whole life?"

"I know. It's been more than twenty years."

"So, where are they going to go?"

"I don't know. I'm pretty worried. I'm worried about the physical toll. But, I also have no idea if they can afford anything else in the neighborhood."

I think my angels must be laughing at the irony. I quickly decide not to tell her that I may soon be in the exact same situation. There's no reason to put more worry on her plate.

"I have some money," she says, "I could give them extra money. So could Ela. But they won't take it from us. Ela and I discussed it. We know you're having some difficulty right now but Mom said it's possible they would accept money from you because you don't have your own family, yet."

I feel like my head is going to explode. I don't even have enough money for myself.

"I'll take care of it, Eliz," I say. But, I have no idea how I'll do it.

***

The next day, when I return from the computer lab, Mrs. Hardwick meets me at the door, again.

"I'm sorry to tell you that Dr. Tiller passed away. He was . . ."

I nod my head as she gives me the details of what happened, how he passed so quickly, but I'm not really listening. I feel nauseous as I think about how Dr. Tiller died alone in a strange bed in a strange room surrounded only by doctors and nurses, no family, no friends. And I never visited him.

On the way to my room, I stop in front of Dr. Tiller's door, resting my palm on it. *Maybe this is all a bad dream; maybe he's still in there.* I almost want to knock. *He had so much knowledge. So much experience. And yet he died penniless, living in a windowless room that most people would use for storage. No wife. No kids. No family. And his one friend, you . . . you Adem, you let him die alone among strangers in a hospital.*

***

After work the next day, the third time in four days, Mrs. Hardwick greets me at the door. I take a deep breath.

"I have some additional news for you today," she says. I cannot imagine what it will be and feel my heartbeat quicken. "I am moving to Florida," she says, sounding incredibly happy, an emotion I wasn't sure she possessed.

"Warmth and sunshine," I say, smiling, my shoulders relaxing. "No more winter boots and winter coats."

"That's right. That's why I'm moving. Better for my joints, you know."

"It sounds like a good decision then, ma'am."

"You've been a good tenant, Adem. I wasn't so sure about you. You know—I don't like immigrants . . . especially ones like you who don't speak English. *Didn't* speak English," she says, correcting herself. "You can stay 'til the house sells," she adds.

I look at her, my eyes darting back and forth, trying to read the expression on her face. *Stay 'til the house sells?* "I'm sorry. Excuse me. I don't think I understand."

"I am moving to Florida, which means I will be selling the house. Once I sell, you will have to move. You won't have to move right away. The house may sell next week or three months from now. You're welcome to stay until the sale is final."

"Excuse me?" I say, again, sounding like I still don't speak English. I may be more shocked by this news than the news of Dr. Tiller's passing.

"Yes, it's been in the works for a while, my plan to sell the house and move to Florida, that is. I didn't want to move while Dr. Tiller was still living here. It would have been too hard for him at his age, with his health issues. He'd been living here for so long, fifteen years almost, I think. So I committed to waiting until Dr. Tiller chose to move or passed away," she explains.

"That was kind of you," I muster, trying to remain polite while a panic sets in. *Where am I going to live?*

"That's all for now, Adem. Have a good day," she says, turning and walking away.

I stand there in the foyer, frozen, staring into the room that is off-limits to guests, watching the dust mites swirling in a sunbeam. *What am I going to do?*

The cheapest room available around here is $300 per month. I don't even need to check the real estate section of the paper; I know this for a fact. I've seen the numbers, the rents and sale prices, and they aren't going down. I can hardly afford more than the $110 a month I'm paying now without my job at the Blues Saloon. I'm only making $440 per month. With my last paycheck from Dan and my latest paycheck from the computer lab, I'll have $400 in my bank account. I still owe friends and family more than $3,000 and I need tuition money for next semester. After four years in the US, this is what I have accomplished. Not only do I have less money than the $800 I arrived with, I also have more debt, a lot more.

I must make America work. I cannot go back home without making it in America. I just can't.

Sweat collects on the back of my neck. I need some fresh air. I turn around and go back out the front door and just start walking, heading nowhere in particular. I wonder where Grandma's angels are right now. *Do I really have them, even one of them? Do you hear me if I talk to you, angels? Do you see me or are you just a make-believe story to make children feel better, safer? Are you looking at each other and shaking your heads at me and saying, "What're you doing, man? Even we can't do anything about this mess, it's all too much."*

Without realizing it, I find myself standing in front of the hot dog display at a 7-Eleven, I'm already near Georgetown. This is the store I used to stop by after my shift ended at the Blues Saloon at 3:00 a.m.; this is where I'd buy a quart of milk and an apple before sitting down on the bench in the park to wait for the Metro to start running for the day. I buy two hot dog sandwiches, a small bag of Ritz crackers, a soda, and a newspaper. I walk over to Dupont Circle, looking at the homeless men gathered. At this point, $400 separates me from them. I find a bench and put together my concoction, then toast my dear friend. "Here's to you, Dr. Tiller," I say. "Your passing has taken a big bite out of my life. Cheers." I clink the air with my hot dog and take a bite. I spread the newspaper out on the bench next to me. As I turn the pages to the help wanted section, a familiar face grabs my attention. The headline under the photo reads, "Dr. Harold Tiller, 85, Physicist, Student and Colleague of Albert Einstein, Dies." Princeton, Berkeley, Los Alamos, the war, the bomb— Dr. Tiller's whole story—it's all there in the article. *An accomplished life. You had an accomplished life, Harry. But, what did you think of the end?*

***

By the time I get home, I've convinced myself I need to do what I did when I first arrived in America: go door to door and ask businesses if they need help. Only now I don't need to be nervous about what to say and I can pick up the phone and call places I know are looking because they've advertised their needs. And, I don't have to limit myself to dishwasher jobs. I'm way ahead of where I was when I first arrived here. That's one big plus I need to remember. I'm not a failure yet.

I circle twenty possible jobs in the paper and dial one business after another. It takes all afternoon, but by the end of the day, I have five interviews lined up.

It takes three busses and two hours to get to the first job interview. It's a satellite company in Virginia. When I arrive, I find out it's not an interview at all, but rather a test which they ask me to sit for, right there on the spot. *Did I misunderstand or did they mislead me?* The test is all about satellites, about which I know nothing. Halfway through, I know I have failed.

I fare much better at the second interview. It's at a cartography firm. First, it's easy to get to because it's right in DC. Second, it's actually an interview and not a test. They spend a lot of time selling me on the job—which sounds extremely tedious—and not really asking me about me. When I leave, the interviewer tells me, "We'll get back to you by Monday." It feels promising that they'll offer me the job even though I really don't want it.

My third interview—"three's the charm" as Dr. Tiller used to say—is just over Key Bridge in Rosslyn, Virginia, and is later that afternoon. It's an easy walk from Georgetown over the Potomac River. The job is computer based; if I'm hired, I'll be monitoring inventory for cargo ships and inputting data. The interview goes well, and they schedule me for a second interview, immediately, one with the "big boss," who offers me the job. When I tell him I don't have a visa, he rescinds his offer on the spot. It was the one job that I was interested in. Apparently, three is not the charm, after all.

I'm still waiting for a call back from the cartography firm when I'm offered a job as a waiter at an expensive French restaurant. The manager has no issues with my illegal status and hires me right away. She asks me to come for my first shift that evening, but I'm fired by the owner five minutes after I show up for work. "You can't work here; you have no experience with French food," he tells me, unapologetically. He's not wrong.

A week and two days after leaving the Blues Saloon, I finally land work at an oriental rug store. My job includes loading and unloading the truck, doing inventory, setting up the retail store, and working as a salesman on the floor. It's a small operation. The owner; the sales manager, whose name is Otto; and me. Since I'll only work the floor some of the time, the owner says he'll pay me $200 a week salary plus 5 percent commission on the rugs that I sell. He says Otto works on a straight commission.

On my first day, Otto tells me the job keeps him fit. "Sometimes I'll move fifty rugs for a customer in less than thirty minutes," he says. While I find this hard to believe, I quickly find out what he's talking about. To learn the process, I follow Otto and his customers around and do all the grunt work for him, pulling out the carefully folded carpets from six-foot stacks one at a time until reaching the carpet the customer wants to see. If the customer doesn't want the rug, it needs to be folded, all eighty pounds of it, back onto the pile. The process happens over and over again with each customer, all day long.

After a week on the job, Otto pulls me away from inventory to help a customer. Within five minutes, I've shown her at least ten rugs. "Too busy," she says. "Too flowery," "Too bold." "Oh, wait, I love that one," she points to a carpet at the bottom of the stack. I move a dozen carpets to get to it. I feel perspiration dripping from my forehead; while she studies the carpet, I turn away from her and pull a handkerchief from my pocket to wipe my brow. "Oh dear. You know. It wouldn't go with the wall paint," she says, shaking her head and making a face. I don't know why she couldn't have figured that out from the colors that were poking out from the stack.

"Well, buying a rug is an investment," I explain, remembering a key line Otto taught me. "With simple care it lasts a hundred years or longer, but a machine carpet, you'd have to replace a dozen times by then. And this rug is handmade; it's hard work. And it's artwork. It's really about whether you love the rug and the design. Wall color can be changed easily and inexpensively. An oriental carpet is an investment," I say, throwing in a little extra flair to the responses Otto has taught me.

"How about this one?" she asks, ignoring me and walking over to another pile and pointing. I have no idea if she has even heard what I said. I follow her, trying not to sigh in frustration. I glance at my watch. I've been with this customer for forty-five minutes. I pull out the rug she likes and then a dozen more. "I'll come back tomorrow with my husband," she says. "I just can't make a decision on my own."

"I won't be here tomorrow," I say. "But I can help you the following day."

"That's okay. I'll just get one of the other salespeople to help me," she says, as if we're all interchangeable. "Toodles," she says. "Thank you for your time."

"Toodles," I repeat, hiding the disappointment in my voice.

By the end of my second week, I haven't sold a single carpet, so my paycheck is a flat $400. At the end of week three, I finally sell a rug. It's a small one, but

I'm happy that my paycheck will bump up by at least $50, more if I can sell another before the end of next week.

The following Friday, payday, the owner finds me on the floor to tell me he doesn't have my paycheck. "Sorry kid. I'm working with the accountant on a new system," he says. "I'll get it to you as soon as I can."

I continue to work hard, trying to improve my sales techniques. I'm inspired by Otto, who makes it look so easy. I write down things he says to customers and try to practice his words and his tone. I make two sales and come close to five more.

Over the course of the next two weeks, the owner says nothing about the new accounting system or my paycheck, which will include what I'm owed from the last pay cycle, $450, and this pay cycle, my flat $400 plus $175 with my two commissions. On payday, Otto waltzes by me as I'm fixing a stack of rugs. He's holding his paycheck high in the air in celebration. "1,000 smackers," he says, high fiving me. I wait patiently for the owner to find me and give me my paycheck, but by the end of the day, when my shift is over and I'm already late to my job at the computer lab where I'm scheduled to tutor Joy, I still haven't received my check. I knock on the door to the owner's office to let him know I'm leaving for the day.

"All right, Adem. You're back when?"

"Tomorrow at one o'clock, sir."

"Right. Yup. You are right. That's what the schedule says. Okay. See you then."

"Sir. I didn't receive my paycheck today. Today's and the last one too, from two weeks ago."

"What are you talking about? I gave you your paycheck earlier today," he says, his voice louder, deeper.

"Excuse me, sir?"

"I . . . gave . . . you . . . your . . . paycheck . . . earlier. Learn to speak the damn language, Adem. You're in America. We speak English here."

"No sir, I understood what you said. But, you did not give me my paycheck."

"You callin' me a liar?"

"No, I am not, sir. But I did not receive my paycheck."

He gets up from his desk and brushes past me to the open door. "Otto!" he yells out toward the sales floor. "Did you get your paycheck today?"

"Yes sir. And thank you very much!" Otto calls back.

"See. I handed out the paychecks. You may want to get yourself checked out, Adem. I can't help it if you're having memory problems. Leave now. And shut the door behind you."

What the h— what's going on?

When I get home, I call Roberto and tell him what happened. "Yup. That happens. Lots of bad people here, Adem. Some bosses, when they know you are illegal and they know there's no one you can complain to, they cheat you. If you turn him in, he turns you in. It's a screwed-up system."

I'm speechless.

For all his faults, at least Dan was honest. Instead of cheating me, he gave me raises. *What is that expression Dr. Tiller taught me? "Careful what you wish for"? No, that wasn't it. "The grass is always greener on the other side." That was it. I quit the Blues Saloon because I thought there was something better out there for me. Dr. Tiller warned me about it and I didn't heed his warning. Even Dan warned me. And now look where I am. I came to this country, this place I've called home for four years, and again I'm in a worse place than when I arrived.* I quit the job and take the loss. Actually, I don't even quit, I just don't show up ever again.

***

Financially, I'm in trouble. If Mrs. Hardwick's house sells, my living expenses could double. And, I can only keep the job in the computer lab if I am a full-time student, which means I must take at least three classes. But I don't make enough to pay for the classes that will allow me to keep the job. And, now I'm down $1,025 for the month after being stiffed on the job.

"Try to think positively, Adem," Dr. Tiller used to tell me. "There's power in positive thinking."

Okay. Positive. You can speak English now. That's a positive. What are some other positives? Um . . . you've learned to program computers. That's something, right?

"Adem . . . Adem?"

I turn toward the voice. Dazed, I realize I'm sitting in the computer lab with Joy. *Wow, maybe there is something wrong with my brain.*

"I'm sorry. So sorry."

"Are you okay?"

"Yes. Absolutely. I apologize."

"Good. Well, I was asking you if you think I will be able to pass the test."

"Yes, yes I do," I tell Joy. I run my fingers through my hair and shift in my chair.

"Okay, well. I need to get home. I want to get a good night's sleep before the test."

"You'll be great. You'll see."

I spend the whole walk home trying to figure out what I'm going to do.

I open the fridge door and squat down. There's a red plum. Today is not a plum day. It's tomorrow. I cut it in half and have it. I wrap the other half for tomorrow.

19

THE CON ARTIST

It's been forty-two days since I quit my job at the Blues Saloon; forty-one days since Bonnie said she's moving to Colorado, leaving me; thirty-nine days since Dr. Tiller died; thirty-seven days since Mrs. Hardwick told me she's selling the house; and a week since I was cheated out of a month's salary.

For the past five days I've gone to the newsstand to buy the *Post* to look at the help wanted ads. I hate the expense, but it's an investment in the future or, as Dr. Tiller used to say, "the cost of doing business." I'm surprised to see a front-page article about Turkey in an American paper. I read through the first half of the article about the humanitarian costs of the military junta-backed government's three-year reign, a bloodbath. As far as I know, Turkish newspapers haven't written anything about the half a million people detained—both Nationalists and revolutionaries. One hundred thousand of the detained were put on trial, fifty executed, the article in the *Post* reports. Thirty-one journalists were sentenced to prison. The article also says that nearly two hundred people were killed during interrogations, and nearly three hundred died while in prison—some murdered, while others killed themselves. I had no idea things were this bad, this violent. Neither Demir nor Izzy's letters ever mention how bad things at home have become, nor Dad's, nor Ela's. The article gives hope that the new civilian government that formed after the parliamentary elections a year ago will help transform Turkey.

Before paying for the *Post*, I glance at the *Nation's Daily*. A small headline about Savas Kartal catches my eye. There's a photo of him and his followers, including Mr. Kaya, although the caption doesn't name him. I pick up the paper and start reading the article, looking up to make sure the newsstand owner doesn't notice. "After a three-month trial, the court declares Savas Kartal innocent. All charges against him have been dismissed and he has been exonerated of his previous murder conviction." The article says that, upon his release from the Istanbul prison, he was greeted by a crowd of cheering people. And then, I'm shocked by what I read. Savas Kartal announces, right there in front of the prison, where he was held for more than four years, that he plans to run for office.

I'm dumbstruck. And I don't know what's more upsetting. That Savas Kartal has been released from jail or that a murderer could, one day, run my country.

I put down the paper. *If I hadn't saved him from drowning, how many people would still be alive? Would Turkey have gone through its three-year reign of terror? Savas was the fire starter, and his gang was the kindling. I'd never thought of this before: I saved Savas's life and he used his life to kill people. What would that make me?* I feel like an accomplice.

I want to go home and take a shower to wash off this horrible thought, but I need to get to work. *This is not my fault. It cannot be my fault. I was trained to save people, like an emergency room doctor who operates on a criminal. I cannot put the weight of my country's problems on my shoulders.*

I pay for the *Post* and head to the computer lab, walking straight back to the office to spread out the paper on the desk and start rifling through the help wanted ads. I have $240 left.

Minutes later, there's a loud rapping on the main door to the computer lab. I jump and run to the door.

"I'm so sorry," I say, unlocking and opening the door for a professor and his assistant standing in the hallway. "I must have forgotten to unlock it."

Get it together, man. The professor nods hello; I can't tell if it's a thank-you for letting them in or if he recognizes me from the courses I've taken from him. As they sit down, I walk around the room, turning on the computer terminals.

"There . . . there it is. That. There's the message!" I hear the professor say to his assistant. "That's the message John sent from the library." His excitement draws me in and I edge closer, pretending to straighten out the chairs at nearby workstations. "Okay, now, let's see if the code works to reply to him," the professor says in a more hushed tone. *That would change how people communicate in the future!*

"I passed!" I turn around to see Joy standing in the doorway. "I passed . . . Thanks to you! It's all thanks to you," she says, holding her arms out wide as she enters the lab.

"Congratulations!" I say, pulling myself away from the professor's project and trying to equal Joy's unhinged glee. She sounds like she's had ten cups of coffee in the span of an hour.

"I wanted to come here in person to tell you," she says, enveloping me. I hold my breath to avoid overdosing on her perfume.

"Well, I'm glad you did," I say, not sure that I am. "Come. Let's go back into my office so we don't bother these folks," I say pointing toward the professor.

"Here's why," she says, without missing a beat, still talking as I walk away from her. "Here's why I wanted to come in person." Her heels are clickety clacking so loud on the linoleum floor that I'm missing some of what she's saying. "Because I want to . . . Okay, hold on. Let me back up a little. So, I told myself, if I passed I would . . ."

"Here, please, sit down," I say, pulling out the chair in front of my desk.

"Thank you, Adem. So . . . I told myself if I passed I would offer you a job. Actually, whether I passed or not, I told myself that," she says, speaking quickly.

What?

"Telling myself I would hire you if I passed was a great incentive, because I really want you to come work for my company."

What?

"Come work for me, for us," she repeats.

"Um. Wow!" I stutter. "I don't know what to say. You are offering me a job?" I ask, equally surprised and skeptical.

"Indeed I am!" she trills. "At First Manhattan Bank. Did I say that? Did I tell you where I work? Well . . . doesn't matter, that's where the job is."

"First Manhattan?"

"Yes! First Manhattan."

"Wow," I say again. A real, real job. She's offering me a real job! "But, I'm not . . ." *I'm not legal. Do I say that? Do I tell her?* "I'm not . . . well, I'm not . . . an economist or even a finance major," I say, instead.

"No, no, not for that. It's for the computer department, we're expanding, we support the bank's worldwide computer operations."

It's really a real job!

"You'll just interview with my boss and maybe my boss's boss. But you will come into those interviews very highly recommended by me," she says, standing up.

I stand up, too, and shake her hand. "This is completely unexpected. I'm . . . surprised. Honored. I don't know what to say."

"Say yes!" she shouts, and the professor at the far end of the room whips his head around.

"Sorry," I say in a whisper in his direction.

"Okay, so. I'll arrange a time to have you come in for an interview."

"Thank you, Joy. Thank you!"

"You know what? Come to my office at 10:00 a.m. tomorrow morning instead," she says, handing me her business card. "Let's just get the ball rolling on this. Tell the guard in the lobby you are there to see me and they'll give you a guest pass. My office is on the twelfth floor," she says, pointing to the address on the card.

And, just as quickly as she appeared in the doorway, she turns on her heels and click-clacks her way out of the lab.

I stand there, stunned. Frozen. *Is this real? A real interview, for a real job?*

***

I know that the suit I wore to my interviews two months ago isn't going to cut it for a bank job. My necktie and dress shirt are fine, but I'm going to need a new suit for an interview like this. *An interview at a bank!* After work, I run over to the Macy's on Twelfth Street to buy a new suit. I find a dark-blue Yves Saint Laurent suit on sale for $207, including same-day alterations. I tell the salesperson I'll be right back with the money if she can hold it for me for fifteen minutes. I find an ATM about five blocks away and take out $220. I have only $20 left in my account. I'm going all in, betting almost everything on this interview—playing poker with my life. My mind flashes back to the drunken nights I spent smoking and betting at the backroom casinos in Istanbul. *There's no one funding this bet but me. I can't afford to screw this one up.*

Back at the computer lab, I fix up my résumé, removing my work at the Blues Saloon and the six weeks at the oriental carpet store. I focus instead on my professional work experience and education:

- Technical University, Istanbul, mechanical engineering degree
- Project Engineer, Soner Ozenli, Istanbul
- Graduate Technical Assistant, Washington University, Washington, DC

To my current position in the computer lab, I add "tutor," as well.

In the morning, I put on my new suit and head to First Manhattan Bank. The new suit feels good on me. And it seems to change how people see me. Actually, I think it's that people actually *see* me now. I'm not an invisible immigrant wearing a T-shirt and jeans.

I arrive at the office, pass muster with the guard, sign in and go right up on the elevator. I'm five minutes early. "On time is late, five minutes early is on time," my dad used to say. Joy's secretary greets me at the elevator doors and leads me to Joy's office.

"Joy, Adem Bayer is here."

"Finally!" Joy says, her back to me. "It's about time you visited us!" she says, excitedly whipping around in her chair. She gets up and extends her hand. Her grip is hard. *Do women in corporate America have to practice their handshakes?* "See this, Adem? You can have a view like this if you want," she says, sweeping her arms in the direction of a wall of windows. It's spectacular. One can see all the way down Pennsylvania Avenue to the White House.

After a short conversation about the weather, Joy walks me over to an empty office with a desk. There's a stack of papers on the desk and a pen. "This is just a formality, Adem, for corporate, for human resources, you know. As soon as you are done, bring it back to my assistant. Take your time. There's no rush. I'll be in my office."

I fill it out; I'm careful not to misprint anything, cross over things, or ask for a fresh form. I want to get this one right the first time. I'm hyperfocused. I'm all in. I need everything to go right today.

The application form is long; from time to time I feel like shouting, *I'm illegal! I'm illegal! I can't work here!* and just leaving. I cement myself to the chair.

When I finish, I turn the form in to Joy's secretary. "Okay," I hear Joy say, from inside her office, "let's meet the boss." Joy comes out of her office. "Annie, I'll be back in a few," she says tapping her nails on her assistant's desk.

Joy leads me down the hall to an office that's even nicer than hers. "Nancy, this is Adem Bayer. He's applying for a job in my section. Adem, this is Nancy, my boss and our international operations manager."

"Nice to meet you, Adem. Please, have a seat," Nancy says, motioning to a chair on the other side of her desk. I look over at Joy, waiting for her to sit first.

"Thank you, Joy, I'll take it from here."

"You are in good hands, Adem. Have fun," Joy says. *Joy is leaving? She's not the one interviewing me?* Butterflies take over. Joy pats me on the back and leaves and I feel like little Adem, standing in the doorway of my new school as a six-year-old, staring at a classroom of eight-year-olds, my mother shoving me into the room and leaving me. *Breathe, Adem; you are not a six-year-old anymore. You can do this.*

"Do sit, please, Adem."

"Thank you."

I'm illegal. I'm illegal! I can't work here. I don't know if I should tell her. *What was I thinking, buying a new suit when there's no way they can hire me? Well, they could. I mean, the school hired me to work at the computer lab. Maybe the bank is the same? There's no way. Get it together, man! Just tell her. Don't make a big deal over it. Just get it over with and tell her. Don't waste everyone's time with this farce of yours just to see how far you can go.*

I remain silent; as silent as I was with Francesca after Savas Kartal shot at us in the car. *Will I ever learn?*

"So, I see that you went to Technical University," Nancy says, looking down at a piece of paper. Her tone is quiet, pleasant, the opposite of Joy, who is so frenetic and loud.

"Yes, ma'am. That's right. With a degree in mechanical engineering."

"And now Washington University, computer science?"

"Yes, ma'am majoring in hardware, software, and systems."

"You're an assistant there?"

"Yes, ma'am, I'm a graduate technical assistant. I help students with their homework."

"How long have you lived in the United States?"

"I'm going on four years, ma'am. I came here because it's been a dream of mine ever since I was a child."

"Well, Adem, let me say this. Your résumé is looks good, your English is excellent, and Joy has not stopped talking about you since you started tutoring her. I don't usually make such a quick decision about a hire."

It's been no more than five minutes. Is she going to hire me? She's asked me four questions.

"Usually it takes me a good half hour to figure out if I think a person will work out. But, I'm going to offer you the job right now. No hesitation."

I got the job?

"We would be happy to have you join our computing services team, Adem," Nancy says, standing up and reaching out to shake my hand in congratulations. I stand up quickly and extend my hand.

She's really hiring me! I got the job!

"I am building a new investment research support team, and that's where you will start. You will develop applications to assist our financial analysts in identifying investment opportunities worldwide."

"Thank you, ma'am," I say, shaking her hand. I can't believe it. *Say it now, Adem. You have to speak up now. Just say it, con artist, say it.* "Ma'am. I, um . . . I have one issue I do need to discuss with you."

"The salary. Yes, of course. You will discuss that with human resources."

"Oh, that's not . . . the salary isn't . . . Thank you. No, it's about my status in the United States."

"What do you mean?"

"I'm not . . ." *Adem, just say it, man!* "It's just . . . I do not have proper papers. That is, I don't have a visa. The university has accepted my status and allowed me to work in the computer lab. But it's clear to me that . . . Well, I understand from my time in America that each business, each entity, might be different. Might have a different policy, that is."

"Ah," she says. And then she is silent. She turns around and looks out her window and I watch her gaze. "That could be a problem," she says, finally, turning back to look directly at me. She bites her cheek. "I'm going to have to talk with legal about it. It's not the kind of decision I can make. There are protocols. Rules." She pushes a button on her phone. "Get me legal please," she says to her assistant.

She's calling them right now? "Would you like me to step out?" I ask. She shakes her head and motions for me to sit back down as she sits too.

She swivels in her chair and I listen as she explains the situation quickly and succinctly, then, she spends the next few moments listening to the person on the other end. She scribbles some notes I can't read. A minute later she hangs up the phone and looks at me with pursed lips. "I'm sorry, Adem. We cannot hire you without the proper paperwork. You need to have a valid visa. It can be a . . ." she looks down at her notes, "student visa or a diplomatic visa, an H-1 worker's visa. Any visa would work. But you need a visa or you cannot work here, no matter how perfect you are for the job. And, well . . . you are perfect."

"I understand," I say, feeling red-faced with embarrassment. "I'm sorry I wasted your time."

I get up and say goodbye. I want to just sneak out without seeing Joy again. I head to the elevators but decide that would be pitiful. I turn back and walk over to her office. She's not there. *Should I write a thank-you note that explains the problem?* I look up to find Joy's secretary looking at me. "Would you thank Joy for me, for the opportunity?" I say. *Nancy will tell Joy what happened.*

As I walk out of the building, I realize how close I got to shifting my life from that of a struggling immigrant to that of a comfortable professional. I got close. It's no longer me standing in my own way, as I feel it's been my whole life; it's bureaucracy, rules, policies, and paperwork.

***

Despite warnings—especially from my friends at the language school—on Monday morning, I decide to go to the immigration office to fix this; to get the proper paperwork. "Don't do it," Roberto told me, not just once, but over and over again. "If you don't have a valid visa, never, ever, ever go to the immigration office." Instead of heeding his warning, I put on my suit, grab my transcript, my passport that expired three years ago, and my revoked US visa, and I head out the door to the one place I've been warned not to go. All I need is a student visa, even for a week, for Nancy and First Manhattan Bank to be able to change it to an H-1 worker's visa and hire me. That's all I need.

Within a half hour of arriving at the immigration office, my number is called. *This is it.* My legs are shaking as I walk over to the window. "Hello, ma'am. Here is my passport; it has expired. Here is my visa; it has expired. I am a student. I have been a full-time student for the past four years since I arrived here from Turkey in 1980. I brought my transcript with me. Look, here are my grades—I have good grades."

I push the pile of papers closer to the clerk. She says nothing. She doesn't even pull her eyes away from her computer. With one hand, she pulls the pile closer to her keyboard. Then, slowly, she picks up each item, one at a time, and types something in.

The silence is almost too much for me. She continues to type, ignoring me. *Don't say anything. Just let her work.* "Is there any way you could give me a visa?" I blurt out, breaking the silence, unable to hold my tongue. My words sound too loud in the quiet room. She looks up but is otherwise unresponsive; then, she continues typing. She gets to the last item in my pile and finally looks at me.

"These cases are handled in the basement. You need to go there," she says, pushing my papers back across the desk in my direction. "One flight down."

The basement?

I head down the stairs and I step out into a large space. There's no one down here but a sharp-looking uniformed officer. Even sitting, I can tell he's a big guy. Like a gym rat. His shirt is white and perfectly starched and ironed.

His shoes, which poke out from under his desk, are shiny against the matte black of his pants.

"Hello, sir," I say into the cavernous room as I approach him. "They sent me here from upstairs. Here are my expired passport and visa," I say, holding out the papers. "I am a student. I study computers. I have always been a student while in the US. I need a valid visa so I can continue my studies. Even a temporary visa. I hope you can help me." *Please help me.*

He looks at me, hesitates, and then takes my passport and expired I-94 card, the one the immigration officer attached to my passport at Kennedy Airport when I first arrived, "Welcome to the US, JR," he said. I can't remember if I smiled. I do remember being scared, thinking I was going to be hauled off to immigration jail.

"Follow me, please," he says, in a voice that's kind but confident. I follow the officer as we walk across the large room lined with empty desks.

When he gets to the end of the room, he turns around. "This way, sir," he says, holding out his arm and pointing left. I turn the corner and right in front of me are iron bars, floor to ceiling. It's a jail cell. I stop.

"Step in here, sir," he says.

I look at him, then step in. *What just happened? How did this just happen? I'm in an American prison? I'm in an American prison! Roberto, man, why didn't you say, "They will put you in a jail cell"? If you'd told me that, if you had just said "jail," I would have listened.*

The officer shuts the gate and locks it. He says nothing, doesn't even look at me in my suit and tie and pressed shirt. I listen to his footsteps fade away until there's complete silence.

My face feels hot. My whole body feels hot, as if someone has just poured a bucket of boiling water over my head.

I'm all alone in a small cell in a large silent room.

What's going to happen to me?

I sit down on the bench. There's an exposed toilet in the corner of the cell.

Will they deport me? Where will they send me? Istanbul? Or can I choose my destination? Would they send me to Greece if I asked? Could I live out my life in Greece? Would I need a visa there too if Dad is from there? I laugh out loud at how absurd I'm being. *Don't I get a phone call? Who would I call?*

Think Adem, think! Can I call overseas? How would that help? Who would I call? Roberto? Trip? I get up and start pacing the cell. *If they kick me out of the country, do they pay to deport me? I mean, who pays for my ticket if I don't have the money? Or, do they keep me in jail until someone sends me the money?*

My mind is racing. Panic is setting in. I keep pacing. *If I'm sent to Istanbul, what will happen to me there? Will I be grabbed up by the military police and sent to military prison for being a deserter? Or, would they just send me to boot camp? Am I going to be on this cycle for the rest of my life, running from immigration officers and the Turkish military?*

I stop pacing. I grab my head, trying to stop my thoughts, which are sending me off the rails. *Or are my thoughts themselves off the rails?*

Why didn't I listen? Why didn't I listen to all the warnings about the immigration office? Why didn't I listen to the dangers of coming to America? I never listen to anyone—do I? I mean every single person said, "Don't go to the immigration office without a proper visa." They all said it. Why don't I listen? Maybe that's the formula to my life, "You don't listen so you lose." And, while I've recovered in the past, recovered from not listening to warnings in the past, this is it. I've come to the end of the line.

I resign myself to my fate and lie down on the bench without even taking off my suit jacket. *What difference does it make now?*

20

SEVENTY-TWO HOURS

I CLOSE MY EYES, THINKING ABOUT MY FAILED ATTEMPT TO MAKE it in America and what it will be like to return to Istanbul, the shame that will bring to my family. And then I hear the click of a door opening and footsteps approaching. "Bayer," the immigration officer says, appearing in front of the jail cell.

"Yes. Yes!" I say, jumping to my feet and checking my watch. I've been here almost three hours.

"Okay, so. This is what's going to happen. Here, you can keep this," he says, reaching his hand through the bars and handing me back my passport.

"Thank you," I say, unclear about what this means.

"And this piece of paper here. This is your hearing date," he says, handing me a piece of paper.

"Thank you," I say, taking the paper from him and looking at it.

"That's a hearing date. You are entitled to a hearing before a judge," he says. Then he steps a little closer and, in a quiet voice, says, "You do not have to go to your hearing. I'm going to unlock this door and you will be free to leave. If you choose to stay in the US, I will not come after you. If you leave the United States on your own within the next seventy-two hours, all of your visa violations will be erased. If you apply for another visa to the US, these violations will not be counted against you. In fact, this violation will not be on any record. Do you understand?"

"I don't..." I start saying, confused. But, as I see him reach for his keys and start unlocking the jail cell, I change my answer. "Yes. Sir. I do. I understand."

He hands me the rest of the papers I had given him earlier, pulls out a card from his shirt pocket.

"This is my card. You are free to go. Go now. Good luck," he says, holding open the jail cell door.

I look at him, confused, but try to hide it. I step out of the cell slowly, waiting to be punched or struck by the officer or others I can't see yet, so they can accuse me not only of being an illegal immigrant, but for attempted escape and assault of an immigration officer.

"C'mon, let's go," the officer says, placing his hand on my shoulder gently.

He leads me across the room. As we walk, I look around for the other officers, still expecting to be jumped, but the room is empty. We get to the stairs and the immigration officer turns to me. "Good luck to you, man," he says, holding out his hand. I still don't really understand what's happening. I look down at his hand, which remains extended. I shake it, but I don't move. "You are free to go," he says. Then, leaning in, he adds, "Remember what I said." I look at him and he motions for me to walk up the stairs.

I step slowly, looking back a few times. The officer nods and I keep climbing, taking the steps now two at a time. I walk out into the sunshine, with my passport and my papers in my hand, trying to process what just happened, looking around, still not sure that I will not be grabbed suddenly. *I was in jail. But am I free now? I don't understand.* I look over my shoulder, then at the officer's card. Richard Wilken, Criminal Investigator. "Remember what I said," he told me. *What did he say?* "You can continue to stay here, illegally. But if you leave the US within 72 hours..." *What did he say? Think.* "If you leave the US within 72 hours ... your current visa violations will be wiped from your record"?

I have $20 in the bank. $20, that's it.

I need to leave the country by Thursday, the officer put down the time, 6:00 p.m.

I call Roberto when I get home, but he doesn't pick up.

Then I try Trip. I tell him about the job offer and the problem with my visa. And then, even though I wasn't planning on telling him about the immigration office, I tell him about being thrown in a jail cell. And, I tell him about what the immigration officer said.

"What's he saying? What happened?" I hear Melanie asking in the background.

"He's got a job at a bank but they can't hire him because he doesn't have a visa," Trip says. "And he was thrown into jail."

"What?" I hear Melanie cry.

"He got a job at a bank. But they can't hire him because he doesn't have a visa!"

"Tell him to go to CRS."

"What? CR . . . who?"

"Let me have the phone," I hear Melanie say.

"Adem. Hi. Listen. Go to CRS—Catholic Relief Services. They have volunteer immigration lawyers there. They'll help you. It's free. It's right near the Capitol Building. I don't know the exact address, but it's on the northeast side of the Capitol."

"I'm not Catholic." *I'm not even Christian.*

"It doesn't matter. They'll help you."

"Really?"

"Really. Yes. Truly. Adem, they'll help you figure this out."

"Thank you, Melanie. I hope so. Should I go now? Today? Do I need an appointment?

"No. No. Go now. Just walk right in."

"And where is it again? I'm sorry. I'm just having trouble thinking. Can you tell me again?"

"I don't know the exact address, it's on the northeast side of the Capitol, Second Street and Maryland Ave., maybe. You'll see it."

"Okay. Thank you. I can figure it out. Thank you."

"Call us back and let us know what happened."

"Okay. I will. Melanie, thank you," I say again.

I gulp my tea, grab a handful of crackers, and head out the door, not having a clue about what to expect.

***

When I arrive about thirty minutes later, I explain to the person at the front desk that I have an immigration issue. An attorney on duty takes me in right away. The first question she asks me is if I speak English. I nod my head. "Do you need a translator? For a little extra help?" she asks. Her voice is warm. Kind.

"No thank you. I can speak English. But thank you."

She nods, "Let's get started then. Please sit. The first thing I want you to know is that I am here to help you. We are not the law. Okay?"

"Okay."

"The more honest with me you are, the better I can help you."

"Okay."

"So, tell me why you are here."

I tell her my story, trying to be brief. She interrupts a few times, asking me pointed questions, which I do my best to answer. She takes notes on a legal pad. I tell her briefly the things that have happened since I came to America, how I was drafted into the military and couldn't afford to go, how my passport expired and my visa because of it. I tell her the jobs I've had, the classes I've taken, my job offer from the bank, being in immigration jail this morning and the officer's recommendation—to leave the country within seventy-two hours.

When I finish she simply says, "Okay," and smiles. "First thing you need to do is get a current Turkish passport." She turns a page on her legal pad. "I'm going to write this down," she says, writing down "1" and then circling it. "Turkish passport. This is important." She underlines "Turkish passport."

"Second," she says, writing "2" and then again, circling it, "go back to your prospective employer and ask them to send a cable to the US consulate office of your overseas travel destination. Can you travel back to Turkey?"

"No," I reply.

"Okay, I won't even ask why. That doesn't matter. Which country can you go to? It has to be an overseas flight. Mexico and Canada don't count. That's the law."

I think for a second. "I can go to Germany."

"Okay, Germany. The cable would say to the consular in Munich, Frankfurt, or wherever you'll go, 'Please provide a visa for' . . ." she looks down at her notes, "Adem Bayer. Once he has a visa, we plan to hire Mr. Bayer for a full-time job as a . . . what?"

"Computer programmer."

"Good. The cable should say, 'As a computer programmer for our company. If you give him a visa, we have a job for him here.' " She jots down the words, rips the paper off the legal pad, folds it once, and hands it to me. "You are going to be fine. Okay?" I nod, thanking her profusely.

She doesn't realize she's wrong. I'm not going to be okay. As a military deserter, I'm not going to be able to get a new Turkish passport. The very reason I lost my US visa in the first place was because I didn't have a valid Turkish passport. That's something I know she can't help me with.

"I need a miracle," I say out loud as I walk out of the CRS.

And then I hear it. The ding, ding, ding of the yellow Volkswagen bug that I used to hear all the time when I worked in Georgetown. I haven't seen it in months. I've never seen it anywhere but Georgetown. "The end is near!" comes the booming voice from the loudspeaker as the car pulls up to a red light. "The end is near!"

"You've got that right," I say and a guy standing next to me starts laughing. "Good one," he says, and I smile, though I'm being completely serious. The light turns green and the car, loudspeaker still blasting, "Repent and turn to God," pulls away. As I start to cross the street, heading home, trying to figure out what I'm going to do, I stare blankly at the "Bug" as it drives away and then I come to an abrupt stop, right in the middle of the street, awestruck. The license plate! "ELA-190." How had I never seen that before? A car honks, and I realize that I'm still standing in the middle of the street and the light's turned red. I run to the sidewalk and keep staring at the yellow Volkswagen as it disappears into the distance. *Is this a sign? It's got to be a sign! But what's the message?*

By the time I've arrived home, I've decided that the message is to call Ela. I stay up until 1:00 a.m. to catch her before she leaves for work. I tell her about the job offer, the problem with my visa and my expired passport. And then I tell her about the Volkswagen and the license plate with her name on it.

"Call me crazy, but I think it was a message for me to call you," I tell her. "I mean, I know there's nothing you can do to help me fix my expired passport, which is the crux of my problem. But, lacking any other—"

"Adem, oh my God . . ." she says, interrupting me. "I don't know, maybe this is just a coincidence, but maybe it was a sign?"

"I'm listening."

"Last week Kaan and Funda, you remember them? From my brunch club."

"I remember," I say, wishing she would get to the point.

"Well, they just arrived in Washington for a month. They were planning to call you when they got settled. But, Adem, call them! I think Funda can help you. She's the organizer for the annual Turkish-American convention. She knows pretty much everyone at the embassy, even the ambassador. The ambassador, Adem! Maybe she can help you."

"What? Are you kidding me?"

"I'm not kidding. They are staying at the Mayflower Hotel. Call her, Adem. I know she'll be able to help you."

"That's unbelievable. It *was* a sign!"

"Sign or no sign, Adem, just call 'em."

"I don't know if I ever told you, but the last time I saw them, Kaan told me to leave Istanbul, to follow my dreams. Ela, this is crazy. He told me, 'This country is too small for you, Adem, you've got to go to America.' He was the only one who told me to go."

"I do remember that. You told me that. I remember. Call them. Oh my God."

I hang up with Ela then turn on the TV. It's well past midnight, already Tuesday. I set my alarm to call Funda at 8:00 a.m. and pace the room trying to figure out what I'm going to say. I don't fall asleep until after five.

***

By 8:15 a.m. I'm off the phone with Funda. An hour later she calls me back to tell me I have a meeting scheduled with an officer at the Turkish consulate at eleven thirty. I can hardly stand still. I can't believe it.

"Bring two passport-sized pictures of yourself to the meeting and your expired passport. Can you get the photos?"

"Yes. Yes. I can do that," I say, trying to sound calm.

"When you get there, ask for Mr. Brikan. Give him your old passport; he will give you a new passport."

"I don't understand. That's all I need to do?" I can't believe this. *This is too good to be true.*

"Don't be amazed," Funda says, as if reading my mind. "I told Mr. Brikan about you and about your job offer. They are always on the lookout for good—no, great people from Turkey who will become successful. You, your job, and your potential success are in the best interest of Turkey."

I thank Funda again and again, finally ending the call. Based on the countdown clock set by the immigration officer, I now have fifty-eight hours to leave the country. If I don't leave, I fear I will lose my shot at one day becoming a legal resident.

Right away I put on my new suit, which until this moment I'd been thinking hasn't served me well, and go to the photo booth at school. I take four passport pictures that don't look flattering, but I don't care; it costs $4, leaving me with $16, and I don't want to spend another $4.

For my 11:30 a.m. meeting, I walk over to the Turkish consulate, which is housed inside the embassy on Q Street. The street is lined with a half-dozen foreign embassies, all with varying architecture that represents their different cultures. After the circle on Massachusetts Avenue, which the locals call Mass. Ave; now it makes more sense, Americans shorten words to save time and effort, dozens of embassies follow. I'm amazed by the realization that each of these buildings is its own little country where the rules of that country apply, not the rules of America. I pass the Embassy of Nicaragua then the Embassy of Greece and before I know it, I'm standing in front of the Turkish embassy. I announce myself to the guard, in Turkish, and tell him I have an appointment with Mr. Brikan. I'm buzzed through the gate and walk across a courtyard before entering the building, where I go through security. I'm told to sit down in the waiting area.

A few minutes later, from behind a glass partition, my name is called. I walk over to the window. "Passport please," the man says in Turkish. I place my expired passport and my new pictures on the steel tray, which he pulls inside. He shuffles my items around and doesn't say anything else; I keep quiet too. "Please have a seat," he says before disappearing into another room.

Can this man change my future?

I walk slowly back to the chairs, feeling like I'm teetering on the precipice of my life, with no clue which way I'll fall. Though I'm sitting here alone, and though I flew off to the US alone, I'm not alone in the world. I didn't really do this alone at all. Yes, it was me, I am the one who took the risk, who moved from a country I knew so well to a country I didn't know at all. Yes, I was the one who learned English and worked as a dishwasher and slept on park benches and Roberto's single bed, and my single bed under the fuel lines. But, without the help of Zeki, Demir, Ela, Eliz, the Pan Am flight attendant, Roberto, Dan, Paul, and now Funda, and a handful of strangers—the immigration officer, the lawyer at CRS, and even this Mr. Brikan—I would not be here today, possibly on the verge of getting a good job at a bank. I would never have met Joy and had this job offer that could help me stay in the US had it not been for Liban. I would never have been able to help Joy had it not been for Trip, who recommended me for the job in the computer lab. I wouldn't even have had the ability to leave Istanbul had it not been for Zeki, who got me the visa I needed. And how about Eliz and Ela, who loaned me the money I needed in the first place? Dozens of people have helped me, if even just for a moment, like my many moments with Dr. Tiller, and they have helped change the trajectory of my life. I guess the reality is, everyone but my parents helped me get to where I am. And perhaps that's why I felt I was alone in this. Because my parents were so uninvolved. Yet in some way it was my parents' lack of interest in me that made me independent enough to "run away" in the first place.

And, I have to wonder, if there had been different people in my ESL classes or different students in my graduate school classes, or different immigration officers on duty at the airport and in DC yesterday, would I have made it this far? Is my life just a series of coin flips, hits and misses, accidents? Is this why Mom told me I was an accident? Was I an accident from the get-go? Is that why I am a nervous wreck—because I'm not the only one in control of my own destiny? Is that the formula then, destiny minus accidents equals life?

Sitting there waiting for Mr. Brikan, I get up to look at the photographs of home hanging on the walls. One is a view of the Bosporus. I walk closer, and staring at the photo, the grainy dots of pixels playing tricks on my eyes, I can see Francesca. I close my eyes to absorb the moment; there she is, standing on the patio at the club. I think of the way she talked, the way she walked, her smile, her clothes, her skin, her smell, her grace, her brain. The dinner, the swim, the bike ride, the boat ride to Sedef Island, our car dates, her kiss, her breasts touching my back when I carried her, when we rode Demir's motorcycle together. It was the first time in my life I had felt like a man; I was taking care of a woman, a woman who adored me, loved me.

I check my watch. It's been twenty minutes and I'm still waiting. I have fifty-four hours to leave the country. "No news is good news," Dr. Tiller had said when I had asked him if his doctor had gotten back to him with results from a blood test. Is no news always good news? I walk over to another group of photos and see that some are drawings. I stare at the images. Istanbul, the Bosporus, the bridges, the Golden Horn, Topkapi Palace, the Cisterns, Galata Tower, Dolmabahce Palace, the Blue Mosque. And some other towns that I haven't been to—Antalya, Alanya, Fethiye, Gocek, Datca, Marmaris, Bodrum, Kusadasi, Ephesus. There's a picture of Mount Ararat where some believe Noah's ark landed a long time ago and where Dad was stationed until 1956, two years before I was born.

Do I miss home? Is missing home different from not wanting to live there? America is home now, not Istanbul. Istanbul is where I am from, but America is my home.

"Bayer?" I hear.

"Sir, here I am," I say, prying myself away from the images and my thoughts and rushing over to the counter.

"We come from a beautiful country, don't we, Adem."

"Yes sir," I say, smiling.

"I'm Brikan," he says, switching to Turkish.

"A pleasure to meet you, sir," I say, trying not to sound nervous. My heart is pounding. I'm sure he can hear it, even through the glass partition.

He's not smiling. I quickly wipe my own smile from my face.

This is it. He's not smiling. It's over. I've failed. I'm going home. I came to America for the American dream and I have failed. "Okay. Here is your old passport," he says, pushing it toward me under the glass on the steel tray. "And, here is your new passport."

I look up at him, confused. Then I look down at the two passports in front of me. The new one is crisp, a little smaller. "I'm giving you a one-year passport," he whispers. "If you tell anyone, I will lose my job."

"I want you to be successful," he continues. "The embassy wants you to be successful. Your country wants you to be successful."

I reach for the passports. My hands are shaking.

"I will, I will be successful, sir," I say, although I don't know what that means. "Sir, thank you. Thank you." I want to hug him or at least shake his hand.

"Make our country proud, son."

I nod and slip the passports into my jacket.

I'm still shaking when I walk out of the consulate. There is a smile on my face that is so wide, my cheeks are hurting. I have a valid passport again. I finally have a valid passport.

I go back to the house in a trance, I think I may have skipped down the street at one point. I call Nancy at First Manhattan immediately. Her secretary puts me right through.

"Adem. Good to hear from you. What can I do for you?"

"Ma'am, I am wondering . . . I don't know how to ask . . . Is the position you offered me still available—as long as I have the proper paperwork?"

"Yes, absolutely. If you have the right paperwork, of course, we would love to have you work for us."

"I think I have solved the problem. But, if I could be so bold, I do need a little help from you," I say.

"Go on . . ."

"Ma'am, in order to stay and work in the country, I actually need to *leave* the country for a few days."

"That's an odd twist."

"Yes. Indeed it is," I say. "I don't quite understand it, myself, but I hope this course of action will be the key to being able to pursue my eventual dream of becoming an American citizen. I have chosen to go to Frankfurt because I have family there. What I need from you, if I could ask you, is a cable to the US consulate in Frankfurt saying if they issue an H-1 visa to me, you will hire me."

"Okay. Sounds like you do have a plan laid out. Let me check with human resources and also legal. I will call you back."

I turn on the TV but don't pay attention. I pace the room. *This, this, is where everything can change for me. A "yes" from Nancy, from First Manhattan, is the final step to securing my American dream story. This is it. If I get a "yes," I will have made it.*

Nancy calls back within the half hour.

"Yes," is the only word I hear her say. *Yes. Yes!*

I let out a loud sigh. I'm speechless.

"It's good news, indeed," Nancy says in response. I let out a laugh that's full and powerful. She laughs, too.

"I am so sorry," I say. "This has become such a roller coaster ride for me," I add, using one of Dr. Tiller's favorites.

"I understand," Nancy says. I can hear her smiling.

"Nancy, thank you for this opportunity, and for this extra step that will help secure my ability to stay and work in the US."

"You are absolutely welcome, Adem," she says emphatically. "We very much want you on our team. The one thing you will need to do is come in and sign a contract. Can you come in tomorrow, 9:00 a.m.?"

"Tomorrow, yes. Absolutely."

"Perfect. We will send the contract with a cable to the US consulate in Frankfurt along with a visa request."

"You don't want to jump the gun here, Adem," I can hear Dr. Tiller say. I still need three horseshoes and a horse to get going. I need to leave the US, get a brand-new visa in my brand-new passport, and return. Okay, maybe just two horseshoes and a horse. Because I already have my new passport.

"Thank you, Nancy. Thank you so much. I will see you tomorrow. Thank you," I say as I hang up the phone.

Funda. Adem, you need to call Funda and tell her.

I pick up the phone again and call Funda to let her know, to thank her profusely. I explain that I'll need to be out of the country for a few days and that when I return, we can celebrate, "on me," I add. Then I call Eliz and tell her I'm on my way to see her in Frankfurt. She screams so loud that my ear rings for the next half hour. Her baby is due in two weeks.

In the morning, I put on my suit and head over to First Manhattan. I look around, taking in the marble walls in the lobby and the leather chairs at the reception desk—I will be working here. Not to mop the floors, but as a professional.

I head straight for human resources, with a plan to stop by Joy's and Nancy's once I've signed all the necessary papers.

"Here is your contract," the personnel officer says, pushing a two-page document in my direction. "Let me go over the highlights for you and then you can read through the contract in its entirety. We are prepared to offer you a salary of $30,000 per year." I try not to react. *$30,000! I'm rich!* I swallow hard. "You will have comprehensive health care and dental benefits." *Insurance? I will have health insurance!* "You will receive fifteen days of annual leave plus ten days of sick leave per year. Overtime pay is 1.5 times your hourly average—"

"I accept," I say, interrupting him. *I'm rich!*

"I haven't finished yet," he says. "There's more."

"I accept. Whatever the terms, my answer is, yes." I would be willing to sign a blank piece of paper at this point.

"I am required to read the offer in its entirety," he says. I nod, trying to pay attention. He is speaking painfully slowly, and I am trying my best not to shift around in my seat. I keep nodding and saying "Yes" every time he pauses and looks up at me. "Yes, yes, yes!" I want to scream. I need to get this signed before someone walks into the office and says, "No, no, he can't work here because of blah blah blah."

Finally, he finishes. "Now that I've explained the terms of the contract, I recommend you read the document yourself," he says. I scan the contract quickly then sign my name, my John Hancock, Mr. Tiller called it. I am about to triple my salary. I will go from earning $5.50 per hour to $15 per hour. But really, I'll be earning six times more because I'll go from twenty hours a week to forty. *Six times more.* Plus benefits. And, I will work in a suit. This job—no, no, this *career*—will allow me to eliminate my tuition deficit and my debts and will allow me to send money to my parents. Plus, I will finally become legal in the US.

But, I know I can't count my chickens yet because they haven't hatched—another Dr. Tillerism. First, I have to leave the country. Such a twist, as Nancy said. A bizarre twist. Second, I need to go to the US consulate in Frankfurt and obtain an H-1 visa, and then come back to Washington without a mishap. That's one last hurdle, but it's a big one. Four horseshoes are in the bag; all I need is a horse.

I now have thirty-two hours to leave the country.

How am I going to do that? I've been so focused on getting the passport that I forgot to think about how I was going to pay for the airfare to Frankfurt.

I have to figure out how to buy a ticket, fast.

21

ROUND TRIP PLEASE

Early afternoon on Wednesday, I call Pan Am to find out how much a Washington–Frankfurt round trip ticket costs. After fifteen minutes on hold, I decide to go over to the Pan Am ticket office, hoping for inspiration along the way. I need money for a visa from the German embassy, too.

The ticket office has a short line, so it's only a few minutes before I find out that I need $800 to save my future, to salvage my American dream. I leave the Pan Am building deflated and dazed. I have twenty-nine hours to get out of town and I have $16.

What am I going to do? Where am I going to come up with $800? I walk past the Capital Hilton, where I got off the bus from National Airport and transferred to the bus that took me out to Rockville, to Demir, almost four years ago. *You were able to figure out how to find Demir without speaking English, Adem. Figure this out. You can figure this out.* I start thinking of everyone I know, people who came through when I needed money: Roberto, Bonnie, Trip—they are all off the table. I can't keep bothering them.

Could I ask Mrs. Hardwick to loan me the money? That's an absurd idea,

Adem. That's more than the monthly rent she collects from the entire house.

There's Paul from the bar, but I haven't seen him since leaving the Blues Saloon. I really need to call him. Maybe when I get back I'll . . . Adem, focus!

There's always Ela or Eliz. I know they'd loan me the money. But could they wire me the money in just a few hours? I wouldn't know how to do that, or even if that's possible.

Would Nancy be able to give me a salary advance? That would be a pretty embarrassing way to start a new job.

I'm still walking when I find myself back in front of the ticket office. *Come on, angels, Grandma's angels, where are you? I need a miracle.* I look around for the Volkswagen, listening for its message of doom, but all I see is a city bus.

Then I look again. On the side of the bus is an ad for a credit card.

Wait a minute. Wait a minute! That's it! My American Express card! Could I use the American Express card to pay for my ticket? I've never thought to use it before. But, isn't that why people have credit cards? I wouldn't have to actually pay for the ticket for an entire month. And then, if all goes well, if I get the visa and start working for First Manhattan, I'll have the money from my first paycheck to pay the bill. Could this work? Yes, it could work!

Feeling triumphant, I walk right back into the Pan Am office and up to the ticket counter mustering as much confidence as I can. The same clerk who told me it cost $800 is behind the counter. I'm not sure whether he recognizes me or he just doesn't care.

"I'd like to travel to Frankfurt, one person, the first available flight tomorrow," I say, "round trip, please. I'd like to return on Sunday."

"Yes, sir. Of course. It'll be the 5:05 p.m. flight. That'll be $804," he says. "How would you like to pay for that?"

I hand him my American Express card, acting like paying by credit card is something I always do. I watch as he places the card into the imprinting device, adds the three-page paper form, and slides the handle with a big thump, just like I'd seen the waitstaff at the Blues Saloon do hundreds of times.

"Okay sir, sign here and you'll be all set," he says. I sign the slip and he hands me my ticket, my receipt, and my American Express card. It looks greener, shinier.

I take the ticket, my student ID, my new passport, and the job offer letter from First Manhattan, and half-run, half-walk over to the German consulate. It's only a matter of minutes before I walk out with a one-week visa.

***

Somehow, I managed to get everything done within the seventy-two-hour time frame required by the immigration officer. My flight leaves in four hours, fifty-five minutes before the deadline. I need to pack. And, I have just a few loose ends to tie up.

First, I call Nancy's office and leave my travel information with her assistant. Then, I call the school and tell them I'm resigning from my assistant job, effective immediately, apologizing for not giving them two-weeks' notice. I recommend a few classmates for the job. I ask the person on the phone to transfer me to the registrar's office. I need to put a hold on my classes. I don't want to drop out, but if I don't return, I won't be able to continue with my classes anyway; if I do return, I suspect I won't have time for three classes with my new job.

Third, I call Bonnie. We haven't talked since she told me she was moving to Colorado. "I can't believe you didn't call me to tell me, Adem," Bonnie says. "Maybe I could have helped you." *Why is she always nicer on the phone than in person?*

"Well, actually. You can help me, still. Um . . . If I can't get a US visa in Frankfurt, would you come to Germany to get me?"

"What do you mean?"

"I mean, would you . . . I wouldn't be able to return without your help. What I mean is . . . would you marry me?"

"Yes," she says, without any hesitation.

"Really? You would?"

"Yes. I really would."

"I don't know what to say. I'm . . . I guess . . . I'm touched, Bonnie. Thank you. I can't . . . that's a huge relief."

"We'd have a long-distance marriage, unless you want to come to Colorado with me," she says, laughing.

I laugh too, then tell Bonnie I need to get off the phone. "My flight leaves in about three hours, and I still need to call my sister in Frankfurt to tell her when my flight lands," I say. "Thank you for coming to rescue me, if I need to be rescued."

"Anytime, Adem," she says. "Call me when you get back. Because I know you'll be back in three days," she says and we hang up.

The last call I need to make is to Trip, to update him and to thank Melanie for her recommendation.

"It's been a whirlwind. I'm sorry I haven't called until now," I say, giving him the details of the last few days. "Please thank Melanie for the recommendation to go to CRS. And, fingers crossed, I'll be able to return."

"You'll be back. I know you will. Melanie and I will pick you up from the airport and we'll celebrate. Okay, man?"

"Okay."

I hang up the phone and for the fourth time since I bought the suit a week ago, I pull it out of the closet along with my only tie. *Should I wear the suit or pack the suit?* I walk over to brew some tea while I think about it. *Wear it, Adem. You know it's a difference maker.* I quickly pack up my suitcase, double check that I have my ticket, my new passport and visa, and my contract with First Manhattan. I take a sip of tea while I unfold the yellow note the lawyer from CRS wrote:

1. Turkish passport. Underlined. I take out a pen and put a checkmark over the "1." Then I draw a line through the whole sentence.

2. Cable from First Manhattan to the US consulate in Germany. I put a question mark next to the "2." I'm relying on Nancy and my future employer to do this for me. I simply have to have faith that they will do this.

3. Get your H-1 visa from the consulate in Germany.

I fold up the yellow paper, stuff it inside the pocket of my suit jacket along with my notebook, grab my suitcase, and head out the door. I run back quickly to leave a note for Mrs. Hardwick that I will be gone for three days.

***

In front of the Capital Hilton, I board the bus to the airport. The damage is $11. I have $5 left. That's it. That's all I have. I get to the airport an hour and a half before the flight leaves. The ticket line to get my boarding pass is almost nonexistent. As I walk past it, I notice that the security line is short as well. Things are moving along smoothly. I'm looking forward to sitting down on a plane for seven hours after running around DC for three days like a crazy person. I might even go into one of the airport stores and buy myself a magazine with my credit card. In a few days, I'll be earning a corporate salary. Now I have not only the four horseshoes, but the horse too. I just have to saddle it without getting kicked in the face. Then I need to climb on and ride. In an American film, the image would be of me riding off into the sunset.

"Next please!" the ticket agent calls out. "Sir." The suit is definitely a difference maker.

"Good evening," I say, shocking myself with how jovial I sound. I smile and place my ticket and my passport on the counter.

"Thank you, Mr. . . . Bayer," she says, looking at the name on the ticket. She opens the passport and I smile at her again to assure her that it's me in the photograph. *Yes, yes, that's me with a new passport, a new visa to Germany, and a round trip ticket to Frankfurt. And I have a $30K signed contract in my jacket's pocket, if you'd like to see that too! That's me, Mr. Adem Bayer.*

"Sir, you do not have a proper visa."

"What?" I exclaim, inadvertently pounding my fist on the counter. The ticket agent jerks her head up in response. My heart drops. "Ma'am?" I say, in a hushed tone, trying to sound calm. *Don't cause a scene*, I think, quickly realizing that I still fear the immigration police. My heart is now racing.

"Once you leave the United States, you may not be able to return to the US. Are you aware of that?"

"Oh. Yes," I say, taking a deep breath. "Yes. I am aware. Yes, ma'am. Thank you, I'm aware," I repeat, visualizing myself at the ticket counter in Frankfurt for my return trip, holding the H-1 visa I need to return to America. *Will this plan work?*

The ticketing agent hands me back my paperwork, my passport, and my boarding pass. A few minutes later, I'm through security and walking down a corridor just like the one I walked through four years ago as a young, hopeful immigrant, worried about the missing $400,000 and unable to reach Demir on the phone, with only a few words of English in my vocabulary. *Look how much things have changed.* I stop for a moment and a woman behind me almost crashes into me.

"I'm sorry," I say, and step to the side, looking around at the people coming and going. *Soon I will be able to come and go freely too. Look at what has happened.*

Twenty minutes before the flight is set to take off, I've settled into my seat on the plane and worry sets in again. *If I can't get a visa back to the US, will America be my epic failure? Or, will Bonnie rescue me, come to Germany and marry me so I can return to the US? If she doesn't, can I stay in Germany? Would they let me stay or would I have to return to Turkey, where I'll be immediately taken upon landing and thrown into military prison as a military deserter?*

I fall asleep worrying, waking up to the smell of dinner being served. I eat then close my eyes again.

I'm woken up by the flight attendant asking me to return my seat to the upright position. Not sleeping much over the past week made for a fast flight. I check my seat belt and prepare for landing.

I'm about to see someone from my family for the first time in four years. It's hard to believe.

***

Eliz and her husband, Erman, greet me at the airport at 6:00 a.m. Eliz is so big she looks like she'll give birth at any moment, though she assures me she still has ten days to go before her due date. The way Erman is driving—the speedometer shows over 200 km/h on the Autobahn, though Porsches are whizzing by us in the left lane—it's as if he were racing Eliz to the hospital, fearing the baby was about to be born in the car.

They bring me to their apartment, where Eliz serves breakfast and tells me she is making my childhood favorites—meatballs and borek, as well as some German favorites, chicken schnitzel and spätzle for lunch. "A home-cooked meal is such a wonderful thing," I say. "Thank you. But first I need to get to the US consulate office."

At 9:00 a.m., after Eliz's giant breakfast, they both leave for work; I head off to the US consulate in my suit, which Eliz has pressed for me.

The woman behind a glass partition extends a steel drawer toward me. I place my new passport, along with the bank's employment contract, into the drawer.

"Ma'am, have you received a cable from First Manhattan about me? I'll be working there. They said they'd send a cable message here."

She takes a look at my documents briefly. Then she punches her keyboard, readjusting the screen a few times. "Yes," she says, finally, "we have received it."

"You are a Turkish citizen," she says, a statement, not a question. "Why didn't you go to Turkey to obtain a US visa?"

I don't know what to say. I wasn't prepared for this question; I should have prepared for it. *Adem, how could you not have known this would be a question?* Out of desperation, I say, "I have come to visit my sister. She's having a baby in a few days. Her first baby . . . but it's the third time I'll be an uncle," I say, rambling.

"Oh, okay . . . Okay, then. Well, congratulations on the baby. And, of course, on your new job," the woman says. She goes back to the keyboard and I shift back and forth, watching her type. "Okay, sir, Mr. Bayer. You are all set. Here is your visa." I watch her hands move as if in slow motion as she slides my future onto the metal tray and pushes it out toward me. *This is happening.* I pick up my passport with the H-1 visa and kiss it, standing right there at the window, right in front of her. She smiles and I thank her. I want to drop to my knees, I'm so happy.

***

Back at Eliz and Erman's, we eat and talk until late at night. I try to shift to German time and go to bed when Eliz and Erman retire for the night, but give up at 4:30 in the morning; it's only 10:30 p.m. for me. I grab my sneakers and head out for a run.

The next day is a blur. We talk and walk along the Main River. I feel the baby kicking and realize that I am genuinely excited about being an uncle, a third time, even though I have yet to see any of the kids. Eliz catches me up on her life in Germany, on Ela and our parents. She takes me shopping; I buy some clothes using my American Express card. *Such an invention!* On the last night, Erman returns home with champagne. "To toast your future, Adem," he says. He pops the cork, and we laugh as the bubbly spills over. "Go," Eliz and Erman say, joyously, as we toast to my visa, my new job, and America, clinking our glasses. "This kind of opportunity doesn't come often."

Eliz and Erman drive me to the airport Sunday morning. Sitting in the backseat of their car, I think *I'm going home*; DC is home. We hug and Erman promises to call as soon as the baby is born.

On my return trip I don't sleep at all. I'm too excited that my future is about to start.

***

When Trip pulls up in front of the boardinghouse, my throat is dry from talking nonstop. I hug Trip and Melanie both and, as we make plans for drinks to officially celebrate my return and my job, I notice Mrs. Hardwick standing out front. "Did you sell the house, Mrs. Hardwick?" I ask as I wave goodbye, preempting her announcement. I've been waiting for this scene to play out for more than seven weeks.

"Yes. Yes, I did, Adem. How did you know?"

"Well, it was either you missed me while I was overseas for three days or the house was sold," I say with a smile. "I had a 50-50 chance of getting it right." She laughs and I realize it may be the first time in the three and a half years living here that I've ever heard her laugh. And then, I keep smiling because for what seems like the first time since moving to America, news like this is something I can handle. *I'm moving up in the world. Literally. I can afford a place now without overhanging fuel lines, without busted coils in the bed, with a real fridge, maybe even wall-to-wall carpeting. And, not a room in a basement.* "Congratulations, Mrs. Hardwick. Florida will be wonderful! I will start looking for a new place right away." *Oh, and have red plums whenever I want them!*

"The sale won't be final for about thirty days, so you have some time."

"That sounds fine, Mrs. Hardwick. I have a new job working for First Manhattan. I think it's time for me to move anyway."

As I pick up my suitcase to take back to my room, she stops me. "Oh,

Adem. I almost forgot," she says, handing me an envelope with my name on it, written in calligraphy. "It looks like you have a friend getting married."

I take the letter from Mrs. Hardwick and look at the envelope with my name handwritten beautifully. *Who could be getting married?* "Thank you," I say, distractedly. Roberto? Paul? Dan? I laugh out loud, my guffaw echoing in the cement hallway in front of my room. *First of all, who could fall in love with Dan? Second, as if Dan would invite you to his wedding . . . Addo?* I look at the lettering on the front again to see if it says "Addo Bayer," then laugh again. I set my suitcase on the floor and open the envelope. It is, indeed, a wedding invitation . . . to *my* wedding. From Bonnie. My wedding . . . *to* Bonnie. I can't believe she's done this. She made a marriage appointment for us at the Frankfurt consulate. She was planning to rescue me. I'm dumbfounded. I re-read the invitation about ten times. I just can't believe she's done this. The ceremony is set for next week, April 3, 1985. *Should we do this regardless? Could we change the venue to DC?*

"Should we do it?" I say when Bonnie picks up the phone.

"Adem?"

"I got the invitation. I can't believe you did that, Bonnie. I just . . . I'm . . . I don't have the words." *Why am I choking up? Pull it together, man.*

"Well, maybe . . . maybe we should talk about it," she says. Despite my jetlag, we decide to meet for coffee an hour later. Bonnie pulls out a legal pad and we spend the afternoon writing a "pros" and "cons" list. After a few hours and two full pages of reasons why and why not, we decide to meet the next evening, after my first day at work, after we've both slept on it.

***

We go to her favorite place, an Ethiopian restaurant in Adams Morgan. Her face is blotchy and her eyes are puffy. "I didn't sleep last night, thinking about it." We admit we're both scared. "I mean . . . I know that we could make it work. And I would have married you so you could stay in the US. But, it's not true love, is it? We're friends. And we're good at making love—or sex, really. But, if you can stay in the US without me, without us marrying, I think it's best for both of us to not do this, to not get married."

"I don't think it's going to work, Adem," Bonnie concludes an hour into our talk.

I agree with Bonnie that it's complicated, but I don't know if I agree that true love is necessary for marriage. Plenty of marriages are simply business contracts, I think. Anyway, it doesn't matter what I think. We decided it would only take one of us to say "no," to end things for good. That she'll be moving to Colorado will make our goodbye easier.

"There's no time to grieve, Adem," Bonnie says, giving me one last hug. "I'll be driving off to Colorado in a few days and you'll be settling into your new job."

***

Four years after arriving in the US for the first time, I have a job in an office. Each morning, I choose from four suits in my closet. I have my own cubicle and an Ivy League–educated supervisor. For the first few weeks at First Manhattan, I arrive at work before anyone else arrives and stay well past the last person has left for the day. I keep my head down, do my assignments, follow the rules, do as I'm told. I don't interact with any coworkers except my direct supervisor, Jonathan, who is the antithesis of Dan. I hardly ever see Joy, who is my boss, or Nancy, who is her boss.

Life feels different. My posture has changed. I notice that I stand up straighter. I feel like a regular person who fits in. I no longer feel ashamed of my accent. I'm more confident. While I'm not a permanent resident, I am legal. Uniformed officers no longer make my heart race, worrying that they are going to stop me and question me. I no longer look over my shoulder when I walk around. I've jaywalked, which is technically still a crime in DC.

I eat better too, and more. The bank's cafeteria has a large salad bar. A three-vegetable plate is only $2. Sometimes I get two vegetable plates, plus a giant salad. "Are these all for you?" the cashier asks me every time. She's started winking at me when she asks, and I laugh with her at our inside joke.

On the wall near the entrance to the cafeteria are bulletin boards filled with notices, some, it appears, placed there by the bank—instructions on what to do if someone's choking, continuing education classes the bank hosts in the evenings, and a calendar of the bank's holidays; others look like they've been placed there by various associations or perhaps even people who work at the bank: roommates wanted, tutors wanted, volunteer opportunities. I study the board every day that first week and make a mental note that once I've settled in here at the bank, I'll start tutoring again, and maybe even do some volunteer work, if I can. I even consider calling a few of the people who have posted the "roommate wanted" notices. I have about twenty days left to vacate Mrs. Hardwick's house.

***

With my first paycheck, I pay my American Express bill which includes the $804 airfare, the cost of the visa in Germany, the clothes I bought there, and a few other items I charged when I only had $5 left. I call Paul and we put a date on the calendar to grab a beer. "Anywhere but the Blues Saloon," I say, laughing. I make a date to take Melanie and Trip out to dinner. I call Roberto and take him out for drinks and tell him I'm indebted to him for letting me sleep on his couch for five months after Demir left. I know he won't accept cash from me, so I give him a card. "I don't want to get all sappy on you, so I wrote you a thank-you note. Open it when you get home. Not here. I don't want to watch you cry," I say, laughing. Inside the card are three $100 bills. I figure his couch was worth at least $50 a month.

The next day, feeling a little sluggish after our night of way too many beers, I sit down to write out a debt-repayment schedule that will allow me to live comfortably and pay down my debts quickly. I sip tea as I jot down my plan and add up the numbers. And I feel a kind of calm take over. I have this odd memory of being a kid and joining a group of boys for a pickup soccer game, just for fun, no refs, no rules. I have no idea how paying IOUs as an adult and kicking around a ball as a kid are analogous, but the feeling is the same. I feel carefree. Not necessarily stress free, but empowered, conscientious.

With the second paycheck, I make a plan to pay Ela back the $800 I borrowed four years ago and send Eliz $200 toward my $2,500 debt. After the third paycheck, I will increase the amount of money I send Eliz each month to $400. And, then I'll send $950 after the fourth paycheck and the final $950 after the fifth paycheck. And, I write in my ledger, "$200/month parents." The Turkish lira has been devalued so much that $200 in Istanbul will be like $1,000 in the US. To be able to support my parents, finally, even with a small amount of money each month, is like a breakaway goal in a soccer game. I've won my war on poverty. It's an absolute victory over indigence. I can support myself—housing, food, school, living expenses—pay off my debts, and support my parents. It's the American dream.

I find a rental opportunity near Dupont Circle just a few blocks from Mrs. Hardwick's. The man who is renting the two bedroom town house and subletting the second room works at the Commerce Department and travels overseas frequently. He tells me that I'll have the house to myself except for a few days each month. The sublet, at $300 a month, is for the smaller of the two bedrooms. With lush wall-to-wall carpeting, it beats the red-painted cement floor and ripped runners I'm used to. There's also an en-suite bathroom, a large closet with mirrored doors, and a huge, queen-size bed. And tons of sunlight. I stand there looking around. *It's luxurious!*

"I'll take it," I say, shaking my new housemate's hand. "Thank you. It's perfect."

***

Two weeks later, I say a tearless goodbye to my landlady and hop in a taxi for the short trip to my new place. With me are all my worldly possessions: two suitcases, including my mother's from home; a box of books; a coffeepot; Dr. Tiller's TV; and my telephone.

22

A NEW PLAN

THAT NIGHT, THE FIRST NIGHT IN MY NEW HOME, I PULL OUT THE notebook I brought with me on my flight to America. I think it's been more than two years since I reviewed the list. Because I know I've finally accomplished most items—the plans I had made on the airplane before landing in New York for the first time—I open the book with gusto. I'm curious to see what I expected of myself.

November 7, 1980

"Get into the US (Today)." There's a check mark by the notation.

"Get a job." In a different color ink, I've checked it off and written, "The Blues Saloon" and "March 25, 1981," the date I started the job. *I didn't remember that.*

"Speak little or no Turkish." Check.

"Survive and learn English." Check.

"Save money for graduate degree." Check.

"Pay off debt to Ela." I add a check mark and today's date, "October 20, 1984."

"Pay off debt to Eliz." I write, "In progress; $200 paid," and today's date.

"Send parents money." I write, "$200 per month starting today," and I write today's date.

I stare at the list. *How am I the same person who came here to America? How have I done all of this?*

Then, for the first time since I arrived in America, I write out a new plan.

October 20, 1984

1. Fix military service situation
2. Buy house
3. Start business
4. Obtain green card
5. Send parents more money

On my regular Saturday call to my parents, I ask whether they need anything, how their health is, and if I could increase the amount I'm sending. "No," they say, "no son, we don't need a thing, you save your hard-earned dollars for the future." Persuading them to accept more money from me could prove to be a challenge. I feel that they don't believe I have that much money, so I would have to sacrifice to send them more, they believe. But persuading them is in my plan.

"It's better to have a wrong plan than no plan at all," Grandma used to say. "One can always change plans if necessary."

I've learned that changing plans isn't a bad thing. And, having a professional job has also made me feel more flexible. It's changed my perspective on almost everything. I feel a kind of security I've never felt before, so I can be more flexible about other things. I try to remember how I felt when I was washing dishes, cleaning windows, or mopping floors. I don't want to forget how hard it was—is—to start out, to be invisible. I make a commitment to myself to *see* those who are struggling to make it so at least one person around them acknowledges them, so they don't feel as invisible as I did for so long.

***

At work, I write computer code. I've not been told what the final product is; I only know about the small piece I've been asked to work on. But I'm fast. And, with each assignment finished, my supervisor begins to let me in on the bigger picture, even calling me into his office to work with him to solve some serious technical problems.

As summer 1985 nears, I decide against registering for the fall semester. Work is busy. I still want to finish graduate school, but also need to focus all my efforts on my job at this juncture. While I'm working fourteen-hour days, I'm only paid for eight hours. Overtime is reserved for when they ask an employee to work beyond those eight hours. But, it's an investment in my future; my degree can wait. I'm committed to putting in the extra time to prove myself—to show Joy and Nancy that going out on a limb to hire me was a good move. Some days, I don't go home at all, using the shower at the office gym and continuing to work straight through the next day without a break.

***

After six months at First Manhattan, I receive a 15 percent raise. I've saved $7,200. With the raise, I'll be able to save another $9,000. I begin to memorize my money rounded to the nearest one thousand: $7,000.

I buy the *Nation's Daily* several times a week. No longer does the clerk at the newsstand eye me and snap, "You read, you buy." I've been following the rise of the current prime minister who studied and worked in the US. He has, on his political agenda, a fresh approach for those people who have, for decades, been called "military deserters"—those called to mandatory military service while working or studying outside of Turkey; people like me who never served because it would have meant quitting school or losing a job. There are apparently thousands of us living all over the world, from Australia to Sweden. We all need our legal status. The prime minister's plan is a win-win. His government, which needs money, would earn $5,600 from each "deserter" and those Turkish expats, in turn, would complete their military service in only two months instead of fifteen. If the majority of expats take advantage of this amnesty deal, it would be a financial windfall in valuable foreign currency for the Turkish government, while we each would earn back our legal status as a Turkish citizen. We would be able to go home again.

In June 1985, the prime minister's plan passes and the new military rule for deserters becomes law. My heart is pounding as I read the article. I need to jump on this. I need to figure out how to take two months off from my job at First Manhattan.

With the newspaper still tucked under my arm, I go right to Joy's office. I explain the situation and she tells me I need to speak with Nancy who tells me I need to speak with human resources. Human resources lets me know it will take a few days for them to look into my request. "We need to determine what 'mandatory military service in Turkey' means," one of the personnel officers tells me after I've filled out a three-page form. "You say it's 'really necessary,' " she says, holding two fingers up and making air quotes. "But, I need to understand what 'really necessary' means," she says, doing the air quotes again. I take a deep breath. "You're asking a lot from us. You're asking us to approve a fifty-five-day leave."

***

It takes an unimaginable two weeks to get approval. But, in September 1985, I board the plane home—to Istanbul. It's been nearly five years since I left. The missing $400,000 has been found, Savas Kartal no longer wants to kill me, I have a passport, a US visa, and more than enough money to return to the US.

I'm greeted at the airport by Ela, her husband, and their children—a son and daughter—who are holding up a sign that reads "Uncle Adem." As I approach them, I see Ela pointing to me and they start shouting "Uncle, Uncle! Uncle is coming!" Ela envelopes me in a hug while the children jump and chant.

As we drive from the airport, me squeezed in between my niece and nephew, I stare out the window, trying to assess the changes that have taken place over the last half decade. Istanbul is more crowded than I remember, not just with cars and traffic, but with people too. There are new bridges, tunnels, and roads to accommodate those people. "The population is two million more than when you left," Ela tells me. "I think the official number is six million, two-hundred thousand. The economy is booming."

"Everyone has color TV," my nephew, Metin, tells me. "Except for Grandmother and Grandfather." I'm sure that's what Mom and Dad want to be called. No "Grampa" and "Granny" for Teoman and Meral Bayer.

Halfway through the ride, I notice both children have fallen asleep leaning against me. The image leaves me with a goofy grin on my face.

As Ela pulls the car into the apartment complex, I suddenly get very nervous. *I haven't seen Mom and Dad in five years. Will they look old? What will they think of me?* "You're living the American dream, man, it shouldn't matter," I mutter to myself.

"What's that, Adem?" Ela asks.

"Oh, nothing, just excited," I say, "happy to be here."

I grab my suitcase with one hand and Metin pulls me by the other hand. "I'll show you, Uncle. I know where to go. You follow me."

"Yes sir," I say, and he pulls me a little harder.

When we exit the stairs, I can see that the apartment door at the end of the hallway is open. "That's the one, that's the one!" Metin shouts, letting go of my hand and skipping down the hall into the apartment. The open door and the smell of homemade cooking is the most wonderful welcome home. "Is it meatballs and potatoes in tomato sauce?" I ask Ela, who has caught up to me; her daughter, Berna, fast asleep in my arms. She shrugs at me, a huge smile on her face.

I place my suitcase near the wall in the foyer and stand in the entryway, taking in the scene in front of me. Their new apartment has a different layout but, with all the same furniture, it feels and sounds and smells like the apartment of my childhood. As I stand there, my feet rooted on the foyer floor, Mom emerges from the kitchen, her arms out. She looks exactly as I remember her on the day I asked for her suitcase and ran out of the house with hardly a goodbye. She grabs me and kisses me.

"Don't go away for so long, ever again . . . Okay?"

I nod, tears in my eyes, unable to speak.

"Promise me," she demands in a tone that's half angry.

"I promise," I choke out.

She lets go of me and pulls me into the apartment. In front of me are Eliz and Erman and the new baby sitting on the couch. "What . . . wait . . . what are you doing here?" I exclaim, truly surprised.

"You think we would miss your homecoming?" they ask, almost in unison.

"And here's your newest nephew," my sister says, showing off the sleeping baby. "You can hold him later. Say hello to Dad first."

I hadn't even seen him, sitting in a chair in the corner. "Dad!" I say and I walk over to him with my hand extended. He gets up, grabs my hand and pulls me in for a hug. My eyes fill with tears. I don't think he's ever hugged me like that before.

After a shower, I walk around the apartment, peering into rooms I don't recognize. The dining table is all set up with my mother's special china, a sight that surprises me. "Fancy dishes are reserved for fancy people. And, you, my American, my American Adem, you've arrived in your fancy suit," my mom says. "You are now a fancy man. And, for the fancy man, I have prepared a fancy feast. Come," she says, pulling me to the table.

My mother has made an eleven-dish banquet. She always makes one more dish than the number of people invited. "Just in case someone doesn't like something," she used to say, "they can have something else." There's shepherd's salad, shredded carrot salad in olive oil and lemon dressing, red beans in olive oil, stuffed grape leaves, stuffed green peppers, fried eggplants with yogurt sauce, lentil soup—soup is always part of every meal because Dad just loves soup that much—cheese and spinach borek, white rice topped with chicken, meatballs with potatoes in tomato sauce—my favorite—and for dessert, a crowd favorite, kunefe, and freshly cut fruits.

"She's been cooking for three days," Ela says to me as we sit down at the table. My cheeks hurt from smiling. I look around the table at my family, at these children I don't know—my niece and nephews—at my sisters and my parents. I'm not the same boy who ran away five years ago. I look at Dad. The smile hasn't left his face. It's the same smile that I saw once before, when I was six years old and he took me to the local school to be tested. That smile is "the picture of happiness," as a poet said.

***

For two days we eat and talk, hardly sleeping as we try to squeeze five years of not seeing each other into the forty-eight hours we have together before I need to leave for two months of boot camp. We do our best to cover a lot of territory, but two days go by quickly. Both my mom and dad hug me goodbye. Two hugs from my parents in two days; I believe it's a record.

***

Bootcamp turns out to be no more than a morning and afternoon jog, with some work in the kitchen in between—pretty much my job at the Blues Saloon: floor scrubbing, potato peeling, and dishwashing. There's some crawling on the ground and some shooting of rifles, too—which reminds me of Trip's cousin's house in Pennsylvania—and a lot of joking around with fellow soldiers. They take us to military maneuvers, where we watch artillery guns and tanks destroy targets miles away in the mountains with pinpoint accuracy. With each fired missile, the ground shakes like an earthquake, whipping up dust and blowing smoke in our faces. It surprises me that I can feel the sound in my chest, as if I've received a good punch.

And then I'm done. It was that simple. Two months of exercise and I'm now a legal Turkish citizen again. I've done my military duty. Dad has that big smile again; Mom cries and hugs me when I tell her that, while I will be going back to America, soon, I will be able to come back to visit her as often as she wants.

I spend another week in Istanbul before returning to America. I go to the Bosporus and watch the ships from Lovers' Leap. I spend time with childhood friends, Demir and Izzy and "the girls"—only, the girls are no longer girls, they are now their wives. We go to the Corner Tavern for fish and raki and slide right back into our past lives as if five years hadn't separated us. We drink and laugh and drink some more. Demir makes me speak in English to show off my command of the language, then imitates the way I used to speak when I first arrived in America. Izzy almost falls off his chair, he's laughing so hard. We skip the disco, not because Demir and Izzy are worried that I'll get into a fight with a random bully, but because they have to get back home to their children.

And then, it's time for me to return to my life in America. Istanbul is still home. I'm home, here in Istanbul. *Can't I have two homes?*

23

BETTER DAYS AHEAD

It's late November when I return to Washington with my military buzz cut and a heavy suntan. The first morning back in the office, I bump into Joy as I'm getting my second cup of coffee. Joy does a double take, then gasps when she realizes it's me, in a new designer suit, standing next to her. Impulsively, she grabs me and welcomes me back with a hug.

As I walk through the office to my cubicle, I shake hands with my colleagues who seem pleased that I have returned. "James Bond!" someone shouts out. "Lawrence of Arabia," another person says. I laugh all the way down the hallway.

Before sitting down at my desk, I walk over to Nancy's office to announce my return.

"With all the chatter and buzz out there, I thought the president had swung by for an unannounced visit," she says, getting up from behind her desk and laughing. "Welcome home," she adds, patting my shoulder as she shakes my hand. "You've been missed."

"Thank you. It's good to be home."

"I hope it was a successful journey."

"Yes, it was, thank you. Good to see my parents, too, after five years."

"I'm so glad to hear it," she says, sounding genuine. "Now, gimme ten and get back to work!" she says with a chuckle.

"Yes, sir, ma'am," I say, saluting her while clicking my heels and trying not to smile. I march back to my cubicle. I can hear her laughing behind me.

It's as if I never left.

That is, until I notice what's going on around me at First Manhattan. A PhD mathematician is writing computer code that makes two mainframe computers—an IBM 3080 and a Burroughs A15—speak to each other even though each speaks a different language, in a way. It's like an automatic translator, converting one machine's data into the other's, on the fly.

I think of the emerging personal computers and local area networks. So mainframes can communicate with one another and PCs can communicate with one another. I wonder if mainframes could communicate with PCs too? *Of course they can. But the real question is, can I write the code to make that happen?*

I ask Joy if I can stay late at the office and write computer code using their equipment. And then I dig in.

***

I don't have much free time nowadays. I feel like a loom weaving back and forth between the office and home, making knots at each pass.

After three months of working fourteen-hour days, eight hours at my bank job and another six hours a night on my coding project—with a weekly brunch at McDonald's to catch up with Trip, though I've canceled on him four times, I finish writing the code. The program takes data from the mainframe, sends it to a personal computer, converts it to any word processing software, formats it to any specification, and delivers it to the PC user. It's completely automated and it takes just a few seconds. I codename this application *Link-Mail*. As in linking computers, as if to mail a letter, a statement, or a bill. If the application my professor and his assistant were developing in the lab became mainstream someday, *Link-Mail* would be even more useful.

My next step is to present *Link-Mail* to Joy and Nancy and explain to them as part of the presentation that this code would allow all monthly statements, for example, to be electronically generated and distributed to clients, potentially eliminating all printing, sorting, and mailing, saving the bank not only time but, more importantly, money. In addition, financial analysts can receive the results of their models and projections directly on their desktop computers, daily. No more printing, no more paper, no more printed internal office mail.

I explain that while similar code could exist, if First Manhattan uses *Link-Mail*, we won't have to acquire the expensive technology from elsewhere and we will have the source code for customizing and enhancement for our future business needs.

Nancy and Joy are reserved in their excitement. They don't jump up and down or dance like Trip and I used to do when we solved a tough problem. They seem impressed, but they are quiet about it. Nancy tells me she wants me to present the software to her boss, James, who is the head of computing services. I've only met him once, in passing.

Even before the presentation, my hands are sweating; I feel my fingers trembling from the moment I begin the presentation all the way through to the "show and tell" portion. James remains stone-faced. Nonetheless, he agrees when Joy and Nancy suggest I present to a group of C-suite executives at the bank. I find this puzzling, but I don't say anything to Joy or Nancy about James's reaction. *If they want me to present it to the higher-ups, then that's a good sign, right?*

I meet Trip for lunch and show him the program. "This is genius, Adem. Your bosses think so too, that's why they are sending you to the big guns to show them."

Three days later, I take the elevator to the fourteenth floor—the part of the building that houses the executive suites. I'm greeted by big windows, lots of leather, and an executive assistant who leads me to a glass-enclosed boardroom with more leather chairs. Eleven men and one woman, all dressed in dark suits, are sitting around an oval table. Nancy is there too, sitting off to the side. James appears out of the far corner and shakes my hand, acting chummy and making me a little uncomfortable. As he introduces me to the group, an older gentleman at the end of the table interrupts him and gruffly tells me to begin.

My nerves calm as I launch into my presentation. I focus on what I am saying rather than the looks on the faces of the people around the room. When I finish, the room erupts in applause; a few of the executives even stand up while they continue clapping. My mouth opens in surprise, and I shut it just as quickly as I also try to suppress a grin. James walks to the front of the room to stand by me. He shakes my hand and slaps me on the back. "The potential of this software is obvious," he says to the room. Then, turning to Nancy, he says, "And thank you Nancy, for conceiving and commissioning this project."

I feel my stomach jolt. *Nancy? What? This was my idea entirely!*

And then I realize what I should have understood from the start, what's written in the contract I signed more than a year ago—the one I skimmed over. The code I've written belongs to the bank; all the code I write here is the property of the bank. I haven't been paid for the hours before and after work that I spent writing the code for a concept that will make—or at least save—the bank millions of dollars. I signed the contract, grateful for the job; it's fair enough.

On my one-year anniversary at the bank, I receive a promotion and a 35 percent pay raise. Joy becomes my direct supervisor. I move out of my townhouse share and into a spacious, three-bedroom apartment. For the first time in my life, at the age of twenty-eight, I am living all by myself—no parents, no sisters, no roommates, no lurking landlady. I buy furniture that I like and the newest thirteen-inch Sony TV. Color. Another first in my life—a color TV. I set it up close to my bed so I can fall asleep to *The Tonight Show with Johnny Carson.* When I can, I catch an NBA game or two.

I fill up my closet with designer suits and shirts and I fill up the fridge with red plums every time I go to the grocery store. And, I finally buy a car, a three-year-old Impala with a 5.7-liter engine and a four-barrel carburetor. I drive to work and park in the garage in my reserved parking space. What would twenty-two-year-old Adem think of me?

I quickly find out that Joy is difficult to work for. She tells me to do something and a few days later, sometimes even a few hours later, she says to do the complete opposite. When I point this out to her, she tells me it's my fault, that I didn't understand the assignment and that I'd better get my act together. Each day becomes a frustrating exercise in futility. With each assignment I deliver—on time and well prepared—I come to expect I'll be admonished and have to start from scratch. I'm doing twice the work and, with each assignment turned in, Joy makes my deadline tighter; so, I have more and more work to do in less and less time. She's constantly yelling at me for my poor performance, and I fear that she's going to fire me. I'm considering filing a formal complaint with human resources. But how could I complain about the person who changed my life? She gave me a job that commands respect—even if she herself doesn't respect me.

I need this ridiculous cycle to end, but Joy is the reason I have this job, she's the reason I'm making all this money, she is the reason I'm in the US legally, she's the reason I'm debt free, and she is, by all calculations, the reason I'm living the American dream. She's given me a job that has allowed me to save $40,000, most of which I've invested in stocks. Now I round my savings to the nearest $10,000.

When I was illegal, I understood that I needed to suck it up, all the abuse dished out by employers like Dan or the outright dishonesty of people like the rug store owner who said he paid me when he didn't; I had to accept their treatment because without them, I would have been left with nothing, or worse, they could have reported me. But now? Now that I'm in a professional job, now that I have a Turkish passport and a US visa, now that I'm in America legally, shouldn't I be able to work without always having to worry about how today's abuse will play out? I may not be a citizen, but I am a person. Shouldn't that vise-grip be loosened by now? Shouldn't I be able to put away that tightrope I had to walk for five years and finally be able to join the masses on the sidewalk?

While I continue to pander to Joy, nearly every day I contemplate discussing the "Joy situation" with Nancy, even James, and filing a formal complaint. But, at the end of the day, each day, I say nothing. Without this job, my H-1 visa would become null and void. I need to keep Joy happy to keep the job and to stay in the US. *Will I ever have the same peace of mind as a real American?*

***

The stress at work has made me start glorifying my life in Istanbul. I convince myself it was better than it was. I realize I'm doing it but I can't stop. "The grass is always greener on the other side," I keep thinking. It's been seven months since I was back, and I think it's time for another trip home. After all, I tell myself, I have six years to make up for.

I put in for vacation starting the Friday before July Fourth, which will give me more than a full week while only missing four days of work. I book a round trip ticket for $1,000. I don't even flinch at the price tag.

On Thursday, the day before I leave, Joy walks into my office and tells me that I must attend a meeting the following morning. I remind her that I have the day off, that I put in for vacation a month earlier and will be traveling to Istanbul on Friday.

"You're wrong Adem. I gave you Friday *afternoon* off and the following week. But, I did not give you Friday *morning* off. The meeting is mandatory. I'll see you tomorrow morning," she says, giving me no time to respond. I watch her walk away.

Did I make the stupid mistake of telling Joy when my flight was? Did I step right into a trap and hand her this opportunity to make my life more difficult? Is she gaslighting me? Is that what she's been doing all along—giving me assignments and then telling me I didn't understand her, I misheard her? Or, is she simply a bad boss with bad organizational skills and a bad memory?

And then, she appears again in my office. Her arms are flailing, and she has a furious look in her eyes. "And, if you are not there," she says, wagging her index finger at me, "don't come back after your vacation. Consider yourself fired." My eyes pop open in surprise at her sucker punch. Joy is always a little off from center, but she's never threatened to fire me before. At this point, I honestly don't know if it was easier working for Dan.

Since I have no choice, on Friday morning, I put on my suit, grab my two suitcases, passport, and tickets and head to work even earlier than usual. I'm at my desk by seven. Joy will have no additional ammunition to fire me, not today.

At 9:20 I walk into the meeting room, ten minutes early, playing Joy's game, making sure I do nothing to jeopardize my trip home or my job at the bank. Joy waltzes in, unapologetically, at 9:35. An hour into the meeting, not one item discussed has had anything to do with any of my projects. At 10:40 I mouth to Joy, "May I leave now?"

"No," she says out loud, shaking her head.

At 11:30 a.m., she passes me a note. "Write down your parents' phone number," it reads. "Just in case I need to get in touch with you while you are absent from work." I know English well enough to catch the meaning behind her word choice—suggesting I'll be "absent" from work rather than "on vacation." I get three weeks of paid vacation a year as part of my contract, and I planned this one well in advance. And, as far as I understand it, a vacation is a break from work—that is, I'm not supposed to work while away. Yet here she is telling me—without actually saying it—that she's going to make me work while I'm on vacation. I try not to shake my head. I don't want her to see any sign of insubordination. I write down my parents' phone number, hesitating for a second and trying to decide if I should write down the wrong number. But I can't play games like that, so I resign myself to the inevitable and jot down the house phone number. Then, on the bottom I write, "I need to leave now, please. My flight is in an hour and a half." It takes thirty minutes to get to the airport. I'm pushing it even if I leave right now.

I pass the note back to Joy and watch her read it. She mouths, "No."

The meeting ends fifteen minutes later, at 11:45 a.m. Not one of my projects ever came up. My flight is in an hour and fifteen minutes. I grab my notepad and make a quick exit and Joy calls me back. *She's going to give me a heart attack!*

"The bank's chauffeur, a driver who is reserved for the C-suite folks, is going to take you to the airport. You're welcome," she says. The undertone of her smugness, the alleged favor she is doing for me, is jarring. "He is pulling up in front of the building now. Hurry up or he will leave without you." I run to my office, grab my jacket, stick my briefcase under my arm, grab my suitcases, and run for the elevator. *Is she off her rocker?*

I arrive at the airport fifty minutes before my flight, thank the driver, and run to the ticket counter. I hand the ticket agent my ID and my ticket.

"And your passport, please, sir."

I reach inside the breast pocket of my jacket. Nothing. It's empty. I pat myself down, front pockets, back pockets. No passport. I open my briefcase. Nothing. I rifle through my suitcases. Nothing. My passport is nowhere to be found. I run to the nearest pay phone and call the office. Joy answers the phone, which is odd since I've called her assistant's desk. "Wait, hold on," she says, "I'll have someone check your office."

And then, she starts to talk to me about work, shooting the breeze as if it's a typical workday. A few minutes later she interrupts herself. "Annie says it was on your desk," Joy says. "I'll have the driver bring it back to you. Just wait for him at departures, outside. You're welcome. Again. You really are quite careless, Adem. You need to work on that." I hang up the phone and stand there in disbelief. I've missed my flight to New York. That's a foregone conclusion. As I'm trying to figure out what to do to rectify the situation, I hear a boarding announcement for a commuter flight to LaGuardia. "This is the one o'clock commuter flight. Next flight leaves at 2:00 p.m." I run over to the ticket counter to see if I could buy a one-way ticket to LaGuardia. If I can get on the 2:00 p.m. flight and grab a taxi over to Kennedy, I think I could make my 5:15 p.m. flight to Frankfurt and my connection to Istanbul. If there's not too much traffic, it could work.

I buy a ticket to LaGuardia and then go outside to wait for my passport to be delivered. I stand there, in front of departures, and replay my morning over and over. I don't remember ever taking my passport out of my jacket and putting it on my desk.

A few minutes later, the bank's Town Car pulls up. The chauffeur rolls down the passenger-side window and leans in my direction, handing me my passport.

"Joy says, 'You're welcome,' " the driver says with a shrug.

"Excuse me?"

"I don't know, sir. All she said was to relay that message. Have a good trip," he adds, rolling up the window and driving away. I'm left standing on the curb with my mouth open. *Did Joy pull my passport out of my jacket?*

***

I think about Joy on the flight to LaGuardia, in the taxi to Kennedy, on the flight to Frankfurt, and on the connecting flight to Istanbul. I want to get her out of my system so I can enjoy my vacation at home.

I arrive at my parents' to find, once again, the whole family there, including Eliz, who has flown in from Germany with Erman and their son. And, once again, my mother has planned a feast with all my favorites and the good china on the table. As Mom offers me dish after dish, I look down the table at Dad; he's beaming. "He is so proud," Eliz whispers, leaning over to me. "In a moment of weakness, maybe he was tired, maybe he's just turning into a softy in his old age, he told me how proud he is of all of us—three children, all college educated despite a shortage of funds, three grandchildren, a fourth on the way," she says, touching her stomach.

I squeeze her hand, and then I realize I'm beaming, just like my dad. I sit there, watching everyone at the table talk at the same time again, except Dad, except me; we both watch. Whether I like it or not, I'm a lot like my dad.

After dinner I make a game out of unpacking my suitcase. I've brought fun things for my sisters' kids and presents for the adults, too. Perfume, little basketballs and soccer balls, coloring books, pens and pencils, and T-shirts with iconic images of Washington, DC, from the Capitol Building to the cherry blossoms at the Tidal Basin.

On Monday morning, Joy calls. She asks me a technical question; it's a question she could have asked anyone on the team. Dad overhears my end of the conversation. "You're calm and confident," he says when I get off the phone. And that's all that he says.

Joy calls me the next two days in a row with nonsensical questions. While I'm annoyed, my parents are impressed. On the third day, I hear Dad say to Mom, "Adem is important. He is needed at work." I walk into the living room, and they smile at me. My dad puts down the paper and gets up to shake my hand; he doesn't say a word.

"I want to start sending you more money," I tell my dad. "$100 more a month," I say, lying. I actually want to send them another $200 a month until I hit $1,000.

"Keep your hard-earned dollars, son," Dad says.

I look at Mom. "Do what your father says, Adem. We are fine." But I see the worry in my mother's eyes. I decide, right there, to send them the extra $200 a month anyway. They must have spent half that on the food for my welcome dinner alone.

I walk back to the living room and pick up Dad's paper. Savas Kartal's picture stares back at me. "Savas Kartal Is Elected Deputy President for the Nationalist Party," the headline reads.

24

THE SPEED OF SOUND

What I have learned about myself is that not only do I not understand the politics of my country, I do not understand corporate politics. I have a sinking feeling that eventually I will fail in corporate America or corporate America will fail me. Until that happens, I decide to become an ostrich and stick my head in the sand, burying myself in my work while catering to Joy's whims. It's the same strategy I used with Dan, and it worked until it stopped working.

The project I'm working on is a buzzword among programmers—an executive information system. Each day I work round the clock on the software, this time knowing well that this is not my intellectual property. It's only my job. Yet I continue to stay after work to develop the program.

When I'm done, ten months later, I've developed a program that instantly displays information about a customer with a single click, an enhancement for the work that a customer representative or salesperson at the bank does.

Before presenting it to Joy and Nancy, I ask Trip to pilot it for me. He's blown away when his computer monitor displays my name and address, previous purchases, product preferences, likes and dislikes, and family members' names—all made up for the test. His reaction instills confidence in me. "Show them! Show them!" he chants from the other end of the phone. "I'm dancing, man. Get up and dance with me," he says, and we both start laughing.

I schedule a meeting with Joy and Nancy to present the new system. Joy is not very enthusiastic; Nancy appears more interested and suggests a two-week pilot program for a few account managers. I leave the meeting flustered by Joy's reaction, trying to focus instead on Nancy's more positive response. Immediately, I put out a call to twenty account managers and by the end of the day I have five volunteers. I spend two days installing the software on five computers, then spend the third day working with my volunteers in what amounts to a training session. I send them off to use *Exec-info*—Nancy's nickname for it—and ask them to report back to me in two weeks.

Three days later, I'm surprised to see one of the account managers standing in my doorway.

"Is there a glitch?" I ask, getting up from my desk.

"Far from it, Adem. It works great. I just had to come down and tell you. On Monday I entered my customer notes into the program just as you trained us to do. Then I started making some calls. I just, well, I really just wanted to tell you immediately what happened. Is that okay? Do you have a minute?"

"Yes. Sure. Come in. Absolutely. Fire away."

"I'll make it quick. Well. So, the first client, I asked her how her mother was doing after her knee surgery. We had a great conversation. It was more personal than usual. Then, I called another client and talked with him about his daughter's first year of college. It's an amazing program, Adem." He steps closer, reaching across my desk to shake my hand. "I love it. Congratulations."

Throughout the week, several others call me to tell me it's a hit. I swing by Nancy's office as I'm heading out for the day to tell her that a week in, the analysts are already excited about the software. I say nothing to Joy.

With the pilot completed and rave reviews, James fast tracks *Exec-info*. Within a month it's the preferred tool for account managers and sales professionals at First Manhattan's DC office. Two weeks later, James tells me he's been flooded with requests to use the program at First Manhattan's affiliate banks not only in the US, but also internationally.

The enthusiasm for the software propels James to weave together the bank's upcoming international expansion—his pet project for more than a year—with the launch of *Exec-info* internationally. He asks me to join him the following week for a one-month tour of Eastern Europe; while he opens new branches and offices, I'll train personnel on how to use the software.

"We're going to start with four cities in Europe—Prague, Budapest, Warsaw, and Tallinn," he tells me. "Give your passport to my assistant; she'll get the proper visas for you. I think we're booked on Air France. My assistant is taking care of everything."

I give my passport to James's assistant, who returns it to me in five days—with multiple visas to multiple countries. I've never in my life gotten so many visas, and so easily. Along with it, she hands me several booklets of airline tickets, Air France and Lufthansa.

***

On Monday morning, a limousine picks me up in front of my house and drives me to National Airport for my flight to Kennedy. James is already in New York for a series of meetings, so we're meeting at the airport. Before leaving home, I double-check that I have my passport.

As the limo approaches Dupont Circle, I crane my head to see the homeless people, some standing, some sitting on the benches that surround the fountain. It's been six years since I fell asleep on those benches myself. Now, I'm sitting in the back of a Lincoln, wearing a suit and being driven to the airport for a business trip to Europe. *How did I get here?*

When I arrive in New York, I walk over to the Air France counter and present my ticket, as instructed by James, and passport to the ticketing agent. "Mr. Bayer, if you could, please follow me, sir."

As I follow the ticketing agent through a doorway and down a long hallway, I have a flashback to immigration prison: the guard politely asking me to follow him across the room, never once mentioning where we were headed. I have no idea where I am headed now as I follow the ticketing agent down a corridor decorated with iconic images of Paris punctuated by signs that read "Restricted" and "Authorized Personnel Only." Finally, we get to a doorway at the end of the hall. She opens the door and sunlight streams into the hallway. "You can wait for your flight here, Mr. Bayer. Enjoy your flight on the Concorde."

What? What did she just say? The Concorde?

I walk up to the windows on the far side of the room. Outside on the tarmac, just about a hundred yards away, is the Concorde. *The Concorde, Adem! You are flying on the Concorde!* I can't stop staring. That's an $8,000 ticket per person and the bank is sending three of us! I do a quick calculation to figure out how long I would have had to work at my engineer's job in Istanbul to make the amount of money to fly on the Concorde. 3.3 years is the number I come up with, and that doesn't include food or other living expenses. Plus, it would be one way only. To return I'd need to work another 3.3 years. I turn around to look at the other people in the waiting area. They seem oblivious to the adventure that lies ahead of us, while I feel the need to scream like a little kid. I turn back to the window and continue staring at the plane.

"It's pretty incredible, isn't it?"

I turn to see James standing next to me.

"I didn't realize we were flying on the Concorde!" I say, unable to suppress my excitement. "Can I admit to you how excited I am without sounding like a ten-year-old?"

"You can say it, Adem. Say it over and over. I've been on this bad boy five times and it's still a thrill."

"Excuse me, gentlemen, champagne and caviar?"

I turn to see two flight attendants, one with a tray of champagne flutes and another with a tray of caviar. We both nod our heads and reach simultaneously for a glass. I think I see James wink at me. "Champagne wishes and caviar dreams," I hear Robin Leach say in my head. *Am I dreaming?*

I wonder if I'll ever get tired of being treated with respect. No more "Addo." No more "Yo." I'm sir. I'm Mr. Bayer. Like everyone else in America, Mr. and sir, Ms. and ma'am. I'm beginning to feel like I belong now.

A few minutes later a flight attendant announces that it's time to board. I hang back, hoping that I can trick the rest of the passengers into thinking that this experience is no big deal for me. I'm the last one to climb the stairs and I duck my head as I enter the plane through its narrow doorway. I'm struck by how small the interior of the plane is, much smaller than I expected. The single cabin has twenty-five or so rows of four seats each, wide, comfortable, and stylish—two on each side of the aisle. As I begin looking for my seat, I suddenly stop, taking a deep breath. *What is that smell? I know that smell . . . that beautiful . . .* I take another breath in through my nose. It's so familiar. I whip my head around, first left, then right. *Where is she? That's her smell. It's Francesca. I'd know that smell anywhere. Even eleven years later, I recognize her smell.* I look around quickly, again.

"Excuse me, sir. Can I help you?" I hear someone behind me say.

"Oh, I'm sorry. No. No . . . apologies." *Man! Adem. get a grip. Francesca isn't on the plane. It's just her perfume, man.* This time I take a breath to calm myself down. I check my seat number again and hurry to it, looking up to see James and his assistant who are seated near the front of the plane.

Really, how is it that she still has such a hold on my heart after this long?

"Champagne, sir?" a flight attendant asks, interrupting my thoughts. "And, caviar? Some smoked salmon?" I help myself to a glass and a plate and I try to find something else to think about that will cancel out the sweet smell of Diorissimo and painful memories of my first love. *The plane. Think about the plane. Okay . . . that's good. The plane. Soon, we will be flying twenty-five hundred feet per second; almost as fast as a bullet. It's a crazy engineering marvel.* I try to imagine what happened to the poor sap, or possibly saps, who suggested humans could fly like birds. "Let's build a tube that can carry hundreds of people at a time," I can hear them say. "Like a bird, soaring through the air and over water to another part of the world." *How many geniuses were thrown into insane asylums before the Wright brothers came along?*

The plane begins to taxi. Other than a muted wheezing of the engines, the cabin remains quiet. After a couple of minutes, the plane makes two left turns on the runway and stops. "We're next," the captain announces. "Sit back and enjoy the three-hour-and-twenty-minute flight to Paris, folks. Flight attendants, prepare for takeoff." The engines gently roar, like a sleeping tiger. Then, the plane accelerates rapidly, and I feel the g-forces kick in. After a few more seconds, the plane is in the air. I prepare my ears for deafening noise, but the noise never comes.

On the wall ahead of me I notice there's a light-blue digital screen displaying the Mach speed in large white numbers. Right underneath, in smaller numbers, the altitude is displayed. I've read that the takeoff speed is 0.3 Mach and that once the plane reaches sixty thousand feet, we'll be traveling at 2.02 Mach. As we climb, I watch the digital screen display our increasing speed—0.8 Mach, then 0.9 Mach. I wonder what the sonic boom will feel like. I keep watching the numbers climb—1.0 Mach, 1.05 Mach, thirty-two thousand feet. *Where's the boom? Are we flying faster than the speed of sound?*

I look around to see if anyone else is watching the screen and my eyes catch those of an older gentleman across the aisle. "Cheers," he says, holding up his champagne and smiling. "So, come here often?" he asks, laughing at his own joke. I chuckle.

"I'm a first timer," I say to him.

"Ah, and where are you from? I detect an accent."

"Turkey."

"Oh, I want to visit there one of these days."

"You should. It's a beautiful country. But of course, I'm biased."

"Steve Harrison," he says. "Chief engineer, the *Orbiter*, the space shuttle program, NASA," he says. I try not to choke on my champagne. *Chief engineer—what?* "I can't afford this $8,000 flight, of course. NASA doesn't pay me that much." He pauses to laugh. Even though I don't find that funny at all, I laugh along with him. "This trip, it's courtesy of my wife. We're meeting in Paris. She's already there on business," he tells me. "What do you do, son?"

"I work at First Manhattan. Computing department."

"Oh yes, the big conglomerate, that's good. My wife is also a banking executive." Then, lowering his voice and leaning toward me, he says, "She's in France working on some multibillion-dollar loan deal with the up-and-coming companies of Eastern Europe."

He gives me his business card as the plane's speed approaches Mach 1.7 and an altitude of fifty thousand feet and I write down my office phone number on a piece of paper and hand it to him. *I need to order some business cards too.* I excuse myself to use the restroom and notice that sitting behind me is a French Olympic ice-skating champion. When I get back, I lean over and tell Harrison. He tells me that sitting a few rows ahead is the US ambassador to France.

Familiar feelings of uneasiness and discomfort come over me. *I don't belong here.* I try to relax, lowering my shoulders, unclenching my jaw, and I take in a deep breath. As I breathe in the lingering scent of Diorissimo, I'm transported back in time to dinner at Francesca's parents' house. I felt so inadequate, so out of place. *Re-focus, Adem. You belong here. You were invited here. You are wearing a suit, you have many more suits in your closet, you are called "sir," you are not an imposter.*

***

Our mission is a success. *Exec-info* is well received in Europe. "I think there's another raise and promotion for you on the other end of our trip," James tells me during breakfast on one of our last mornings at our hotel in Prague. I try to digest what he's saying, to take stock in his comments. My development, *my concept*, is increasing profits for the bank. *You did that, Adem.* I realize, after more than twenty-five breakfast conversations with James, that we have "gelled," that I feel comfortable with him. In fact, he reminds me of Paul the bartender, the kind of person who will always look out for me. We fly back home on the Concorde, leaving Paris at 11:00 a.m. on a Friday morning. I'm back at my desk in Washington at 10:30 a.m. the same day. I've gone back in time. It's mind boggling and I wonder if there's an underlying message in that phenomenon. You can never go back in time? Or, the only way to move forward is to go back in time and fix the mistakes of your past. *You are overthinking things again, Adem. There's no message; it's simply an engineering marvel.*

***

I'm not rested but I'm ready to get back to work. And, as James promised, about a week after our return, he calls me into his office to tell me I'm being promoted and earning another raise. And, he tells me, I'll no longer be reporting to Joy, but rather to him. The second he tells me that, the best news

I could have imagined, I stop paying attention. Of course! The raise and the promotion are good, but untangling from Joy is . . . oh my Lord, joyous!

"But Adem, Mr. Graves isn't an easy assignment," James says and I realize I've drifted off, missed what he's telling me. "Mr. Graves thinks his office is being taken hostage by the computer people. While our job—your job, that is—is only to write computer software to support his investment advisers, he knows his people are becoming more and more dependent on your work, the work of programmers, computers. He's old-school. It's a little bass-ackwards, because our new programs are helping his output, but it's a major problem for him."

"Okay," I say, not really understanding.

"It's almost as if the computer support people are running the show. That's what Graves thinks, anyway. I heard him say it in passing, never directly to me. Just keep it in mind as you deal with him. He's not easy."

"Ah. Okay. I understand. Be a good soldier."

"Right. Yes. Exactly. So . . . the promotion. You are going to be selecting the team and you are going to be running this team. You can bring in two new programmers from outside. Make sure your programmers don't get too cocky. Keep them in line. Create a code, if you will, call it the Graves Effect or something. I don't know. No, don't name it that, maybe the Gray Zone. I don't know. Just keep your team in line."

"Okay. I've got it. Thank you for having faith in me, James."

"You're a good egg, Adem. You're going to be the lead programmer. The other five will report to you. Remember, you are handpicking your team. Think about it carefully. Let me know in a week who you've selected."

25

SEED AND HARVEST

I HEAD BACK TO MY OFFICE AND IMMEDIATELY START MAKING A list of the top ten programmers from which I would choose five for the project.

"So, you're going to lead the team that supports investment research, huh?" With no knock, Joy has thrown open my office door. No "excuse me," no "hello." No nothing. "You'll be in Graves's office. Careful what you wish for, Adem."

"Good morning, Joy," I say. *Should I tell her that she can't just barge into my office anymore now that I no longer report to her? Is it too soon for that?* "Good luck with that," she says, still talking, though I'm hardly listening. *Oh my Lord, it's such a relief that I no longer have to deal with her.* "The man hates me. Mark my words, Adem, you are going to miss me. You think working for me is hard?" *Who told her that?* "You have no idea what's about to hit you," she says and, without waiting for me to respond, she turns and walks out. I get up and close my door.

By the end of the week, I've narrowed down my list and had it approved by James, and I call a meeting of my new team. I explain the situation to them. And they don't seem to care. I mean they really just don't. They *are* cocky. My speech has no impact on them, whatsoever. Since I don't seem to be getting through to them, I let them go and swivel my chair around to stare out the window. *How am I going to reel them in, keep them in check? Maybe I'm that cocky too. Am I that cocky?* "Don't become a cocky SOB now, Addo," Dan used to say after I came up with an idea for him that I knew he liked. Dan was the cocky SOB, not me; but he loved to get in my head. The memory makes me smile, which makes no sense at all. Still, there's something about that time in my life, my new American life, that was grounding.

I get up and walk down to the cafeteria for a cup of coffee. There's a janitor pushing a mop and bucket down the hallway. His head is down. I keep walking. I say nothing as I pass him, just walk right by. *What the h—Addo, you just walked right by that man without saying hello? That's it. That's it right there. You know what, Adem, you are cocky. You're out of touch. That used to be you, head down, invisible. Now you've put on a suit and you've become cocky. You promised you wouldn't do that. You promised you would see people. You've forgotten where you came from. Remember where you came from, Adem. Remember your struggle.* I consider turning around and saying hello to the janitor, but decide that I will say hello on my way back to my office. Then, for the first time in a long time, I stop at the community bulletin board.

I glance at the continuing education classes—classes on how to create and deliver a better presentation, how to improve writing skills, management skills, communication skills, negotiation skills, and more. And then my eyes settle on a notice with the headline, "Volunteer Tutors Needed, Baptist Home: Physics and Math."

That's it. That's what I need to be doing! That's what's been missing from my life.

I quickly memorize the phone number and head back to my office to call the Baptist Home. I stop to say hi to the janitor, and we chat for a minute. Once in my office, I call the Baptist Home and make an appointment for an interview at eight o'clock the following evening.

***

As I drive up to the main building, streetlamps cast shadows over a baseball diamond on one side of the driveway and a soccer field on the other side. I'm greeted at the door by a man in blue jeans. I'm pulled in by his demeanor; he's calm and quiet, with a melodious voice. We chat for a few minutes and then he offers me a tour of the campus. It hits me halfway through one of the buildings—"Where Sunday services are held," he tells me—that there is no "Mr. Baptist" who started a home for children; "Baptist" is church. I don't know much about Christian denominations, or other denominations. *If I'm going to tutor here, I'll need to learn about the Baptists.*

At the end of the tour, we walk into a room that has a large table in the middle, where two men greet us. One of the men shakes my hand. "Welcome to Baptist Home. I'm Reverend Franklin, and this is Mr. Nichols, the head administrator. You are . . ."

"Adem Bayer, sir."

I sit down for an interview with Rev. Franklin, then Mr. Nichols asks more detailed questions. He asks me about what I do for a living, how long I've lived in the US, why I want to become a volunteer tutor. And, they tell me more about the Baptist Home and the children who live there—eight girls and eight boys.

"This is Tom," the administrator says when a young man, a boy really, appears in the room as if on cue. "Tom, this is Mr. Bayer." Tom is quick to extend his hand; his grip is strong, confident, even. "Tom is fifteen and takes college-level math and physics. We do not have any volunteer teachers who can guide him in his studies. We are hoping you are the right man for the job."

"Well done, Tom," I say. I don't know what I was expecting, but he looks like a typical fifteen-year-old kid, shorter than me, but I can tell he will get taller, and skinny with a baby face and a touch of acne. "I was ahead by two grades myself, so I know what it feels like to be surrounded by older students whom you automatically assume know more than you do." Tom nods and offers a slight smile.

"If you have some time tonight, maybe you and Tom can hang out for a few minutes, he can show you what he's learning and then we can see if you can work with him," the administrator says.

"Sounds like a plan," I say, smiling, trying to make Tom feel more comfortable.

The administrator leaves us to chat and I end up staying for almost two hours. Part of the time, Tom and I study, part of the time, we just talk. My most successful students back in Istanbul were the ones with whom I developed a personal relationship, so I focus on letting Tom know that I can be his friend as well as his teacher. He tells me he was born here in DC to parents who were Chinese immigrants and who were killed in a car crash. Tom was only two years old and in the back seat; he somehow survived. The story that he's been told is that while he was in the hospital, officials tried to find relatives to take care of him, but when no one stepped up, he was brought to the Baptist Home. He has no memory of having ever lived anywhere else. He sounds comfortable with his plight. In a way, I think he's fortunate that he was so young when his parents died that he doesn't have memories of a life with them. Then again, maybe not having memories is just as painful.

At 10:00 p.m. the administrator comes by to announce that it's time for Tom to get ready for bed. I shake his hand and, shyly, he asks me if I can come back and be his regular tutor. I smile and say yes a little too loudly.

We set Wednesday nights at 8:00 p.m. as a study time. On the way home I feel happy. Grandma was right. I had never really understood what she called her "Seed and Harvest Story." But now, I understand. If you give away your time, your effort, your help, even your money—that is, plant a seed—you can reap a harvest, get it back and then some, many times over. Your one seed can turn into an entire harvest. Perhaps that's what I'll earn from working with Tom. Maybe I need to do other things, too, other than work. Spend more time with my friends and not just work round the clock. I need to stop canceling on Trip and reach out to Roberto and get back in touch with Paul. I haven't been swimming for years. I haven't dated anyone since Bonnie left for Colorado. All I did was work and watch my stocks and cash exceed $500,000. Now rounded to the nearest 100,000. I haven't even taken a course since putting school on hold. I make a mental note to check out the community board and sign up for one of the bank's continuing education classes.

The following Wednesday I head over to the Baptist Home again. Tom and I meet in the same room where I was interviewed and afterward we studied.

A younger boy walks in, "My roommate Shaun," Tom says. I find out Shaun is only twelve. Shaun asks if he can sit with us quietly while we study for a test Tom has the following week, which reminds me of how I used to sit and watch my sisters study more than two decades ago. When we take a break, Tom asks Shaun if he understands anything we've been studying.

"I don't think I understood any of it," Shaun says, with an embarrassed laugh. "But it felt like I was watching TV, so it was fun."

"We don't watch much TV here," Tom says to me, by way of explanation, I think. "Just on Sunday evenings, we watch Bible study."

"Bible what?"

"Bible study."

"I don't know what that is."

"Oh. Um. Well, it's an evangelist preacher on TV, he teaches about the Bible."

"Aren't those the people who sell keys to the doors of heaven, cheat widows out of their Social Security checks, and live lavishly?" I ask, smiling when I realize that the teacher has just become the student.

"No, not this guy. He doesn't ask for money."

"Excuse me, gentlemen," one of the prefects says from the doorway. "Unfortunately, Shaun, it's time for you to get ready for bed. Tom, you have another half hour with Mr. Bayer and then it's time for you, too."

"That was a lot of fun, guys. Thanks for letting me listen. Maybe I absorbed more of that than I realize, and I'll grow up to be as smart as Tom so I can go to college before I'm eighteen too."

"I worry about him," Tom says, once Shaun has left the room. "His mother died when he was six. His dad's not in the picture at all. When he arrived here, I sort of took him under my wing. I'm sort of a big brother to him. That's why they roomed him with me. He'll be only fifteen when I leave here."

"What do you mean?"

"That's the rule. I have to leave here when I'm eighteen. Then I'm on my own. All of us," he says, "we are only here 'til we're eighteen." *I had no idea. Wow. All alone in the world at eighteen?* "I want to finish college and get a good job before I have to leave here so I don't have to worry about taking care of myself," he adds. "And, if I can, I want to help other kids with their transitions out of here, especially Shaun."

"That's very admirable," I say. "That's a ridiculous thing to say. I'm sorry. What it is, is . . . it's incredible, really. I have no doubt you'll do it."

"I'm going to do it."

"Yes . . . yes you will."

"Um, before you leave, I'm wondering if we can change the schedule for next week. Can you come on Tuesday *and* Wednesday to help me study? I have a test next Thursday and I might need the extra study day."

"Tuesday? Yes. I think I can. Definitely," I say. "I'll see you then." As usual, Tom extends his hand to shake goodbye and then hands me a book.

"A Bible, for you. I have another one," he says.

I think about Tom the entire way home. His dedication to his studies inspires me. Though I know there's no way I could go back to school and complete my graduate degree with the workload I have at the bank, I decide I really *should* take a class, perhaps one of the ones listed on the bank's bulletin board.

The next day, I mull over the list: presentation skills, writing skills, management skills, communication skills, negotiation skills. I read through all of the course descriptions. I settle on "Effective Communications." The first class meets that night in the bank's training room.

During the first, hour-long class, we are handed reference articles on related topics. Afterward, I mingle for a few minutes to thank the teacher and meet a couple of the other students. It feels good to be social.

When I get home, I make myself some tea and sit down at my kitchen table. I pull out the articles and start scanning them. There's one on human brain development that catches my eye. I pick up the article and start reading it. It says different faculties in children's brains develop during different ages. 3D visualization, for example, begins to develop at around age eighteen. *Hmm, I didn't know that.* I think back to my struggles during my first few years at Technical University. Perhaps it wasn't that I was stupid or lazy, but rather, as this article suggests, that my abilities hadn't fully developed yet. According to the article, I literally couldn't visualize the engineering problems while my older classmates could.

I finish the article and pick up another one. It's entitled "Hyperlexia."

I'm about to pass on this one and move on to the next article in the pile, but the words "Precocious reading ability" and a subheading down the page, "Why reading early isn't necessarily a sign of genius," catch my eye. "Hyperlexia is defined as precocious reading ability accompanied by difficulties in acquiring language and social skills." I quickly read through the introduction and then jump to the section with the subheading, "Some children simply read very early. Parents are proud and may believe their children to be geniuses; witnesses are often amazed when a three- or four-year-old child reads to his nursery school class and, further, can comprehend and explain the themes of the story. While hyperlexic children are bright, they may fall within the spectrum of autistic disorders . . ." I read the paragraph in its entirety two more times. Stunned, I glance back down at the keywords popping up from the page at me: "autism," "genius," "developmental disorder." I sit back in my chair and close my eyes and see myself as a three-year-old sitting on the floor in the living room reading a book, then taking the test to get into school, then the first day of second grade—a six-year-old in the classroom among all the eight-year-olds. I take a sip of my tea and continue reading. The research was conducted in 1967, three years after I'd started second grade. It shows that there is a subset of the population that develops a fascination, even an obsession, with numbers or words or both, six months to four years before the general population. I'm stunned. *Hyperlexia is defined as advanced reading ability accompanied by difficulties in acquiring language and social skills.* I feel like I'm reading about myself and I can't stop. I've never heard the term "hyperlexic." I go back up to the top paragraph and reread it. "While hyperlexic children are bright, they may fall within the spectrum of autistic disorders . . ." I then scan through the article, again, finding myself described within the paragraphs: "do arithmetic at these early ages," "exhibiting impressive skills," "not geniuses," "normal intelligence," "autistic."

26

LIVE AND LEARN

THE FOLLOWING DAY JOY CALLS ME INTO HER OFFICE. BEFORE SHE even utters a word, I can see she's furious. I brace myself. "Look at this," she says, balling up a piece of paper and throwing it at me.

"Asshole . . ." *Man, she's such a piece of work. Calling me into her office just to call me that?* I stand there staring at her. "Read the piece of paper, Adem!" she says. I unwrap the paper, an office memorandum, smoothing it out while I read it. "Programmers like Mr. Bayer and his team are simply pieces of equipment and they are dispensable . . . They believe themselves to be indispensable, but they are not. They are merely robots. We are a bank founded by people, by financial experts, not robots . . ." Before I get to the end, Joy says, "He's such an asshole."

It's a scathing review of me and my team written to senior management. The focus is on me.

"Who gave this to you?" I ask her.

Shaking her head, she says, "I can't tell you. I have my sources. You always need to watch your back, Adem. Always." Instinctively, I turn around. "Not actually watch your back, Adem. Are you an idiot?" Joy asks.

I look back down at the memo, scanning the words again. "Mr. Bayer is inept," he is "odd" and "self-unaware."

Slowly, I put the paper down and walk out of her office in a daze.

"Don't take it personally, Adem. He's an asshole," she calls to me down the hall and I wonder who is worse, Mr. Graves for writing what he wrote, or Joy for showing it to me. I walk straight out of the office and keep walking—twenty blocks—to the library. I find as many books on autism as I can, choose five, and while standing in the check-out line, peel through a few of them.

***

The next morning, I don't get out of bed. I turn on the TV and call in sick to work. It's the first time in my life that I've ever done that. "Inept, odd, self-unaware." The words keep rolling around in my head.

I lie in bed all day hoping the phone will ring. Hoping I'll get a call from Trip, even Bonnie, or from Ela or Eliz, even though I don't want to talk to anyone. Does everyone think I'm odd? Inept? I pull out the article on hyperlexia and read it again. I devour the library books. And then again and again. I think of my mom's seven-foot jumps when she was pregnant with me, to lose me. "To drop me," as they say in Turkish. *Is it possible I got some brain damage during her jumps? Am I autistic? Is that how it happens?*

Is that why my parents let me be; and my sisters treated me like I'm that . . . inept, self-unaware? Is that why Savas Kartal hated me and wanted to kill me, Demir and Izzy shook their heads at me, and Polat nearly killed me? Is that why Dan was mean to me, I had fights at discos and bars, Bonnie left me, and Joy mistreated me? Is all that because I cannot connect with people? Is that why Francesca didn't want to have anything to do with me? Is that why I'm still hurting eleven years after she left me? Is it because I'm autistic, dysregulated, impulsive, as the articles explain?

Reruns play on TV and the sun begins to set. I haven't moved from my bed all day. I haven't eaten. As the room darkens, I don't turn on any lights. I fall in and out of sleep.

The next day, I don't get up again.

Am I a word? Is that all I am? Hyperlexic? Autistic? With three billion letters, times two, with a four-letter alphabet, my DNA is a word. *Is my word misspelled so I'm hyperlexic and autistic? Every word is a number too. Is that why I loved numbers and words when I was little? Am I merely a number? What is the formula that results in that number? Who knows that formula? Does everyone have to figure out their own formula and I'm just late to the game, as usual? Do all people spend their lives trying to figure out their own formula? Or, is this an affliction of mine? Can a formula exist on its own without anyone knowing it? Einstein discovered the formula that specified the relationship between mass and energy. The formula was there before he found it . . . before he unearthed it, defined it. I mean the relationship already existed, he illustrated it, explained it. But was there anyone before him who knew this formula, or better yet, created the formula altogether? If energy must exist for mass to form, and vice versa, how can either one exist without someone making them and setting the formula and put things in motion?*

I roll over in bed. My head hurts.

Do my angels exist Grandma even though I can't see them? I can't see atoms either, but they're there. Science tells us they are. *If I talk to my angels, can they hear me? Can they talk to me? Are they talking to me now and I'm not hearing them? Or, hearing them but not listening?*

"You are a spirit," Grandma says.

"Grandma? Oh Grandma! I've missed you so much. You are the only one who has ever protected me."

"I am here now. To protect you."

"Tell me about the angels. Tell me about my spirit."

"You are a spirit, Adem. You have a mind, and you live in a body. Your body is upright and moving because of your spirit. Your mind works because of your spirit. When you die, your spirit leaves your body, it rises and your body falls. But your spirit, it lives forever. Your spirit has power over both your mind and your body."

"Will I get a better mind, Grandma? One that isn't autistic?" I ask her.

"If you keep your spirit strong, your mind will obey your spirit and be sound, and your body will obey both and be sound. Think of a person addicted to alcohol, or gambling, or anything else. Their body tells their mind, 'Do this' and they do it. Instead, they could train their mind to tell their body, 'You don't get what you want, you get what I tell you to get.' The way to train your mind is to keep your spirit strong, to tell your mind and your body both, 'You don't get what you want, you get what I tell you to get.' The way to keep your spirit strong is by spending time in scripture, listening, and praying. I didn't go to college, Adem. But I know things. God made you because he loves you. You must be worthy of his love and love him back and keep your spirit strong. If your spirit is strong, your mind and your body will be strong also. If you are strong, you can become a blessing to others. Can you do that, Adem?"

"Yes, Grandma. I will try. I promise, I will try."

"That's a good boy, Adem," she says, pinching my cheek. "I have to go now."

"No, Grandma. Don't leave me, I can't do it alone. Please stay."

"I have to go now . . ."

"Grandma!" I scream, as tears stream down my face.

***

My pillowcase is wet and my eyes are burning. I roll over in my bed yet again and look at the clock. It's 7:30 a.m. and the sun has risen. I reach over to my nightstand and pull out my notebook from three years ago.

October 20, 1984.

1. Fix military service situation

2. Buy house

3. Start business

4. Obtain green card

5. Send parents more money

I rifle back to the pages before.

I stare at the list, then fold the book closed and hold it against my chest. *If I'm so inept, how did I prevail? How did I come to America and learn the language and get a professional job and earn a decent living and fill my closet up with suits and ties and buy a state-of-the-art television?*

I pick up one of the library books and read a little:

"Difficulty understanding nonverbal communication, including facial expressions and/or body language."

"Difficulty understanding how to interact in social situations."

"Trouble maintaining relationships with others."

I don't realize I've fallen asleep reading until the ringing phone wakes me up. I let the machine pick up. "Where the hell are you, man? I'm here at McDonald's, waiting for you."

I grab the phone. "Oh sh—, Trip. Sorry. I'm not feeling well. I should have called."

He asks me if I need anything, asks me if I've been eating or called a doctor. I rush him off the phone, apologizing again. And go back to sleep.

I'm woken up, again, by the ringing phone. Groggy, I reach for the phone and knock the clock off the nightstand. I can see sunlight peeking through the sides of my drawn shades. I let the answering machine pick up. It's James.

"Hey Adem, James here. How you feelin'? I know you called in sick on Friday, but we didn't hear from you today. Call me back. I want to know that you're alive. Just kidding. I know you're alive. Well, actually, I guess I don't know that. Okay, never mind, just . . . just call me back when you get this."

I lean over the bed and look at the clock. It glares at me angrily. It's 3:21 on Monday?

I don't call James back. Instead, I turn over and go back to sleep, my body sticky with sweat, my hair matted.

Early on Tuesday morning, I call the answering service to leave a message for James to let him know I won't be coming in again today. I roll over and fall back asleep, waking up only to re-read my list as Mr. Graves's words roil in my brain. My body is aching from lying in bed for so long. As night falls, the only light in the room comes from the glow of the TV, which I haven't turned off since the morning.

On Tuesday night, I'm still in bed. When the phone rings, once again, I let the machine pick up.

"Hi Adem. It's Tom. Um . . . I got your number from the minister. I'm really sorry for calling, but I think we're supposed to be meeting tonight to study for my test on Thursday. And . . ."

I sit up in bed. Tom. Tom! I grab the phone. "Tom, I'm so sorry. I'm . . . I'm not feeling well. I've been in bed for a few days. I'm sorry, man. I should have called. I meant to call. I'm sorry. I'm . . . can we reschedule for tomorrow night?"

"Sure. If you think you'll be better."

"Yes. Yes!" I say, shocking myself with the force of my conviction. "Yes. I will be there. I'm feeling better."

We hang up and I throw the covers off. Something about Tom's voice, the urgency, his expectation, pierced my numbed brain.

He's my student, Grandma. I seed wisdom of math and physics in his life. He doesn't think I'm inept. To Tom, I'm not inept. He needs me.

That I'm hyperlexic may be a fact. That I'm autistic may be a fact. What's a fact? Does fact equal truth? "No," Grandma said, "facts can change from person to person, place to place, or time to time; but truth never changes."

She said, "God loves you and that's the truth." She said, "You're sick. That's a fact. You are healed. That's the truth," All I have to do is to believe in God. Truth takes over and changes the facts. I begin reading my Bible—Tom's Bible—and pray until I fall asleep.

I get up early Wednesday morning on legs that are wobbly from lack of use. I step into the shower then shave off the beard that's overtaken my face. I strip my bed and throw in a load of laundry, remake the bed, tidy up my desk, and rearrange the books on my shelf.

I call work and leave a message with James's assistant: "I'll be in the office tomorrow."

At 6:00 a.m., I collect the article on hyperlexia and the library books on autism, put on my sneakers, and run to the library. I return the books through the afterhours return slot. Then, I ceremoniously tear the hyperlexia article into shreds over a garbage can on the corner and continue my run.

I think about Tom, Shaun, the other children at the orphanage. If these young men can be thrown into the proverbial lion's den, then I need to throw myself out there, too. I've relied on myself in the past to pivot and start from scratch. It's time for me to do it again, to work on computer innovations that I own, that I can sell.

I think about Tom's goals, his mission, a mission not only for himself, but for the other children, the children who are younger than him. He's so committed to himself, his direction. My mind jumps from Tom to myself as a six-year-old in Istanbul, my own goals, my own direction. My mind races and my pace speeds up as I remember the conviction I had as a twenty-two-year-old arriving in America, how I saved money, learned English, and enrolled in graduate school, the list in my notebook of all the things I accomplished. I quicken my pace again until I begin panting.

"I'm not inept, Mr. Graves. That's your opinion, Mr. Graves. But it's not who I am at all," I say out loud.

When my side begins to cramp, I walk a few blocks until I spot a McDonald's. Then I remember I haven't eaten much in the past few days. I grab a couple of Egg McMuffins and scarf them down. I walk slowly back toward the library and stop. *It's time. You're ready. You've been preparing for this for the last five years. Just like Tom. You know what you need to do.* I turn and I walk up the steps and wait for the doors to open.

27

END OF THE TUNNEL

"I'm going to call it lincom," I tell Trip the following Sunday, in between bites of my Quarter Pounder. "Because my first important project was linking computers. I'm going to start my own company," I say, pausing for effect, "... and I want you to do it with me."

Trip stops chewing midbite.

"What the f—?"

"Hear me out. I'm going to stay at First Manhattan until the business is up and running. I've spent the past four nights reading about how to set up a corporation. I know there's a niche here. And I know you can help me fill it. I know what I'm good at and I know I can't do it alone. But, I also know that with every new program I write for the bank, it's theirs. It's my intellect but their property. I want to do one for myself."

"Go on," Trip says, taking a sip of his soda.

"There are several small companies out there contracting to maintain the software used by large financial institutions. By hiring a contractor, these institutions save money and avoid the headache of having full-time employees with benefits, severance, and other overhead expenses. They do not have to find and maintain talent either, the contractors do that. We could earn $75 an hour per programmer. I can write and maintain the banking software, but I don't know about the rapidly growing local area networks. That's where you come in. We should be more valuable having knowledge in two areas: software maintenance, that's me, and local area networking, you."

I hand him the proposal I've drawn up. While he reads, I get up and order a fish filet. He's still reading by the time I've finished the sandwich; I get up and start pacing. "Adem, sit down man, you're making me nervous."

"Don't worry about me, just read." I start pacing again and Trip laughs.

"Well?" I ask when he gets to the last page. "What do you think?"

"Genius, Adem. Genius. I'm in. We're going to do this!"

"Okay. We're in it. 50-50. And your dad? Do you think he'll be our financial adviser?"

"You know what, I just think he might?"

"Okay. And, I was thinking we also need a sales guy ... My friend Roberto, from my ESL class. I think he's our guy for sales. Yes? No? Maybe?"

"I think yes, because you're on fire, man."

"Yes!" I say. "I'll give him a call this afternoon."

"What about your visa? What happens if this works and you quit the bank, what about your status?"

"I'm glad you asked. Our business can sponsor me for a green card."

"Really?"

"Yup! Crazy, right?"

"Well, as far as I'm concerned, that's the best reason to start this business."

We agree to reconnect later that afternoon after he's talked to his dad and I've talked to Roberto.

***

Over the next couple of weeks, we put the word out to fellow programmers. They recommend us to their employers, and by word of mouth, we win a network upgrade contract from a national association.

We work overnight so we can upgrade their systems after the staff have left their offices for the night. Since we all still have day jobs, working overnight is optimal, both for us and our clients; we just lose quite a bit of sleep. By morning, we've upgraded the association's server software, added new wiring, and new workstations. Trip is an expert at this and when I can, I watch him work so I can learn.

The association pays us $1,000.

Immediately, we realize this is where the hidden treasure lies: DC is home to hundreds of national and international associations and they all need upgrades to their local area networks. Associations become our sweet spot.

Depending on the size of the network, we make $1,000 to $2,400 per night. Roberto wants us to charge even more. "Larger companies are charging much more for the same work," he says. "And we are doing a better job."

Within three months we've doubled our prices; our upgrade packages run from $2,000 to $4,800. We give Roberto a 10 percent commission, pay Trip's dad 3 percent to do our accounting, and Trip and I split the rest. With Roberto booking us one to two upgrades a week, Trip and I are each raking in between $8,000 and $16,000 a month.

Within a year Roberto has landed us more than sixty clients and we're booking two months out. Trip and I continue to do the work overnight and somehow manage to keep our day jobs, though we're making enough money that we can both quit. Admittedly, I'm not pushing as hard at First Manhattan, just doing what I'm told; nothing extra. I remain surprised Mr. Graves hasn't fired me. The less I'm involved with important projects and the less work I do, the happier he seems.

Trip buys a farm in West Virginia, a dream he's always had, and we boost Roberto's cut to 12 percent. Roberto quits his day job and after a few weeks of pushing us to do the same, Trip and I decide it's time.

James organizes a farewell party, which Mr. Graves doesn't attend. Joy tells me I'm making a huge mistake. Nancy reminds me of our first meeting and says she always knew I'd make it big one day. James tells me he worried about this day, my departure, from the moment he saw my *Link-Mail* demonstration. I leave the party promising to stay in touch.

***

Nine months later, Trip and Melanie have a baby boy. And a month after that, Trip drops a bombshell.

"I have decided to retire, Adem. Melanie and the baby and I are moving to West Virginia. I'm going to raise my child, enjoy time with my wife, and live a life of leisure."

"You're leaving? O . . . kay," I say, waiting for him to elaborate.

"Yeah. I'm moving to West Virginia, to the farm. I've made my million, I'm ready to enjoy life."

"I don't know what to say."

"Say, good luck, Adem. I'd say it to you, but I don't think you need it."

Trip leaves his share in Lincom to me. I tell him he should sell it to me, but he says he doesn't need the money; he's set for life, thanks to our venture.

His departure dredges up every moment I've ever felt abandoned—my mother leaving me at school, Francesca leaving me and disappearing back to Italy, Demir moving back to Istanbul. I'm afraid Roberto will also leave me. He's been talking about going back to Bolivia.

I don't know if I can do this alone.

***

After Trip's departure, I rejigger Lincom's focus. Local area network hardware and software—Trip's specialty—changes at lightning speed. I can't keep up and without Trip, I can't compete with the in-house computer geeks.

I think about the *Link-Mail* program I wrote for First Manhattan and wonder how I can apply the same idea to banking software, its internal production processes. Between and among money transactions, there's a lot of software that runs overnight on mainframes, often multiple mainframes in different locations. Some software applications run simultaneously; some run contiguously because one process has to wait for another process to finish. Computer programmers keep monitoring these processes and if one is successful, they trigger the next process. I think I can automate this entire workflow. I think I can write a program that enables a mainframe to report a successful completion of or an error in a process, then have the PC "make a decision" about what to do next—send a signal to the same mainframe to repeat the process, abort the programs, or to start the next process. The program, if successful, would save businesses thousands, if not millions of dollars; no more need for programmers to check each process round the clock. In fact, it's possible all that checking could be eliminated.

I go over to the Library of Congress to do research, reading about the latest computer technologies, hoping something will jump off the page to confirm this idea. There are several papers on automated processes. For a full week I can't get this concept out of my head. I debate whether I've learned enough about computer coding that I could write software for it. Despite the business being good and Lincom doing well, Mr. Graves's words still haunt me. *If it hasn't been done yet, what makes me think I can do it?*

I codename this project *Skipper*, because it directs multiple resources from a central location and makes the ship sail.

My research sparks another idea. I believe with my knowledge of image compression algorithms, I could develop a prototype application for video teleconferencing. The program would enable companies and individuals in different locations to meet live on screen. I dub it *Video-call*.

***

By 1988, eight years since I arrived in the US, my net worth reaches two million dollars.

The first million took me thirty years; the second, only one year, thanks in part to my soaring stock holdings.

If only Mr. Graves could see me now.

28

THE END IS NEAR

BY 1989, MY *SKIPPER* AND *VIDEO-CALL* PROTOTYPES ARE READY TO go. I rent an office on K Street and hire an artist who etches *Lincom* on the glass wall at the entrance. I also hire two programmers away from the bank and put the word out that I'm seeking three more. My business plan calls for five programmers by Lincom's three-year anniversary. It also calls for feedback—lots of feedback—from investors; so, my next step is finding and scheduling clients for presentations and demos.

But, my growth takes a hit three months later when Roberto tells me he's moving back to Bolivia. His mother is ill and he needs to go home to take care of her. "You've given me the ability to help my mother, man. You're a rock star. I wish I could stay, but it's time for me to go home."

Despite the training courses I took at the bank, I still feel I'm not good at sales. If I learned anything from the oriental rug store—other than that many bosses are crooks—I learned that sales is not my forte. I don't have the stamina for it, the confidence. Roberto was excellent at it; he never once took it personally when someone said no.

After about a month of cold calls and only a few interested clients and even fewer booked appointments, I feel like I'm spinning my wheels. I need a better, faster, more structured pitching system.

I mention my dilemma to Leo Goldstein, a semiretired attorney who co-founded the law offices with whom my new company shares a floor. Benowitz, Edelman, and Goldstein is a boutique law firm that represents investment bankers and other financial institutions. The first time we met, we were in the elevator. I pressed seven and he immediately mistook me for a new client and introduced himself.

"Actually sir, I'm the founder and CEO of a new company, Lincom. I just rented the suite of offices down the hall from your firm."

"Those offices have been empty for months," he told me. "So, congratulations are in order. Come by my office after work today and we'll toast your future success," he said as the doors opened. "Work hard and you'll be like me one day, rich enough to work a few hours a day and play golf all afternoon. Imagine a world where every day feels like a weekend. My firm's been around for more than thirty years. I was a strapping young man like you when my partners and I founded this firm." Leo and I ended up chatting for about two hours that first evening. And then, we fell into a bit of a routine, meeting for a glass of bourbon in his office once a week.

When I ask Leo for advice on my client acquisition issue, he suggests that I apply to attend an exclusive investment forum in New York City. "On the first Saturday of each month," he says. "Investors listen to fifteen-minute project presentations from entrepreneurs. You have to pass the screening process first; they don't let just anyone present. But if your project passes muster, you can be chosen to present your idea. It can't hurt to apply."

I send in my application to present both prototypes, and within three weeks *Skipper* is approved. I'm scheduled for a presentation the following month.

***

On my drive to New York City, it occurs to me that I've never actually been anywhere other than New York's airports. I decide that no matter how the presentation goes, I'll spend the night in the city so I can finally see it.

During my fifteen minutes with investors, I present *Skipper*. Leo has warned me to be sure not to speak down to them, and not to be so technical that they have no idea what I'm talking about.

When my time is up, they ask me to stay for another 15 minutes. They want me to demonstrate *Video-call* also. I fire it up, and it's an immediate disaster. The application runs poorly; the video is monochrome, choppy, and keeps freezing.

I leave the meeting feeling like my entire presentation was a colossal failure; I am sure my *Video-call* debacle tainted my *Skipper* demonstration. I contemplate breaking my promise to myself to stay and walk around Manhattan. But, in a moment of clarity, I realize that instead of focusing on what went wrong, I could focus on what went right. I treat myself to a steak and a glass of red wine. "Here's to you, Adem."

***

The following day, I'm up and in the car by 5:00 a.m. for my drive back to DC. I arrive at the office a little late and a little sluggish from my round trip to New York. There's a message on my desk that I missed a call from a Mr. Harvey Carlson from Allied Atlantic Capital, a New York-based venture capital firm. In the memo section the receptionist has written, "He was at yesterday's meeting. Call ASAP."

I don't take off my coat, I don't sit down—I dial. "We'd like to buy *Skipper*," Mr. Carlson says when I get him on the line. "We're looking for all future rights to the software." I listen as he goes into more details about the deal they're proposing: Lincom would have the option to continue maintaining the code, but Allied Atlantic Capital would call the shots as to what would be done to it and how it would be used. And that's when I stop listening. I don't interrupt him, I let him keep talking, but I know my answer is no.

"Four million is what we're offering," he says.

"No deal," I say without any pleasantries. I've learned from American TV that these Wall Street types don't like to waste time. "I'd consider it for five million, but I don't want to maintain it," I say, as if I'm talking about Monopoly money.

"You can't be serious, Adem; this is a very generous offer," Mr. Carlson says.

"I'm 100 percent serious, Mr. Carlson. Call me back when you can make me a serious offer."

I hang up the phone wondering who I am and where I learned to talk that way.

Two days later Allied Atlantic calls back. They've raised their offer to 4.5 million.

"Push it to 4.8 and you have a deal," I say, sitting back in my chair. "And, please don't call back unless you can get to that number," I say, hanging up the phone without letting Mr. Carlson respond and without even saying goodbye.

"Welcome to the US, JR," I say to myself.

Two days later a courier drops off a twenty-page contract. 4.8 million in a single transaction.

I round my money to the nearest million, 7.

It's time to celebrate with a trip to Istanbul. It's been more than two years.

***

The Istanbul Yesilkoy Airport, now called Ataturk Airport, has become much larger, with a new wing that's just opened. The city has changed, too. New, taller high rises have left the skyline of my youth unrecognizable. The roads are more congested, despite more new highways, more bridges, and more tunnels. While my bank account was growing in DC, Istanbul was growing into a raging metropolis.

The first morning home, I wake up before my parents. I walk until the sun rises then flag down a taxi. I have an urge to see my parents' old apartment, the street, the corner where the mailman handed me my university entrance test results, my elementary school, middle school, the traffic lights where Savas Kartal shot at me, almost hitting Francesca, and the block where he chased me on rooftops, trying to kill me. I want to see the coffeehouses where I gambled, the movie theater where I saw *The Deer Hunter*, and the cafeteria that served animal parts to people who are drunk or high or both, all night. I want to see my childhood. I want to understand where I came from so I can find clues to how I got to where I am now.

When I see the middle school up ahead, I ask the cab driver to pull over. The school is freshly painted and the trees out in front that used to offer no respite from the sun, now tower like giant beach umbrellas, casting a shadow over the whole building. I look across the street and see that not only is the wall to "The Promised Land" gone, but the soccer fields and basketball courts are, too. Now in their place is a contrived-looking town center, a hub that simply looks like it's trying to be something it can't be. There's a multistory shopping mall and a multistory carpark, a food court, and movie theaters. There's a large courtyard with grass and benches. A few people are out for an early morning stroll, some walking their dogs. I walk by a woman selling flowers. "A rose for that special lady," she calls out to me, "may your belly buttons come together for life." I haven't heard that for more than a decade. I should have taught it to Dr. Tiller; he would have loved it!

***

By the time I've returned home, Mom and Dad have left for the club. There's a note asking if I can meet them there.

I turn on the TV and see a familiar and unpleasant face.

The chyron at the bottom of the screen reads, "Live: Istanbul Sports Arena, Nationalist Party Annual Convention." The arena is filled with a sea of signs and waving flags. The announcer introduces Savas Kartal and the low roar crescendos into an almost uncontained mania. *They are screaming in support of a murderer.* The one I saved from drowning, the one who almost killed Francesca, the one who tried to kill me, who abducted me, and who single-handedly assassinated dozens, and possibly strategized the murders of thousands more. The people who support him are either crazy or as clueless as he is maniacal.

Finally, the crowd quiets; Savas launches in to a sea of signs and waving flags. "Dear Mr. President, my fellow party members, and citizens of our free republic. In the beginning of our fight fourteen years ago, we promised that we would defeat Communism in our country once and for all. And we did. We had many casualties; we had many martyrs. We first defeated the internal enemies, then defeated the external enemies who supported them. No weapons could stop us. No jails could contain us!"

The crowd roars. Thousands of people begin to stomp their feet in excitement and the reverberations are so strong that the TV cameras vibrate. "Savas, our leader!" the crowd chants, whipping itself into a collective frenzy of adoration for this man they consider their hero.

Savas Kartal waits patiently for the crowd to quiet down, holds his left coat pocket with his left hand, raises his right arm and as he pumps it in the air, he continues, "And I promise you now, in our country, Communism will never come back! Communism will never show its ugly head, ever again. We will never allow that to happen."

The crowd goes wild again. Savas Kartal gives a brief nod in acknowledgment.

"Throughout history," Savas resumes as the crowd hushes again, "Turks have built thirteen different states. We are now the Republic of Turkey. Never have we been ruled by another nation. Never will we be ruled by another nation. It is the same today, and it will be so tomorrow. We are free. Together, we will take this freedom and unify our forty-nine million citizens to build a great state of arts, commerce, and sciences! I also promise you today that together, we will make Turkey one of the wealthiest and most powerful countries in the world. And throughout this journey, our Nationalist Party will lead us into the future!"

Savas is on track to become the leader of the Nationalist Party. A man who took the lives of my friends and fellow students may one day—and soon—run my homeland. I don't know how to make sense of this except to say that it all comes down to money. It's all about money. Money is power. Money can make a murderer a legitimate politician.

The cameras follow Savas as he walks off the stage, his right hand caressing his jacket's pocket flap; four bodyguards surround him as he walks out of the arena. The video cuts to a different camera, and I watch as Savas emerges out of a dark tunnel and onto the sidewalk. Savas and two of his guards climb into a limousine; the two remaining guards take up positions on either side of the car as the driver slowly pulls out. People stream from the building into the streets running behind Savas's car, the guards unable to stop the crush of people. The car moves forward, slowed by crowds of adoring supporters. I'm dumbfounded by the mania. People continue to peel out of the arena and surround Savas's limo, and to lunge toward the vehicle with outstretched hands. The limo inches forward so slowly that it's almost not moving.

And then there is an explosion. I watch as a pedestrian in a raincoat standing to the side of the limousine opens fire. The cameras witness the entire execution as the bullets rip into the back seats of the limo, one shot after another. My jaw drops and I step closer to the TV. The shooter is holding what looks to be an automatic assault rifle.

A stampede of screaming people run in all directions away from the scene. Abruptly, the live broadcast cuts off, switching back to the studio where the camera accidentally catches the anchor's reaction to the horrific scene for just a split second before she regains her stage face. As one pundit after another is brought in to discuss the unfolding events, I'm gripped. Every few minutes, the station replays the clip in a loop, over and over. I can't move.

The journalists on the scene report that Savas Kartal was in the back seat with a security guard; another guard was in the passenger seat. The shooter, he says, sprayed the car with a thirty-round magazine, then replaced it, and as he moved closer to the car, began shooting again, sweeping back and forth. In less than a minute, it was done. A traffic officer shot and wounded the assailant, then arrested him.

Everyone in the car was killed. Several bystanders were injured and transported to the hospital. Eyewitnesses say they're amazed that more people weren't injured or killed with the amount of gunfire they watched in horror.

I'm in shock.

For the next week, a quiet descends upon the city.

A funeral service for Savas is broadcast live on TV. Government officials, politicians, businesspeople give speeches about Savas Kartal's contributions to freedom and democracy. No one mentions the dozens of people Savas killed or the seven thousand who died in opposition to or in support of him and his party. Instead, the news media reports that no high-profile politician has ever before been killed in Turkey. The news media begin referring to him as a martyr executed by a crazy man.

I leave Istanbul wondering what has happened to my country. And I can't stop thinking about how many people might still be alive if I hadn't been on the beach that day and saved a drowning man.

29

BACK TO THE CLUB

THOUGH I'M BACK IN WASHINGTON, IN MY HEAD, I FEEL STUCK IN Turkey. I buy the *Nation's Daily* every day on my way to work to see what's happening there. The police have identified Savas's bodyguards killed during the attack as Tunc Solak and Volkan Aytekin—the men who kidnapped me.

The killer is also identified: Aslan Ozkan. The name sounds so familiar. I put down the paper. *Aslan Ozkan.* Who is that? *Aslan Ozkan. Ozkan.* It's a common name; maybe it's just that I've known a number of people with that last name. Pars, my roommate a lifetime ago. His last name was Ozkan. There was also an Ozkan in my navy high school and I think one in my elementary school.

I keep reading, my mind drifting back to the day Polat Mardin held a gun to my head and how the rest of the gang mistook my desire to die, still crushed over Francesca, as bravery. *Ozkan.* Who else do I know with that name?

"The lion with true blood, Pars is gone, Pars is gone," I say out loud. *What was that?* I keep reading, the words stuck in my head with a strange, distinct rhythm. And then, suddenly, I drop the paper. *Oh my Lord.* That's what Pars's brother was reciting after Pars was killed, his father came to pick up

Pars's belongings; I tried to kick a soccer ball around with his little brother to distract him. "Maybe you and Aslan kick the ball around outside," Polat had said as Taner and I stood in the front hall looking into Pars's father's bloodshot eyes. *Aslan*, that was his boy's name. *Aslan Ozkan. Aslan Ozkan killed Savas Kartal. He avenged his brother's murder.* I don't know what to think.

Who was Savas? He's from near Oren, where my dad and Zeki used to hang out when they were cadets. Dad could have known Savas's father who was a police officer. A young Communist rebel shot and killed the man and Savas vowed to kill all Communists. I could have known Savas from Oren too, in fact I knew him in a way, he was the drowning man I rescued. Yet he wanted to kill me. Then he let me go. Were we enemies? We could have been friends. Who is the one that turns potential friends against each other, sows strife and hatred, tempts and entices people, and divides them—left-right, Communist-Nationalist, worker-boss, man-woman? Who is this devil?

***

I return to DC. Allied Atlantic wants to acquire *Video-call* now. They've upped the stakes and I feel it's time for me to do the same. "I'll have my lawyers get back to you," I tell Mr. Carlson, then walk across the hall next door to Benowitz, Edelman, and Goldstein.

"Good morning Mr. Bayer," the receptionist says, looking at her watch. "I think you are a little early for cocktails with Mr. Goldstein."

"Ha!" I say with a snort. "Believe it or not, I'm here on business. Is he available?" She buzzes his office and just a few seconds later Leo comes out in a slow jog with a big smile and a handshake. "Adem, my friend. What a nice surprise. What can I do you for?"

"I'd like to hire you, your firm."

"Well, okay then," he says, and his face grows taut, serious. "Let's sit down in my office."

I tell him about Allied Atlantic, Mr. Carlson, about the sale of *Skipper* and the new offer. After a quick demo of *Video-call*, I hire him, just like that. We shake on it. Before I'm even out the door, I hear him ask his assistant to arrange an immediate call with Mr. Carlson at Allied Atlantic.

***

Later that same day, Leo calls me. "They are interested in both the *Video-call* and Lincom itself, including the programmers, and you," he says. "You can stay and continue to run the company if you want, but they would own it. They would pull all the strings, and of course make all the decisions. We can negotiate that."

"That's not a problem for me," I tell Leo. "They can make the decisions." I miss writing code. I miss the challenge of finding a need and writing the code to solve the problem.

We go over the details of their offer, everything from *Video-call* itself to Lincom's software maintenance service contracts with local banks. We make a list of the things I won't budge on and things I don't care about, for Leo to keep in mind during negotiations.

"Okay. I think I'm all set. I'm flying to New York tomorrow morning to meet with them," Leo says. "I'll report back to you as soon as I can."

***

Leo is still in New York the next day when he calls. "Okay. We had a good conversation. We discussed a lot of different scenarios," he says. "It's all about valuation, Adem. The value of *Video-call* is based on several factors, basically what they get. Is it your staff alone? You? The entire company? Also, they want to look at the source code to see how well it's constructed. And, how close it is for prime time, whether it could be repurposed, reused."

"How much are they considering?"

"They don't know yet. That's why they want to take a microscopic look, have the application evaluated," he says. "Right now the price tag falls within a wide range."

"So, how much?" I ask again. Standing up from my chair, I begin to pace the room.

"Are you sitting down?" Leo asks. "I want you to sit down. You should sit down for this."

"I'm good, go ahead," I reply, although I'm still pacing.

"Are you sitting? Really, you need to sit for this."

"I'm sitting," I lie. "No, wait . . . I lied, I'm not sitting, I can't sit."

"Well, I think you're going to need to," he says, pausing. "See, the thing is, congratulations are in order, my friend. Adem, they're estimating Lincom to be worth between 60 and 100 million dollars."

I take a deep breath. I feel dizzy. I walk back to my chair and sit down. I'm silent.

"Adem?" I barely hear Leo say. My ears feel clogged.

"Ex . . . excuse. What?" I say, stumbling on my words.

Leo laughs. "You heard me. Between 60 and 100 million. Don't worry about the wide range in the value, I will bill you accordingly," Leo says with a chuckle.

I surprise myself and laugh too.

$4.8 million for *Skipper* had sounded excessive. *60 to 100 million?*

"I've just found out that they're going to use this software in video games, not in telephone calls. They have nothing to do with telephone calls. They think it's never going to be possible to transmit video information over telephone lines. They want the image compression algorithms for their video games. Would you believe that?"

"This is crazy, Leo! Video games? Is there any money in video games? One plays and earns no money, what a waste of time!"

"I haven't a clue! Listen, I'm coming back to Washington this evening. How about dinner tomorrow night to celebrate?"

"Yes. Sure," I say, still in shock. *Video games? Huh!*

"You're buying!" Leo says, and hangs up while still laughing.

The next day, I invite the programmers out to lunch and give them the news that some good things are coming our way.

"I have an idea how to celebrate. I really want to show all of you my appreciation for the hard work, the long hours you've put in, the sacrifices you have made to create *Video-call* and get it ready for the marketplace. I want to take everyone—all of you and your families, children, but no pets," I say with a smile, "back home with me—to Turkey. We'll go to Greece, stay three days in Santorini, then board a boat for a 'blue voyage' in the Aegean. The trip will end by sailing north to Istanbul, from which I emigrated in 1980." There's silence. I look around the table, trying to gauge the reaction of the staff. "Five weeks. No work. All play. We have room for up to twenty people. You can bring your nannies and babysitters so you can truly sit back and enjoy yourselves. What do you say? On me. No one here will spend a dime. No work. The break you all deserve."

A slow rumbling of shocked reactions resonates around the room, "I can't believe it, Adem, really? . . ." "Are you kidding? For us, our families . . ." "Five weeks? That's unbelievable . . ." "I've never even been out of the country . . ."

"And, I forgot to add, it's a paid vacation. You will be paid for playing."

The table erupts in cheers and hoots. One by one each staff member comes over to me to shake my hand, hug me. "Champagne. Let's have some champagne. The workday ends now," I announce to another explosion of cheers.

As Leo negotiates the final numbers with Allied Atlantic, I prepare for the five-week cruise and a five-week closure of Lincom. The answering service will handle all calls; a sister company we work with will fill in for our programmers. I plan to make this a true vacation for myself as well and decide I'll call in to get my messages at the end of the day, once a day only, and only when we're on land. I tell the concierge service to leave voice messages on my answering machine and to tell Leo Goldstein to do the same.

I call my parents with the news of my cruise.

"I'll see you at the club thirty-three days from now," I tell my dad.

I can hear my mom in the background. "What's he saying, what's he saying?"

"He's coming to visit. Now, hush, I can't hear him." I roll my eyes and smile. They haven't changed a bit.

"I'm arriving by yacht. We'll dock at the club and I'm scheduling our arrival for dinner. I'm bringing ten guests with me, plus three children—school age. They'll be staying at the Ritz-Carlton next to the club. I'll stay with you, if that's okay."

***

A week later, we fly to Paris, then on to Santorini where we stay at one of the island's best hotels. I've scheduled bus tours along the cliffs followed by lazy afternoons on the volcanic beach. Some join me for a swim in the Aegean during a gentle rain. Every day starts with thank yous and "I can't believe we are here," and "this is the most incredible experience of our lives." While I try to absorb the kind words and accolades from the staff, I feel like one of them, like someone else other than me has footed the bill for this grand experience. *How could I be the one who has made this all possible?*

After three nights in Greece, we climb aboard the yacht for the "blue voyage." It is, without a doubt, even by Robin Leach's standards, the most exclusive way to see the Aegean. For our fourteen, there's a crew of six plus the captain. Everything we could need or want is provided, including five gourmet meals a day. On our way to Istanbul, we sleep, eat, tan, tan while we sleep, swim, play, party, dance, and drink. Every night, I read my Bible and pray until I fall asleep. We stop to rest and explore the islands of Naxos, Paros, Ikaria, and Khios, then continue making our way north to Turkey, through the Dardanelles past Gallipoli, to the Marmara Sea.

We arrive in Istanbul three weeks after leaving Santorini. Just before we enter the Bosporus from the Marmara Sea to the south, the captain veers into the Golden Horn, tracing its shore. It is a glorious late-spring afternoon with views of Europe on one side and Asia on the other. At full throttle, the engines push against the current, gliding the yacht past the majestic Dolmabahce Palace as the sun begins to set and the lights begin to come on in the palace gardens and on the Bosporus Bridge. I stand on the deck as my home, my former home, my birthplace, rises up in front of me. We pass by the Rumeli Hisar, and new waterfront hotels built out of renovated old palaces, then under another, new bridge, that I haven't yet crossed, that connects Europe and Asia.

Finally, with the currents behind us, we approach the dock where I used to swim. As we glide closer, my heart begins to race and my stomach lurches; it's been over ten years since I've stepped foot at the club.

I notice there's a yacht moored at the dock and make my way toward the bridge to the captain. "Maybe we should dock at the Ritz-Carlton right next door," I suggest. "It's a short walk to the club from the street."

"We'll just ask the crew of the other yacht if we can double-dock, it's not a problem," the captain says. "We do it all the time." I walk to the front of the yacht and watch the club grow bigger in front of me as the engine cuts and we glide to lock in with the docked yacht.

One by one, my guests disembark, stepping across the neighboring yacht to make their way to the club's patio. I let everyone else go first; and, while I watch them hop from one boat to the next, I look up to see my parents standing at the farthest end of the patio, their mouths agape. My dad's wide smile exposes his white teeth. Mom waves discreetly. I hold my hands out in show, then look down and prepare for my jump onto the neighboring yacht, stopping short in midstep when I look up at the captain's quarter and see the name: *Francesca II.*

Francesca. Is it possible that's my Francesca? Is Francesca here at the club?

My legs weaken. I grab the railing, almost falling between the bobbing vessels. My knees are trembling, and I don't seem to be able to control them. It feels like my heart might explode. *Could she really be here? Is it truly possible?*

I step off the yacht and onto the patio. The ground still feels like it is moving under my feet. I don't know how much of that is nerves and how much is sea legs—but I resolve to use the latter as my excuse if I see Francesca.

Will she recognize me? It has been thirteen years; she's twenty-nine years old now. *Is she married? Does she have children?* I hate myself for thinking, wondering if she's gotten fat and unattractive. But I think it anyway, and I can't figure out why. *Will I be glad then, that I haven't been with her all this time to see her change? Or, does she have the same eyes, the same lips, the same smell? Will the love that gripped my heart unleash itself again and expose me to relive the pain of our breakup?*

I'm distracted as I receive a warm welcome from the staff, some of whom remember and recognize me. The headwaiter, looking grayer but otherwise the same, slaps my outstretched hand away and envelops me in a hug. "She's here," he whispers.

"Who?" I say, pretending I don't know. He lifts his eyebrow and I lose the act. "I saw the yacht. I haven't seen her, though." I shake out my hands and crack my neck. "Changing the subject," I say with a smile, "how are you? And how did he do?" My voice is cracking. I try to clear my throat.

"Electrical engineer. Thank God. He's in Munich, working for a big electronics company; they paid for his graduate school." I shake his hand in congratulations then excuse myself as I see my parents walking toward me. The headwaiter steps back, and, as they approach, says, "May your days be happy like this, always as you celebrate the arrival of a long-gone son." Dad is smiling—that smile that I have become so fond of, that I saw so little of as a child. He shakes my hand, Mom air-kisses me superficially. "We don't show affection in public," she whispers to me as a reminder. "It's gauche."

I bring my parents over to my guests and introduce them. Chatter rises into the air as, one by one, they deliver to my parents the Turkish phrases I've been teaching them over the course of the past month. My parents respond with a few English phrases they know—saying "Hello, how are you" and "nice to meet you."

And then I see Francesca through the glass doors of the clubhouse. I gaze in her direction and quickly find it impossible to look away. She's a young woman now, her silhouette hinting at how kind the last decade has been to her. I stare at her through the glass. *How is it that she can still take my breath away?* I feel powerless, all strength sucked from my body. I have no authority over myself or the situation. I have no wisdom; I do not have a clue what I'm supposed to do. *Grandma—help! My angels—help! I have no power, no authority, no wisdom. My spirit is crushed, my mind is blank, my body is trembling.*

I watch her as she holds a glass of wine in her right hand and gestures with the other—her arm sweeping up and down, waving and arching with the grace of a ballerina. *Is it possible that she is even more beautiful?* I've loved her for so long and from so far away. And now she is standing only a few feet from me like she did so many times in so many dreams. Her hair, a little shorter than when she was a teenager, shines in the light. The gold dress she is wearing clings to her breasts, her hips, her stomach then flows softly down to her knees, caressing them, exposing her tanned legs. *I would trade the riches of the whole world for a single kiss from her.*

I walk down the marble walkway toward her. The magnolia trees arch above me, painting the air with their sweetness; the roses climb their trellises, the buds on display hiding the thorns that line their stems. The lilies of the valley sway in step with me.

My knees have stopped trembling, but I still feel shaky as I step closer to the clubhouse doors. I test my voice. "Hello, how are you?" I say, my voice cracking. "One, two, three . . . testing," I say, as if I'm speaking into a microphone. I try to clear my throat but can't. I laugh at myself. *You're pathetic, Adem Bayer.*

The glass doors of the clubhouse slide open as someone walks out, and Francesca turns in my direction. I stand perfectly still, falling into her eyes the way I did the first time I ever saw her. She looks at me, smiles a polite, passing smile, then turns back to the woman she's with. As the clubhouse doors close in front of me, her aroma embraces me. It's not Diorissimo, it's Francesca. I close my eyes and breathe her in.

The doors open again and someone else walks in, and I open my eyes. She's looking at me, her head tilted as if in thought. My heart lurches. I feel faint. *Get it together, man.* I watch her face and try to read her expression. She holds onto my gaze for an extra second and then I see it. Her eyes widen and her eyebrows arch. Her head straightens and a smile emerges. She turns back to the woman, kisses her on both cheeks, and then starts walking toward me. *She knows who you are.* My feet are cemented to the ground as they were thirteen years ago. I watch her walk through the open doors.

"Hi," she says, in Turkish. "Wow. Is it really you?"

"That's exactly what I was thinking," I say, and we both laugh. "And your Turkish. Your accent is so good," I add. My arms dangle at my side. I want to reach out and hug her, but I remain planted in place. She smiles. *Why did I say that?*

"You look beautiful," I blurt out, my brain and heart unleashed. "I'm sorry. That was rude," I say. "I think part of me is still eighteen."

"Not rude at all. Very kind, in fact. Thank you. Life has been good to you as well."

"I can't complain." I twist my body to point my arm toward the yachts. "Thank you for letting us dock . . . I mean the captain, the crew . . . your crew." I'm unable to stop myself from babbling. ". . . I mean, thank you too." I feel like I'm in quicksand. The more I speak, the more I sink.

She nods, looks over my shoulder toward the boats, and then looks back at me. Her eyes are moving gently around my face, as if to examine it. She raises her eyebrows. I'm thankful she can't see the scars inside my heart.

A soft breeze moves between us and a curl of hair dances in front of her face. As she lifts her hand to tuck the errant strands back in their place, I notice a wedding band on her ring finger. My heart jolts. *You cannot be jealous, Adem. Seriously, man. No, no . . . I'm happy for her. You could never have made her happy, Adem, you know that. She moved on. Of course she moved on.* But, I want to know if she thought of me the way I thought of her almost every day for the last thirteen years. I want that to be true of her, as well. I need it to be true. *If I could know that she didn't forget me, would it help release me? Can I ask her that?*

"I've heard you're doing well in America," she says, switching to English—British English, not American.

How would she know I moved to America?

"My grandmother," she says, as if in answer to my thought. "I ask her from time to time." She takes a step closer. *My Lord, she's too beautiful.*

We stroll over toward the pier and walk by the spot where we had our first dinner. I want to rewind time, relive that summer over a candlelit dinner with her. And then I want us to board one of the yachts and sail off to the Greek Islands together.

"I moved to London," she says.

"I remember you wanted to do that."

"Yes, I moved right after our summer together, I moved there for school." *Right after our summer together.* "I stayed there for graduate school, and I now work there as a journalist. For the *Times.*"

Not meaning to, I look at the ring on her finger. She twists it. "I met Trevor, he's my husband, at the newspaper's annual party, and we got married four years ago."

"Is he here?"

"He flew to London for a trial last Sunday and will be back here Friday evening."

"I would have liked to have met him. I'm sure I would have liked him."

"He reminds me of you."

He reminds you of me? He reminds her of me!

"Unfortunately, I need to leave now. I have dinner scheduled with my father and grandmother."

"Please send my regards."

"Of course. I will . . . um, it was good to see you, Adem. Really good. You look good. You seem happy."

We part, saying we hope to see each other again in the future. I'm left standing there alone, the clubhouse doors opening and closing behind me as if she is coming out again to greet me. I watch her walk away, but her perfume lingers, stays with me. *This is the last time we're ever going to see each other. I'm on a one-way trip; I can't go back.*

My mom notices me standing by myself and she comes over and whisks me over to the table, her arm tucked in mine. "We are ordering drinks," she says. "Remember your guests." If I weren't so numb, her mild manner would shock me.

We walk over to the table and sit down for dinner. At the dock, I watch the club staff climb over Francesca's yacht to retrieve my guests' luggage and wheel it over to the hotel.

We finish dinner with a toast to the company as I struggle to find the words to express my appreciation. As I hesitate, I look around the table and I see the faces of happy people, even my parents. A tear pushes against my eyelids and I stop myself. *Make it personal, Adem.* "Cheers," I say, and that's it. *I will pull each person aside this week and thank them personally.*

"To our esteemed host," they call back at me. And, a little tipsy, they break out in song. "For he's a jolly good fellow . . ." I look at my parents. *What are they thinking right now?*

As my guests leave to check in at the hotel, I rise from the table and head over to the edge of the patio.

The air is warm and humid, my shirt is sticking to my skin. It's summer in the Bosporus Strait.

I remember feeling uneasy here, inside the gates where only the wealthy and influential belong. But not today. And, maybe never again.

I savor every step along the path that runs along the Bosporus. And, I notice the changes that have occurred since I left ten years ago—the new lounge chairs, new tables, new flowering plants I don't know the names of, that seem to have seamlessly found a place among the roses, magnolias, and lilies of the valley. I can hear the chatter from tables behind me on the large patio. As I walk along, the sweet scents of flowers give way to the stronger smell of sea kelp. The Moody Blues quietly sing in the background. *"Each and every heart, it seems is bounded by a world of dreams. Each and every rising sun is greeted by a lonely one."*

My heart may be lonely but it's happy. It has been a long time since I thought of being happy or not. It may be because I was too busy carrying out my plans or because Grandma had said, "It's not about you, don't even think about yourself. It's about God, how much He loves you, and how much you love Him, and His people."

"If God is happy with me, I'm happy," she said.

The last time that I remember asking myself if I was happy was eight years ago, while sitting on a park bench at 4:00 a.m. in Dupont Circle. Why shouldn't I have been happy? All I had ever wanted from life was to be in America, have a minimum-wage job, and save enough money to buy myself a 1970 Dodge Challenger. I was happy then, and I'm happy now, but also content.

Once I reach the edge of the patio, I look down into the water, to the school of fish under a lamppost. I want to estimate how many fish are visible.

"Your mother and I were talking . . ." I hear, and turn around; Dad has followed me.

"You know those houses Mr. Baris built on the hill? Remember? You played ball there during construction."

"I know those houses, Dad. They're beautiful."

"One of them has come on the market. You said you wanted to invest . . ."

"Which one, which one?"

"Lot three. Do you remember? You were little. You know you could . . ."

"Tomorrow morning, Dad, we're going. You and me!" *They are going to be neighbors with Francesca's parents.*

I want to buy that house with the view. Mom will love it. Then maybe I will move to Paros or another Greek Island.

"You know Adem, the staff here were always asking about you. Members too. You know your mother doesn't like to brag about her children's . . ."

"Success. I know Dad." *It's gauche.*

"It's just that you were not like your sisters, son, you were different."

"I didn't listen."

"No, you wouldn't listen."

"And I didn't study."

"No. You wouldn't study."

Should I try to explain who I was to my dad? *I was autistic, Dad. I was hyperlexic and autistic.* I wouldn't know where to begin. I decide to remain silent.

"But this?" he continues, spreading his arms out and sweeping them across the Strait in the direction of the yachts. "This makes me realize your difference, your differences, your approach, wasn't bad. It was just . . . different."

I glance over to him and then look ahead at the black water, and above it the lights on the Asian side.

"I'm proud of you," he says. "Your mother and I, both, are proud of you."

"I know, Dad." *I know.*